Count Angelo

By Makala V. P. Thomas

For

Nathan Walcott

Sherene Williams

Shannon Thompson

Makeda Farrell

Sade Thomas

Madalene Aza

To the London Borough of Hackney. No matter how far I go in life, I will never forget where I came from.

x-x-x Mwah x-x-x

COUNT ANGELO   MAKALA THOMAS

Prologue

I am Count Angelo Heathen. I live with my elder brother Cormier in a dark, dark castle, which resides in the dark woods of Pennsylvania... where my family, the dreaded wolf pack, lives.

I have lived there for two hundred years with Cormier, but haven't touched the skin of a human's neck in almost six years. I, a vampire, have never bitten any living creature in six years but the cows on Penny's Farm, who provide me with what I desire when the time comes. I am not like my brother, who had once been obsessed with drinking the blood of humans, and so formed the Vampire Community. There are only two hundred humans left in our town.

The rest... are vampires.

* * *

"Bianca!" yelled her father Samuel as he drove the caravan up the brick path. "Wake up, for the thousandth time!"
Bianca Davis pulled her duvet over her head, only to have her father's mother Beverly pull it off as she sighed "Up now, dear. I sense something dark about this town…"
"Cut it out Gran," said Ricky, rolling his eyes. "Apart from the choice of structure, colour and the weather, there's nothing dark about here. Bianca."
"What?" she groaned, sitting up. She loved her big brother so much she wouldn't think twice about responding when he called. "I'm up, ok?"
"Good. Dad, where are we staying?"
"In a park this time. Not far from this town… just beyond the woods."
"Ick," muttered Richard as he stared out the front window. "The woods are like… on top of the hill. Do we have to go through them?"
"No," said Gran sharply, before Samuel could answer. "We shan't take any shortcuts to the camp- we will travel *around* the woods."
Samuel scowled, but he said "Fine."

* * Count Angelo * *

"Angelo, wake up," Cormier said curtly, rapping on his door. "We're going to check this park out. About fifty humans are there, Jessie told me. Fresh blood, hmm? I can smell it already."
Angelo could smell it too, but he refused to take it in. "I'm staying."
"You cannot," Cormier said abruptly. "As the elder, I order you."
Angelo sighed. "You speak as if I am still twenty."
"You became a vampire on your twentieth birthday," Cormier said amusedly. "Technically, you still are twenty. You don't look a day older."
"Nor you twenty four," Angelo replied as he sat up. "Must I go?"
"Yes. Who knows, you may see a pretty neck itching for your bite."

* * Bianca * *

"I've been busy up all day sorting my stuff out- do we have to go?"
"Yes," said Ricky, amused as he helped her step down from the caravan. "Come on, Dad's there already with Gran. I bet he's made a load of lady friends."
"Me too."

* * Count Angelo * *

"A fantastic change from the normal city life you all are used to!"
Cheers went up, Cormier's eyes glowing scarlet as he gazed around. Angelo shook his head, knowing he'd already spotted at least three people he'd make it his duty getting to know before biting them.
Angelo sniffed curiously as the wind blew. "Cormier?"
"Yes Angelo."
"What is that scent in the air?"
Cormier smelt, frowning. "All I smell is blood. Do you?"
"No; I smell things aside from blood. I smell a bored person, smell their sweet, floral scent. It's a lovely scent, Cormier." Angelo sighed. "If only we could feast on the scent rather than the blood."
Cormier shook his head, amused as he looked to the crowd. "I suppose."

* * Bianca * *

"Oh, my." Gran clutched her son's arm. "Darkness is upon us, Samuel."

"Yeah; night time," muttered Ricky, and Bianca smiled. Ricky didn't take Gran seriously, but sometimes she felt the old woman knew what she was saying. Bianca sighed, looking around. If darkness were upon them, at least her boredom would vanish... and darkness would probably be in those trees...

Bianca's heart almost stopped as she made out two tall figures standing there, still as ever. It didn't look as if they were part of the crowd...

She stared, about to nudge her brother. Then she stopped, knowing Ricky would freak out. Bianca watched as the figures, obviously male, were joined by a shorter, feminine one.

* * Angelo * *

"Hello, Angelo."

"Greetings, Marissa," murmured Angelo, taking her hand and kissing it.

"How are you since we last met?"

"Perfect now that I'm with the Grand Vampire of Pennsylvania."

Cormier rolled his eyes. Her lust for his little brother was unmistakable-he could smell it a mile away. Damned if he let him fall for her...

"Aren't there any other men in the vampire community that you'd rather chase, Marissa Bennett? You are wasting your time with my brother."

Marissa turned her cold gaze on him. "You think so, Cormier Heathen?"

"I know so. You know as well as I that a vampire takes longer than a human to get over the loss of a loved one."

Marissa laughed. "Yes, you would know."

"Indeed," smirked Cormier. "If I had a heart your sister would surely have torn it out the day she confessed she'd found a new lover."

"I'm nothing like Patricia."

"So you think."

Marissa's eyes flashed. "You think otherwise?"

"The way you chase Angelo reminds me of her. I always wonder if she chased Brian like that, behind my back."

Angelo remained silent, searching for the source of that sweet scent.

"I'm surprised you didn't attack Brian."

"He had no clue of my and Patricia's relationship."

Marissa closed her mouth. "I see. So when you and your idiot friends speak ill of myself and Patricia-"

"I speak ill of Patricia only," Cormier said, scowling at her as the fiery red glow in his eyes died out. "Whatever you have done to earn those callous comments is your business. Angelo."

"Yes brother?"

"I'm going home. Whenever I come across Marissa, she spoils my appetite."

Cormier vanished in a puff of black smoke, gone. Angelo watched as the bat took to the skies, vanishing into the woods. Sighing, he said "You seem to get under his skin more and more, Marissa."

"Cormier knows he can't have me," Marissa answered. "It was for that reason he turned to Patricia instead, but Patricia knew it wasn't her he wanted. She hated to feel unloved, which is the reason she found *true* love, Angelo. She and Brian will be wed in October."

"Congratulate her on my behalf."

"I will."

They turned back to the giant crowd, listening to the leader speak jovially.

"And now, it's time to swarm around the campfires! Make new friends! Find out who comes from where you came from! England!"

Cheers went up. Angelo got a whiff of that scent again.

"You seem distracted," Marissa observed, as he stared around. "Angelo?"

"Help me, Marissa. Can you not smell that glorious scent?"

Marissa tilted her head, inhaling deeply. "I smell it."

"Where- *who,* should I say- is it coming from?"

Female vampires had higher senses when it came to hunting. Marissa's eyes burned scarlet as she nodded in the direction the scent came from.

"She stands with a boy her age, a man... and an old woman." She grimaced. "Be careful, though- the grandmother's clairvoyance hits me smack in the chest. She already senses darkness here in Pennsylvania."

Angelo nodded, taking that into account. "The last time someone mystical came to this town, many friends received the dreaded stake."

Marissa nodded. "Feed well. Throw the body into the woods for our wolf friends and family."

Angelo nodded, though he had no intention of biting the girl at all.

"Come to my castle tomorrow if you are not feeding."

"I think I will be, but I'll send word if my plans change."

Angelo smiled and morphed into a night bat, eyes glowing. Marissa waved as he took off, his senses much higher.

* * Bianca * *

"Oh, oh!" cried Gran, making everyone turn. "Darkness has arrived!"
"For God's sake- Ricky, get her back to the caravan," snapped Samuel, Ricky cursing as he grabbed his grandmother by the arm and roughly steered her away, Bianca behind.

* * *

"Shut up, Gran- get in the bed." Ricky forced her down furiously. "I saw a cute girl looking at me and then you had to mess up!"
Gran glared at him, doing as she was told. "I'm telling you-"
"Here you go Gran," said Bianca soothingly, handing her a mug. "I've made you some tea. You always like a hot cup of tea before bed."
Gran smiled at her as she took the mug. "And I always tell you and Ricky a tale before we sleep."
"Uh… not tonight Gran," Bianca said apologetically. "I've got a slight headache- I'm staying outside the van for fresh air."
"Me too," Ricky said quickly, but Bianca said "No, Richard. You have to keep an eye on Gran."
"Yes dear," smiled Gran. "Come and hear this tale."
Ricky glared at his little sister. Smiling sweetly, Bianca left the van.
She walked for fifteen minutes before flopping down on the grass, sighing "She seriously needs to calm down with all that. I don't know if I can take months of Gran going on about darkness arriving."
"I apologise for startling her," a voice replied, making her jump and scramble to her feet, looking around wildly. There was no-one there.
Bianca remembered the figures she saw by the trees- this had to be one of them. Darkness, just like Gran said- they apologised for scaring her!
"So- so darkness really is upon us?" she asked as calmly as she could, though she was shaking as she scanned the grass for a weapon.
There!
Before she could seize the branch the voice said "No, please. You'd waste your energy trying to duel with what you can't see. I advise you not to waste your energy. I just… wanted to know your name."
"If you're the Devil you should know it," Bianca said, staring around. She really couldn't see anything but grass, let alone signs of movement.
"I am not the Devil."
Bianca dived and grabbed the branch, holding it up wildly. "But you don't deny you *are* darkness!"
"No, I do not deny it. Darkness, as you call it, has not arrived. It has resided here in Pennsylvania for almost three hundred years."
"I've read a few stories. But-"

"What exactly is your name?"

"My name?"

Don't give your name to strangers.

"I'm not a stranger- at least, I won't be if I befriend you."

"Oh hell no," Bianca said, growing angry. "You can read minds?"

"I can do a lot of things you mortals would deem impossible."

Bianca was intrigued, but she didn't let her curiosity get the better of her.

"I'm not giving my name to something I can't see."

"I am not a something." She noted the voice sounded annoyed.

"What, so you're a *someone?* Not a monster?"

"I am a someone, not a monster," the voice replied calmly. "But others like me... some can be monsters when the time arrives."

"Time for what?" Silence. "Time for *what?"*

"Time..." she heard them take a deep breath. "To bite another."

"Bite??" Then Bianca realised. "You... you're a... a vampire?"

* * Angelo * *

"I," Angelo said as he took shape, "Am Count Angelo Heathen, the Grand Vampire of Pennsylvania."

The girl's jaw dropped. Then she smiled. "Wow."

Angelo frowned at her. "Is this not the part where you flee screaming?"

"Do I look like a child?" she demanded. "I'm not scared at all."

Angelo smiled, and he caught a whiff of that wonderful scent along with something else: her attraction. He seemed to have made an excellent first impression on her. Cautiously stepping closer, he asked "Do I have the pleasure of knowing your name? You are exquisite."

"No I'm not," she said, though she smiled shyly. "I'm not good looking."

"Beauty is in the eye of the beholder," Angelo answered, "And from what my eyes can see, you are extremely beautiful."

She smiled, looking away. "My name is Bianca. Bianca Davis."

"A pleasure to meet you, Miss Bianca." Angelo took her hand and kissed it. "I could smell your beautiful scent far away in the trees. I had to meet you, even if you did flee."

Bianca smiled as he freed her hand. "I'm uh... flattered."

"Why, Bianca?"

Bianca snapped out of her dreamy stupor. "Because I am."

Angelo laughed, his teeth flashing. "Very well. Unfortunately, I have a meeting to attend-"

"You're going?" she said disappointedly, and he nodded.

"I will return, of course. Possibly tomorrow, depending on the outcome of the meeting."

Suddenly he was very far away from her, walking slowly. Bianca hesitated, then she called "Count Angelo!"

He looked back.

"I just- I mean, you're a very good looking vampire. Nothing like the ones in Dracula."

Angelo smiled, dissolving into nothingness. Bianca had a split second view of the bat before it was camouflaged in the night sky.

* * Bianca * *

"And where was *you* for half an hour?" demanded Ricky, as she reached the caravan. "Looking for mice or something?"

"Ha ha, very stupid." Bianca looked up at the sky before shaking her head. "No, I just took a quick walk and back. Dad must have gone to the campfires with the rest of the crowd."

"That sucks," said Ricky angrily. "He could easily have taken Gran and let us go. He normally does in the other countries-"

"You know he loves this kind of thing. Come on, it's Pennsylvania. Everyone knows about the Dracula thing."

"Dracula," Ricky said as he rolled his eyes, "Is the same as the Easter Bunny, the Tooth Fairy, and Santa Claus. Not real."

"Ok, maybe Dracula isn't. But vampires-"

"Aren't real either."

Bianca sighed. Though they were just one year apart, it felt like fifty.

"Forget we ever had this minute discussion. I'm going to bed."

"Yeah, me too."

* * Cormier * *

Twelve vampires sat around the long table, waiting for the head chair to be filled. Cormier looked at his watch, then he got up.

"I will retrieve him. He must be daydreaming again."

The vampires nodded, understanding totally. Angelo often daydreamed about life before the after-death.

"Angelo?" Silence. "Angelo! Brother, are you here?"

Cormier walked straight into Angelo's suite without knocking this time.

"Angelo-" he stopped abruptly, staring at the bed. "My word."

Angelo lay perfectly on top of the duvet, fully clothed, fast asleep. Cormier quietly closed the door, rapidly going back to the meeting.

"It seems my younger brother is exhausted. From what, I have no clue. For I woke him up three hours ago the maximum."

"We should have known," said Sebastian, a close friend of the Heathen brothers. He ran a hand through his silky black hair, saying "It is time for Angelo to feed. You must get him to the farm soon, Cormier. He will have fainting fancies next if you're not careful."

"Yes. Yes, I know. If only he decided upon feeding on a human again-"

"We have tried to persuade the Count for six years," Clover said quietly, a stunningly beautiful vampire of twenty five. That is, she were twenty five when she became prey to Sebastian, who was so in love with his childhood friend he refused to go on without her. After almost thirty years of bearing hatred for him, Clover melted down and let him back in her heart. She knew where Angelo was coming from. "It will take perhaps thirty to convince Angelo to come back to his ways."

"He will not." Cormier sighed, shaking his head as he sat at the table. "Ever since Alicia walked towards dawn and her death, he vowed never to bite another human again."

"We all say that-"

"But he is the only one who lasted longer than three months," Marissa said smoothly, speaking for the first time. "I do believe Angelo will keep his word- and we all know his word never breaks."

There were murmurs of agreement, Cormier irritated.

"I have faith in my brother. He will bite the neck of a human again-"

"But that human will surely die," Clover said softly. "We are talking years without their blood- even the largest human will not have enough to supply."

Cormier grinned. "Then we will finally see the Count go on a rampage."

Everyone laughed, Marissa trying not to smile. Cormier didn't notice.

"Maybe," said Sebastian, "It is because he once had a broken heart. He is scared to treat it as loosely as he once did before."

"I believe he will love again," Cormier said, folding his arms. "Do not

15

argue with me on the matter. Angelo will surely love again."

"And you, Cormier?" Marissa asked coolly. "Will *you* love again?"

Silence, everyone looking at Cormier.

"Meeting adjourned," he snapped, and they hopped to leaving.

One by one they vanished in puffs of black smoke, screeching as they flew through the open window into the night sky.

* * *

"Brother," called Angelo, walking about the house. "Cormier?"

I sleep, young one. Come to me tonight at nine.

Angelo sighed, checking the time. It was soon five a.m. He walked into the kitchen and went to inspect the fridge. Raw meat? Mmm…

Angelo selected a pork chop and took a large bite, chewing slowly as he thought of Bianca Davis. If she were in his day, they would probably be wed by now. He was only two years older than her. Even though time had passed, his age had not. As the clock struck five, he felt his limbs grow heavy- but he was not completely exhausted yet.

Still he had better climb back into bed before he crumpled to the floor in a heap. He'd done it a number of times this year already, always forgetting that daylight always arrived fully at around seven a.m.

He'd give anything to see daylight again. Maybe that's what made Alicia do it… she must have been delighted before she was snatched away.

Angelo sighed, legs shaking as he finished the chop. He really had to get back to bed…

* * Bianca * *

Bianca tossed and turned all night, dreaming weird dreams.

A wild party of some sort was going on, loads of people dancing the night away, drinking, joking, having fun. Suddenly the man standing near the bar pulled the string of a massive bell, shouting "Dawn is near! The club ends now!"

Was that Count Angelo? No... but he sure looked like him...

One by one the people vanished into clouds of black smoke, filling the entire club. When the smoke cleared, the club was spotless. And empty.

A girl was walking serenely atop a mountain to gaze at the sun rising. She smiled contentedly as the light fell on her face- before she burst into flames and ashes fell to the ground, then the wind blew them away.

Bianca gasped and sat up, sweat trickling down her forehead. She checked the time: it was ten past five in the morning.

She got up quietly, grabbing her dressing gown before slipping outside.

* * *

"Bianca," a voice murmured, and she turned and saw him.

"Count Angelo!"

Before she knew it she was running towards him, and he held his arms out. Bianca flung herself into them as if they had known each other for longer than ten hours.

"I had these crazy dreams that frightened me-"

"Yes, I know. I knew it the minute I saw you."

"Do you know what they were?"

"No. Would you mind coming to my grand abode?"

"I'd love to," she replied, while her mind screamed *don't do it!*

Angelo took her hand.

* * Angelo * *

Angelo glanced skyward: it was getting light. His limbs were growing heavier by the second. It seemed weird to him that Bianca followed him straight into his room, not asking where the spare one was.

She waited until he slid under the duvet before she got under herself, snuggling up close to him, not as afraid anymore. Angelo laid on his side, holding her close to him as he murmured "What were these dreams?"

Bianca described each one in full detail, leaving nothing out. By the time she finished the first few sentences, Angelo heard nothing more.

* * Bianca * *

Bianca finished, taking a deep breath. "Do you think they're real?"

Silence.

Bianca turned to stare at him. "Count Angelo?"

Angelo was fast asleep.

Her jaw dropped at the sight of his perfect face, eyes closed, peaceful. Angelo was fast asleep.

He looks like an angel, Bianca thought amazedly. A fallen angel.

She hesitated, then she reached over and turned off the lamp on her side, leaving his on so it looked like light radiated from him. Bianca hesitated, then drew out her camera phone.

Angelo was oblivious to the photo-shoot he was currently starring in: Bianca took many. Then, quite cheekily, she tiptoed around his home and took much more of each room, stopping at the only room with a closed door. The plate on that door read "Cormier."

Cormier? She thought as she placed her door on the handle- and suddenly she found she was staring at Angelo again, fast asleep. She looked around amazedly: she was back in the Count's bedroom.

Bianca shivered, climbing back into bed and switching off all the lamps. She didn't need to be told twice: intruders weren't welcome in Cormier's room.

* * Cormier * *

Cormier rose slowly, yawning. "What time…?"

He glanced at the clock on his wall, and immediately felt annoyed.

"I am one of the few vampires who manage to wake hours before nightfall, yet I cannot go outside. Nonsense if there ever was any."

Cormier stopped, sniffing the air. "What on earth…?"

He paused, wondering whether he should do it. Then he decided he should- he was the elder brother, after all. It was for the greater good.

Cormier focused on Angelo's unconscious mind, breathing in and out slowly. Images flashed before his eyes rapidly, almost uncontrollably.

It wasn't spying, not really. The smell of lust shot up his nose as the images slowed, then he saw the pretty brown face of a girl, with big brown eyes and a cute smile. Angelo's lust.

"Oh," smirked Cormier, rubbing his hands with glee. "Marissa Marissa, Angelo has indeed fallen for another. And not any other. A *mortal.*"

Laughing, he made his way towards Angelo's room to meet her.

* * Bianca * *

Bianca walked out of Angelo's bathroom fresh and clean, but still in her pyjamas. "I should have brought some clothes with me."

"Indeed you should have," said a voice amusedly, and she spun round.

Cormier was leaning against the doorframe, arms folded. "Hello."

"Hello," said Bianca nervously. "I… are you Cormier?"

Cormier was pleased. "Angelo has told you about me, yes?"

"Uh… no- I mean, I've just met Count Angelo. We met not even twenty four hours ago."

"I see." Now Cormier was interested. "And… for *some* reason, the pair of you share a bed as if you've known each other longer than two years."

"Why are you up in the day?" Bianca answered, though she smiled.

Cormier smiled back.

"I'm a blessed but cursed vampire. Come, Bianca. Are you hungry?"

"Very," she answered, wondering how he knew her name.

"We vampires have many skills," Cormier answered for her as he walked out of the room. "Our senses are much, much higher. We can do all sorts."

"Like read minds?" Bianca said amusedly, and he nodded with a smile.

"I think we'll get along perfectly, Bianca. Yes, like read minds."

"So… you know what I'm thinking?"

"If I focus I'll know everything." Cormier opened the fridge, taking out a carton of milk and tossing it to her. "Have a bit of milk. Vampires love milk, Bianca. Milk gives us energy when we aren't feeding on another."

"Cool," Bianca said. "May I have a glass?"

Cormier smiled before going into one of the cupboards. "Angelo asks the same. He hates when I drink milk out of the carton."

Bianca smiled and poured the milk. "Have a glass as well."

Cormier sighed and obeyed.

* * Angelo * *

Angelo woke drowsily, mumbling "Bianca…"

No answer.

Angelo sat up. "Bianca?"

Silence.

Oh no. Angelo scrambled out of bed and into the bathroom, sorting himself out quickly. *She must have ran like the wind back home, frightened when I wouldn't wake- or disgusted she shared my bed.*

Angelo dressed quickly before dashing into the corridor, his cape flying behind him as he called "Brother!"

"Yes Angelo. We're in the living area."

"We're?" asked Angelo curiously, turning into the living room- then he gaped at the scene in front of him. "Bianca?"

"Hey Count Angelo-" Bianca sipped her milk, smiling at him. She'd had a lot of milk since she woke up- and she found it made her feel great. "Me and Cormier was just talking about where you used to live- I mean, how it was before you became a vampire."

"Indeed," said Angelo coldly, looking at Cormier. "Good things, I hope?"

"Of course," said Cormier, smile fading. "Er… Bianca, my good friend." Bianca smiled up at him as he stood. "I must leave now, to go to the club."

"Club?" asked Bianca, then she realised. "Oh my- *club!*"

Cormier and Angelo frowned at her as she said "I dreamt about you!"

Cormier smirked. "Many women daydream about me, my friend."

Bianca laughed. "No, Cormier- I mean I actually had a dream-"

"You were telling me about these dreams," Angelo cut across. "Earlier this morning, before I fell asleep."

"Yes," Bianca said nervously, Angelo looking at Cormier.

"I should be going," Cormier said, getting the message without need to read his brother's mind. "Until next time, Bianca Davis."

"Bye Cormier," smiled Bianca, annoying Angelo greatly.

"Yes, Cormier. Goodbye."

Cormier smirked and bowed, then he vanished in a puff of black smoke.

Angelo looked at Bianca, who averted her gaze as he said "I see that you and Cormier have taken to each other… quite nicely."

"He kept me company while you was asleep," Bianca said, smiling again.

"I don't know why, but he made me feel so warm inside."

Angelo couldn't help scowling. "Did he really."

"Yep. I really like your brother, Count Angelo." Bianca leant back in the armchair, relaxed. "I feel like we're the best of friends."

Angelo's jaw clenched: she hadn't even looked at him as she said all of that. "Bianca, will you please look at me when you talk to me?"

Bianca looked at him, apologising. "Sorry, Count Angelo."

"Please, call me Angelo." He sat in the chair opposite, smiling at her. "I'm sorry I fell asleep while you explained such important things."

"It's ok- I forgot you need to sleep in the day. You was exhausted."

"Yes," said Angelo, raising an eyebrow slightly. "You understand me already."

"And you understand me." Bianca smiled, and he smiled back.

"I didn't mean to be so cold."

"It's fine. I'm cranky when I wake up too."

Angelo smiled, getting up. "As it's night time, would you like to go on a walk with me? Nowhere frightening, I assure you. Just the forest."

"The forest?" she repeated incredulously. "That's not frightening?"

Angelo started to say no, then he realised what he was saying.

"Uh… that is- if you were Marissa, I'd gladly have taken you-"

"Who's Marissa?" Bianca asked coldly, eyes narrowing. Angelo tried not to smile as he watched jealousy swirl around her, a vivid green smoke in his eye. Bianca could see nothing. "Angelo?"

"Marissa is a close friend," Angelo said, wanting to laugh. He hadn't laughed since the death of Alicia- he refused to do it. "She and I go way back. We have been friends for many, many years."

Bianca scowled, not answering him. Angelo reached out and took her hand, suddenly serious. "Bianca."

"Yes?" she said stiffly, and he sighed. Females were so complicated. You had to explain every little sentence or they'd find their own explanation.

"I have many female vampire friends. And we all go way back. Don't you think, that if I wanted any, they'd be the Countess of Pennsylvania?"

Bianca's expression cleared as she thought about that. Angelo smiled.

"Come, we go now."

"Wait- I don't… I mean-" Bianca gestured at herself hopelessly. "I don't have any clothes to wear out."

"That's fine, there is one outfit I'm sure will fit you perfectly. Come."

Bianca followed Angelo as he strode into his suite and opened his wardrobe, then he stopped.

This was to be his gift to Alicia, but dawn snatched her away before he had the chance to give it to her. It was very modern, black jeans with a red belt laced with a heavy black outline, a superb red corset with black designs on it, along with a black shawl for the cold and matching shoes.

Bianca's jaw dropped as she stared at the clothes. "Angelo, I-"
"You will wear them?" he asked, turning to her with shining eyes. Too
shiny for Bianca's health. *Red* shiny. Bianca backed away from him, eyes
full of fear. "Bianca?"
"Angelo, you- you look different-"
"How different?" he said with a smile, amused. "Do I seem fully awake?
My senses seem much higher now."
Bianca stared at his mouth, at his unsheathed fangs which she was sure
were *very* sheathed seconds before he pulled open the wardrobe.
"Angelo, I... I have to go home. My father and the rest must be very
worried."
"Oh," said Angelo disappointedly. "When will I see you again?"
"I- you won't be seeing me again."
"What? Why not?" Bianca bolted, startling him. "Bianca!"

* * Bianca * *

 Her footsteps pounded the grass as she ran, his call echoing in her ears as
she raced through the tourist parking lot towards her sacred caravan.
She was almost there- ten seconds away-
Angelo rose out of the ground in front of the door, cape billowing.
"Bianca, what-"
"Get out of my way, Angelo!"
"Please, just tell me what the matter is!"
"Oh, *you* don't know what the matter is?" The ghetto side of her was
coming out now. *"No guy, no matter how piff he is- will bite my neck!"*
"What on earth are you talking about??"
"Bite your lip!" she snapped, as the lights went on in the van.
"My lip?"
"Bite it!"
Angelo obeyed quickly, wincing. "Ouch!"
"Yeah!" said Bianca, as he held a coin to his eyes. The unmistakable
scarlet glow reflected, stunning him. "Take a damn good look!"
Angelo dropped the coin, not knowing what to say. "Bianca, I-"
"Bianca!" shouted Ricky, bursting through the van door. "Where the hell
have you been?! Everyone's been out searching like mad-"
"Don't- I'm fine," muttered Bianca as he hugged her; Angelo was gone.
"I'm all right- uh... I felt unwell and I crashed out near the trees."
"And they're so dark too- and so are your pyjamas!" said Ricky furiously.
"This is exactly why we tell you to wear bright clothes, but *no-"*
"Shut up, Ricky. Jeez. I'm alive and healthy, and tired. I need to sleep."
"I'll make you some tea," called Gran, not even getting up. "Come in."
Bianca obeyed, Ricky behind as they went in. Then Bianca turned back,

looking at the grass.

Angelo's silver coin sparkled merrily, flashing bright colours.

"I forgot something," she said, quickly darting back and scooping up the coin. "Gran, can I have herbal tea please?"

She didn't see the dark mist hovering just out of light's reach as she closed the van door.

* * Angelo * *

Damn her brother, thought Angelo furiously. Damn myself. Damn her for running away! Damn Cormier for winning her affection. Damn it all!

"Oh my," said a very amused voice. "Why all these damns, Angelo?"

"Marissa," he breathed, relieved. "Come, let us talk."

* * *

"It seems you really like this mortal," Marissa observed. She didn't feel jealous at all. "Nearly as much as you liked Alicia, but in such a short space of time."

"Yes," admitted Angelo. "And we barely know each other. It hasn't even been two days-"

"Meaning she had every right to flee," Marissa said, amused once again. "Angelo, you forget she is a mortal. And she has no experience of our kind. How would you react if you were her? Or how did *you* react?"

Angelo thought back to when Beverly, his first love, bit both him and Cormier- in the same night.

"I attacked Beverly when her eyes started to glow," he said thoughtfully. "She was very surprised, yet she was ready to battle."

"Just how you were surprised, but was ready to pursue Bianca," Marissa said with a smile. "Angelo, give her time. Do not approach her too soon."

"But we got off on such a good start," Angelo said wistfully. "She shared my bed, Marissa. Even *you* aren't brazen enough to share my bed without asking my permission first."

"And I have not shared your bed," smiled Marissa. "But I am brazen."

"Is that so?" smiled Angelo, looking at her. "Are you brazen enough to dance with the Grand Vampire at the club he owns, all night until light?"

Marissa smiled back. "I think I am."

* * *

"Brother!" shouted Cormier over the loud music. "Where is Bianca?"
"She fled," Angelo called back. "My eyes decided to light."
Cormier burst out laughing. "Don't dwell on it! Come, have a drink!"
Angelo and Marissa left the dance floor to accept Cormier's drink.
"Why are you behind the bar tonight?" asked Marissa, cold as ever. She liked having a drink when it got too hot, and if Cormier was behind the bar, he'd probably be crude as usual when he served her.
"Yes, why are you?" asked Angelo amusedly, and Cormier grinned.
"I created my own drink- my own recipe! Vodka, Alizé, Rum, Coke and Moét champagne all rolled into one! It's a blast, Angelo! Try?" Angelo shook his head. "Come on, little brother! Don't get depressed over Bianca. She'll be back, just give her two weeks."
"Two weeks!"
"Two weeks," Cormier said with a nod, and Angelo looked at Marissa for confirmation. She nodded, then he looked at Sebastian. He gave the thumbs up from the dance floor, nodding too.
"Fine," sighed Angelo. "Come Marissa, let us sample Cormier's drink."

* * Bianca * *

"If you ever run away like that again I'll lay you in front of the van before I run you over!" shouted Samuel, beside himself. He'd been so worried, and relieved when Bianca stepped into the caravan- then his relief turned to rage very quickly. "And then I'll- don't ignore me when I'm speaking to you, Bianca!"
"I'm going to bed," snapped Bianca. "Leave me alone, Dad!"
Gran covered her son's mouth as he nearly flipped his lid. "Samuel, Bianca is exhausted. We'll settle this in the morning."
Samuel scowled, Bianca pulling the duvet over her head. "I guess, but-"
"No buts. You've been yelling for over an hour, and I have a headache."
Ricky was listening to his iPod to shut out the noise, on the top bunk. He hadn't heard a word since Samuel's jaw dropped at the sight of Bianca.
Bianca shut her eyes tightly, hugging her teddy and squeezing the coin before she slipped it in her breast pocket.
I'll forget all about him. I mean, vampires aren't even meant to exist.

* * Angelo * *

A week later Angelo sat reading in his library, with a glass of milk and a slab of raw meat on a saucer. He felt very light, content. Cormier's drink had done wonders for him- he felt stress leave his body moments after he'd downed the whole glass, one each night after Bianca fled.

Marissa sat opposite him, reading too. It was quiet, peaceful, and Angelo loved every moment of it.

"It's very serene, is it not Marissa?" She nodded, smiling at him. "I don't feel too anxious about Bianca anymore."

"That's good. And I don't mean it in a spiteful way when I say that."

"Yes, I know."

"But Angelo, you do know why you feel this way, don't you?"

Angelo started to nod, then he shook his head. Before Marissa could explain Cormier strolled in, so arrogant he couldn't see he'd interrupted something. "Why so cosy in the library? We do have a living area."

"Yes, we know. Marissa was about to explain why I feel so calm."

"Was she really," smirked Cormier, and Marissa glared at him. "Angelo, it's obvious. You and Bianca seem to have a bond of some kind; you already feel you understand, possibly know each other well. It's possible you feel the same way she does. When she starts to miss you, you may start to miss her also."

"Or the effects of your ridiculous beverage is still in his body," Marissa said coolly. "As they are in mine and many others."

"*And many others,*" mimicked Cormier. "I feel fine."

"You always do," Angelo murmured, turning a page of his book. Once again, he kept out of Marissa and Cormier's bickering.

"By tomorrow many including myself will have a hangover," Marissa said with a shrug. "Not that I'm irritated with you for being the cause."

The sarcasm rolled off her tongue like stones down a slope. Cormier scowled at her, saying "If Angelo has a hangover then he is my problem. I will tend to him like I always do."

"Indeed you will," said Marissa coldly. "By serving him another drink."

"I did that once," snapped Cormier. "To help him puke. Vomiting clears the system, and Angelo was fine afterwards."

Angelo sighed, picking up his glass. How did the subject of their arguments always land on him?

* * Bianca * *

It had been two weeks- for Bianca, a cold, miserable two weeks.
Ever since she fled from the Grand Vampire like the coward she was,
Bianca felt dissatisfied with her life. Knowing more was out there, more
she'd just begun to discover before throwing it away, she was growing
more and more upset and angry with herself. All she had was his coin-
"Bee?" She jumped, slipping the coin in her pocket. "Bianca, what is it?"
Bianca sighed and turned away. "Nothing."
Ricky joined his sister at the table as she stared out the window sadly.
"Something happened when you went missing, didn't it?"
"No, I- Ricky, I told you what happened already." Her big brother didn't
answer, making her look at his dubious face. "Don't you believe me?"
"I want to, I swear. I just don't get it, I mean… if you crashed out the
whole time, why would you be so tired when you got back?" It was
Bianca's turn not to answer. "I would have been up all night."
"Drop it, Richard. Please."
"No. And don't call me Richard like that. You sound like Gran."
Bianca laughed, making him smile. "I do, don't I?"
"Yep." Ricky got up, feeling a little better. At least she laughed. "And
Bee, if you don't want to tell me, then tell Gran. You know she won't
tell."
Bianca nodded, then she remembered Gran's dramatic behaviour the
night she met Count Angelo. She clutched her heart and cried darkness
was upon them, attracting attention to herself and the rest of the family.
Nope. She couldn't tell Gran either.
As Ricky left, she took out the coin and gazed at it again. The silver coin
flashed bright colours, winking merrily at her.
"Silver coins don't normally act like opals, do they Bianca?"
Bianca jumped again, whipping round. Nobody was there. Sometime
during her brooding, the sun had set. Ricky had gone and met Dad and
Gran at the camp with all the other tourists, while she stayed home.
It was dark… meaning Count Angelo was awake. Fully awake.
Bianca got up, holding the coin tightly as she said "No they don't."
"Does it belong to you?"
"No," she said heavily. "You can have it back if you want it."

* * Angelo * *

Angelo smiled, taking shape. "I missed you."

"I missed you too- uh, that is, if we knew each other properly. Yeah." Bianca held up her chin, holding onto what was left of her pride. "If we knew each other well, I probably would have missed you too."

Angelo laughed. "You don't have to pretend, Bianca."

"I'm not," she lied, as he gazed around the caravan. "I wouldn't pret-"

"You live here?" he asked, cutting her off. She nodded. "Permanently?"

"No," she said, amused at his disdainful tone. "When we travel, we travel in this caravan. It's nice and cosy."

"Indeed," said Angelo, eyebrow raised as he took in every tiny detail- without the lights on. Bianca swallowed, making him look at her.

"What's the matter? Are you still afraid? Are my eyes alight again?"

Bianca shook her head and said no. "You're just frightening. Can Cormier do all that? See in the dark like you can?"

Angelo said no as well. "Being a Grand Vampire... it's very tough. My father chose me to be the next, and I inherited his power the minute he resigned."

"Where is he now?"

Angelo looked away. "Gone."

"Was he staked in the heart like the vampires in the books?"

The books, Angelo thought amusedly, then his smile faded. "Yes."

Bianca could tell it was a painful subject, and didn't ask anything else. They stood in silence, the dark enveloping them. Bianca fidgeted, then she said "Is the offer still open?"

A smile tugged Angelo's mouth. "What offer was that, Bianca?"

Bianca smiled back. "The walk at night."

"Of course," smiled Angelo. "I see that you are fully dressed."

"Yep."

"And fully awake also."

Bianca smiled, repeating herself. "Yep."

"Then let us go."

* * Bianca * *

Bianca hung onto Angelo's arm, content as they walked- through the woods. "Why do they say the wolves are family to the vampires?"
"Some relatives are wolves," Angelo answered, and she nodded.
Then she stopped dead. "Wolves as in *wolf* wolves? Or wolves as in… you know- *werewolves?* "
"Both, but werewolves originally. When in wolf form, the werewolves join with real wolves, most of the time producing offspring."
"Wow. And they know you're relatives?"
"Of course. Look, there's a cub waiting for me."
"Wow," whispered Bianca as she gazed at the grey and white cub, with it's tiny white paws. "It's beautiful."
Angelo smiled and knelt. "Come, Joseph. Don't be afraid."
The baby wolf looked at Bianca nervously, then padded forwards. Bianca could feel eyes on them, shifting as close as she could get to Angelo.
"Don't be afraid," Angelo repeated, though he was addressing her this time. "They won't hurt you."
"Do they talk? The werewolves' baby wolves?"
"Yes. But Joseph is very still young. Where is your mother?" he asked the cub gently, stroking him as he stared intently at Bianca. "Come, Bianca. He likes the look of you."
"Can I touch him?" she asked, though she was addressing a female wolf, which had just walked out of the trees next to her.
"Be my guest," the wolf answered, her voice so soft and feminine it startled her. Joseph the cub licked Bianca's palm happily as she knelt to stroke him, beside Angelo.
"How are you, Claire?" Angelo asked the wolf, handing the cub to Bianca and standing up. Bianca couldn't help but cuddle the cute cub affectionately, Joseph content in her arms.
"Fine as always. As usual, when winter approaches it gets harder to find food for the young ones. I'm so glad I only have Joseph to look after: many friends have children aplenty."
"You may always come and stay at my castle," Angelo murmured. "How is that cousin of mine? Still giving you trouble?"
Claire sighed, turning her blue eyes towards the dark trees. "Trevor cannot help the female werewolves. I suppose, because they can morph back into a human like he can, and I cannot-"
"Rubbish," spat Angelo, and Joseph whimpered. Angelo glanced at both the cub and Bianca, then regained his cool. He couldn't afford for both to flee- it would be much harder to find Bianca than Joseph, especially if she fell into the wrong paws- or hands.
"Claire, is that what he tells you?" The wolf hung her head. "Ignore him."

"He constantly talks down to both me and Joseph. He even disclaims our baby as his own. Oh Angelo, I know he is your relative, but I can't take much more of Trevor's behaviour."

"But you don't let me leave," snarled a voice, making everyone turn.

A handsome man stepped into the clearing, Bianca's jaw dropping at the sight of him. Then she scowled.

All the good looking guys are gits.

Angelo looked at her, arching an eyebrow. Bianca smiled, hastily correcting herself for his sake.

Most of the good looking guys, anyway.

His expression didn't change.

Who aren't vampires? She tried, and he smiled and looked away.

"And who is this beauty?" Trevor asked, looking at Bianca. "Cousin?"

"A friend of mine," Angelo replied. "Trevor."

"No." Trevor turned to walk back into the trees, near enough causing Angelo to lose his temper.

"Trevor!"

"No, Angelo!" he spun back round angrily. "I wait and I wait for the woman to dismiss me as her own, but she does not. So I am bound to her and the cub!"

Angelo looked at Claire, who hung her head. "I love him, Angelo."

"Yet you cannot take his behaviour. This relationship is failing, Claire. You may as well rid yourself of the burden my cousin is to you."

Bianca nodded, Trevor thankful. "Even the mortal knows it."

"Quiet," snapped Angelo. "Claire?"

Joseph wriggled in Bianca's arms, making her let him go as he bounded to Trevor happily, yapping. Trevor sighed, kneeling down to pet him.

"It's not that I don't care for them, Angelo. But-"

"I understand," said Angelo curtly. "Claire, please- rid yourself of my cousin. Werewolves can be savage when they want to be; you don't want Joseph hurt. If Trevor is always annoyed with you as a human, imagine him as a werewolf. One night in wolf form his temper, much higher, could snap."

"I- I..." Trevor waited, hardly daring to believe it. Claire looked away from him, then she walked back into the trees. Joseph hovered, unsure whether to stay with his father or go with his mother.

Angelo pointed at the trees, looking at him. Joseph padded after Claire, then he looked back at Trevor, who sighed, waiting.

They heard Claire's voice, loud and clear: "I dismiss you as my lover. You are free to do as you please, Trevor Gordon- on the condition that you stay away from both myself and Joseph."

"I will," Trevor said, though he didn't seem so sure.

"Come, Joseph," said Claire gently, and both dogs vanished into the trees.

Trevor sighed, rubbing his neck.

"I'm free. And yet-"

"Don't approach Claire or Joseph," Angelo said coldly, knowing full well he was regretting having Claire dismiss him. "This may have been a heat of the moment situation for you, Trevor- we all know fatherhood can be frightening. But many wolves, even if they do fool around, stick to the mothers of their children."

Their baby mama's, Bianca thought to herself, Angelo frowning at her.

"What?"

"It's a term for 'mothers of their children,'" Bianca explained, wanting to laugh. "The modern term young people use."

"I see," he said curiously. "Let us go, Bianca. Trevor, we will meet again."

"Of course," murmured Trevor. "Goodbye... Bianca."

"Bye," Bianca said, feeling sorry for him as he left.

Angelo sighed, taking her hand. "Are you ready to go home?"

"Home to mine?" He nodded. "No, not yet. I'll go when I can't stay with you anymore. How's Cormier?"

Angelo cringed. "Cormier is fine. He has been busy with his many lady friends."

Bianca didn't seem to care about that. "Is he at home?"

Angelo scowled, but he kept his tone the same. "Of course, but he may be going out shortly after we arrive."

* * Cormier * *

"Cormier!"

"Ah, look who it is," said Cormier lazily, standing as she ran to him. He embraced Bianca warmly, ignoring Angelo's annoyed face. "How have you been, my little chick pea?"

"I've been great, you?" Bianca hugged him back. "I missed you."

Cormier sensed the fury which exploded within his brother, and immediately knew she had said otherwise to him- or said the same with a twist to it.

Angelo smiled coldly, saying "Make yourself at home with Cormier, Bianca."

"I will, definitely."

"If you need me for anything, thought I doubt it, I shall be in the library."

"Uh... ok," she said uncertainly, and Angelo turned on his heel and left. They watched his cape billow behind him, heard a door slam.

Bianca looked at Cormier, confused. "What-"

"Never mind him," said Cormier amusedly. "Would you like a *real* tour of the Heathen Manor? Even though you acted like a brilliant tourist the first time, taking so many pictures and discovering rooms-"

"Sorry," she said embarrassedly, but he waved that off.

"Come, chick pea. Let us go on our tour."

* * Angelo * *

Angelo tried to read, but he couldn't concentrate. Why Bianca seemed to like Cormier so much, he had no clue. Maybe Grand Vampires weren't supposed to have lovers? His father definitely didn't have time for his mother after Grandfather gave him the job of it.

And Angelo was the same. If Cormier didn't live with him, he probably wouldn't have time for his brother either.

Bianca's shriek of laughter made him look up sharply, getting to his feet.

* * Cormier * *

"And then, they'd dip low like this-" Cormier spun Bianca around before he dipped her, Bianca laughing even though his face was so close to her. "And vanish. They'd drop the women on the floor like they were nothing!"

"Why?"

Cormier shrugged. "Vanishing seemed to be the spectacular thing to do when one finishes dancing with his lover, but not if the woman ruins her frock."

"Did they try something else in the end?"

"Of course," said a voice coldly, and they looked up and saw Angelo. "They'd vanish with their lover instead. It was better that way."

"Oh- ok." Bianca and Cormier righted themselves, Cormier amused.

"Brother, come and demonstrate for us how the vampires dance at a ball."

"No."

"Fine," shrugged Cormier. "Then go back to the library. You're only interrupting the Heathen Tour."

Angelo glared at him. Being the elder brother, Cormier didn't waver.

"As I was saying Bianca, that was the ridiculous way they ended a dance."

Bianca was enthralled once again. "Why don't you demonstrate the dance, Cormier?"

"I would, my little chick pea, but I need a partner to volunteer."

Bianca lifted her hand, playing along. Cormier laughed.

"You, young one?" She nodded. "Do you dance?"

"I've done ballroom dancing before-"

"Perfect! Let us begin."

* * Angelo * *

Rage coursed through Angelo as the lights dimmed, slow, taunting music playing. Cormier was going to pay as soon as Bianca left their home, he'd make sure of it.

He did his best to look nonchalant, but when he was shaking with anger it was pretty hard.

Bianca and Cormier looked perfect together as they moved across the dance floor, Bianca caught up in the romance, the pleasure, the moment.

"You'll have a fit if you watch any more of their behaviour," Marissa said softly, invisible to their eye. "Come, Angelo."

He obeyed, storming away into his bedroom.

"I'll kill Cormier!" he exploded furiously, pacing the floor as Marissa materialised, calmly closing the door behind her. "How could he?"

"Cormier likes to wind people up, it's an uncanny habit of his," Marissa replied. "Which is why I wouldn't court him even if I wanted. He would interact with other females just to taunt me if we argued, to make a point as he is doing with you- his younger brother."

"Which is why you want someone staid, like the Grand Vampire."

"Yes," she said with a shrug, being totally honest. "I don't deny it."

"Well, Bianca seems to have chosen which of us she prefers. She wants someone to make her laugh, feel at ease- like Cormier. All I seem to do is frighten her." Marissa didn't reply, waiting. "Maybe it's better they like each other so much. That way, I can move on... to another."

"Another... such as myself?"

Angelo shrugged. "I see no harm in it."

"Kiss me," Marissa replied, hearing the falsehood in his tone. "Now."

"Why?"

"It's the only way I can believe you, Angelo."

Angelo took her in his arms, taking a deep breath.

But he couldn't. Bianca's pretty face danced across his brain the same way she danced with Cormier: slowly, tauntingly. He couldn't kiss Marissa, his close friend. Their whole relationship would alter.

Marissa nodded, speaking quietly. "I thought the same."

Before Angelo could release her his door burst open. Cormier and Bianca fell through it, laughing.

"Brother, you must keep Bianca. She's-"

Silence fell, Cormier and Bianca staring at the vampires in front of them.

Bianca was the first to react. "What the hell?"

"Yes, exactly!" Cormier said, trying to sound stunned too. "What the hell, Angelo."

Bianca stared at him as he released the beautiful woman- she looked about twenty two- older than Angelo but younger than Cormier.

"I- I don't... Cormier, can you take me home?"

"You're not going anywhere," said Angelo quietly, as Marissa vaporised.

"What- Marissa!" Silence. "Damn it- she left me. Bianca-"

"I want to go home."

"No- and if you flee you won't get very far," Angelo warned. "I will make each door become the one to this room, where I will wait for you."

Bianca looked at Cormier disbelievingly, who said "It isn't a joke- I am a frequent victim of his mind tricks."

"Get out," snapped Angelo, glaring at Bianca. He couldn't even look at his brother right now, he was that angry. "Set up the club, brother. It's soon eleven."

Cormier scowled and vanished in a cloud of black smoke, obeying. Bianca wanted to say "Don't leave me!" but he flew through the window as a night bat before she had the chance.

"Now, you." Angelo's glare intensified. "Explain your behaviour."

"Oh, oh- I should explain *my* behaviour?" she said furiously. "I was about to say the same to *you!"*

"I shouldn't have to explain a thing. What you witnessed was nothing compared to you and my brother."

"What?"

"Don't give me that, Bianca!" Rage spilled through the Count's lips, his eyes lighting up. Bianca recoiled as he said "From the moment you met Cormier, all I've witnessed is the love you both express for one another-"

"What the hell are you talking about??"

"You prefer Cormier to me!"

"What!"

"It's fine, I can cope with that- but did you have to be so intimate in front of me?" said Angelo angrily. "Slow dancing like the perfect couple?"

"All right Dracula, listen up." Now Bianca was just as mad. "I see why Cormier ignores your behaviour towards him sometimes. You overreact!"

"I do not!"

"Ok fine, you're jealous! For no damn reason! Shut up!" she said angrily, as Angelo opened his mouth. "Don't you think that if I'd rather- you know, be involved with Cormier, it would have been him I was missing so much it bordered on depression? Yes, I missed his jolly nature- but it was you I wanted! Guys!" she said furiously, before he could answer. "This is exactly why I don't bother with them!"

Angelo calmed down. "I apologise, Bianca."

"Get stuffed. Now, if you'd please let me out so I can go home?"

Angelo hesitated, then he obliged and removed the charm on the doors. Bianca stormed out, then she stopped and looked back.

Angelo just watched her. He knew full well she wanted to stay with him. Bianca refused to do it. "It was nice seeing you again-"

She shrieked as Angelo vanished and reappeared in front of her, grabbing her by her shoulders and slamming her into the wall of the upper corridor. "If you dare tell me I won't be seeing you again like before," he growled, "I'll kidnap you. And I always keep my word, Bianca."

Bianca struggled, but he was too strong. "Let me go, Angelo! You can't just-"

Angelo crushed his mouth to hers before she could react, releasing his firm hold on her shoulders only to hold her tightly by the waist. Bianca's arms curved around his neck, pulling him closer urgently- but Angelo pulled back.

She whimpered, making him smile. "Now you may leave."

Bianca's mind was spinning, her mouth tingling. "What just happened?"

"You experienced the pleasures of the mouth only the Grand Vampire could give," smirked Angelo. "Now, with me knowing you'll be thinking about it and wanting more, wanting me more than anything, you may leave and go home confused."

Bianca stared at him, Angelo's smirk growing. "Go, Bianca."

SMACK!!

He stared at her, stunned, face stinging. "Did you just slap me?"

"Yes I did! Get out of my way." She pushed him roughly- to her, anyway.

Angelo laughed: her hands tickled his stomach.

"I'll see you again, Bianca. Very soon."

Bianca stopped as the clock in the lower hall chimed eleven.

"The club's open now?"

Angelo frowned, nodding. "Yes. Why?"

"Then I'm going to hang out with Cormier. Which way is it?"

Angelo tried his best to remain calm. "You are not going to my club."

"Why not? Because you're insecure about Cormier?"

"Actually my little dove, my club is for vampires only. Each night at least four of them grow bloodthirsty. If you'd like to walk amongst us in the night, never to see sunlight again- by all means, go. But I will not come to your rescue."

Bianca stared at him, unsure whether he was bluffing or not.

"Have fun," Angelo added, and she scowled and started walking, surprising him. "You're still going to go?"

"No. I'm going home."

"Even though you want more than anything to stay with me?"

"Yep."

Angelo smiled, shaking his head. "May I walk you home?"

"How about you walk me to the guest room instead?" said Bianca, noticing the full moon outside through Angelo's three storey window.

Angelo threw back his head and laughed, Bianca puzzled.

"What's so funny?"

"You," said Angelo, laughing. "You're unbelievable, Bianca Davis."

"Why?" she asked, though she smiled back.

"You expect me to allow you to stay after you annoyed me greatly?"

"You don't have to, but... the full moon's out. And we have to walk by the woods, and- and there's werewolves out- I don't want to-"

"Shh," he said soothingly, realising she actually thought he'd make her leave. "You're not going anywhere, don't worry. My bluff."

Bianca smiled, shaking her head. "You're unbelievable, not me."

"Well, a real life vampire is very unbelievable." Angelo laughed again, Bianca watching him with a smile. "Don't you think?"

She nodded, smiling still. Angelo frowned at her again.

"Why do you look so relaxed? Content when you were raging less than an hour ago?"

"I like when you laugh," Bianca replied, and he smiled.

"I haven't laughed in six years."

"Shut up," she said, her jaw dropping. "Are you serious?"

Angelo nodded. "You make me happy."

"You say that, but we've only seen each other twice."

"Ah, but two days are like two months in the mind of a vampire."

"That's why everyone's hitched?" Bianca wanted to laugh again. "What happened to Cormier?"

"Cormier prides himself on being the Bachelor of Pennsylvania."

"He gave himself that name? Typical Cormier."

"Yes, exactly. You aren't tired?" Bianca said no. "How about we have some warm milk and meat- well, you may have biscuits."

Bianca smiled, taking his hand. "Ok."

* * Cormier * *

"You disgust me, Cormier Heathen."

Cormier rolled his eyes before looking at Marissa. "Why now, woman?"

Sebastian grinned, and Marissa glared at him. "Don't say one word, Sebastian- you haven't a clue what I talk about."

"Indeed I do," Sebastian answered, serving a customer some vodka and ice from behind the bar. "Cormier has been keeping me nicely updated."

"Then you agree that he was out of order with the mortal?"

"I agree that Angelo was very jealous," Sebastian replied, "Just as he was when I used to greet Alicia lovingly. Clover was too," he added thoughtfully. "But then, they found out she was my second cousin on my mother's side, and their envy vanished."

"Yes, but Cormier had no right to-"

"Blah blah blah," Cormier said, infuriating her. "The club is for fun, Marissa. If you've come just to give lectures then get out."

"How dare you," hissed Marissa, eyes lighting a furious burgundy. "Your brother is finally starting to love again, but you decided to grab the mortal before he had a chance, just as you did with Alicia."

The music faded away, everyone looking at them. Nobody but those who attended the Grand Meetings knew the true story of Alicia Peters.

"The mortal has a name," Cormier said, starting to grow angry too. "Angelo should know I have no intention of stealing the girl like I did Alicia. It was a mistake, a stupid mistake-"

"And she couldn't live with herself, so she walked to her death!"

Cormier's eyes lit too. "You're barred from my club!"

"I'll think you'll find it is *my* club, brother."

Everyone turned to see the Grand Vampire leaning against a post, half hidden in the shadows. Angelo stepped into the light and swept past everyone towards the bar, ignoring the bows and murmured greetings the vampires gave him.

"You are not barred," Angelo said calmly to Marissa. "I think Cormier is the one who needs to stay with myself at home for a few nights. Sebastian will be in charge until he returns."

"What? But I did nothing-"

"Come," Angelo said, still calm as ever. He took Marissa's hand and kissed it. "Until again, Marissa."

She nodded, Angelo and Cormier vanishing. They took to the skies, Angelo far in front. Cormier could be heard screeching furiously.

"Well!" said Sebastian, clapping his hands. "Drinks all round?"

* * Angelo * *

"You had no right to attempt barring Marissa."

"Angelo, she is a menace. She approaches me only to argue!"

"You don't get along, so steer clear of her. When she does approach you, ignore her. You could have easily continued serving drinks and monitoring the club as you always do when she nears you."

"Yes, but usually Marissa gets her drink and moves away again!"

"You angered her as you angered me," Angelo said flatly, sitting down.

Cormier remained standing. "You may be the Grand Vampire, but I am the elder brother. Don't bother instructing me to keep away from Bianca Davis. How to interact with her is how I always interact with females."

"And somehow they end up in love with you," Angelo said as he picked up the local newspaper for vampires, delivered at one a.m. once a week always. "Yes Cormier, I know."

"That wasn't where I was headed, Angelo. Alicia-"

"Don't," said Angelo, shaking his head. "I don't want to hear it. You and she both had the same version of the story- that's good enough for me. She wasn't forced, she fell in love. That's all there is to it."

"You still resent what happened?"

"No, Cormier. I got over what happened before Alicia's death. I still resent the fact that my brother, my hero for twenty decades, stabbed me brutally in the back."

"I see." Cormier looked away. "Well, if your wish is for me to keep away from Bianca-"

"I wish nothing of the sort. I wished nothing with Alicia as well; I clapped when you danced together and called bravo, I laughed at your silly jokes and said you both were a delight to have in the same room. I trusted you, Cormier. But I don't trust you now. You did the same with Alicia as you do to Bianca, but now I cannot let it skip over my head."

"Then... why do you refrain from ordering me away from her?"

"Because she is nothing like Alicia. She told me, when we have only seen each other twice, that it was me she wanted. Not you."

"And Alicia...?"

"Said otherwise when I confronted her."

"I see," said Cormier. "Where is Bianca?"

"Asleep in the guestroom."

Cormier grinned, amused. "Bit of a step back from the last time she was here."

Angelo scowled at him. "Be quiet."

* * Bianca * *

She was sobbing, Angelo so angry his entire body as well as his eyes were glowing a deep, frightening red. His fangs were unsheathed, he couldn't control his anger.

Ornament after ornament exploded, the girl screaming "Stop, Angelo!"

"How could you, Alicia?! How?!"

"I love him," she wept, Bianca confused. Was she Angelo's sister?

Wait- wasn't that the girl who burst into flames in another nightmare?

Cormier appeared exactly in front of her, blocking her view from the girl before she could get a better look. "Angelo, please stop!"

He vanished just as quickly as Angelo sent an ornament rushing for him, the giant vase speeding towards Bianca's face-

She gasped, sitting up. Sweat trickled down her forehead, Bianca quickly walking into her bathroom and washing her face, her neck- then she jumped into the shower instead before putting the robe Angelo gave her back on, and clean underwear.

Cormier laughed at something, then she heard Angelo's voice.

"Why, it's only two a.m. Time seems to be going slowly this night."

Bianca trudged down the corridor, then stopped and looked over the banister curiously. Downstairs looked so empty, so cold. Didn't they ever go down there apart from when they left the house?

And they didn't even have to, she thought to herself. They can fly through an upstairs window if they want.

"Bianca!" said Cormier, popping his head round the dining area door with a broad smile. "Must you think so loud?"

"I don't know how to think quietly," she retorted, smiling back at him. "Where's Angelo?"

"Right here," smiled Angelo. "We could hear you miles away."

"I don't know how to think quietly," she repeated, pouting. "I thought inside the head was quiet enough, but there you go."

Both brothers laughed, making her smile.

"Come, we was about to have our supper. When was the last time you had a full table of food, my dear?" Cormier asked. "All the meats you can possibly think of-"

"Raw?"

"For us, yes." Cormier's smile grew. "For you, no."

"You have a weird stomach," smiled Angelo, and she looked at him.

"Me!"

They burst out laughing again, then Angelo looked at the robe.

"This won't do. You cannot come to supper in just a robe, Bianca."

"Oh, I didn't know-"

"Go and change at once!" said Cormier, feigning strictness as Angelo

added "And don't come back without socks on."
Bianca played along, saluting them and bowing before she jogged away, both brothers laughing as they watched her go.

* * Cormier * *

Cormier smiled at his little brother. "It's good to hear you laugh again."
"It is," agreed Angelo. "Come, let's be seated."
He rubbed his neck as he looked at the table with uncooked food, raw vegetables, raw potatoes, raw everything. Angelo raised a hand, then he lowered it.
"We may as well startle her."
"Yes, let's," Cormier said, as Bianca walked down the corridor.

* * Angelo * *

Angelo was surprised at himself. When did the loving Count reappear? Angelo was sure the old Grand Vampire, the lovable, enjoyable Angelo Heathen who everybody loved to death, died the minute he discovered Alicia's betrayal.
No wonder Father refused her as the Countess. He must have foreseen the whole incident. Now I don't think that was strange at all.
Then Angelo frowned.
Strange though, after he'd wiped his hands of her and Cormier, he was brutally staked.

* * Bianca * *

Bianca turned into the room, Cormier beaming as her jaw dropped at the underdone feast on the table, everything raw.

"You're not serious."

"We certainly are," smirked Cormier. "We will eat, you will starve. Right brother?" Silence, Cormier looking at him. "Angelo?"

"Hmm?"

"Where were you?"

"Far away in my thoughts. Where were *we?*"

"About to eat while Bianca starves."

"Indeed. It must have slipped my mind-"

"Hey!" she said indignantly, and Angelo laughed as he waved a hand over the great table.

The food burst into colour at once, meat steaming.

Angelo pulled out Bianca's chair for her, Bianca smiling as she sat.

Cormier inhaled deeply, reaching for the potatoes. "I'm starving."

"So vampires eat normal food?" Bianca asked as she pulled the pork chops towards her, taking one up with the large fork provided. "That isn't meat, I mean. I know you eat it raw."

Angelo reached for the same platter with pork chops: as soon as the chop hit his plate it was wiped of its colour, returning to it's soft, pale, red state.

Bianca stared at it, shocked. "Um… how did it go from cooked to raw?"

"Angelo has many powers," Cormier said proudly. "Sometimes I am afraid of him."

Angelo cut his chop, saying "It's not easy being me, Bianca. I know some are very envious out there of me. Some smiles are genuine, some fake."

"I know what you mean. I used to get that a lot before I started travelling with my father."

"Why did you?" asked Cormier, interested. "To get away from it?"

"No, to see what was out there. Mum was too perfect, her house too clean. Everything was so… stuck up. I hated school, I hated the snobby students. I didn't fit in. That's why I left with my dad and Ricky."

"You both walked out?" asked Angelo, but she said no.

"I had to wait until I was eighteen. Ricky went a year before me."

Cormier nodded. "And you missed your brother."

"Naturally," Angelo said, frowning at him. "You always state the over-obvious, don't you brother?"

"Be quiet and eat, Angelo. You're so slim. Try fattening up a little."

Angelo rolled his eyes, Bianca smiling at him.

Who'd think he'd change so much in the blink of an eye.

"Certainly not Cormier," Cormier said, highly amused as she scowled.

"I forgot my thoughts aren't private when I'm here."

"Speaking of *here,*" Cormier said innocently, "Are you returning to your family this night? Or will you stay with us again?"

Angelo looked at her as well.

"I'll go in the day," Bianca said, reaching for a glass of wine. She felt so grown up right now. "That way I won't have to get emotional saying goodbye to you two in person."

"Smart," Angelo commented, and she smiled at him.

* * *

Angelo laid on his side, arms around Bianca. She enjoyed his long fingers combing through her hair, almost falling asleep when she was struck by a sudden thought, suddenly wide awake again.

"Angelo?"

"Mmm?"

"Do you think this relationship... is too fast?"

"How do you mean?"

"I mean, you know. People don't usually get hitched the day they meet."

Angelo smiled. "You don't believe in love at first sight?"

"Well... no," she admitted. "Not really. But Gran does."

"I think your grandmother is a very gifted woman." Angelo spoke with much honesty. "I only hope that, as she senses the dark energy of us- the undead, vampires roaming this large town- that she doesn't gather many tourists and villagers together to attempt destroying us."

"Gran would never do that, I promise."

"I believe you," Angelo said uncertainly, "But-"

A fierce howl sailed through the open windows, followed by many others.

"Angelo!" bellowed Cormier, running down the corridor. "Claire has been savaged! You can hear the pain in her howl- we must go!"

Angelo was up right away, Bianca scared. "Angelo?"

He turned as he pulled his fastened his cape, swearing inside his head. He'd forgotten her being with him.

"You cannot come, Bianca-"

"You must bring her," said Cormier angrily. "She cannot stay alone in this castle when the werewolves are headed for it!"

"What? Why are they headed here?"

"To eat the meat we so graciously give them when they need to savage a human being," Angelo said, taking a small, very feminine cloak out of his wardrobe. Another of his to-be gifts to Alicia. "Put this on, Bianca. Whatever you do, don't lower your hood. They may smell fresh, human blood, but they won't be able to tell you aren't a vampire unless they see the mortal in your eyes."

"The mortal in- huh?"

"Do as he says," said Cormier steadily, pulling his own cloak on.

Angelo straightened up, then he turned. Bianca's jaw dropped at the sight of him- he really did look magnificent in his black suit with a red shirt and shoes, upturned collar with his cape flying behind him, with gloves on his hands and all the rest of it.

He held out a hand to Bianca, and she took it. Cormier stepped forwards and adjusted her hood, saying "I'll lead."

Angelo nodded as Cormier morphed, waiting for the smoke to vanish.

Cormier flew through an open window, staring down as he flapped his tiny wings. He screeched at Angelo, Angelo lifting Bianca into his arms.

"Our savage relatives are almost here... hold tight."

"What- why should I-?"

Angelo burst into full speed, running straight at the open window. Bianca flung her arms around his neck, shrieking "You gotta be kidding me!"

Angelo dived through the window, Bianca screaming.

* * Ricky * *

Ricky stopped and stared up at the crazy silhouette falling against the moon, breathless. Was that Bianca who screamed?

The silhouette vanished into the darkness, tourists holding their lamps up fearfully.

"Did you hear the howling?"

"What's going on?"

"Richard!" called a girl, running up to him quickly. "Hi! Do you want to share my tent? My Dad'll be out looking for your sister, so we can-"

Ricky pushed her away angrily, looking around in vain. "How can you think about me at a time like this! I'm not thinking about *you,* I'm thinking about my sister!"

"This is the second time she wandered off!" said Samuel angrily, then he stopped. "Where's your grandmother?"

"She's sleeping in the van-"

"Get inside with her, Ricky!!"

"What about Bianca?!"

"I'll look with the boys!"

* * Angelo * *

Cormier swore angrily, outraged. "No! Who did this?!"

Claire's torn body lay under the stars in the clearing she and Bianca met, her blood shining in the moonlight.

Angelo was much calmer, looking at the wolves who surrounded her, heads bent with sorrow as he asked "Where is Trevor?"

Bianca heard a snuffling sound, turning to see Joseph, the baby wolf.

"We haven't seen Trevor since Claire detached him from her life."

"He wouldn't do this to her," a male wolf said sharply. "I know Trevor."

"We all know Trevor," another wolf said, and all the dogs nodded.

"He may have grown restless, but he did care about his family."

Bianca took a few steps back, into the darkness. She held her arms out to Joseph, who recoiled with a small whimper.

"I won't hurt you," she whispered, cautiously reaching out and scratching him behind the ears. "Don't be scared."

Joseph padded forwards, into her arms. He was shaking, Bianca realised. Did he witness his mother's onslaught? Was it a human who did it? Is that why he's scared of me?

Angelo turned almost as soon as she thought it. "Joseph."

The cub flinched, Angelo walking into the darkness and kneeling next to Bianca, the same way she knelt next to him the first time.

Cormier spoke to the other wolves angrily, but none had seen the actual attack. Phoebus, the wolf who had spoken sharply- and the leader of the pack, looked over at Bianca holding Joseph protectively, whispering words of comfort in his tiny ear. Amazed, he asked "The mortal isn't afraid of anything that has taken place? She won't flee?"

Bianca looked at him, and she shook her head. "No."

There were low murmurs of respect at that, Cormier saying "As relatives, we will take full responsibility for Joseph. Even if Claire is gone, her bond remains. Trevor cannot come near his son once he is free of her."

"There is one way," Angelo said quietly, and everyone looked at him. "Trevor still loves Claire. I doubt he has any idea of what went on. The least he can do is solve the mystery of his late wife's onslaught, his last display of love to her. Only that love," he said firmly, "Can give him what he is possibly yearning for."

Everyone looked at Joseph, who was sniffing the air curiously.

"Once then, he can communicate with Joseph," Cormier said, Angelo nodding as he added "If what Bianca thinks is true and Joseph did witness the attack on his mother, then Trevor could surely confirm whatever his belief will be."

"What of Joseph?" Phoebus said sharply. "Your intentions are very much approved of, but let's not forget that you certainly won't be able to function in the day. Who will tend to Joseph?"

"I'll will," Bianca said firmly, and everyone stared at her.

"You? A mortal?" Phoebus asked dubiously. "Tending to a baby wolf?"

"Yes."

"Bianca," started Angelo, but she cut him off, eyes shining angrily.

"Don't tell me you're going to leave him in the forest or something! Whatever killed Claire, it might be because they was jealous of her!"

Talk broke out, the wolves confused.

"Jealous?"

"What is she talking about?"

"That is so silly and typically mortal-"

"This is exactly why we keep to ourselves and don't mix with the non-magical-"

"Enough!" barked Phoebus, and silence fell. "Don't think, that because she is a mortal, that the mortal-"

"Bianca," Cormier said irritably. "She has a name."

Angelo was just as annoyed. Phoebus apologised.

"Bianca, we will say from now on, may be correct. We all know of Trevor Gordon's many lovers- but the Bond of Wolves and Joining would not allow him to conceive with any other but Claire."

"That's exactly my *point,*" Bianca said, hurt that they thought she was clueless. Cormier took Joseph off her gently as she said "Maybe they think that if they kill his family, Trevor won't *be* bonded anymore."

Silence, Angelo nodding furiously.

"Is the silly typical mortal who knows no magic so silly now?"

"Count Angelo, forgive them," a wolf said quietly. "Forgive us all."

"I will think about it."

"It's ok," started Bianca, but Cormier shook his head.

"If Angelo thinks it's not ok then that's what it is."

"Joseph is now my responsibility," Angelo said coldly; no one argued. "Once the werewolves leave and the castle returns to it's normal state, we will take him home."

Bianca smiled at him, Cormier holding Joseph in one arm as he said "Let us be grateful we dined already. Come, we go to Sebastian's."

* * Bianca * *

Bianca felt nervous being around the vampires as they spoke heartily, instead keeping her attention on the baby wolf.

Angelo stood by the window, his back to them as he gazed up at the moon. Bianca knew he was thinking about Claire.

She felt angry. She didn't even get to know the wolf, who seemed so calm and tranquil- they could have talked about things, she was sure of it.

Angelo sighed as Joseph whined dolefully, hanging his head.

"Hush, Joseph. You'll be all right."

Clover squeezed Angelo's arm. "I'm certain it wasn't Trevor."

"We all are," Angelo replied. "But none has seen him-"

"I'll check the castle with Sebastian," Cormier said. "It's been an hour now, and day will soon arrive. We must get home."

"Angelo, cheer yourself," Sebastian said, looking at him. "You cannot blame yourself for what happened."

"I know."

Clover turned her hazel eyes to Bianca, who avoided her gaze.

"You're afraid, Bianca?"

"No, but... I'm scared I might get bitten by a vampire real soon."

"Your teeth," murmured Angelo, and Clover ran her tongue over them. She laughed at Bianca's worried face, explaining "Teeth are nothing to be scared of if the eyes aren't glowing. Sometimes, even if they *are* aglow, it may be because a vampire is merely thinking of a really special time, or person. The way your eyes would light up at a gift, for example- but a vampire's eyes really *will* light up."

"Oh," mumbled Bianca, and Clover laughed again as she sat next to her, then embraced her in a tight hug. Letting go, she said "I will make sure a vampire doesn't hurt you, little sister."

"Sister?" she repeated amazedly, mind spinning. "How- we've just met-"

"And I know everything about you already. Come, you must be tired. I doubt you'll be going back to the castle- and the path to your truck is dangerous when the full moon is out."

Bianca let herself be led away, amazed.

Vampires are way too weird.

* * Angelo * *

Angelo struggled to keep his eyes open as Clover entered his room to check on her husband, and the Grand Vampire with his brother.

His gaze was unfocused, but he recognised her outline in the doorway.

"Where... where is Bianca?"

"Fast asleep," Clover said quietly: she was another gifted vampire, like Cormier. She fell asleep later and woke earlier than normal vampires. Something in her fought the spell of day, for almost three hours.

Cormier could only resist sleep for almost one, but he did wake up three hours before nightfall.

Clover knelt next to Angelo, murmuring "Sleep, Count Angelo."

"What... what happened to... to Joseph?"

"Joseph sleeps at Bianca's side," Clover answered. "Don't fight it anymore, Angelo. Close your eyes."

Angelo felt himself slip away as he did as he was told.

* * *

When he woke, it was dark again. Sebastian and Cormier was gone. Angelo sat up, running a hand through his trimmed hair. It tickled his neck and shoulders as he rose from the bed, already thinking of her.

As he made to leave the room, Sebastian walked in and pushed him back.

"Whoa, Master Heathen. I know you yearn for her, but at least fix up and look sharp before you go to Bianca."

"Is she all right? Has she been fed? What-"

"Everything's fine," Sebastian reassured him. "I took the night off so I could look after Joseph for Bianca and the rest."

"Bianca and the rest! Where is she?" demanded Angelo, and Sebastian stalled time, knowing Angelo would go crazy.

"Clover has taken Bianca under her wing. She's fine."

"Where is she?" Angelo repeated, Sebastian squirming under his glare.

"With Clover Angelo, I told you. Come and eat some-"

"Don't make me force it out of you, Sebastian!"

"I- I... all right," Sebastian said quickly, as Angelo took a menacing step forwards. "They went to the night club with Cormier."

"What!"

* * Cormier * *

"And that is why your nose will never be perfect," Cormier told Marissa. "No matter how much you try to tweak it, your nose will always be…"

* * Bianca * *

Many fit guys asked Bianca to dance eagerly, taking her waist as soon as another song started. Some even fought for her.

Right now, she was dancing with a handsome man, very handsome. And Hanson his name was! Very, very spooky.

He'd given her a drink of Tequila, served by whoever it was at the bar. Not knowing that he'd drugged her, Bianca was having the time of her life.

Angelo slipped out of her head, along with Cormier, Clover and Sebastian. Even Claire and Joseph she had no clue of.

All she wanted was Hanson- all she *needed* was Hanson.

"You have such soft skin," Hanson said as he trailed his index up and down her neck, making her shiver elatedly.

"Thank you."

They were in a dark corner of the club: Hanson was sure Cormier couldn't see them.

"You are exquisite, Bianca Davis."

"Thank you," she repeated, gazing at him. "Don't you want to go somewhere more… private?"

Hanson smiled, a very scary smile. Bianca thought he was glad she suggested them being on her own, and thought nothing of it as he took her hand, saying "Come then, we'll go for a walk."

* * Cormier * *

"And no matter how much you add powder, your neck will still have that horrid birthmark which is shaped like a banana-" Cormier stopped abruptly as Angelo entered the club, heading straight for the bar with Sebastian, who had Joseph in his arms.

Marissa was livid: Clover was trying to calm her down.

"Ignore Cormier, Marissa- he loves to get under your skin. Angelo!"

"You're awake," smiled Cormier, then he stopped as Angelo looked around the club, saying "Where is Bianca?"

"She was dancing with Romeo," Clover said as she looked, but the dance floor wasn't occupied right now. Everyone was sitting, exhausted.

Angelo grabbed Cormier by the collar, lifting him high off his feet as he dragged him over the bar. Glasses fell, smashing as silence did the same.

"Don't you ever let Bianca come here unless I am informed, Cormier!"

"Much absorbed," said Cormier weakly, and Angelo dropped him as he looked around the club. Furious, he realised Bianca was nowhere in it.

"Who was she last with?"

"Hanson," called the DJ from the mini studio. "They left ten minutes ago."

Angelo cursed violently, pushing Cormier roughly as he stormed out of the club.

"I'll have your head if she's hurt, Cormier!"

Annoyed, Cormier said "I'll have your *eyes* if this jacket is ruined!"

Angelo didn't answer, morphing into a night bat. Cormier followed suit, irritated.

He'd better remember who is the elder!

* * Bianca * *

Bianca gasped as she pushed him away, swaying on the spot a little.

Ever so innocent, Hanson asked "Are you all right Bianca?"

"Y-yeah," she said shakily, head spinning. The tender kiss on her neck had rocked her senseless, her head feeling like it would burst as the soft nip which caused so much pleasure pricked her flesh, causing her to gasp in pain and fright. "What... what happened?"

Then, as though she'd been doused with cold water, she remembered Hanson was a vampire- and he'd just kissed her neck!

"Did you bite me?!"

"No," a voice said; before Hanson could react he went flying, crashing to the ground in a heap before he leapt up and rushed at his attacker.

Bianca staggered away from Cormier and Hanson's furious duel, falling into Angelo's arms. His face swam in and out of focus as he stared down at her.

* * Angelo * *

"He- he... Angelo, I don't feel well-"

"Shh," he said gently, holding her up, but her knees gave way. "Bianca, you'll be fine. I'm taking you home."

* * Ricky * *

"Oi!" screamed Samuel, beside himself as he recognised his daughter in the young man's arms. "Let go of my daughter!"

Ricky and some others charged forwards, stopping with fright as another guy grabbed a man who struggled to get away, but he opened his mouth to reveal glimmering white fangs, clamping down on the man's face.

"Take Bianca, Angelo!"

"*Give* Bianca!" yelled Ricky, as the guy gathered his sister into his arms and turned, his back to them. "Give my sister!"

The man ignored him, cape billowing as he stared up at the moon.

* * Cormier * *

Hanson slammed onto the ground, his face a mass of blood. He didn't move again.

Breathing hard, Cormier said "He's stronger than he makes out."

Angelo didn't answer, Bianca turning her head weakly to look at the gathering crowd- of tourists!

"Dad... R-Ricky..."

"Dadricky?" Cormier said, perplexed. "What language is that?"

"She's talking about the men who shouted out," Angelo said, still with his back to the tourists. "One is her father, the other her brother."

"Ah," said Cormier. "And... will you return Bianca to them?"

Angelo hesitated, then he said "No."

Furious talk broke out, Ricky shouting "She's our responsibility!"

"She is weak," Angelo replied, in a voice of deadly calm. "She has been drugged magnificently by the brute you see lying before you. Bianca must rest. I assure you she will be home by nightfall tomorrow."

Cormier scowled as Ricky looked at his father. "Dad?"

"Who are you?" spat Samuel, glaring at Angelo. "How do you know Bianca? Turn around so I can see your face!"

"If I turn, you will not forget this face," Angelo said. "It is best you recognise me from behind. My elder brother's face you may scrutinize. He shall be the one to return your daughter to you."

Cormier stared at them all angrily, mouth tightly closed.

"We saw the fangs already," snapped Ricky. "Don't think you're going to get away with this. When Bianca comes home, you'll be staked in the heart! Nobody- and I mean *nobody*- hurts my sister!"

* * Angelo * *

"An idle threat," Cormier said angrily, pacing Angelo's bedroom. "Why the boy thinks he is any match for us I have no idea."

Angelo said nothing, holding Bianca's hand as she slept. He'd licked the wounds on her neck so they healed, but Bianca was still weak as ever.

"She must eat very soon," he said to Cormier worriedly. "Healing alone will not give her strength back."

"I agree. Wake her up, Angelo. I'll bring in a little something."

Angelo hesitated, then he obeyed. "Bianca."

She stirred, mumbling as she turned under his quality duvet.

"Bianca, honey. Wake up."

Bianca struggled, then she opened her eyes wearily. "Angelo…"

"Shh," he said soothingly, gently pulling her up. She slumped against him, head on his shoulder. Speaking gently but firmly, Angelo said "Bianca, you need your strength. You must eat something."

"I don't want anything…"

"Yes, you do." Angelo hoisted her up as Cormier entered the room holding a tray.

"God, she looks terrible. Do you think we should take her to the hospital?"

Angelo shook his head. "She just needs to eat. Bianca, hold on to me. I'm going to help you sit, ok?"

Bianca made a weak noise in reply, Angelo carefully lifting her up and onto his lap. That way, he could hold her upright.

"Where is Hanson?" he asked Cormier, fury bubbling in the pit of his stomach as he stared down at Bianca's ashen face. "Did he flee?"

"Flee he did, right into the jaws of Trevor. Our cousin saw the whole thing, but he was afraid he'd savage Bianca if he intervened."

"That was very smart of Trevor," Angelo admitted as he held Bianca, who was slowly dozing off again. "No, Bianca. Wake up."

She opened her eyes wearily, then closed them again. Angelo sighed.

"Set the tray on the side, Cormier. We don't have long before we must return her to her family."

Cormier obeyed and backed out of the room, worried at Bianca's state.

Angelo picked up the glass of orange juice, Bianca resting in the crook of his other arm as she breathed slowly.

"Drink this, Bianca. You'll feel much better afterwards."

All she could do was open her mouth, Angelo gently tipping some in.

* * Bianca * *

Her throat was dry. The cool liquid seeping down there seemed to heighten her senses: Bianca opened her eyes properly to look into Angelo's, who was watching her with bated breath.

Instead of saying something she may have wanted to hear, he said "Drink some more."

She obeyed, Angelo holding the glass for her. Bianca felt like she was three again, in the high chair being fed by her mother.

"Now eat some of this. It's meat- cooked meat for you."

Bianca chewed slowly, unable to speak just yet. She was thinking of Hanson. And did she see Dad and Ricky? Or was that a dream?

"Not a dream," murmured Angelo as he popped another piece of meat in her mouth. "Your family want you back by midnight. They'll make you tell all, Bianca- and you may be forbidden to see me ever again."

Bianca didn't respond, chewing slowly. She couldn't understand him well, and it was hard for her to say something.

She could feel the dizziness leaving her. She opened her mouth, Angelo feeding her silently as he brooded.

* * Cormier * *

"She's doing ok, I think," said Cormier to Clover and Sebastian, who was a few doors away from Angelo's. "Clover, relax. She'll be fine."

"This is all my fault," said Clover agitatedly. "I vowed not to let a vampire harm her, and still the worst happened!"

"It's not the worst," Sebastian said reassuringly- Clover rounded on him furiously.

"It wasn't any vampire, Sebastian! It was that rogue, Hanson! He'll be back for Bianca just like he was back for Marissa-"

"What?" said Cormier sharply, and they looked at him.

"You don't know Marissa's story?" said Sebastian incredulously, Cormier annoyed as he answered "No I do not-"

"And you need not know it," Marissa said coolly, materialising next to Clover. "My story has nothing to do with this vile behaviour of Hanson."

"He was bloodthirsty," Sebastian said reasonably: Clover glared at him.

"As he is every night. Many of us were victims of Hanson!"

"Bianca will not be next," said Cormier angrily. "Hanson won't be coming near here anytime soon: Trevor will make sure of it. Hanson is his bone."

"His bone?" asked Clover confusedly, Sebastian grinning. Cormier smirked, explaining "Our cousin is a werewolf, is he not? A savage dog at the full moon, a calm dog whenever he feels like turning into one.

Dogs like bones, do they not? Hanson will do for Trevor when the full moon is out."

"That's horrid," said Clover, and Cormier scowled at her.

"You, cousin Clover, are too soft. Hanson's attempt to bite Bianca was horrid!"

"He didn't succeed?" asked Marissa curiously, Cormier saying no.

"He'd just started to play his teasing game-"

"The nipping and kissing etcetera," Marissa said lazily, and he nodded.

"Exactly. He'd pricked her a bit too hard, and she pushed him away. That's when Angelo and I arrived. Angelo threw him high, and I took over as Bianca's legs gave way."

"Angelo caught her?" asked Clover, Marissa saying "Naturally."

"So Hanson is Trevor's hostage?" asked Sebastian, and they all burst out laughing except Marissa, who gave a fleeting smile.

"I wonder how she is?" Clover said, Cormier saying "Much better."

"And how would you know?" Sebastian said amusedly, Cormier saying "Because Angelo is with her."

* * Ricky * *

"She was weird when she came back! Why didn't I clock before?"

"Because you don't believe in that kind of thing," Gran said calmly, sipping her tea as she watched her son and grandson fume as if their life depended on it. "You laughed at me when I tried to tell you darkness was upon us, and you didn't want to listen. Now Bianca is in the hands of a Count, and it's all your fault, Samuel."

"Me!" shouted Samuel, leaping to his feet. "Why is this *my* fault?!"

"Bianca is only eighteen!" snapped Gran. "She's not a full grown adult, Samuel! How you let her wander off by herself I have no clue-"

"That night!" said Ricky, realising something. Samuel looked at him. "What?"

"Like… the night we met the tourists and Gran made a scene, Bianca said she had a headache to get out of hearing Gran's story. She said she was stepping out the van, but she was gone for half an hour," gushed Ricky. "She must have met him then! She mentioned vampires when she got back- Bianca wouldn't do that. I mean, she stopped the fantasy thing when she was thirteen, remember?"

Samuel nodded, thinking hard. "And that night she came running in-"

"Like she saw a ghost from the dead or something!" said Ricky, nodding. "She was gone for the whole night- maybe he frightened her!"

"He must have," said Samuel, remembering the terrified look on Bianca's face as she entered the caravan that night. "She's scared of him!"

"Well, if he did scare her, why would she go back to him then?" Gran asked, rolling her eyes. "Samuel, Ricky. He didn't kidnap her-"

"He did! He said he wouldn't give her back!"

"But didn't he also say he'd return her midnight latest?"

"Gran," said Ricky, annoyed. "You're not helping the situation!"

"Well, I just think that the young man has the right frame of mind. Obviously he doesn't want to return her unwell. He wants her to be fit and healthy-"

"Gran!"

"And there's nothing wrong with that," Gran said loudly, over Samuel's cursing. "And killing the boy won't help the situation-"

"Boy! Mom, he's a *monster!*" said Samuel angrily. "He refused to show his face- spoke with his back to us all the time! He must have a hideous face- he said we wouldn't forget it!"

"And his brother is savage!" Ricky said angrily. "I saw his teeth- he shredded that guy up! I bet he was helping Bianca get away from them!"

"Have a cup of tea," said Gran in reply, and both men swore angrily.

"Mom!"

"Gran!"

"Tea!" she snapped, and they both obeyed reluctantly, fuming under their breath. "And stop the cursing too. Killing the boy won't help!"

They didn't answer, knowing if they argued they'd lose the battle.

* * Angelo * *

"Blah," said Bianca as she left the bathroom; Angelo burst out laughing.

"How charming. Blah is the first word you speak after you get your strength back?"

"Yep!"

He laughed again, pulling her towards him and giving her a quick kiss.

"Everyone is waiting for you. I spoke to them while you bathed."

"Everyone like who?"

"The vampires you know: Clover, Sebastian, Cormier-"

"Great!"

"And Marissa."

"Cool," said Bianca as she brushed her hair to the side. "Where's Joseph?"

"Joseph is having his... do I call it lunch? For you, it is dinner."

"Let's just say he's having a meal," said Bianca, growing confused. "Ok, now you have to get out so I can get dressed."

"Of course," said Angelo quickly, and she smiled at him.

"You're a really nice guy, you know that? Real gentlemanly."

Angelo smiled back shyly, walking to the door and closing it behind him. His heart seemed to beat faster as he walking into the living area.

"How is she?" asked Clover, and Angelo took a shaky breath.

"She... she's much, much better."

"Good," said Cormier, staring at him. "Why is your heart thumping?"

"You can hear it?" said Angelo, rubbing his chest. "It's Bianca."

"Yes," said Clover, amused. "What did she do, Angelo?"

Angelo didn't know himself. Saying he makes her shy wouldn't be right.

"What is another word for shy, Marissa?"

"Bashful."

"Yes," said Angelo, nodding. "She complimented me, and I felt very strange afterwards."

"You felt shy?" said Sebastian; Cormier cracked up.

"Bashful," snapped Angelo, glaring at his brother laughing. "She makes me bashful. Why does she make me bashful?"

"It's a female thing," said Sebastian, chortling at his friend's confused face. "They have the power to make you feel things you shouldn't feel."

"Indeed," said Cormier; Marissa glared at him. "Every time I look at Marissa I have an overwhelming urge to slap her senseless."

"Just as I had the overwhelming urge to convince my sister to leave you,"

Marissa replied coolly. "The only difference between you and I, Cormier Heathen, is that I went with the urge."

"You-!!"

"Enough!" said Angelo angrily, then he shook his head. "Can you both get along? Just while Bianca is here?"

They both looked at him and said no.

"Fine, at least tolerate being in the same room with each other."

Silence.

Annoyed, Angelo snapped "That's an order from the Grand Vampire!"

"Order obeyed," Marissa said through gritted teeth, Cormier as well.

"I'm going to see Bianca," Clover said as she stood. "I bet Joseph wants to see her, do you not?" she asked the cub with a smile. "Come and see Bianca."

Joseph bounded after her as she left.

Seconds later they heard Bianca's delighted exclamation, Joseph yapping excitedly.

* * Bianca * *

"Little sister, I am so sorry about what happened," Clover said, eyes welling up as she looked at Bianca cuddling Joseph. "I had no clue you left the club with that rogue: I thought you was still on the dance floor."

"He drugged me," Bianca said with a shrug. "Because I was so drowsy, you and Cormier couldn't hear my thoughts. I couldn't think at all, and it was dark. You couldn't possibly have known I was gone."

"That sounds like something Angelo would say."

"He did. Word for word," smiled Bianca, and Clover laughed.

"Are you ready to go home?"

"No, not yet. I want to spend a bit more time with Angelo."

"Alone?" smiled Clover, and Bianca smiled back embarrassedly. Clover went to the door, saying "I will get him for you."

"Don't make him if he doesn't want to-"

"He does, I assure you. Wait here."

* * Angelo * *

Angelo walked towards Bianca's room before Clover even opened her mouth.

"Are you going to the club tonight, Clover?"

"No, cousin. I need to rest."

"I shan't go either," Sebastian said, and Angelo said "That's fine. There is always extra staff there, so the club should be fine. Otherwise close it for tonight."

"Yes sir."

* * Bianca * *

Bianca rubbed her neck, so smooth when she was sure it bled the minute Hanson kissed it.

He bit me, she thought with a shudder. Well, he pricked me.

Angelo entered the room, closing the door behind him. "Hello."

"Hi," she said, smiling. "Can I have a hug, Angelo?"

"A hug? Whatever for?"

"I have to go home soon. And you said I won't be allowed to see you, so-"

"It's not the end," Angelo reassured her. "Your father is very angry, and so is your brother. They plan to stake me and my brother."

"They wouldn't," said Bianca uncertainly. "Dad's just angry, and Ricky-well, he's the younger version of Dad. They're hot-headed."

"I believe them when they say they'll attempt murdering me, Bianca."

"They won't," she said firmly, covering his mouth with her fingertips. "Shut up, Angelo- don't say that. Don't ever say that again."

"All right," he said in a muffled voice, taking her by the wrist and removing her hand. "I won't say it again."

Bianca raised an eyebrow, folding her arms. "But you'll think it."

"I can't win," said Angelo, highly amused. "I obey you and you still manage to twist the order. Now I can't think of it?"

"Now you have to kiss me."

Angelo laughed before he obeyed, giving her a soft, tender kiss.

"There. Now, are you ready to leave?"

Bianca turned and walked to her window, looking out. "No."

Angelo sighed. "Bianca, I told your father I'd return you tonight."

"I know, but that doesn't mean I have to want to go home."

"Yes, I know."

"Can we have one last walk through the woods?" she asked, looking at him. When Angelo said no, she grew annoyed. "Why not?"

"Don't, Bianca. You sound like a spoilt child." Angelo didn't mean to sound so cold, but he did. "You are going home to your father, and if he forbids you from seeing me, then so be it."

"Fine," she said bitterly. "Fine- I'm going. You don't have to take me, Angelo. I know my way home."

Angelo didn't let his frustration show. "If you want to alone then go."

Bianca put on her jacket, not knowing why she wanted to burst into tears. She picked up her bag, then she looked at him.

* * Angelo * *

Angelo said nothing, staring through the window at the dark courtyard. He didn't know why he didn't stop her from leaving.

It's my pride, he realised. *I can't become head over heels in love with her like I did with Alicia. I won't allow it.*

* * Bianca * *

Bianca crept past the living area, then she bolted like she did the first time. She'd just reached the door when Cormier morphed in front of her, arms folded as he glared at her furiously.

"You weren't going to pull the same stunt like time uno, were you?"

"I- no," she said meekly, as he took her arm and frog-marched her back up the stairs and into the library, where Angelo sat reading.

"Reading!" she burst out incredulously. "You would've let me go?"

"No," he said calmly, "But I would have let you get so far for fun."

Cormier grinned, then quickly hid it as Bianca looked at him.

"Can you believe him, Cormier?"

"Let's not argue," said Cormier, as Angelo was about to speak. "I'm going to say goodbye to our guests, and then take Joseph for a walk. When I return, I want you both to say goodbye in good spirits-"

"Good spirits!" said Angelo disbelievingly. "She'll be forbidden to see me again! There's nothing to be good spirited about, Cormier!"

"Brother, brother. You bend rules better than I do," Cormier said amusedly, and Angelo smiled. "You know very well this isn't the end, so don't act like you cannot do a thing about it."

* * Angelo * *

When Cormier left with Joseph, Angelo looked up at Bianca. She was still standing with her arms folded, but she said nothing. She wasn't even looking at him.
"Bianca, what's the matter?"
"Nothing."
"No, tell me." Angelo closed his book and stood, going over to her. Bianca didn't react when he touched her cheek gently. "Bianca?"
"I feel like you don't care if I go or not. Like... I'm nothing to you."
Angelo was surprised. "Weren't you the one who was talking about things happening too fast? We haven't even known each other a month."
"I don't want to go," mumbled Bianca, and Angelo smiled.
"You heard Cormier. I'll bend the rules if you are forbidden to see me."
"And I will be. I know my father- he must be really, really angry."
"Never mind that," said Angelo, not wanting the dark cloud above his head to grow while he was with her. "Let's... I don't know... watch TV."
"You have a television?" she said amazedly, Angelo smiling at her.
"Of course. In the Electronics Room. Well, it's really a lounge."
Angelo took her hand and led her down the corridor into the room at the very end. Before he let her in, he explained "I seldom watch TV."
"I kind of figured."
Moments later they sat with a glass of milk each, watching the television contentedly. Angelo had almost forgotten Bianca was leaving, but then Cormier strolled in, clapping his hands.
"Ok lovebirds, your time is up."
"Five more minutes," begged Bianca, but Cormier put his foot down.
"No. Midnight it nearly is, Bianca- and it is midnight you must be back."
"Fine," she said sulkily as she got up: Cormier laughed.
"You look just like Clover when her mother caught her with Sebastian after hours. Her face when she had to go home!"
Angelo laughed as well. "Wait for us by the exit, Cormier."
Cormier rolled his eyes before leaving, calling "Don't get carried away, brother! Five minutes!"
"As you wish."
Angelo listened, ears pricked. Hearing nothing, he smiled and took Bianca in his arms. "One last kiss before we depart?"
She smiled back, nodding her consent.

* * Cormier * *

Joseph padded around the place, sniffing every large object curiously. Cormier watched him, tapping his foot as he waited.

Before he knew it, Marissa Bennett appeared. "Where is Angelo?"

"Saying goodbye to Bianca," he snapped. "Is this your abode, Marissa? The last time I checked, you always made sure you alerted Angelo first before coming here."

"That was one hundred and nine years ago, Cormier. Me and Angelo grew much closer in that time. Now, I may stop by whenever I please- so long as he is around. That's why his charm doesn't affect me."

Cormier's jaw dropped as he realised that. Any other trespassers immediately teleported back to where they came from moments after they reached the Heathen Castle uninvited. But not Marissa...

"Bianca!" he called, looking at the clock. "Time to go."

Bianca left Angelo's room reluctantly, Angelo at her side.

"Take care of her, Cormier. Be civil to her relatives, even if they provoke you. You have a very short temper- once you are angered, that's it. I don't want anyone hurt."

"You mean you don't want the situation to get out of hand before it has even become apparent," Marissa said amusedly, and Angelo nodded.

"Exactly. You have a knack for stretching my lines, Marissa."

"It's a natural talent. But thank you all the same."

"You're very welcome."

Bianca and Cormier both scowled, Cormier saying "We're leaving now."

Angelo nodded, saying to Marissa "Would you like a beverage of some sort?"

"Red wine will do nicely."

"Follow me."

Bianca couldn't help staring as they walked away, Cormier taking her by the arm and pulling her through the door.

* * Bianca * *

Gran embraced Bianca, eyes filling. "I'm so glad you're all right."

"Did they hurt you?" demanded Ricky, as Samuel looked at Cormier and snapped "You're late!"

"It's ten past the hour," Cormier said calmly. "If you are over-punctual, that isn't my problem. Bianca was reluctant to leave my younger brother."

"Who is he?" said Samuel angrily. "This brother of yours?"

"You need not know his name."

"Then who are you?"

"Cormier Heathen, his elder brother by four years."

"And you're a bloodsucking monster like he is?"

A muscle twitched in Cormier's jaw, Bianca saying "Angelo isn't a monster, Dad-"

"That's his name?" snorted Ricky. *"Angelo? Real scary."*

"I'm glad you think so," said Cormier coldly, looking at him. "If angered Angelo will become the most frightening person imaginable. He has powers unknown to any man, including the Counts before him. I imagine his son or daughter will inherit them."

"Son or daughter?" Samuel repeated, then he pulled Bianca away. "Not from mine!"

"I said nothing of the sort," smirked Cormier, and Samuel suddenly grew afraid.

"Are you psychic? Can you see something? What can you see?!"

"Maybe two bloodsucking monster grandchildren, maybe nothing at all."

"You're full of crap!" spat Ricky, but Cormier didn't take his eyes off Samuel's, who tightened his hold on Bianca.

"Cormier, thanks for bringing me," she said weakly, and Cormier smiled at her.

"It was my pleasure. Hopefully we'll meet again-"

"In your dreams," spat Ricky, Gran apologetically saying "Unfortunately for your brother, we've come to the decision not to have Bianca anywhere near him."

"Is that so?"

"Yes," she said politely. "Her father insisted."

"And so did her brother," spat Ricky; Cormier laughed.

"You are the same age as Angelo, boy. You don't intimidate me at all."

"Cormier, just go," said Bianca meekly. "Remember what Angelo said about your temper, ok?"

Cormier turned with a nod and walked away, Ricky goading "We've already seen his temper, Bianca- too bad you was out of it. I feel sorry for the dude that got mangled by that thing you call Cormier."

Cormier stopped, clenching his fists. Ricky smiled smugly, Samuel saying "I hope that bites harder than you do, Cormier Heathen."
Cormier took a deep breath before dissolving into thin air, Ricky looking at their father, who hadn't released his hold on Bianca.
"Dad?"
"Get inside with Gran, Ricky."
Ricky scowled and entered the van with Gran, Bianca biting her lip as she stared down at the grass. Samuel looked down at her.
"Bianca."
She flinched, but didn't respond.
"Bianca, look at me."
Bianca obeyed, eyes filling. "Dad, please don't be angry-"
"What the hell were you thinking, Bianca?" said Samuel, sighing as he stepped away from her. "You're eighteen. I gave you privileges because you were of age- I put my trust in you."
"I know, but-"
"Do you think this is a ride on a ghost train? That those teeth and clothes are just costumes those things get paid to sport?"
"No, but- but they're so nice- and Angelo's really-"
"Angelo disgusts me," snapped Samuel. "Almost as much as I fear his brother, who is a savage brute like I suppose he is-"
"Don't, Dad! Angelo and Cormier are the nicest guys I've ever met-"
"Yes, they tend to hide all flaws until your neck is bared."
"My neck *was* bared," she said frustratedly, stamping her foot on the grass. "It was bared almost all the time- and neither of them cared!"
Samuel opened his mouth, then closed it as he thought hard for a comeback. Bianca waited angrily, Samuel throwing his hands up as he said "They're vampires, Bianca!"
"I know, but Angelo-"
"Angelo?! Enough about Angelo!" he said, heat rising as he saw the exaltation in his little girls eyes as she said Angelo's name. "He could bite you at any time, don't you realise that? Gran filled your head with enough stories over the years for you to know that *this is not a game!*"
"I know it's not a game, Dad! Me and Angelo-"
"Don't you dare pull a love stunt! You've been here almost a month- how many times have you seen him since we've arrived here?"
"This was the second time!"
"Exactly! Do you think this is Titanic?" demanded Samuel. "That you're Rose and he's Jack Dawson?? Well it isn't!" he snapped, as Bianca opened her mouth, half amused. "This isn't a ship, it's a caravan- and you're not in the ocean, you're in Pennsylvania! Get your head out of the clouds, Bianca!"
Bianca knew she wasn't going to win the case. No matter what her

comeback, Samuel, Ricky and whoever else would counter it with "They're vampires."

She sighed and hung her head, mumbling "I'm sorry I upset you."

Samuel sighed too; he could never stay mad at her for too long.

"You scared me half to death," said Samuel gently. "Running off after dark in a country you've never been before isn't what I expected from you, ok?" She nodded. "Go on to bed while I take a breather."

Bianca obeyed, going inside the caravan.

"Shut up," she snapped, when Ricky opened his mouth. "Get stuffed, Richard- don't speak to me for a week."

"Ok," grinned Ricky, knowing she'd never say 'ever again.' "Cool."

* * Angelo * *

"You won't touch her brother," said Angelo, shaking his head as Cormier raged like a madman. Marissa blew smoke placidly, amused as she said "I wonder if Patricia saw you in this state, Cormier? If so, she had every right to flee from your clutches."

"Get out, Marissa!" spat Cormier, and she smirked and vanished. Cormier ducked as the bat sped right at his head, cackling as it flew through the library window into the night sky.

Angelo looked at Cormier as he slumped in his seat angrily, swearing.

"Brother, calm yourself. There's no point fuming at the brother of Bianca. We don't care of him, yes? We care about her. Not him."

"We care about her. Not him," Cormier repeated with difficulty, as if trying to force the line into his brain. Angelo shook his head, turning a page of his book as he said "Sometimes I forget which of us is the elder."

* * Bianca * *

"Can I go for a walk?"

"You can do what you like," Samuel answered as he pulled on his boots. "As long as the sun is out. Be back by nightfall."

Bianca nodded and left, kicking the grass as she walked. As soon as she was far away she muttered "Asswipe."

She saw her grandmother picking flowers just ahead.

I don't want to talk to Gran. I don't want to talk to anyone *right now.*

Gran looked up at saw her, her creased face breaking into a brilliant smile. "Bianca, darling. Do you want to come and help me?"

Bianca shook her head sullenly, muttering "I want to see Angelo."

* * Ricky * *

Gran didn't hear, but Ricky did.

Who the hell is *this Angelo?! I wish he showed his face!*

"Bianca, come on. Pull yourself together. It's been like... a week."

"Go to hell, Richard."

Ricky watched her go, shoulders slumped. He had to admit, since Samuel had scolded her and Cormier left, she hadn't been happy at all. It was a bit like those two weeks she was depressed... probably over Cormier's little brother... that Angelo person.

Ricky didn't know how to talk to her right now. He'd been avoiding Bianca for six days and nights, because since he'd insulted Cormier she'd been giving him the most evil look she could muster whenever they were in the same room.

Gran stopped picking flowers as Bianca became a dot in the distance, still a lone, sad figure from far. Ricky joined her, jamming his hands in his pockets as he said "Gran, what do you think?"

* * *

"I think we may have been too rash when banning Bianca from the vampires," Gran told her son. "I do think she was happy in their company, Samuel."

Samuel shrugged. "I think so too Mom, but that doesn't excuse the fact that my baby was hurt. I saw it. Ricky saw it. Many others saw it too! Bianca was bleeding, unconscious in Angelo Heathen's arms. And Cormier savaged the man who was helping her escape from him."

"How do you know that's how it happened?" demanded Gran, growing annoyed with her son's attitude. "Were you there?"

"Mom! Stop being so optical, for God's sake. I know what I saw."

"Me too," said Ricky, as Bianca entered the caravan silently. They carried on talking. "I saw it with my own eyes: she was out cold. But…"

Gran looked at him. "Yes?"

"If Cormier Heathen really *is* her friend, and Angelo Heathen is too, then doesn't that mean he was angry because… I don't know, that man tried to hurt Bianca? She was bleeding. They can't have been holding her prisoner, because they returned her when they said they would- and Bianca was as good as knew."

Bianca smiled at her brother, and Ricky smiled back briefly before he said "Maybe they really are her friends, Dad. And maybe this Angelo really is her-"

"No, Ricky. Even if what you say adds up, it doesn't mean that Bianca's seeing a vampire."

"He's not any old vampire," said Bianca, heat rising. "Angelo's the Count of this town- and he's also the Grand Vampire of Pennsylvania."

"Goodness," said Gran, as Samuel and Ricky's jaws dropped. "He rules the land, darling?"

Bianca nodded, Samuel looking disbelieving as he said "How did he fall upon you, Bianca? How did you meet him?"

"Ricky told you already, didn't he? He's been going over it with you all week."

"And he's right."

"Yes Dad," said Bianca calmly. "He's right. That's how we met."

Samuel sighed, looking out the window at the dark night. "We've still got another few months until we leave here. I don't doubt you'll see him again…" Bianca yawned, rubbing her eyes as he spoke. Samuel noticed, but pretended not to as he carried on speaking. "Well, not if I can help it."

"But Dad, that's not fair! Ricky gets to see Catherine all the time!"

"Catherine," snapped Samuel, "We can see in the light of day! Her teeth are perfect! She's not a savage monster like your new friends, Bianca!"

"They're not savages!" she said, eyes filling. "Stop insulting them!"

Not in the mood for another argument with his daughter, Samuel simply said "Go to bed, Bianca. Look at you. You've been out since eight a.m.- you must be exhausted."

Bianca was, so she didn't hesitate to obey. She'd gone to the Heathen Castle, getting as far as she possibly could before she whizzed back to where she started- far away. Not put out, she decided to do a bit of experimenting with Angelo's charm.

She'd worked out the farthest point she could go: about forty yards from the gigantic gates. Bianca sat there every day instead, hidden in the trees as she gazed up at the windows, knowing there was no way Angelo or Cormier would be staring out...

Bianca rolled over, eyelids growing heavy as she thought about them. How brilliant Angelo was to all the vampires in the community, and to her. And how funny Cormier was, and weird too. How is it he was awake three hours earlier than any other vampire? Three hours before nightfall?

Bianca smiled, settling down for a long, warm sleep.

Hours later, as dawn was breaking, Bianca snapped awake.

Three hours before nightfall.

* * Ricky * *

"Gran, do you think we was a bit harsh on her?" Ricky asked hesitantly two days later, and she looked at him coldly.

"Harsh? Richard, you were demonic. You made the vampires look like gentlemen, which they were. Bianca is safe and sound, like he promised."

"Who are you talking about, Cormier or Count Angelo?"

"Both," snapped Gran. "The Count promised to return Bianca to us, and his so-called savage brother brought her back with no complications at all. It was *you-"* Ricky flinched. "Who threw insults at the poor thing. Forgetting what he is and what he is capable of- you stupid, stupid boy."

"But-"

"And to add the icing to the cake, Bianca is so distant and depressed now. I believe she needs to see her Count Angelo, no matter what you or your father think."

"Like I haven't been trying to visit him," Bianca said, heat rising as they turned. "Discussions again?"

"No," began Ricky, while their grandmother said yes.

"There must be a reason behind his staying away, hmm?"

"Angelo knows what he's doing," Bianca said angrily. "He's probably going to find me real soon, maybe when everything dies down."

* * Angelo * *

"She's been trying to reach you."

Angelo didn't turn around as he said "I know."

Cormier raised an eyebrow. "Just what are you planning, Angelo?"

"She'll forget me if I don't respond to her calls."

"Her calls??"

"Her soul screams my name. I hear her voice whisper it every night, as she sleeps. I see her in my dreams, when she attempts reaching me."

"Then… you are bonded like you and Alicia were…?"

Angelo stiffened. "Yes, until I no longer heard Alicia whisper my name. I heard Cormier instead from her soul."

"Yes, well…" Cormier hung awkwardly, then he turned and walked away. Then he spun back round, demanding "When are you going to let this go?"

"Cormier, I cannot trust you. I had faith that you'd respect a relationship of mine, but you get on too well with Bianca and that's the truth."

"Trust," said Cormier angrily, "Comes with love and friendship. Are we not the best of friends?"

"Yes."

"And do you not love me, your elder brother?"

"Yes, but-"

"But you don't trust me with any woman you know at all, any! Why?"

"You know why!!"

"Don't talk rubbish," spat Cormier. "Go and argue with Bianca over nonsensical insecurities. You have already argued and settled before arguing again and settling, uprooting the calmness of her family and making them wild over what? The memory of Alicia?"

Angelo didn't answer.

"It's only you who's hurting, brother. She'll gradually forget you, grow old, die…" Angelo cringed. "And you'll never forget her."

"What time is the meeting?" Angelo said through gritted teeth, and Cormier glared at him.

"Ten to eleven, then I go to the club. You?"

"Never you mind."

"You go to Bianca." Cormier couldn't help smirking. "I thought as much."

"Get out, Cormier."

* * Bianca * *

"Bianca, eat something," begged Samuel, but she ignored him as she gazed out the caravan window. "Bianca!"

"We need to call Count Angelo," said Gran worriedly, Ricky saying "Or Cormier, he'll definitely know what's wrong with her-"

"What is it with you and that- Cormier?" demanded Samuel, wheeling round to stare at his son. "Ricky!"

Ricky didn't answer, joining his sister. Both gazed out the window.

* * Angelo * *

"They are both in a trance," Marissa said softly at the table. "Now would be the right time to bite-"

"Nobody touches Bianca," Angelo said firmly. "Or her brother. Feed off the other families staying here if you wish, let them become a part of our world. But none touch that family. I want them alive- all of them."

"Brought to you, sir?" a meek looking vampire asked far down the table. "Kidnap the lot and bring them alive?"

"No," said Cormier, rolling his eyes. "That is not a pro, but a con."

"He's right. I will visit Bianca tonight, and snap her out of her stupor. Maybe her brother should keep in a trance," Angelo said broodingly. "He is the hyper-active one."

"Brother, let him out of it. I will see to him," Cormier said, smirking. "After all, I am less than he. Am I not the thing you call Cormier?"

"Indeed you are," Marissa said, making him scowl. "Angelo, what of Joseph?"

"He is walking with Clover. So... Sebastian, the round up?"

Sebastian cleared his throat.

"The club is closed the night after tomorrow. Nobody touches Bianca or her family. We must make sure they are kept safe from the hunger of our people."

"Is that all?"

"Yep."

"Meeting closed," Angelo said as he stood, and everyone vanished in puffs of black smoke.

* * Bianca * *

"Bianca," he murmured softly, and Bianca whipped round, staring at thin air.

"Count Angelo?"

"Yes. How have you been?"

"Miserable."

Angelo laughed, materialising in the kitchen section of the caravan. "And why is that, my darling Bianca?"

"I've been trying and failing to reach your castle. I was obsessed with-"

"You were suffering," Angelo cut across, "From what we vampires call Count Syndrome."

Bianca raised an eyebrow. "Excuse me?"

"You were in a trance," explained Angelo, "Because you were craving contact with me, The Grand Vampire. Like many other vampires do-"

"Especially Marissa." Bianca scowled as she said it. "She'd better find a cure for her syndrome, because I snapped out of it-"

"As soon as you saw me," Angelo explained kindly. "That is the cure."

"No way. If I saw Cormier-"

"You would have asked for Count Angelo." Angelo looked around the caravan like he did before, with as much distaste as he did back then. "And you would have kept on until you saw my face."

"Your face?"

"You will never forget it once you see it. That is why I did not turn and look at your family."

"Mmm. I guess so." Then she pouted. "Why didn't you come sooner?"

"I foolishly decided to keep away, with hopes you'd forget me."

"Forget you? Why would you want that- why-"

"It was foolish of me and I apologise." Angelo paused, looking around. "Where is your family?"

"Oh, I don't know. Richard's out with Gran, Dad's with a friend. They'll be back soon- real soon probably. They never let me out of their sight after nightfall."

"Hmm. Well, it's nightfall now. Would you like to come home with me?"

Bianca's heart leapt as she said yes quickly. "How's Cormier?"

"Cormier is fine."

Angelo smiled before leaning closer and giving her a quick kiss. Sighing, Bianca said "Let's go."

* * Angelo * *

Angelo ran his hand over the doors: the lock clicked and they both swung open, creaking loud and impressively as Bianca walked through nervously, looking around.

"Don't be afraid," Angelo said softly. "Nothing can hurt you whilst you're with me."

Bianca nodded, then she stood on tiptoe and kissed him. Surprised but pleased, Angelo responded, arms around her.

An amused cough made them break apart and look up, startled. Cormier was leaning over a banister above, grinning.

"So you're back with us, Miss Bianca."

"Yep. I am," Bianca said, smiling up at him. "Did you miss me?"

"Of course I did. Come on up, both of you. I prepared dinner."

"You?" said Angelo, highly amused. "What did you make? Cheese and crackers with milk?"

Cormier scowled as Bianca burst out laughing. "I can cook, Angelo."

"You haven't cooked in years," Angelo said, smirking. "But seriously, what did you make? I don't want Bianca poisoned."

"Rice and paprika chicken," Cormier said huffily, and Bianca smiled. "It sounds delicious."

Cormier smiled back. "Come on up."

* * *

"Amazing," Bianca said, sighing. "You're a brilliant cook, Cormier."

"Indeed," Angelo admitted, and Cormier smiled at him.

"Go and get settled. I'll tidy up before I go to the club."

"It's not open for another two hours," frowned Angelo. "It's almost nine."

"Well I don't want to be in the way of you two lovebirds," smirked Cormier. "Unless you go to the library while I watch the television."

"I'd like that," Bianca said, looking at Angelo. "Angelo?"

"I don't mind," said Angelo, standing and snapping his fingers. Everything on the table vanished, the table sparkling clean. Bianca couldn't help wowing as he took her hand and they left the dining area.

"Angelo?"

"Mmm?"

"Uh… I just… um-"

Angelo looked at her as they walked. "What is it?"

Bianca swallowed. How do you explain you'd rather make out than read? Angelo heard her thoughts, but was puzzled.

"Make out?" Bianca nodded, but he continued to frown. "Make out what?"

"Oh jeez." Bianca burst out laughing. "You wouldn't last a day where I come from."

Angelo pouted but let it go. "I don't understand some of the terms you use, that's all. I think I'd last just fine where you come from."

"Are there only armchairs in the library?" asked Bianca, and he said "No. There is also a sofa here and there. Why?"

"No reason," she said quickly. "Let's go, then."

* * *

Cormier sensed her before she even appeared.

As soon as she did he grabbed her arm and dragged her roughly down the corridor back towards the castle entrance, Marissa struggling, but she wasn't strong enough.

"Cormier Heathen, you let go of me right now!!" she screeched, but Cormier ignored her. "I mean it!"

"Bianca is here," snapped Cormier. "And I know she won't appreciate you coming here to see Angelo."

"Angelo can decide whether I leave, not you!" spat Marissa, and Cormier almost threw her down the stairs instead of pulling her.

"You are not wanted or needed right now. Bianca hasn't even been here a full night. Leave. Now!"

"Angelo wouldn't have me leave-"

"I am not Angelo," snapped Cormier. "If you don't leave by the time I count to five, I promise you all hell will break loose. One."

"You dare threaten me?!"

"Two," Cormier replied, as her eyes lit a deep scarlet. "Three."

"If a battle is what you want a battle is what you will get!!"

"Four, Marissa!"

"I won't leave!"

"Five!"

Marissa smirked. "I'm a female. You wouldn't hurt-"

BANG!!

Marissa dodged the ball of flame, losing her balance- and tumbling down the massive staircase.

Her scream shot through the castle, Cormier yelling her name as he dashed after her.

"Marissa!!"

* * Bianca * *

"What was that?"
Bianca and Angelo looked up sharply, Angelo rising to his feet.
"Should I stay here?" Bianca asked, but he said no.
"Come with me."
"What if it was a werewolf?"
"I doubt it was."

* * Richard * *

"She's gone again," spat Samuel, Ricky scowling too. "He'd better return her like he did before! And how did he reach her before nightfall?!"
"He can't have," shrugged Ricky. "He must have come as soon as he could."
"I wouldn't put it past him."
"Stop this ridiculous hatred," Gran snapped. "Bianca is safe with Count Angelo and his brother. I know she is. I can feel it. I truly believe they will keep her safe from harm."
"Yeah, sure. Like before, right?" said Samuel sarcastically, Ricky nodding too. "Wait until she gets back. Someone needs to nail that girl's feet to the floor."

* * Angelo * *

"What did you do?!"
"Nothing!" said Cormier, as Angelo knelt beside Marissa. "I only meant to scare her, but she lost her balance and fell down the-"
"Be quiet," snapped Angelo. "Marissa, can you hear me?"
Silence.
Bianca stood by Cormier's side, watching with her arms folded.
"Is she dead?"
"No," murmured Angelo, placing his hands on Marissa's body. "She will be fine."
"Unfortunately," said Cormier, scowling as Marissa's eyes flickered, then opened. "She is just a drama."
"Angelo," whispered Marissa, as he helped her up, then she murmured "My apologies for interrupting your reading session-"
"Do not worry about it," Angelo said reassuringly. "Are you fit to travel? To fly home?"
Bianca knew she would say no. She just knew.
"No. I... I feel very weak-"
"Then you will rest," Angelo said. "Come, I'll take you to your room."

"She is play acting," scowled Cormier. "She has been through much worse than falling down the stairs. She is a vampire. Vampires are only weak when they are bloodthirsty."

Bianca could have kissed him. Cormier smiled at her, then he said "I will take Marissa home and stay with her for an hour just to make sure she is all right."

Angelo thought about it, then he nodded. "Very well. Marissa?"

Marissa wanted to refuse, but she nodded.

"Good," Cormier said flatly. "Brother, go back to the library with Bianca. I will make sure Marissa gets everything she deserves."

Marissa heard the indirect threat, and so did Angelo and Bianca, but Bianca didn't care at that precise moment. Marissa was after Angelo. Her man. Her Count. Her almost everything. She wasn't going to let that happen. She was real close to telling the pretty blonde to hit the road.

"I'm not sure I can fly, Count Angelo..."

"Are you serious?" said Bianca disbelievingly, speaking for the first time. "You're not weak at all! You just want to be around Angelo-"

"Leave it, chick pea." Cormier smiled at her. "She isn't staying."

"Good."

Angelo smiled at her. Bianca was so fiery.

Taking her hand, he said "Let's go back to the library."

Marissa gaped as they left, Angelo not looking back. He normally would have let her stay the night, tend to her needs, care for her-

"Yes, well fortunately that isn't the case tonight," Cormier said flatly. "Come."

"I can make my own way home," snapped Marissa. "Leave me be."

"Fine."

Marissa glared at him before she vanished, Cormier amused as he called "So much for not being able to fly!"

He didn't get a reply.

* * *

Bianca was content as she read her book, in an armchair by a warm, crackling fireplace.

Angelo sat opposite her, head propped on his hand as he smiled at her. Bianca didn't notice him looking, turning a page of her book.

"Is it interesting?"

Bianca glanced up at Angelo, smiling as she said "Very."

"What is it about?"

"It's a romance novel. I really love romance novels."

Angelo smiled. "Really?"

"Yep. Everything seems so magical. Nothing like real life. Well, it probably is like that in some people's lives," she said thoughtfully, "But not all. I'd love to be whisked off my feet and taken away by the love of my life. But my father and brother would most likely go ham."

"There you go again, using terms I have no clue of. What do you mean by 'go ham', Bianca?"

"Oh- I mean go ballistic. Lose their cool."

"I see," said Angelo, amused. "You were about to go ham on Marissa, were you not?"

"I- no," she said, as he started laughing his head off. "All right, yes. Well she was getting under my skin. Nothing was wrong with her, she just wanted your attention."

Angelo chose not to answer that. "Shall we have a hot drink and biscuits before we retire to bed?"

"You won't be tired until six in the morning," Bianca replied amusedly, and Angelo laughed again. "We've got like eight hours."

"Well, what would you like to do?"

Bianca shrugged a shoulder. "I'd really like to finish this book."

"You may keep it," Angelo replied, and she gaped at him.

"Really?" He said of course. "Thank you so much!"

"You're most welcome."

"Can you sign it for me?" Bianca asked shyly, and he nodded, snapping his fingers. A pen appeared, and he murmured "Let go of the book."

Bianca obeyed, then she gasped. The book hung in the air, hovering on the spot, before gently sailing towards Angelo, who took it and began writing inside the front cover.

"You are not to read what I wrote until you're back home," Angelo said, amused as he put the book down, and it vanished, Bianca dismayed.

"Where is it?"

"It's in your caravan, under your pillow."

"But I wanted to finish it," she said unhappily, and he smiled at her.

"You was only on page thirty. Shall we see what Cormier is up to?"

Bianca smiled back and nodded, both of them getting up.

* * *

"Brother!"
Cormier lowered the volume on the television as he replied "In here."
Bianca smiled as she entered the giant lounge. "Wow. It's beautiful."
Cormier nodded, smiling back as she looked at the paintings on the walls, the statues, the ornaments.
"So, chick pea. You have come to disturb me, yes?"
"Yep!"
Cormier laughed as Angelo said "Shall I bring in some wine?"
"Champagne," Cormier replied amusedly, and Angelo pouted.
"What are we celebrating?"
"We're celebrating having Bianca back with us," was Cormier's amused reply. "Go on, Angelo. Before I leave for the club."
"You should have your drink at the club, brother. I'm not being held responsible if you go there drunk."
"Fine," Cormier said, highly amused as he stood. "Bring in the champagne anyway. I'm going to go and get ready. Both of you can stay in here with your champagne, and watch a movie of some kind."
Bianca liked that idea. So did Angelo.
Cormier smiled and left, Bianca saying "He seems to be in a real calm mood."
"Indeed," agreed Angelo. "It is rare for Cormier to be this mellow."
"He must have a lot on his mind."

* * *

Angelo was victim to Bianca's scorching mouth as she kissed the life out of him- that is, if he were really alive.
"We must stop," he gasped, as she placed her mouth on his neck to kiss him fruitfully there. "Bianca-"
"Don't make me stop, Angelo…" He shivered at her heated whisper. "I need to feel you want me."
"I do, you know I do-"
Bianca kissed him again, and Angelo gave in, taking control as he pulled her into his arms and turned on the sofa so he was the one on top.
"Angelo, I… I feel weird…"
Angelo kissed her, Bianca quivering underneath him. She'd never felt she wanted someone so much in her entire life.
Angelo broke the kiss, murmuring "Shall we stop?"
"No."

"Bianca-"

"Please, Angelo- don't stop. Please."

Angelo could feel the excitement pulsing through her body. It was raw. It was heated. She wanted him to make love to her, to be her first.

"We can't do this."

"Why?"

"Bianca-"

She kissed him before he could finish his sentence, and his resolve broke.

* * Ricky * *

"I can't sleep. Not while Bianca's out there."

"Ricky, go to bed," Samuel said wearily. "What do you want me to do?"

"Uh… not sure," Ricky said sarcastically. "How about go to the castle and get her?"

"You heard your grandmother. Bianca's safe."

"And what if she doesn't come back?" demanded Ricky. "Then what?"

"She'll probably be back tomorrow."

"Why aren't you worried??"

"Because I trust my mother's instincts. Now go to bed."

* * Angelo * *

There was a knock on the lounge door.

"Brother?"

Angelo and Bianca sat up, Angelo saying "Yes Cormier."

"I leave now, for the club. I-" Cormier stopped, inhaling deeply. Angelo snapped his fingers quickly, making sure he and Bianca looked appropriate before Cormier stormed into the lounge.

He did, the doors bursting open as he strode in.

"The lounge reeks of lust," Cormier said, both surprised and amused as he came in. "You may need to open the windows, brother."

"The windows need not be opened," Angelo said haughtily. "Are you leaving or not?"

"Yes I am. Bianca, are you all right?"

"Why wouldn't she be?" snapped Angelo, when Bianca nodded. Cormier smirked, saying "Remember, you have power unknown to any man or vampire before you. And I have heard about your kisses, Angelo. Just do not overwhelm her."

"I won't. Now leave."

* * Cormier * *

Marissa strode up to the bar, saying "Tequila. Now!"
Cormier smirked as he served her. "I thought you felt very weak, Marissa Bennett?"
"Shut up," she snapped, as he laughed. "I need a drink."
"Aww, are you upset Angelo paid you no or hardly any attention?"
"Cormier Heathen, I swear one day I will just-"
"Hurt me?" grinned Cormier. "I doubt it. Oh, and apologies for making you fall down the stairs. I should have thrown you down instead."
Marissa downed her drink in one gulp and stormed away, furious.
Sebastian burst out laughing. "When will you both get along?"
"We won't," said Cormier amusedly. "But she needs to understand Angelo is no longer on the market. He has found someone."
The female vampires glanced towards the bar, curious as they listened.
"Who is the lucky vampire, Cormier?"
"You need not know her name," Cormier replied flatly. "But Angelo has very strong feelings for her, and she him. He hardly looked at Marissa when she was there. And the lounge reeked of both their lust when I left to come here."
The female vampires hissed angrily.
"It's just curiosity. Count Angelo will get bored eventually."
"Don't count on it," Cormier replied, as they looked at each other.
"I want to know who the vampire is."
"Maybe we should ask around. Cormier will not tell us."
"I never had the slightest idea that Count Angelo found love again-"
"Nor I. I really want to know who she is."
"Leave them to gossip," Sebastian said amusedly, when Cormier opened his mouth. "DJ! Give us some slow music!"
The lights in the club dimmed as the DJ obeyed, the male vampires rising to approach the females and ask for a dance.
Clover approached the bar to talk to Cormier and Sebastian.
"Joseph is with the wolves this night."
"Good," Cormier replied. "And you have come to visit us? Or simply let your hair down and have a good time?"
Clover smiled at him. "Both."

* * Angelo * *

Angelo gasped when Bianca placed her mouth on his neck, emotion coursing through his body like water.

He'd never experienced feelings of this kind ever, not even with Alicia.

What was happening??

Then he realised, shocked.

Love.

He loved her!

"Bianca, stop!"

Bianca obeyed, startled. "What's wrong?"

"I just… I need a drink. My head is pounding."

Angelo got up and left the lounge, shirt undone as he walked down the corridor and into his kitchen, running a hand through his hair.

"I can't believe this is happening to me."

* * Bianca * *

Bianca took a deep breath, waiting. She wore no top, simply in her jeans and bra. She wasn't sure whether to go and get Angelo or wait for him.

* * Cormier * *

Cormier drummed his fingers as he watched the clock.

Sebastian and Clover were on the dance floor, everyone with a partner dancing also or seated watching the dancers dance.

Marissa was glowering as she sipped from a glass of wine. Cormier could see her eyes glowing in the dark. He shook his head, amused.

She wasn't going to let the fact that Angelo hadn't tended to her go.

"Another shot of Tequila, Marissa?" he called, grinning. "The wine doesn't seem to be doing much for your mood."

"Go to Hell, Cormier Heathen," she called back dryly, standing. "I'll have some Courvoisier."

"The hell you will," Cormier replied. "You just want to get totaled so you can come back to the castle and see Angelo."

Marissa vanished and reappeared in front of the bar, startling him as she snapped "Serve me."

"No."

"Now!"

"No!"

"I'll buy you a bottle for a wrist bite, Marissa," a sleazy vampire said, grinning at her, and Marissa smirked.

"Very well. Give me your wrist."

Vampires also bit each other for pleasure, the most raw kind of pleasure one could get without making love, and didn't Cormier know it. The male vampire began to breathe heavily as Marissa pulled his sleeve down, holding his wrist while never taking her gaze from Cormier.

Cormier stared back at her, livid. "If you dare, Marissa-"

"Serve me the drink and I won't," Marissa replied, smirking. "Give me a bottle and I won't bite him. I'll pay you for it."

"So this is how low you'll stoop for a piece of my brother?"

"Indeed."

"Fine," spat Cormier. "Take the blasted bottle. Turn up at the castle drunk. Let Angelo tend to you. But I will be telling him as soon as I can that it was all a charade."

* * Angelo * *

Angelo splashed his face with water, trying to clear his head. He had no idea what to do.

Bianca was still waiting for him in the lounge. It had been over an hour.

Angelo paced his bathroom, not knowing what he should do.

Tell her?

No. He couldn't! They hadn't been together for a lifetime for him to confess he was in love with her. She'd run home screaming most likely.

"Angelo?" said a soft voice, and Angelo whipped round.

"Bianca!"

"I figured something was wrong," Bianca said quietly. "Are you ok?"

"I… yes. I'm fine."

"You're lying."

"I was just a little overwhelmed, that's all. I had to clear my head."

Bianca nodded. "Shall we go back to the lounge? Or we can go back to the library. It's up to you."

Before Angelo could reply Marissa Bennett appeared.

"Marissa!"

"Angelo- help me."

Marissa collapsed on the marble floor and laid there, lifeless. Angelo and Bianca stared down at her, then Bianca said "Throw water on her."

"She must be truly weak-"

"She's drunk," Bianca said flatly. "I can smell it on her. Courvoisier. She must have had an entire bottle to reek that bad."

"Marissa? Can you hear me?"

Silence.

Angelo gently lifted Marissa into his arms and carried her out of the bathroom, Bianca following him down the corridor.

"Where are you taking her?"

"To her room. She just needs to rest."

"Give her a bucket for when she wakes up. I know she's going to chuck up."

Angelo smiled at her. "Yes Ma'am."

* * Cormier * *

"She wants Angelo that badly," Cormier was saying to Sebastian. "She drank two bottles of Courvoisier and a bottle of wine. I hope she stays unconscious for a full seven days."

"Five more likely," Sebastian said as he burst out laughing. "Wow. Angelo has no idea of how much women want him."

"All Angelo wants is Bianca," Cormier replied, then he yawned. "Dawn is near. I am growing weak in the limbs. The club ends now."

* * Bianca * *

"She's not moving."

"I know."

"Like, at all."

"I know, Bianca. She'll most likely remain unconscious for five days." Bianca stared at him. "What?"

"Alcohol has consumed her mind, body and senses," Angelo explained. "It will not leave anytime soon."

"Oh. Wow." Bianca's folded arms dropped to her side. "Why go clubbing if she was supposedly *too weak to fly?*"

"Cormier will tell us after we get some sleep." Angelo smiled at her. "Come, let's go to bed."

* * *

When Bianca woke again, it was dark outside.

She glanced at the clock and saw that it was almost seven p.m.

"Angelo?" she said softly, sitting up, but she didn't get a reply. Bianca rushed into the bathroom and into the shower, dressing quickly before she left Angelo's bedroom, walking down the corridor to the room Marissa was in, because she knew he'd be in there.

Angelo was staring at Marissa's still figure, deep in thought as he knelt beside her. Cormier was there also, scowling.

"Hey," Bianca said, and they both smiled at her. "I guess she's not going to wake any time soon."

"No," Cormier said, and Angelo stood, looking at him.

"You're sure that's how it happened, brother?"

"Oh, I'm definitely sure. You can read my mind if you think I'm lying."

"I do not doubt your word," Angelo answered. "I'm just wondering why she wants my attention so much she intoxicated herself this badly."

"She must be in love with you."

"I do not doubt that either. But Marissa was never one to let her feelings show," said Angelo. "So why now?"

"The answer is blatantly obvious," said Cormier. "It's Bianca."

"Me?" said Bianca, and they looked at her. "Why me?"

"Marissa is starting to envy you," Cormier said, shrugging. "It's not surprising. She has wanted Angelo for years. Everyone knows it. But she seemed fine with just being friends until Angelo was ready to court her."

Bianca said nothing, staring at Marissa.

"And now Angelo *is* ready, but not for her. For you. He has strong feelings for you, Bianca."

"Can we pour water on her in case she does wake?" was Bianca's cold reply, and Cormier and Angelo burst out laughing.

"Come, let's have breakfast. Or supper. Whatever you want to call it. What do you fancy, Bianca?"

"Pancakes," smiled Bianca, Angelo taking her hand as Cormier left the room, them behind. "With maple syrup."

"Sounds lovely."

"It is."

* * Ricky * *

"Can we panic now?" demanded Ricky, glaring at his father. "She's still not back!"

"Richard, go and see your girlfriend," Samuel said wearily. "She's been asking for you non-stop. Go and visit her. Take your mind off Bianca."

"It's like you don't even care!"

"I do care!" snapped Samuel, standing. "What do you want me to do, Ricky? Go storming into the castle and drag Bianca out by her hair?"

"Yes!!"

"No, you idiot! She wants to be with this Count Angelo person and his savage brother! If she didn't, she'd be here! Now stop acting like a spoilt brat and get out of my sight!"

"Fine!" said Ricky angrily. "But if something happens to her while she's with them, then I'm putting the whole blame on you!"

He stormed out of the caravan, Samuel calling "Spoilt!"

Ricky didn't answer him.

* * Bianca * *

Bianca was content in Angelo's arms, both of them watching a movie.

Cormier was munching popcorn, pulling a face at each swallow.

"You don't have to eat it if you don't like it," Bianca said, amused as she looked at him. "Angelo isn't."

"Angelo likes toffee popcorn," Cormier said. "As do I. But this popcorn is salted. I'm simply eating it to give my mouth exercise."

Bianca laughed, Angelo smiling amusedly.

"Check on Marissa, Cormier."

"She hasn't stirred once," Cormier replied without moving. "I know."

"All right."

* * Angelo * *

Angelo dropped a kiss on Bianca's forehead. "Bianca."

"Don't say it."

"Say what?"

"Say that I've been away from my family for over twenty four hours," Bianca said softly. "And don't ask if I want to go back."

Angelo turned to look at her properly. "How did you know I was going to ask that?"

"I just did. And my answer is no. I don't want to go back."

"You'll have to sooner or later."

"But I don't want to."

"Yes, but you'll still have to. Things can't always go your way."
Bianca sighed. "All right. I'll visit them in the day tomorrow and you can pick me up at nightfall."
Angelo opened his mouth, then closed it. "That is a good idea."
"I know," smiled Bianca. "They won't be happy, but it's my choice."
"Bianca, you know your brother is very angry with me. He more or less told your father to drag you out of the castle by your hair."
Bianca burst out laughing. "Ricky's a hot head. Don't take anything he says into account. What did Dad say?"
"He seems ok with the idea that you're here. Well, not ok, but he has accepted the fact you want to be with me and Cormier. I think your grandmother is the one to thank for that."
"I'll definitely thank her."
"Cormier, do you go to the club tonight?"
"No. I'm going to pick up Joseph. He needs to be with us this night."
"Why do you say that?"
"Because the full moon is out. Trevor is a werewolf. And I know he has been missing his son terribly since Claire dismissed him."
"All right," Angelo said evenly. "Go and get him."

* * Bianca * *

"Angelo?"
Angelo looked at her. "Yes?"
"What happens after I leave here? Will that be the end?"
Angelo stared at her. He hadn't even thought of what would happen when the remaining two months were over and Bianca left for England. Now that she'd put it in his head, his mind was already whirring.
"Angelo?"
"Bianca, do not worry about it for now. When the time comes, I will know what to do."
Bianca snuggled into his warm embrace. "All right."

* * Angelo * *

He was warm.
Angelo couldn't help smiling a little. It almost felt as if he were alive. He knew it was Bianca who was making him so. Love, he thought, can do strange things to a vampire.
"You're so warm," whispered Bianca, and he nodded.
"I know."
Bianca took his hand and kissed it gently. "Angelo?"
"Yes Bianca," he whispered, and she quietly said "Can I kiss you?"

Before he could answer they heard a familiar high pitched yapping, Cormier laughing as Joseph's tiny paws pattered, the tiny cub searching for Angelo.

Angelo smiled and pulled Bianca closer before he kissed her tenderly, Bianca shuddering at that simple connection, before Angelo broke the kiss, murmuring "Tomorrow, I will kiss you as much times as you want, and more. For now, let's see Joseph."

* * *

Bianca fell asleep in Angelo's bed, Joseph in her arms.

Angelo and Cormier smiled, at the door.

"Joseph really likes Bianca, Angelo."

Angelo nodded. "As do I."

"And I," Cormier said. "So. She leaves when we are asleep and you collect her at nightfall?"

"That's the plan."

"Are you sure I shouldn't be the one to go? Her family may still be there at the time. If they see your face-"

"If they see it they won't forget it. That is what I want. I want them to remember me years from now. Bianca as well."

* * Bianca * *

Bianca woke up with a smile on her face. She felt so happy.

Joseph the cub slept on, snuggled in her arms. Bianca gently got up so as not to disturb him, or Angelo, then she headed into the bathroom.

Once out of the shower, she gaped at the brand new jeans and blouse hovering in front of her. Black jeans, and a red blouse. There was also a black jacket and an oh-so-sexy pair of black boots.

She knew they were for her.

With just a towel around her, she walked back into the bedroom and kissed Angelo on the lips.

"Thank you," she whispered, kissing him again, before she went and got dressed.

Straightening up, she glanced at the clock. It was eleven a.m. Sighing, Bianca grabbed her shoulder bag. She whispered goodbye to Angelo and Cormier, though she knew they couldn't possibly hear her, and set off out of the castle.

* * Ricky * *

"Richard, calm yourself," Gran said wearily. "Bianca is fine. She's not eight anymore. She doesn't need her boisterous big brother smothering her like he used to when she talked to boys. She's going to be nineteen this year."

"Gran, you're not helping," Ricky said angrily. "Where's Dad?"

"Outside brooding. Go and join him."

"No!"

"Fine," said Gran just as wearily as before. "Then set about making breakfast. Or lunch. Whichever."

Ricky obeyed, scowling as Samuel said from outside "Bianca!"

* * Bianca * *

"Hey Dad," Bianca said. "How are you?"

Samuel knew she was acting like she'd just gone for half an hour rather than almost two days to wind him up. He wasn't going to lose his temper so easily.

"I'm fine. How was your time with Count Angelo and his brother?"

"It was brilliant."

"I can tell from the way you're smiling," said Samuel. "Did Angelo get those clothes and boots for you?"

"Yep."

Samuel nodded. "They look expensive."

"They are," shrugged Bianca. "Where's Gran and Ricky?"

"Inside the caravan. Are you hungry?"

"Yep. I haven't eaten since last night."

"Then go on in. I can smell breakfast."

* * *

Bianca ate slowly and thoughtfully, feeling eyes on her.

Ricky was glaring as he picked at his scrambled egg, Samuel was looking at Bianca as he sipped from a mug of coffee. Gran was eating some toast.

"So how was it with Count Angelo, darling?" she asked, once she'd swallowed.

"Amazing," Bianca replied, smiling at her grandmother. "I had a great time as usual."

"And how is his brother, Cormier?"

"Cormier's ok."

Ricky slammed his fork down. "Am I the only sane one in his van?"

"Ricky," said Samuel warningly, and he said "No, Dad! Bianca, you're not going to see those freaks again. I'm putting my foot down!"

"And you think I'd listen to you?" Bianca asked, highly amused. "I can see whoever I want, Richard."

"The hell you can!"

"What, so you're going to tell Count Angelo he's not seeing me anymore?"

"I would if he showed his bloody face!"

"Good," Bianca said coldly, "Because he's coming here at nightfall."

Ricky stared at her. "What?"

"You heard."

"Count Angelo's coming here?"

"Yep."

"Why?"

"To pick me up."

"You're going back again?!"

"That's right. And as you're so against it, you can tell Angelo he's not seeing me anymore. I really have to see this."

Ricky stared at her. "Why isn't Cormier coming?"

"Aww, you wanted to see the thing I call Cormier? How sweet."

"Shut up," snapped Ricky. "Fine. I'll tell Count Angelo he's not seeing you anymore."

"Dad?" said Bianca brightly. "Are you going to as well?"

"I know what you're doing, Bianca," growled Samuel. "You're trying to make me mad so I blow my top and go nuts, giving you a perfect excuse to run away and see Count Angelo."

"I don't need an excuse to see him," shrugged Bianca. "If I want to see him I will."

Samuel and Ricky stared at her. "What's the matter with you??"

"I'm telling you like it is," Bianca answered as she picked up her mug of tea. Taking a sip, she said "I'm not a child. I'm a young adult. So start treating me like one and I'll treat you the same. Your rules and regulations to me are void. I can do what I want."

"Well said," smiled Gran, and Ricky and Samuel whipped round to stare at her as if she'd gone mad.

"Well said?!"

"She's right," shrugged Gran. "Bianca isn't a child anymore. I was saying this to Richard before she came. And I think it's splendid that we'll get to meet this Count Angelo after hearing so much about him."

"Meet?" said Ricky angrily. "What, so we're going to sit down and have a family dinner or something? He probably eats rats and stuff, not people food!"

"People food?" Bianca repeated, furious, and Ricky snapped "Yes!"

"Angelo *is* a person, you dumb prick!! He eats the same as you and me, and his brother is a brilliant cook! He drinks like you and me as well! He's not a monster, idiot! Just because he's a vampire it doesn't mean-"

"Shut up, Bianca! I'm not in the mood to hear you praise him."

"Do you think the same, Dad?" Bianca asked her father. "You think Angelo's a-"

"I haven't met him, so I won't judge him," Samuel replied. "Well, not harshly anyway."

"Good. And Gran?"

"I think the same as your father, minus the harsh part. His brother was very polite when we spoke to him that night he brought you home. I trust Angelo is the same."

"He's better."

* * Cormier * *

Cormier trundled down the corridor, calling "Joseph!"

An excited yap answered him, and he saw the cub run through Angelo's open door towards him, barking happily.

"Stop that noise," smiled Cormier, looking at the clock. It was four p.m. "Trust me to wake three hours before nightfall."

Cormier knelt and stroked the little cub.

"You must be hungry. Come, it's time to eat."

* * Bianca * *

Bianca read the local newspaper, seated in an armchair. Samuel watched her, slightly amazed.

It was like his little girl had grown into a woman overnight. She looked and sounded so mature. He knew it was down to Count Angelo.

"Bianca."

"Yes Dad?"

"Angelo *can* be in light, can't he? Not sunlight," he added quickly, when she glared at him. "I meant electric lights. You know, light bulbs and stuff. At night."

"Sure he can," said Bianca, glancing back at her newspaper. "Why?"

"Well, I was wondering if he'd like to come in for a drink."

"Really?"

"Yes really."

Bianca glanced at the clock. It was almost seven in the evening.

"Angelo should be here soon."

"Well, we should be dressed properly," Gran said, and Bianca looked at her, puzzled.

"You look fine, Gran."

"In my nightdress?" chuckled Gran. "No darling, I don't want to give the Count a ridiculous first impression. I'm going to change."

"All right. But we're not staying for too long. He's only picking me up."

"I know, sweetie."

Gran left the living area, Ricky glaring at Bianca.

"What are you going to do at the castle, then?"

"That's none of your damn business."

"Dad!" said Ricky angrily, turning to Samuel. "Can't you stop her from going?"

"To be honest I just want to meet this guy," Samuel replied, shrugging a shoulder. "He must be really special if Bianca's speaking this way."

"He's got her under some kind of spell, that's why she's acting like this! He hoodwinked her!" said Ricky angrily. "Wait until he comes! I'll open the door and punch his face in-"

There was a knock on the caravan door.

Ricky spun round, Bianca amused.

"Go on, Richard. Open the door and punch his face in."

Ricky backed away and stood by Samuel, Gran walking in the kitchen wearing her best suit.

"Is he here?"

"I think so," Bianca said, getting up. "Angelo?"

"Yes, Bianca."

Gran quickly sat in a chair facing the door, Bianca smirking at Ricky.
"You sure you don't want to get the door so you can punch him?"
"Shut up!" hissed Ricky. "He'll hear you!"
Bianca opened the caravan door, and Gran gasped.
"My goodness!"
Angelo smiled at her, saying "Good evening. It's a pleasure to meet you."
Gran didn't answer, gaping at Angelo. He was STUNNING!!!
"Angelo, meet my father and brother. Come in."
"Y-yes, come- come in," stuttered Gran, Samuel gaping at Angelo as he
stepped into the caravan. Ricky was shocked too.
"Samuel Davis," Samuel said quickly, holding out a hand, and Angelo
shook it. Ricky's eyes raked over Angelo's body before settling on his
face, unable to speak. "And this is my son, Richard-"
"Ricky," Ricky said quickly, holding out a hand. "Um. I'm sorry for
um... you know. I didn't know you- I just- I mean..."
Everyone looked at him amusedly, Angelo raising a perfect eyebrow.
"Yes?"
"I thought you looked like a monster," muttered Ricky. "You're hot."
Bianca burst out laughing with Gran as Samuel slapped him on the head.
"I think Ricky likes you, Angelo," Bianca said, amused. "Let's go."
"Wait!" said Ricky quickly. "Aren't you going to stay for a drink? Dad
said he wants to have a drink with you, didn't you Dad?"
"I did," Samuel said amusedly. "Um... Count Angelo-"
"Angelo is fine," Angelo said, a small smile on his face. "I was going to
take Bianca for a meal tonight, but if you'd rather we stay here-"
"They don't," said Bianca quickly. "Let's go, Angelo."
"Wait, Bianca. Would you rather we stay, sir?" Angelo asked Samuel,
and once again Samuel was stunned at the young man's brilliant looks.
So was Gran and Ricky.
"Dad?" said Bianca, and Samuel shook himself.
"Uh... no, it's fine. Take Bianca to dinner," he said, swallowing. "Have a
good time."
Angelo smiled and took Bianca's hand, both of them leaving the caravan.
Bianca couldn't help but laugh.
"They're all attracted to you, even my father."
"I know," Angelo said, amused. "So. Will you come with me to dinner?"
"You wasn't joking about that?"
"Of course not."
"But what if we see other vampires? I don't want to be targeted."
Angelo frowned at her. "Targeted?"
"Marissa already put herself in some kind of vampire coma because of
me," Bianca pointed out. "What if another female vampire finds out
we're together? She might do something worse?"

"If she does it is not my problem," shrugged Angelo. "Marissa is a close friend. But I have no time for jealous females. Besides, nobody knows I'm seeing you. They know I'm seeing someone, but they think she is another vampire. They have no idea that you're a mortal."

"Oh. Well, Clover and Sebastian-"

"Are the only ones aside from Cormier and Marissa who know we are in a relationship." Angelo smiled at her. "The others in the meeting assume I will eventually bite you."

"Which you won't?"

"Of course I won't."

Bianca smiled and said nothing as they walked. Then she asked "How's Joseph doing?"

"Joseph is fine. Clover has him for the night."

"Oh. Where's Cormier?"

"Cormier is keeping an eye on Marissa at the castle while I take you out."

"And what made you decide to take me out, Count Angelo?"

Angelo smiled down at her. "Although I could have easily dined alone with you at the castle, I thought it would be nice to take you out for a change."

Bianca smiled back.

* * Cormier * *

Cormier glared down at Marissa's lifeless figure.

"You are a fool, Marissa Bennett. A total, complete fool."

Marissa's pale skin seemed even more pale. And looked... grey. Cormier knew when she woke up she'd be bloodthirsty. Scowling, he said "All of this for my brother, and he doesn't want you. He never has and probably never will. You may as well give up and let him be."

Marissa was still as ever, unconscious. Cormier began pacing the room.

"You could have any man you want, yet you cling to the thought of having my brother like a child holding a toy. Why?"

Silence.

Marissa gave no reply, which he knew wasn't deliberate. If she were awake he knew she'd have plenty to say. Cormier scowled, leaving the room. He was going to ask her the same question as soon as she was fit.

* * Angelo * *

Angelo frowned at his menu.

"Is there anything that isn't swimming in gravy?"

Bianca burst out laughing. "Would you rather Cormier make us a dish?"

"Well, now that you've said it-"

"No!" gushed the waitress, and Bianca and Angelo looked at her. "Count Angelo sir, name any dish and the chef will be happy to make it for you."

"I'd rather not give him the hassle-"

"Please don't go, Count Angelo!"

Bianca noticed the red gleam in her eyes as Angelo sighed, saying "All right. Tell the chef to make us beef lasagna. With his finest meat."

"Yes sir, right away."

The waitress bowed and walked away, Bianca staring after her.

"She's a vampire."

Angelo nodded. "I know."

"Is this a restaurant for vampires?"

"Yes and no. In the day, normal people from all over come here. Especially from the tourist park. I'm sure your brother has been here with that girl he's taken a liking to. But at night, it's open to anyone. Even vampires. And vampires do have night jobs. Like that waitress Morcheeba. But I warn you, do not look her in the eye. I don't want her or anyone to realise you're mortal. Like you said, you may be targeted. And I'm desperate to keep you safe."

Bianca nodded, Morcheeba the waitress coming back.

"Would you both like a drink of some sort, Count Angelo?"

"Yes. Bring us both a Hurricane cocktail."

"Yes sir. Right away sir."

"She loves you," Bianca said, amused as Angelo said "I don't get why."

"You're gorgeous, nutcase. Even my father and brother was gay for thirty seconds."

Angelo burst out laughing, and gasps went up.

"He's laughing!"

"He hasn't laughed in *years!*"

"My goodness!"

"His company made him *laugh?!*"

Morcheeba the waitress returned with the drinks, glaring at Bianca.

"You made Count Angelo laugh easily when others have tried and failed to do so. Who are you?"

"Leave it, Morcheeba," another vampire called warningly, as Bianca hesitated to answer, looking at Angelo.

"I'm just a friend."

"Indeed. Others who are *just a friend* have not made him crack a smile even."

"And how is that my problem exactly?" was Bianca's curt reply, Angelo saying "Leave us be, Morcheeba."

"But-"

"Now," said Angelo flatly. "Do not return without our meal."

It was obvious Morcheeba wanted to say a lot more, but she closed her mouth and bowed to Angelo, turning and walking away.

Bianca nonchalantly reached for her drink.

"Maybe I should stay silent in case I make you laugh again."

"Don't be silly," Angelo said, amused. "My laughter is like music to their ears."

"Oh really."

Angelo nodded, smiling as she took a sip of her Hurricane cocktail, then she gasped at the taste.

"Do you like it?" he asked, and she stared at him.

"Who created this cocktail?"

Angelo smiled. "I did."

"Is that why everyone has ordered it?" Bianca noticed most of the tables sporting the same drink as herself and Count Angelo.

"Yes."

"It's brilliant," Bianca confessed, and he smiled at her.

"Thank you."

"So does Cormier take cocktail making after you or vice versa?"

"It's really vice versa. Cormier makes a new cocktail almost every couple of nights. It's an uncanny habit of his. I only made this one and two others."

"I'd like to try those others sometime."

Angelo smiled as he sipped his drink. "You will."

* * Bianca * *

"Here is your food, Count Angelo and company."

"Thank you Morcheeba," Angelo replied, as the waitress set the plates down without taking her eyes off Bianca. Bianca refused to look at her, gazing out of the restaurant window.

"Would you like anything else, sir?"

"No."

Morcheeba nodded, and, glancing at Bianca again, left their table. Smiling ruefully, Bianca said "Another Marissa."

"Morcheeba is not a close friend," Angelo replied. "Which makes her slightly more of a risk than Marissa."

"Why a risk?"

"She may tell people she saw the Grand Vampire in the company of someone unknown, and that company made him laugh."

"Have you foreseen it?"

Angelo nodded. "I have."

"Well I don't care," Bianca said flatly. "She can tell who she wants. And so can the other vampires here. I really couldn't give a damn."

"Are you sure?"

"I'm definitely sure."

Angelo leant back in his chair, looking at her through his stunning golden eyes.

"I've never met someone like you yet."

"Good," Bianca replied as she picked up her fork. "This lasagna smells great. I can't wait to eat it."

"Nor I."

* * Ricky * *

"He's a god," Ricky said dazedly. "Gran, I... you- you saw what I saw, right? I wasn't hallucinating?"

"I saw, Richard." Gran was still shocked. "He's a beautiful young man. It's not hard to see why Bianca loves him."

"Now hold on," said Samuel sharply, looking at them both. "Bianca doesn't love this Count. She hasn't know him long enough. And stop this gayness, Richard. You can't be attracted to the vampire."

"Why not? You was!"

"For a split second," snapped Samuel, feeling ashamed of himself. They'd all wanted this vampire in a moment of madness, as soon as he stepped into the caravan and smiled. "At least I got to touch him."

"He didn't shake my hand," grumbled Ricky. "Dad, what did it feel like? Was his hand ice cold?"

"Actually, it was warm," Samuel admitted. "But I don't understand why."

"I'm betting it was because of Bianca," Gran said thoughtfully. "Now, I'm off to bed. Richard, are you going to see Catherine?"

"Who? Oh! Catherine. Nah. I'm going to bed too."

* * Cormier * *

Cormier sat watching the television, Joseph at his feet.

Suddenly the cub made a whining noise, and he glanced down, murmuring "What's the matter, Joseph?"

Joseph whined again. Cormier stood, unsure what to do. Sebastian appeared by his side, saying "It is time."

"Time? Time for what?"

"For Joseph to morph into a human."

"WHAT?!!"

"Stay here. I will get Angelo."

"No- he's on a date with Bianca."

"He needs to be here," Sebastian answered. "Trust me."

* * Bianca * *

"That was amazing," Bianca admitted, Morcheeba taking her and Angelo's plates away.

"Would you like dessert?"

"No thank you," Angelo said, as he saw Sebastian hurry in the restaurant, ignoring the people who called him.

"Sebastian! Not with Clover this time?"

"Angelo," panted Sebastian as he reached their table. "You must come."

"What is the matter?"

"It's the cub. Joseph."

Angelo frowned. "What about him?"

"His time has come."

Angelo stared at Sebastian, then he stood. "Come, Bianca."

Bianca stood too. "Is everything ok?"

"Everything will be."

Angelo took her hand and began walking, saying to Morcheeba "I will pay you for your services and food upon my next visit."

"Yes sir," she said humbly, Bianca not looking at her as they walked out of the restaurant.

"Bianca, I am going to teleport with you to the castle. It's either that or I fly," Angelo said, "Which will take longer. I need to get to Joseph."

"Ok sure, but what's wrong with him?"

"His time has come," Sebastian repeated, and she said "Time for what exactly?"

Bianca was suddenly aware of the eyes on them. Everyone was looking at them through the restaurant windows as Angelo pulled her into his arms, staring down at her. Bianca stared up at him too, and Angelo almost kissed her as he murmured "You are beautiful."

"Thank you," she said softly, and they vanished.

Grinning at the vampires at the window, Sebastian saluted them and vanished too.

* * Angelo * *

"He keeps doing that," Cormier said worriedly, as Joseph rolled over on the carpet, whimpering.

Angelo held out an arm to stop Bianca rushing over, saying "Don't."

Dismayed, Bianca said "He's a baby, Angelo! And he's in pain-"

"He is not in any form of pain. He is just scared."

"Scared of what?"

"Scared of changing."

"Changing??"

"He's trying to suppress the change, but he won't be able to for much longer. I'd say twenty seconds max."

Joseph whined again, then he began to glow. Bianca's jaw dropped, like Cormier's. Angelo's expression didn't change.

Joseph's paws began to stretch into tiny fingers, his hair on his body thinning, his nose and ears shrinking... Before a cloud of blue smoke engulfed his entire body before thinning and clearing- Bianca gasped.

There stood a little boy, no older than three, standing there looking at them, melting chocolate skin, eyes dark green as he blinked, looking at them curiously before he smiled at them.

"Hello."

"Hello," smiled Angelo, and Joseph giggled shyly.

Bianca couldn't believe her eyes as she stared at the tiny child that was once Joseph the wolf cub. He wore blue dungarees with a green t-shirt inside, bringing out his beautiful green eyes.

"He's gorgeous," she said softly, and Angelo smiled at her.

"He's human. And he knows you."

Joseph had tottered unsteadily over to Bianca, smiling up at her.

"Hello!"

"Hey," she said softly, and he reached up happily.

Bianca reached down and picked him up, snuggling him close. Joseph clung to her tightly, Cormier and Sebastian touched. So was Angelo.

"Clover will be upset she missed his changing," Sebastian said musingly. "I'm in the dog house for this one."

"She'll get over it," Angelo said, amused. "Joseph must be hungry. He needs human food."

"Cereal?" asked Cormier, and Angelo shrugged.

"That should do for now."

Bianca held Joseph, already loving him like a baby brother.

"Will he change back to a wolf?"

"No," Angelo replied, and she stared at him.

"No?" He said no. "At all?"

"Not until he is around eight."

"But that's years from now!"

"I know."

"So what now? Will he go to nursery? School? Something??"

"Of course he will."

"How??"

"Bianca, do not get worked up. I will think of something."

Bianca was already protective of little Joseph.

"I hungry," said Joseph, and Cormier said "Let me take him, Bianca."

Bianca reluctantly handed little Joseph over, Cormier saying "Let's give you some food."

As soon as they left, Bianca turned to Angelo.

"How is this going to work exactly?"

"I will have to pay a human to mind him in the day, sort of be a nanny for him, while I recharge. It's the only way."

"A stranger?! Angelo-"

"It's the only option. Joseph will needed to be minded at all times. He is only a baby."

"Let me do it," Bianca said, and Angelo stared at her.

"You?"

"Yes."

"No. Joseph is my responsibility. I can't let you, Bianca."

"Look, I'd rather it be me than some crusty old woman who doesn't connect with him the way I do. Don't deny we have a connection!"

"I wasn't going to. But Bianca, listen to me for just one minute."

Bianca sighed, waiting.

"You will be leaving in two months' time. Joseph will most likely never see you again. Nor will I. He needs stability. I won't have him pining for you when you have to leave, missing you terribly, crying every night for weeks. I wouldn't put him through that sort of emotional pain."

"So you won't let me care for him?"

"I can't, Bianca. I'm thinking ahead. There's no point."

Bianca thought about that for a moment, then she said "Then I'll stay."

"Your family would never let you."

"Just how I won't let you palm Joseph off to a stranger!"

"Bianca, don't do this. Please."

Bianca didn't answer, furious. She turned and left the room, Angelo sighing as he let her go.

It was for the best.

* * Bianca * *

Joseph was happily playing with some toys on the library carpet, by the fireplace. Bianca sat watching him almost contentedly, in an armchair near him.

She was seething about Angelo's nonchalant attitude, what he said.

"Joseph will most likely never see you again. Nor will I."

Bianca scowled. So this romance between herself and Angelo, it really would be over once she returned to England. She'd never see him again. Now she knew.

"I guess Happily Ever Afters only happen in the romance novels, right Joseph?" she said, smiling, though her eyes filled over and she found tears coursing down her face.

Joseph stopped playing, staring at her. "Ok?"

"I'm fine," wept Bianca, and he got up and tottered over to her, reaching up. Bianca picked him up and cuddled him, Joseph hugging her back.

"Be ok." He smiled at her, wiping her tears away. "Be ok."

"It won't be ok, Joseph. Angelo's right. I'll never see either of you again," she sobbed. "I don't know if I can deal with that."

* * Angelo * *

Angelo's heart was breaking as he listened, Cormier and Sebastian as well as they heard Bianca trying to pull herself together.

"Go in to her," hissed Cormier. "Make her feel better."

"By lying? I can't," Angelo said quietly. "I can't make false promises, brother. I haven't lied to her yet and I refuse to start."

* * Bianca * *

Joseph was falling asleep as Bianca sung to him gently, rocking him in her arms in the armchair by the fire.
It had been three hours and Angelo hadn't come in to her. Neither had Cormier or Sebastian. Bianca guessed they knew she wanted to be alone.
Joseph sniffed, eyes closed before he snuggled into Bianca, Bianca gently murmuring "I *will* see you again, Joseph... I promise."
She kissed him on the forehead before she leant back and closed her eyes. Both of them fell into a deeper sleep, warm and content by the fire.

* * Angelo * *

It was four in the morning.
Angelo had watched Bianca sleep with Joseph in that armchair for an entire hour before he found that his eyes had filled, making him gasp.
"Tears?!"
A total shock.
He was as upset as she was but had been suppressing his feelings all night. He hadn't gone into her when she was weeping because he thought there wouldn't be any point. When it all came down to it, she would still leave in two months' time and he'd never see her again.
Angelo went into the kitchen to find Cormier creating another cocktail. Sebastian had gone. Cormier grinned at his little brother.
"I'm trying something similar to Pina Colada. But instead of just pineapple and coconut, pineapple, mango, *apple* and coconut. With white rum of course."
"Sounds delightful," Angelo replied dryly. "I need a drink."
"Of Pina Colada?"
"No. Give me something strong."
"Angelo, alcohol isn't going to help," Cormier said firmly. "Stop being a coward and go and talk to Bianca."
"I can't. She's angry with me."
"And she should be," Cormier said, glaring at him. "What was there to gain from telling her you would never see her again after she left for England? Even if it was true? You hurt her feelings, even if you didn't mean to! Go and patch things up with her before she-"
"It's ok, Cormier."
Angelo and Cormier whipped round.
"Bianca!"
"I put Joseph to bed," she said quietly. "Cormier, can I speak to Angelo alone please?"
"I'm making a new drink, chick pea." Cormier smiled at her. "Take

Angelo to the library."
"All right." Bianca looked at Angelo. "Let's go."

* * Bianca * *

"I've been doing some thinking about what you said. And I have a proposition."
"Really," said Angelo. "What is that?"
"Seeing as I'm never going to see you or Joseph again after I leave for England, like you said-"
"Bianca-"
"Let me speak," Bianca said quietly, and he closed his mouth. "I want to spend as much time with Joseph as possible before I leave. Seeing as you don't care about me spending time with you-"
"How can you say that?!" Shocked, Angelo stared at her.
"Because I know it's true," Bianca replied flatly. "You said I'd never see you again. You didn't even make me a false promise. You kept it straight. Which I'm grateful for, but I'm doing exactly the same. And I'm telling you now, I want to spend as much time with Joseph as possible during the two months I have left here. And just so you know, I do plan to see him again. No matter what it takes."
"And what if I do not let you see him?" Angelo asked, eyebrow raised.
"Because it seems to me you haven't listened to a word I said about not wanting to hurt Joseph."
"I listened," Bianca said, heat rising. "You can't stop me from seeing him."
"I can," shrugged Angelo. "He is my responsibility, not yours. And just so you know, I have a proposition also."
Bianca scowled at him. "And what is that?"
"If you want to spend the remaining two months with Joseph, you must spend them with me also."
"What's the point when you don't care about me?"
"I care more than you'll ever know," Angelo said softly. "Please, Bianca. I didn't mean to hurt you. At all. I was being blunt about the whole thing and I apologise. Do you accept my apology?"
"Only if you accept my proposition."
"I will, but you must accept mine first."
"Angelo, you don't have to ask me to spend time with you. I want to. I feel so strongly for you, I…" Bianca shook her head. "You made me cry. No guy has ever done that. We have a connection. I want to be with you, I always have since the day I met you. But it seems like you only want to turn me away."
"I just don't want to get hurt," Angelo said quietly. "Let's make each

other a promise. I promise not to hurt you, to spend each day with you as if it is our last, to protect you." He did not say 'To love you', not wanting to share that information yet. "Do you promise the same?"

Bianca's eyes filled as she nodded. "I promise."

Relieved, Angelo pulled her into his arms and kissed her. Bianca kissed him back, heart racing as Cormier appeared.

"I take it you've made up then?"

Angelo broke the kiss to glare at his elder brother. "Do you not know the meaning of privacy?"

Cormier grinned at him. "I was only coming to tell you both to get to bed. It's soon dawn."

Angelo scowled. "All right. Thank you."

* * Bianca * *

Angelo couldn't sleep.

Dawn wasn't even affecting him like it usually did. He was staring at Bianca, deep in thought.

Bianca slept on, her brown skin glowing. Angelo reached out and caressed her cheek before he stood, going to check on Joseph.

He'd already decorated a bedroom for the happy little boy. It was baby blue, his bed covers green. A giant photo of the full moon took up one wall opposite the bed, so when Joseph woke up he'd see it and be reminded of what he was.

Surprised, Angelo saw that Joseph was awake, sitting up in bed, sucking his thumb as he stared at the full moon on his wall.

"Hello," Angelo said curiously, and Joseph smiled at him.

"Hello!"

"Why aren't you asleep, Joseph Heathen?"

Joseph reached out happily, and Angelo picked him up.

"You're not hungry. I would know."

"Bee," Joseph said happily, and Angelo smiled at him.

"Bianca's sleeping. Just like we both should be. But I'll let you stay with us as long as you behave."

Joseph giggled, Angelo carrying him into the master suite. He placed Joseph next to Bianca, who stirred and opened her eyes.

"Hey," she said softly, as Joseph snuggled up to her happily. "What are you doing up, Angelo?"

"For some reason daylight isn't affecting me," Angelo replied, as Bianca put an arm around Joseph and pulled him to her gently. "And apart from that Joseph was awake. He wanted to see you."

Bianca yawned, then she said "Maybe that's why you're up. Because of Joseph. Maybe something will make sure you stay awake so you can tend to him properly instead of just at night."

"I hadn't thought of that explanation," Angelo admitted. "It's a good one, and probably true, but I'll need confirmation from the wolves."

"The wolves?"

"They know all," Angelo explained. "They are extremely wise. If the curse of the undead has indeed been lifted, then I'd want to hear it from them."

He yawned, then frowned. "I seem to be getting tired."

"Because Joseph's asleep," Bianca said softly, and Angelo looked at the toddler. Joseph was sleeping soundly, in Bianca's arms. Angelo couldn't help but say "I'm sure you'll be an amazing mother."

Bianca smiled at him. "Thanks."

Angelo got into bed, settling down for a good rest.

"Angelo?"

"Yes Bianca?"

"I…" Bianca hesitated, then said "Have a good day's sleep."

Knowing that wasn't what she was going to say but not wanting to pursue it, Angelo said "And the same to you."

He leant across Joseph gave her a soft kiss. Bianca smiled, closing her eyes. She was asleep in minutes.

Angelo sighed, on his back. He watched Joseph sleep for a small while, then he settled down to sleep.

* * Ricky * *

"Dad!"

"What?"

"Is Bianca coming back today?"

"I'm not sure," Samuel replied as he drank his coffee. "Why?"

"I'm just asking," Ricky said huffily, and his father smirked at him.

"You're asking because you want to see Count Angelo."

"That's not true!"

"Sure it isn't." Samuel glanced at the clock: it was almost lunchtime. "Where's your grandmother? I'm starving."

"I can make lunch," Ricky offered, and Samuel frowned at him.

"What will you make?"

"Umm. Not sure. Cheese on toast with baked beans and eggs?"

"Sounds delightful."

Ricky beamed, then realised his dad was being sarcastic.

"Well *you* cook something then!"

* * Angelo * *

Angelo snapped awake, startled.

Joseph was looking at him, thumb in his mouth as Bianca slept. Angelo smiled and gently pulled the infant's thumb out of his mouth.

"No thumb sucking, Joseph. It's a bad habit."

Joseph giggled, Angelo turning his head to look at the clock. It was almost four in the afternoon.

"All right. You're hungry," Angelo said, slowly getting to his feet. "Come."

He picked up Joseph, Bianca mumbling something before she rolled over, snuggling back down.

"Bee," Joseph said happily as he looked at her, and Angelo said "You'll see her when she wakes up. Come."

He carried Joseph out of the giant room, down the hallway and into the kitchen, snapping his fingers.

A high chair appeared, Angelo placing Joseph in it. Joseph kicked his legs happily as he waited, Angelo reaching into the cupboard and taking down a few boxes of cereal, frowning at each one.

"Which is the most healthy?"

Laughter erupted, making Joseph jump as Angelo looked around.

"Brother, just give him the cereal," Cormier said, amused as he appeared, hair tousled. "It matters not which is the most healthy. He is a child."

Angelo pouted. "I don't want him eating unhealthy food."

Cormier rolled his eyes before saying "Give him Rice Krispies then.

105

Warm the milk and add sugar."
"Will he like that?"
"Of course he will."

* * Bianca * *

"Bee?" Bianca stirred, Joseph looking at her. He reached out and shook her shoulder with his tiny hands. "Bee! Ok?"
"I'm fine," she mumbled, and Joseph beamed at her as she sat up, looking around. Angelo stood at the door. Smiling jadedly, she said "Hi."
"Hi," he said quietly. "Dinner is ready when you are."
Bianca frowned at him. "What time is it?"
"Six in the evening."
"Oh God. Was Joseph all right?"
"He was fine," Angelo said reassuringly. "I snapped awake as soon as he woke up, which was at almost four. I fed him already, but me and Cormier beg to differ about the kinds of food he should be eating. Cormier says junk food as he is a child. I say healthy. What do you think?"
"Um. A bit of both really," Bianca said. "He can't always have junk yet he can't always have healthy food. Balance it out and he should be fine."
Angelo smiled at her. "All right."
Bianca tickled Joseph, making him shriek with laughter as she stood.
"I'm going to shower. I'll meet you in the dining room."
"All right," Angelo said again. "Come, Joseph."

* * Angelo * *

"Did you check on Marissa, brother?"
Cormier rolled his eyes. "Angelo, she isn't going to wake. At least not for now. What exactly am I meant to be checking for? A pulse? A heartbeat? What?"
Angelo scowled at him. "I will check on her myself. Seeing as you don't care."
"No. I don't. Because she put herself in this state deliberately. Why should either of us care?"
"Because she is a close friend," Angelo snapped, and Cormier said "She is your close friend, not mine. Where is Bianca?"
"Getting ready for dinner."
Joseph squirmed about in his chair, wanting to play.
"And what does Joseph call us exactly?" Cormier asked. "Daddy to you and Uncle to me?"
"I haven't thought about it."

"Bee!" said Joseph happily, making them turn.

Cormier's jaw dropped as Angelo smiled at Bianca.

"You look wonderful."

"Thank you," she said shyly. She'd styled her hair in curls, which framed her face. Lip gloss shimmered from her lips, which were smiling at Angelo specifically as he gazed at her. This time she wore a white blouse with black trousers and white shoes. "Angelo, you should stop getting me these nice outfits. They're too gorgeous. And the hair stuff is expensive too. I've seen them for mad prices in England."

"Very well. The next time I will poke some holes in a black bag and make you wear it. And make you a comb out of cardboard."

Cormier burst out laughing, Bianca as well as Angelo winked amusedly, saying "Are you ready to eat, Bianca?"

"Definitely. I overslept. I should have gotten up."

"It matters not, chick pea." Cormier smiled at her. "Now we have lamb and roast potatoes with vegetables here. Is that all right?"

"It's perfect," smiled Bianca as she sat down. Joseph beamed at her as Angelo sat next to her, then he kissed her on the cheek.

"Cormier? Will you carve the lamb?"

"Are you sure you don't want to, brother? Seeing as we're going to differ about how much Joseph gets."

Angelo sighed. "How much are you going to give him?"

"Quite a bit. As he is a wolf. A carnivore. Grrr!"

Bianca burst out laughing, Joseph giggling as Angelo said "Fine. But not too much potatoes if he's having a lot of meat. And make sure he gets a lot of vegetables."

"All right all right." Cormier started carving the lamb, Angelo snapping his fingers. The cutest little blue plate and cup appeared with a tiny knife, fork and spoon, Bianca saying "Aww. Cute."

"Mine?" asked Joseph, and Angelo nodded.

"Yes Joseph. Yours."

Cormier placed Joseph's plate in front of him, Bianca saying "I'll feed him. Can I?"

"Of course," smiled Angelo. "Slowly he will learn to feed himself."

Bianca smiled back before she fed little Joseph slowly and thoughtfully, watching as he chewed uncertainly before swallowing, then he smiled. "Nice."

Bianca smiled, loving him so much. "You're too cute, Joseph."

"Won't you eat yours, chick pea?" asked Cormier, and Bianca said "Should I feed Joseph first before I eat mine?"

"You can, or you can multitask."

Bianca stuck her tongue out at him.

* * Cormier * *

Clover arrived at the castle, Sebastian with her.

"I can't believe you two didn't consult me the minute you realised Joseph's time to change had come. Or even after!"

"Cousin Clover, be quiet." Cormier grinned at her. "It is now after."

Clover hit him on the arm. "Where is he? And what of his surname?"

"He is a Heathen of course. Joseph Heathen."

"Will cousin Trevor approve?" asked Clover uncertainly, and Cormier said "Trevor lost all rights as a parent the minute Claire dismissed him. Joseph is our responsibility; therefore, he is a Heathen. I doubt Trevor will be too bothered about his name."

"Hmm. Well, where is the little cub? I want to see him."

"He's in the library with Angelo and Bianca. Bianca is reading with him."

"And Angelo is watching her I presume?" Clover said, shaking her head.

"He is smitten."

"Very smitten," Sebastian said, Cormier saying "Super smitten."

Clover laughed.

"Come, let us join them."

* * Angelo * *

Angelo gazed at Bianca, head propped on his hand. He vaguely nodded when Clover whispered her hello, not taking his eyes off Bianca.

"Choo choo! The train started and pulled away."

"Choo choo!" said Joseph happily, and Bianca smiled down at him.

"Angelo, do you want to read with him?"

Angelo didn't answer, and she glanced at him.

"Angelo? You ok?"

"Hmm?" said Angelo dreamily, and she frowned at him. He snapped out of it, realising she'd asked him if he was ok. "Oh, I'm fine. What did you say before?"

Sebastian and Cormier were sniggering.

"He's on his own planet, Bianca. Keep reading so he stays in a trance."

"Ignore them," Clover said, scowling at her husband and cousin.

"It's time for Joseph to go to bed," Angelo said, glaring at them and standing. "Do you want me to take him for you?"

"I don't mind."

Angelo reached down and picked up tiny Joseph, saying "Say goodnight, Joseph."

"Night night," said Joseph shyly, and Bianca said "Night."

Angelo left the room with Joseph, and Bianca smiled at Clover.

"It's good to see you, Clover."

"I feel the same, little sister. It seems Angelo is really smitten, possibly in love with you."

"You think so?" Bianca didn't dare think of such a thing. "Maybe he's just.... I don't know... Sprung?"

Clover burst out laughing and Bianca smiled shyly.

"Whatever you want to call it. Sprung means smitten I'm guessing?"

"Sort of," smiled Bianca. "On a slightly higher level than smitten."

"Well I have no doubt that Angelo is sprung," smiled Clover, Sebastian saying "Nor I."

"And I," said Cormier, amused. "Bianca, why don't you join Angelo in Joseph's room? He probably won't settle without you."

Bianca smiled and left the library.

As soon as her footsteps faded Cormier said "Angelo is in love."

"And how do you know that?" demanded Clover, Cormier saying "I know Angelo better than anyone. His heart always races when he is near Bianca. What's more, he is emitting body heat."

Clover gaped.

Cormier nodded. "Exactly. He's warm. Almost as if he is alive again. And aside from that dawn isn't even affecting him anymore."

"But that's because of Joseph," Clover said uncertainly. "The wolves said so."

"You've been talking with the wolves?"

"Of course," Clover said. "I was in the woods before I came here. They did say a lot. I need to discuss that with Angelo."

"Angelo would want to hear it for himself," Sebastian said, rubbing his chin. "You know he is not fond of messages, Clover. He goes straight to the person who said it."

"It's not a message. Just an explanation."

"Whatever it is, he'd still want to hear it from the direct person."

Clover sighed. "Fine. I'll tell him to meet with Phoebus."

"Good."

* * Bianca * *

Joseph was sound asleep, holding a green frog teddy.
Bianca stood and watched him for a few minutes, then Angelo whispered "Come."
Bianca looked at him. "Come where?"
"Come with me to the bedroom."
"We're going to bed?" he said yes. "What about Clover, Sebastian and Cormier?"
"I didn't say we're retiring for the night." Angelo hesitated, uncertain if she would come. "I just… I want to be alone with you."
Bianca smiled at the admission. "All right. Let's go."

* * Cormier * *

"And Marissa is still unconscious?"
"Yes," said Cormier, scowling. "If you want to see for yourself-"
"I don't need to. Word has already spread that she's put herself in this condition and is lying unconscious in the Grand Vampire's castle." Clover couldn't help but smile. "Surprising for Marissa to take such drastic measures just to get Angelo's attention, when she never has before."
"Her patience is wearing thin," Cormier replied amusedly, Sebastian grinning. "Oh, and she will definitely be bloodthirsty when she wakes. So be prepared for it."
"All right," Clover said evenly. "Where is Angelo?"

* * Angelo * *

Angelo kissed Bianca tenderly, Bianca's heart racing as he murmured "Bianca, I want you with an intensity that is killing me."
"I feel the same," Bianca said quietly. "But Clover, Cormier, Sebastian and even Joseph can't be here if..."
She trailed off, sighing as Angelo caressed her cheek.
"If?"
"If we make love," she said softly, and he smiled at her.
"When the time comes, I will make sure everything is perfect."
"It's perfect now," Bianca said quietly, but Angelo said "Now isn't the right time, Bianca."
"Don't deny me, Angelo..." she kissed him before he could say something. "Please."
"Now isn't... isn't the right..." Angelo swore quietly as she kissed his neck. "Bianca, you're going to be the death of me."
Bianca smiled as she took his hand and kissed his fingertips, never taking her brown eyes off his golden ones.
Angelo stared back at her, breath held as she kissed his fingers again, then, ever so gently, drew his index finger into her mouth.
"Bianca-!"
She didn't reply, eyes never leaving his face as she sucked his finger gently, watching as he fought to remain in control, Bianca holding his hand and never stopping her sensuous assault on his finger. Bianca's hot tongue circled before she drew his finger in further, moaning the same time Angelo did, closing her eyes.
Angelo thought he would die if he didn't take her this moment. But he was the most practical vampire ever. Right now he was fighting with his heart and his mind. His heart demanded he make love to her this instant, whereas his mind interjected the setting had to be right. He had to stay in control, remember that although she was causing mind boggling pleasure, Bianca was a virgin. He had to make it special.
Angelo gasped as Bianca released his finger, tongue flicking it one last time before she smiled at him, a cheeky, saucy smile.
"Did you like that, Dracula?"
"Don't wind me up, Bianca," growled Angelo, breathing hard. "If you do, I won't be responsible for what I do to you."
Bianca smirked. "I like the sound of that."
Before Angelo could stop her she smiled, biting her lip, before she reached up and began to unbutton her blouse.
"Bianca, don't."
"Why?"
"Just don't."

Bianca ignored him. Angelo swore as he stared at her perfect body, her flat brown stomach and sexy white bra, her chest.

Bianca smirked. "Like what you see?"

"Do not tempt me, Bianca. We cannot do this now."

"Touch me, Angelo." He stared at her, and Bianca smiled, softly saying "Put your hands on me. Feel me. Know how much I want you."

Angelo started to obey, then she said "First take your shirt off."

Angelo almost tore the shirt off his body, Bianca wowing at his eight pac, his muscles, his gorgeous bronze complexion.

Giving in, Angelo reached and brushed her shirt off her shoulders also, pulling her on top of him and kissing her passionately.

Like before, he could feel her excitement. This time, he was too far gone to care.

* * Cormier * *

Clover sniffed the air curiously, Cormier as well.

"Cousin Angelo wants to make love to Bianca, and vice versa," Clover said. "I can practically taste the lust."

"Shall we leave?" asked Sebastian, but Cormier said "No. Angelo isn't going to take it that far. I know he isn't."

* * Bianca * *

Angelo carefully unhooked Bianca's bra, easing the straps down her shoulders and off her arms, so he could properly see her top half... for the first time. He did nothing but stare.

Bianca burst out laughing before she took his hands in hers, raising them to her body.

"Go on," she said softly. "Touch them."

Angelo obeyed, then he sighed. It felt like heaven. Her breasts seemed to fit snugly in his hands, as if they'd been made just for him. Bianca's breathing grew heavier as he toyed with her nipple, rolling it between his finger and thumb before he stroked it gently- then, without warning, he leant forwards and captured it in his mouth the same way she had done to his finger, sucking gently, holding her to him as she writhed about, moaning softly.

"Angelo-"

"Shh," he murmured. "Don't make me stop, Bianca."

"I wasn't going to-" She gasped hotly as he lifted his mouth away, only to put it on her left breast and begin pleasuring her all over again.

"Your breasts are perfect, Bianca," he said quietly, but before she could answer he leant forwards again, skimming his tongue over both her breasts before greedily pulling her nipple into his mouth again and sucking a little harder, making her gasp and moan at the same time.

* * Angelo * *

He could tell from the way she gripped the back of his head and held him to her breasts that she liked the feeling and that he was arousing sensations inside of her. And they were not sensations she had felt before either. He knew it.

"Angelo, please don't stop," she whispered, making him smile.

"I won't."

Angelo didn't plan on stopping at her breasts. There was a direct correlation between a woman's breasts and the area between her legs, which was the reason he knew why she was shifting her legs back and forth as she held him to her.

With every suck and flick of his tongue, heat was gathering near her womb and spreading all over her body. Bianca's scent was getting stronger, flowing through his nostrils and causing him to devour her breasts with inane hunger.

Needing to touch the wetness he knew had gathered between her thighs, Angelo shifted and slowly unbuttoned her trousers with one hand, keeping the other arm around her and his mouth firmly on her nipple, continuing to drive her over the edge and showing her what a perfect multitasker he was.

* * Cormier * *

"You may be the first to try my Cormi Colada, cousin Clover."

"Me?" said Clover, amused. "Which cocktail is this?"

"It's my very own remix of Pina Colada. I call it the Cormi Colada. Come, have a glass."

Clover obeyed, Sebastian saying "Let me know if it's disgusting so I can knock him out for poisoning you, Clover."

"Oh, be quiet Sebastian." Cormier grinned at him as he handed a glass of the orange beverage to Clover. "You only say that because I didn't offer you the first glass. Clover? How does it taste?"

"It's delicious," she admitted, and Cormier's grin grew even bigger.

* * Angelo * *

Angelo slipped his hand into Bianca's panties, and she automatically spread her legs, breathing hard.

When he felt her moist heat, how wet she was, Angelo was filled with an enormous need to taste her in that very spot. To stake his claim, brand her his. Because he knew Bianca was his. There was no going back.

It was a good thing he remembered they were not alone in the castle, because he would have liked nothing more than to make love to her all through the night. Even though he couldn't, he intended to give her something to remember him by.

Giving her breasts a rest, Angelo lifted his head to kiss Bianca as his hands concentrated on letting his fingers pleasure her. She felt hot, swollen and ready; he moved his fingers inside of her, caressing the area he knew would stir a need within her, a thirst only he could quench.

"Angelo!"

Her crying out his name did something to him, and the sound was of an intensity and desperation he hadn't heard from her before. There was a sexiness in her voice, and the more he stroked her, the wetter she became, moaning his name. He knew she was on the verge of the climax he was intentionally giving her.

When Bianca's body moved in a fierce jerk, he knew she was about to let out a scream and he quickly moved up a little to angle his head and capture her mouth in a fierce kiss, smothering the sound, tangling his tongue with hers as she whimpered, enjoying the feel of the aftershock going on between her thighs.

Bianca was quivering as she whispered his name, Angelo gently lifting his hand away.

"Are you all right, Bianca?" he asked softly, and she nodded.

"I... I'm fine."

The air surrounding them had the fragrance of uncompleted sex. Angelo inhaled deeply before he kissed her again, Bianca leaning back and closing her eyes, Angelo murmuring "You came."
Bianca nodded, eyes closed still. "I guess I did."
"Your first time?" asked Angelo, and she nodded again. "I'm glad I pleased you."
"Being with you alone pleases me, Angelo. Sex isn't everything."
"Wise words coming from the girl who begged me not to stop."
Bianca burst out laughing as he smiled at her.
"Touché, Dracula." She stood up, then bent and kissed him gently. "I'm going to get a shower and then check on Joseph."
"All right. I'll go and see what the others are up to."
Angelo smiled and left the room, sighing dreamily.
"I love her."

* * Cormier * *

Cormier smirked when Angelo entered the kitchen. "Are you all right, brother?"
"Why wouldn't I be?"
"You reek of lust. Your lips are shiny, probably from Bianca's lip gloss. Your hair is tousled, and your shirt is undone. I've never seen you looking like this in years. Which is why I asked if you're all right," Cormier said, struggling not to laugh. "Even when you saw other females, you always made sure you looked perfect before you joined others."
Angelo was embarrassed as he realised that, quickly wiping his mouth. "Yes, well-"
"It seems as though you've been using your mouth continuously," Sebastian said, grinning at Angelo. "I know I wouldn't be fine. Bianca must be a brilliant kisser."
"Be quiet! I am fine!"
"We know he's fine," said Clover, amused as Sebastian and Cormier burst out laughing. "Angelo, ignore them. Where is Bianca?"
"She's in the shower."
"You go and get one too, cousin. Don't mind Cormier and Sebastian."
Angelo smiled at her. "Ok."

* * Bianca * *

Fresh and clean in beige pyjamas, Bianca headed for Joseph's room.
Joseph was fast asleep, cuddling his frog teddy.
Bianca smiled and leant down, kissing him on the forehead and tucking him in properly, whispering "Sweet Dreams, Joseph."
"He'll probably wake us up tomorrow," Angelo said softly, making her whip round. He was leaning against the door, in black pyjama bottoms and no shirt. Bianca started to feel hot just looking at him. "But for now, let's go to bed."
"Where's Clover and Sebastian? And Cormier?"
"In the lounge," Angelo said, lowering his voice as Joseph stirred. "Shall we join them?"
Bianca thought about it, then she smiled and shook her head. "No."
"All right." Angelo glanced at the clock, then he said "Bed it is, then."

* * Ricky * *

"Something has happened," murmured Gran, and Ricky and Samuel looked at her, already starting to panic.
"Did the Count do something to Bianca?" said Samuel fearfully. "Is she hurt? Shall we go and get her? Mum!"
"No," said Gran quietly. "I sense something, but it's not negative. I feel… happiness. Contentment. Bianca and Count Angelo are closer than ever."
Silence.
Ricky turned to look at his father, then he said "Dad, I don't like the sound of this. What if Bianca refuses to-"
"Don't say it, Ricky! I don't want to think about that," Samuel said, glaring at him. "If Bianca refuses to come back home then I really will drag her out of there by her hair."
"Her curly hair," murmured Gran, but they ignored her.
"I will let her spend as much time as she wants with Count Angelo. It's what she wants and I can't stop her, like she said." Samuel scowled, rubbing his chin. "But once it's time to leave, we're leaving. And that will be the end of it."

* * Angelo * *

Angelo held Bianca close as she slept, deep in thought about what they shared. He'd never let himself go like that, at least not in a long time.
Not since Alicia.
Angelo sighed. He hadn't even thought of Alicia. Not in a long time. Who'd thought he'd love again. Definitely not him. And the love he felt for Bianca was different. It was so pure. He wanted to protect her, nurture her, love her forever. She was his. And although she didn't know it, he knew he was hers also. He'd do anything for her.
Bianca snuggled closer to him, and Angelo kissed her on the forehead, thinking to himself about when the remaining two months passed and Bianca returned to England.
"I wouldn't be able to bear it," he murmured sadly. "But I have no choice in the matter."
Clover appeared, startling him.
"Clover! You know not to enter my suite unless it's an emergency-"
"This is an emergency," she answered, sitting down. "Angelo, I know."
"You know? Know what?"
"I know how you feel about Bianca. You're in love with her."
"I am not," said Angelo angrily. "Now leave, Clover!"
"Angelo, you don't have to act like you have no feelings. You've been deadpan for how many years and Bianca has brought you back to life. Don't deny it," she said, when he opened his mouth. "I can feel your body heat from here. Angelo, body heat? This is a prime side effect of a vampire being in love!"
"Clover, please. I am not in love. I do not feel a thing. The body heat means nothing. It's probably because of Joseph."
Clover frowned at him. "Joseph?"
"I love him, Clover. Like a son or little brother. That's probably why I have body heat all of a sudden."
"Who are you trying to convince, me or you Angelo?" Clover shook her head. "You shared something with Bianca tonight and I know that it meant a lot to you. *She* means a lot to you. Just say how you feel!"
"I'm done talking, Clover. I do not feel a thing, yes?"
"And what about when she leaves for England?" Clover demanded. "You're just going to move on and forget?"
"That's the plan."
"Angelo-"
"I have spoken, Clover."
Clover sighed and stood. She vanished.
Angelo sighed and got up, going into the bathroom, leaving Bianca asleep as he went and splashed his face with water.

* * Bianca * *

Bianca laid very still as Angelo came back, fighting to stop the tears escaping her eyes. She quickly rolled over, pretending to sleep as Angelo got back into bed, then he put his arm around her.

He must have realised she felt a little stiff, because he turned and looked at her.

"Bianca?"

She didn't answer.

"Are you awake?"

"Yes," she mumbled, and he said "Look at me, sweetheart."

Bianca obeyed, quickly wiping her eyes as Angelo asked "What is the matter?"

"Nothing."

Angelo stared at her, then he realised without having to read her mind.

"You heard me and Clover."

Bianca shrugged, not answering.

"Bianca, I can explain why I said those things-"

"It's ok," she said quietly. "I'm going to go to sleep now, Angelo."

"Would you like to be alone?"

"No," she said softly. "Stay with me. Please."

Angelo nodded.

* * Cormier * *

"Angelo's pride will be his downfall," Clover said, shaking her head as Cormier served her and Sebastian more of his new cocktail. "He wouldn't even admit how he feels for Bianca."
"Leave him be, cousin Clover." Cormier smiled at her. "We all know how he really feels. He isn't fooling anyone."
"He's fooling Bianca," Clover said, folding her arms. "She heard what he said. I can tell."
"They'll work it out by this time tomorrow," Cormier said, shrugging. "Now. Does the cocktail need more rum, less fruit?"
"It's perfect the way it is, Cormier." Clover smiled at him. "Me and Sebastian will head home soon."
"Why don't you stay?" Cormier offered. "Your room is the same way you left it."
Clover said no. "We'll come back tomorrow if you'd like. But Sebastian and I must head home."
"All right."

* * Bianca * *

Bianca couldn't sleep. "Angelo?"
"Mmm?"
"Let's go and read in the library."
Angelo turned and looked at her, a small smile on his face.
"I see you're not tired anymore."
Because I'm annoyed, she thought wryly, and Angelo frowned at her, hearing her thoughts.
"Annoyed? About what?"
"I heard you and Clover talking," Bianca said honestly. "It felt like you really didn't care. Even after we did what we did."
Angelo sighed, deciding not to answer in case it caused an argument. "Let's go to the library."

* * Cormier * *

Cormier safely stored some bottles of his new cocktail in the fridge, then he went to check on Angelo and Bianca, heading for the library.

* * Bianca * *

Bianca read her book in silence, not noticing Angelo watching her dreamily. Cormier watched his little brother, amused. Angelo didn't even look at him, keeping his focus entirely on Bianca.
"May I join you or is this a private session?"
"Join us," smiled Bianca, and Angelo tore his gaze away from her to frown at his brother.
"You hate reading."
"I'm studying," smirked Cormier, and Angelo's frown deepened.
"Studying what?"
You, brother. You are definitely smitten.
Angelo glared at the mind message, Bianca looking at Cormier.
"What are you studying, Cormier?"
"Drinks," Cormier said brightly. "I want to make wine instead of cocktails all the time."
"Good luck," smiled Bianca, and he smiled back at her, then smirked at Angelo.
"Bee!" cried a tiny voice, startling them. "Bee!"
Bianca closed her book and got up, calling "Coming!"
As soon as she left the library Cormier said to Angelo "You love her."
"That's neither here nor there," Angelo replied. "Now leave."
"No no. I want to stay."

* * *

Bianca cuddled Joseph, Joseph hugging her back happily as she carried him into the library. Angelo and Cormier were speaking in low voices, though they stopped their conversation as they smiled at her and Joseph.
"Hello," said Joseph shyly as he looked at Angelo, and Angelo smiled at him.
"Hello, Joseph. Are you hungry?"
Joseph nodded, then shook his head. Then he nodded, giggling, and Cormier stood.
"I'll give him something to eat."
Bianca handed him over, Joseph beaming. As soon as the library was empty Angelo said "Come here, Bianca."
Bianca obeyed, Angelo standing as she neared him.
"Bianca."
Looking up at him, she quietly said "Yes?"
Angelo pulled her into his arms, bringing his mouth down on hers in a passionate kiss. Bianca's arms went round him as she kissed him back, heart pounding furiously.
"Please, Angelo... be my first. Please," she panted, when he released her. "I want you so much..."
"I know you do," he said softly. "I want you even more."
Bianca reached up and kissed him again.

* * Angelo * *

Bianca smiled as Angelo took her hand and kissed it.
"I want the castle empty before I make love to you."
"Not possible, Dracula. Marissa's in a coma, this is Joseph's home, and as for Cormier... well, I don't think he'd leave on our account."
"He would if he's working at the club. And Joseph can stay with Clover."
"And Marissa?" asked Bianca, and Angelo shrugged.
"Marissa isn't conscious so she isn't a worry."
"Great."
"We'll do it tomorrow. I don't think I can wait much longer."
"You promise?"
Angelo kissed her. "I promise."

* * Ricky * *

The next day...

It was almost five in the evening.

Ricky was thinking about Bianca. Everyone was.

"Ok, so if the worst comes to the worst and she refuses to come back to England, then what?" he asked, looking at his father and grandmother. "Mum will go mad!"

"Richard, calm yourself." Gran shook her head. "Bianca won't refuse to come back to England."

"Are you sure?"

"I'm positive."

Samuel didn't take part in the conversation, deep in thought about his little girl.

Ricky wasn't done talking. "I think we should call our mother."

"If we call your mother Bianca will definitely go mad," Samuel said grudgingly. "And anyway, I don't think she'll refuse to come back to England. She's a practical person."

"She's also a dreamer," Ricky shot back. "If she was so practical she wouldn't have gone off with Count Angelo when she'd practically just met him."

"Point taken," Samuel said wearily, not wanting his son to start ranting.

"Mum, are you making dinner?"

"Yes. Now what do you fancy?"

"Rice," said Ricky. "And chicken. And ice cream and macaroni."

"Don't listen to him, Mum. Minus the ice cream," Samuel said, and Gran pouted.

"Well one of you come and help me cook. I only have one pair of hands."

Samuel pushed his son towards her, smirking. "Ricky can help."

"Dad!"

"Well you can either help cook or help clean, or both."

Ricky glared at him.

* * Angelo * *

Joseph's eyes filled as Angelo put on his little backpack, which held some diapers, a fresh set of clothes for tomorrow, his green frog teddy and his bottle.

Angelo smiled at him, then he noticed the tears. "Joseph? What is the matter?"

"Bee," wept Joseph, and Bianca swept him up in a kiss and cuddle.

"You'll see me soon, Joseph. I promise. It's just one night, ok?"

"Ok," he wept, and Bianca kissed him again before handing him to Angelo.

Joseph threw his arms around Angelo's neck in a hug, Angelo surprised but pleased as he hugged the tiny child back.

"There there. You'll be back tomorrow. That's a promise."

Clover smiled and gently took Joseph. "Say goodbye, Joseph."

"Goodbye," wept Joseph, and Bianca's eyes filled over as Clover carried him towards the stairs.

"Maybe he can stay?" she whispered, and Angelo replied "He needs to get to know cousin Clover. She's family. And Sebastian before he leaves for the club."

"All right, fine. Where's Cormier?"

"Cormier is checking on Marissa."

"Tomorrow, Angelo," Clover called, and Angelo called ok. "Farewell, little sister."

"Bye," Bianca called with a smile, then they were gone.

Angelo glanced at the clock. It was seven in the evening.

"Are you hungry, Bianca?"

"A little."

"All right. I'll let Cormier cook us his ravioli."

"Cormier can make ravioli?" said Bianca, impressed as Angelo said "I taught him years ago, and he perfected the dish. He now has multiple flavours of ravioli he likes to cook. He'll probably make all for you to sample."

"I can't wait."

* * Bianca * *

Bianca leant back on the sofa, eyes closed. "Brilliant ravioli."
Cormier grinned at her. "I'm glad you like it, chick pea. Where is Angelo?"
"I'm not sure."

* * Angelo * *

Angelo stared down at Marissa's ashen face.
She was as still as ever, unmoving. Cormier called his name from the hallway, and he reluctantly left the room.
"Brother, why do you bother?"
"I'm just making sure she is all right."
"She's fine," Cormier said exasperatedly. "Trust me. Go back to Bianca. If you want me to keep watch I will keep watch."
"All right. I'll go back to Bianca. What time are you leaving?"
"In an hour," shrugged Cormier, and Angelo frowned.
"But it's hours before the club should open."
"I know. And I know how much you want to be alone with Bianca. So! I'm going to check on Joseph at Clover's. And then I'm going to the woods to talk with the wolves."
Angelo's frown deepened. "You rarely talk with the wolves, brother. They always tell you something you don't want to hear."
"True. But I want to talk with Trevor."
"About Joseph?"
"About anything. He is our cousin. And he's been feeling a little isolated," Cormier said. "He knows we have Joseph, and he has no problem with it. But he has still been feeling very alone."
Angelo sighed. "Now you make me want to come with you to see him."
"No. Stay with Bianca. I'll talk to Trevor and let him know you are thinking of him." Cormier ran a hand through his hair. "I'll go and get ready."

* * Bianca * *

Bianca sat reading contentedly, in the library, warm by the fireplace.
Angelo watched her, invisible. His mind was racing as he thought about what they were going to do when Cormier left the castle.
"Bianca."
She jumped, startled as she looked around, but she saw nothing.
"Angelo?"
"Yes."
"Show yourself," she said nervously, and Angelo obeyed, materialising in the chair opposite her. "What's wrong?"
"Nothing."
"Don't lie to me, Angelo. I know when something's bothering you."
"I'm just thinking about... tonight. Aren't you nervous?"
"If I said I'm not I'd be lying. But I want it so much."
Angelo smiled. "As do I. But like I said, I want it to be special."
Bianca smiled back. "I know it will be."
Angelo leant down and kissed her tenderly, Bianca responding as she dropped her book.
It fell to the floor, Angelo curving his arms around Bianca and pulling her to her feet as a sweet moan escaped her.
"Where will we do this?" she whispered, once he'd released her.
"In my suite for your first time."
Bianca smiled. "And for my second third and fourth time?"
Angelo laughed before he kissed her again. "Up to you."

* * Cormier * *

In a shirt and trousers and polished black shoes, Cormier walked steadily towards the library.
"Brother!"
"Yes," called Angelo, and Cormier said "I leave now."
"All right, fine." Angelo appeared by the door. "Will you stay at Clover and Sebastian's with Joseph tonight for me?"
"What's the magic word?" teased Cormier, and Angelo replied "Promptly."
Cormier scowled at him, Bianca calling "Please, Cormier."
"There, that's better. Come and give me a hug goodbye, chick pea."
Bianca ran and gave him a big hug, Cormier smiling as she let go.
"I trust I will be sorely missed?"
"Of course you will," said Bianca, as Angelo rolled his eyes.
"Cormier, go. Why you must always massage your ego is beyond me."
Cormier laughed before he vanished in a puff of black smoke. When it cleared, he was gone. Bianca didn't even see any sign of the bat that she knew Cormier had become.
Smiling, Angelo took her hand. "Shall we go back to the library?"
"What about-"
"There's no need to rush," Angelo said softly. "When you're sure you're ready, so will I be."
Bianca smiled and nodded.

* * Cormier * *

Cormier and Trevor sat, talking.

"It's best Joseph does not know me. I don't mind him thinking of Angelo as a father."

"And his name?" asked Cormier. "Angelo has named him Joseph Heathen, not Joseph Gordon."

"I don't mind," Trevor repeated. "Just make sure he understands as much as he can about the wolves, vampires, and magic."

"We'll make sure of it," Cormier replied, and Trevor stood. "Where is Hanson?"

"Hanson is in my cave." Trevor smirked, and Cormier smirked back. "He doesn't dare leave."

"He must really fear you."

"Many do." Trevor shrugged a shoulder. "What will you do when you leave here?"

"Go to cousin Clover's before I go to the club."

"And Angelo?" asked Trevor. "What is he doing?"

Cormier knew Trevor was missing his brother. Sighing, he replied "Angelo is with Bianca."

"I see," said Trevor, a smirk playing on his face. "He seems very fond of this mortal."

"Indeed." Cormier glanced up at the sky, at the stars. "He is very fond of her."

* * Angelo * *

Angelo poured Bianca a glass of champagne. Smiling, she took it.
"Thank you."
"You're most welcome."
They were in the lounge, on Angelo's loveseat. Their eyes were on the television, but neither of them were really seeing anything.
Angelo wasn't nervous, but he was still on edge. Bianca didn't seem nervous, but reading her mind, he knew she was.
"Bianca," he murmured, and she looked at him. "If you don't want to do this-"
"I do," she said quietly. "I'm ready."
"Shall we go to the bedroom?"
"Give me five minutes," she said quickly. "I need to... um... change."
Angelo frowned at her. "Change?"
"Yes."
"You mean into something I got you?"
"Something I bought while you slept," Bianca said, and he stared at her.
"You went out of the castle?"
"Yep."
"How did you get back in?"
"Cormier gave me a set of keys," smiled Bianca. "Now give me five minutes."
"All right. I'll wait here."
"Actually, make that ten minutes," she said as she began walking, and Angelo said ok.

* * Bianca * *

Bianca threw the last of the rose petals down before she sprayed the air with her perfume and lit the scented candles. Everything was set up to resemble a lover's haven, and as far as she was concerned it looked fit for a prince... her prince. It was time.

She dimmed Angelo's lights just as he knocked on the door.

"Bianca, may I come in? It has been ten minutes."

Bianca took a deep breath before saying "Come in."

* * Angelo * *

Angelo opened the door and gasped, swallowing with difficulty as he stared around the candlelit room, taking in the sweet scent in the air, the rose petals, his bed.

Everything was drawing him forwards- he looked around his suite in wonder, running a hand through his hair.

"You... you did this."

"Do you like it?" she asked shyly, and he whispered "I love it."

He smiled at her, then his smile faded as he realised what she was wearing. He couldn't do a thing but stare.

She was wearing a short, shimmering, baby-doll-style nightie that seemed to glow on her body. Completely white, the material was a sharp contrast to her dark skin, and he could easily make out parts of her body through the almost transparent material.

She wasn't wearing anything underneath that nightie. Angelo himself only wore a black robe, thinking that if Bianca was going to change then he should too.

"Angelo? Are you ok?" Bianca asked uncertainly, making him shake himself and look at her again- look at the nightie again. He swallowed hard before he moved closer to her and pressed his lips to hers in a soft kiss, then he backed away to look at her again.

"Take it off, Bianca." His words were hoarse. "Please."

She did nothing but stare at him.

* * Bianca * *

Bianca was unable to do anything but stare. Through the haze of passion she saw him, *really* saw him, and knew that he might not love her, but she had something he desperately wanted. And from the way he was breathing and the size of the arousal he wasn't trying to hide, she had something he urgently needed.

A ray of hope sprang within her. Maybe, although he may not love her, she loved him, and maybe, just maybe, she would have enough love for the both of them, love that would see her through when she had to leave him in two months' time, memories she would always cling to.

"Take it off."

His words, Bianca noted, had been growled... through clenched teeth and sharp breaths- total frustration. She would bet any woman in her shoes would already be naked in his bed, not staring at him like a dummy.

I'm not a dummy.

Bianca reached up slowly, easing the spaghetti straps off her shoulders, then she gave the top of her body part a sensuous wiggle, which prompted the gown to ease down past her small waist, past her thighs and land in a pool at her feet.

She met Angelo's gaze when she heard his sharp intake of breath, watching his golden eyes darken to a sexy sort of orange, and she saw how he was focusing entirely on her naked body, looking spellbound by what he saw. His eyes roamed over her like a lover's caress, the deep penetration of his gaze blazing a heated path from the tips of her breasts to the area between her legs.

Angelo came closer. Bianca closed her eyes as he gently reached behind her head and pulled her hair band out so her hair fell around her shoulders.

A thickness settled deep in her throat, and she breathed in deeply. She thought she would always remember this moment when she had openly displayed herself to Angelo Heathen, the man she loved. He was seeing her as no man ever had.

"Now... now it's your turn," she managed to say, in the silence that had settled between them. She watched as he slowly pushed the robe from his shoulders, then he stood before her, all male, naked for her. The glow of the candles reflected off his brown skin.

"I want you, Bianca." His whispered plea made her shiver and grow warmer. "I want to take you in all the ways a man can take a woman. And I promise to give you pleasure of the richest, purest and most profound kind. Will you let me do that? Will you accept me, us, as we are? Accept the things that cannot be and accept that the remaining two months are all we can have together?"

Bianca met his gaze, knowing what her answer would be. This wasn't a hot day in December, and he wasn't coming to her exclusively. Yet she would go to him willingly, without shame and with no regrets.

Right there, right then, she promised herself that after the two months ended, things would be far from over. She'd make sure of it.

And because she loved him, in whatever time he believed they had left to spend together she would be his, the woman of the Grand Vampire, all his, and he would be hers, Bianca's Count Angelo.

* * Angelo * *

Angelo waited for her response. As much as he wanted her, if she denied him he would accept her decision.

* * Bianca * *

Bianca had no intention of denying him. Lifting her head and squarely meeting his gaze, she said "Yes, Angelo, I accept that we only have two months left together. I accept us as we are. I want to experience the pleasure you offer, knowing that is all I can and will ever get from you."

Bianca could have sworn she saw regret, deep and profound, flash across his face just before he reached forwards and gathered her in his arms, sealing his lips with hers.

His skin felt hot against hers, and Bianca moved closer as she deepened the kiss which seemed to go on and on, neither of them wanting to break it. They wanted to savour every moment together and not rush towards what they knew awaited them. The more they kissed the more the fire ignited between them, and they began devouring each other with inane hunger.

When breathing became a must, they broke apart, panting.

"Angelo, I-"

"What is it?" he looked at her, concerned. "Is everything ok?"

"Everything's fine," she reassured him, and he kissed her again.

* * Ricky * *

Ricky gazed up at the stars, deep in thought.
Catherine stood by his side, hanging onto his arm dreamily. "Ricky?"
"Mmm?"
"I was just wondering if you'd like to come to my caravan. It's cold out here."
"The cold clears my mind," Ricky replied. "We can go in a few minutes."
"Ok."

* * Bianca * *

Bianca didn't think her mind or senses could take much more, yet she didn't want Angelo to stop. His tongue skimmed over her breasts lightly, Bianca whispering his name. Displaying an expertise that had her weak in the knees, Angelo paid sensual attention to her breasts, lavishing them with gentle bites and mind spinning licks. The scalding touch of his tongue on her nipples flooded her insides with heat so intense she was sure she would burn to a crisp.
"Angelo…"
Angelo didn't answer. Instead he lifted her into his arms and carried her across the room, placing her on his giant bed.
Bianca drew a deep breath as he gazed down at her.
"Bianca, I… I-"
"Yes?" she said quietly, and she saw him swallow. She had a feeling she knew what he was about to say, and decided if he confessed how he felt about her she would too.
But Angelo shook his head, sighing, and kissed her instead.

* * Angelo * *

He almost told her he loved her.
Angelo took a deep breath before he kissed Bianca again.
"Are you ready?"
Bianca nodded. "I'm ready."
Once again Angelo could feel her excitement, coursing through her body, rampant like his own. While holding her mouth captive in a third kiss, his fingers sought out every part of her body, flicking light touches over her dark skin, trailing from the tip of her breasts, down to her waist and navel and along her inner thigh before claiming the area between her legs.

* * Bianca * *

Bianca broke the kiss, shuddering as a gasp escaped her, feeling Angelo's fingers touch her intimately... stroking, probing, caressing. She closed her eyes as she struggled to breathe, to maintain control and not drown in the sensations he enveloped her in.

Angelo drew a sharp breath, and she opened her eyes and looked at him. His gaze was locked on hers, and she could tell from the tense expression on his face that he was one step away from sexual madness. And she didn't think she could take much more of what he was doing to her.

* * Angelo * *

"I want you, Bianca," he murmured seductively as his fingers continued to stroke her. "I want this," he said right in her ear, and he pushed his fingers deeper inside of her, so she'd exactly what "this" was.

Bianca's only response was a shuddering moan. Angelo slowly moved his fingers in and out of her, relishing the tiny purrs and moans she made, knowing he was giving her pleasure.

A sudden tremble passed through his body, and he knew at that moment he couldn't last much longer. He had to get inside her.

Shifting his body to where she lay under him, he leant back for a moment to admire her, glorying the beautiful darkness of her skin, the magnificent curves of her hips, the flatness of her stomach and the beautiful scent that was totally her.

Her eyes were on him too. They locked gazes, and he saw desire so deep in her eyes he almost lost it. He had to connect with her and sample the very essence of the gift she was offering him.

"Will it hurt?" she whispered, in a voice so quiet he wasn't sure if he'd imagined it. Angelo hesitated, then he said "There will be pain at first, but afterward only pleasure."

Bianca nodded, biting her lip, totally distracting him again as he leant down to kiss her again, in a passionate way that shook him to the core and made everything inside him feel the need for her.

Boldly, Bianca lifted her hips to him as they kissed each other, and he gave up the fight: he grabbed her by the hips and pulled her to him, then, in one hard thrust, he had completely filled her.

* * Bianca * *

Bianca gasped at the first sensation of pain, but it subsided when he slowly began moving inside of her. Angelo broke off their kiss and held her dark gaze in the fiery gold of his.

"I brand you mine, Bianca Davis," he murmured as he lowered his head to kiss her neck, kissing her gently. "Mine."

"Please don't stop," Bianca panted, then she closed her eyes, drowning in the pleasure he was giving her. Her fingers dug deeply into his shoulders, and her legs were wrapped tightly around his waist. Angelo's hands were still on her waist, locking her to him, holding her in place to meet his every thrust.

Bianca opened her eyes again, and their gazes met and fused. He was looking at her, almost into her soul, and she whispered in a voice filled with quivering need, mind-stealing pleasure: "If you brand me, then I brand you too, Angelo Heathen."

* * Angelo * *

Her words sent Angelo's mind reeling and he knew she *had* branded him. Closing his eyes, he focused on his body connecting with hers, becoming a part of her. He was lured to a place he wasn't certain he wanted to go but found himself going anyway.

In the back of his mind he heard her whimpering sounds of pleasure as his body continued to pump repeatedly into hers, taking her on a journey he had never travelled before with any woman. And when he felt the tip of her tongue softly lick the side of his face, tracing a path down his neck, he knew then and there he would always remember this but the memories would never be enough.

"Angelo!"

He felt her draw in a shuddering breath, felt her body tighten around him, clenching him, milking him, taking him to the same plane she was on. Bianca moaned out loud as he inhaled, her scent surrounding him.

Sensations he had never felt before took control, flooding him to the point where he couldn't think, only feel.

The world seemed to explode around him as his own orgasm hit and forged them tighter in each other's arms, as extreme sexual gratification claimed their bodies, minds and senses.

And for the first time in his life, Angelo felt mind-boggling pleasure and total, incredible peace.

He knew there and then he would never get enough of Bianca Davis.

* * *

Angelo stirred awake as the flickering candles cast shadows around the room. He glanced down at the young woman he held in his arms. She was getting much deserved rest.

Angelo gently let go of Bianca and stood, putting out all the candles and leaving on his dimmed lights, then he slipped back into bed with her. Bianca snuggled closer in her sleep, Angelo kissing her forehead.

After making love that first time, they had both quickly fallen asleep, succumbing to sexual oblivion, only to wake up two hours later just as hungry for each other as they was that first time. Angelo had thought that it might be too soon for Bianca to make love again, but she strongly objected and he gave in, flipping her under him and giving her what they both wanted.

Once again he had experienced feelings with her he never felt with any woman before, and knew when they separated he would never find peace. Bianca would be a clinging memory for the rest of his days.

* * Bianca * *

The sunlight woke her up.
Bianca sat up, yawning and stretching. Her limbs were heavy from her actions last night. Bianca smiled, standing.
What a night.
It was four in the afternoon. Angelo didn't move, in a deep sleep. Bianca went and got a shower, deciding to go and see her family... then she decided not to.
She knew where Clover lived. She could pick up little Joseph. Or she could wait for Cormier to bring him back.
Cormier, bring back Joseph. She thought the words long and hard, repeating them in her mind. *Bring Joseph home.*

* * Cormier * *

Surprised, Cormier looked at his cousin.
"I can hear Bianca."
"What is she saying?" Clover replied, and Cormier replied "She is telling me to bring Joseph home."
"Is that possible?" Clover asked, interested. "Mortals cannot send mind messages."
"It is not a mind message," Cormier replied. "I'm just surprised I can hear her thoughts when I am not even present."
"Are you connected?"
"I have no idea. But I'll do as she asks."

* * Bianca * *

"Bee!" Joseph cried happily as he ran towards her, and Bianca knelt, arms held out to the happy little boy. "Bee!"
Bianca swept him up and cuddled him, kissing his forehead.
"Was he ok at Clover's, Cormier?"
"He was very neutral," Cormier said honestly. "He hardly said a word, just sat playing with his teddy. I suppose he isn't comfortable with Clover yet as he hardly knows her."
"He'll warm up," said Bianca. "Is he hungry?"
"He should be. He didn't eat much of his breakfast."

* * Angelo * *

Angelo woke up slowly, satisfied. Feeling like the head lion of a pack. "Bianca?"

"She is with Joseph," Cormier said, appearing at the foot of his bed. "In the lounge."

Angelo frowned. "What are you doing back so soon?"

"Bianca told me to bring Joseph back."

Angelo's frown deepened. "How is that possible?"

"I heard her thoughts," Cormier explained. "Even though I wasn't in the castle."

"Impossible."

"It's true."

"It could only be true if you both were connected."

"Brother, I... don't get angry. But I think we are."

Angelo stared at him. "What?"

Cormier backed two steps before he repeated it, Angelo rising to his feet, still staring- well, *glaring* now.

"I think we are. But not in a romantic way. A strong friendship, a bond. It seems I am one of her closest friends. And you... you are her everything."

Angelo thought about what he said, then he nodded. Cormier breathed out, relieved.

"So how was your night?"

Angelo opened his mouth, then closed it. "That's none of your business."

Cormier laughed. "Come, brother. I made dinner."

"What did you make?"

"Well, I'm not so hungry. But I cooked for Bianca and Joseph especially."

"Are you going to the club tonight?" Angelo asked his brother, and Cormier shrugged. "Is that a yes or no?"

"It's an 'if I feel like it'."

Angelo scowled at him. "Make up your mind."

"Why?"

"Because I order it."

Cormier laughed. "And I should obey you? Don't forget I am the elder brother. I don't need to take any order from a younger sibling."

Angelo's eyes lit scarlet. "It's an order from the Grand Vampire!"

Cormier's body went rigid, unable to move as he forced the words out.

"All right- all right! Order obeyed! I'll go to the club!"

"When?" asked Angelo, smirking as Cormier struggled with the body lock, but it was no use. "I *said,* when?"

"After- after dinner!"

"But you said you was not so hungry. Are you hungry now?"

"Release me, Angelo!"

"No."

"When you release me, I... I swear I will cut your head off!" gasped Cormier, as the pressure of the force increased. He was starting to get a splitting headache.

"Then I'd better keep you as you are for a few hours," said Angelo amusedly. "I'm going to shower and find Bianca."

"Let me out of this at once!"

"No," Angelo replied, going into the bathroom. "Next time you will not be so rash to disobey an order I make."

"I'm going to kill you, Angelo!"

"Of course you are."

The bathroom door closed behind him, Cormier fuming.

* * Bianca * *

Bianca's heart leapt when she saw Angelo enter the lounge, Joseph snug in her arms. Smiling at him, she said "Hey."

"Hey," he responded, smiling back. "Are you all right?"

"I'm fine," she said softly. "Where's Cormier?"

"Cormier is in my bedroom," shrugged Angelo. "I have him in a body lock."

Bianca burst out laughing. "Why?"

"Because he disobeyed an order."

Bianca laughed again. "Don't be mean, Angelo. Let him out of it."

Angelo pouted, but he obeyed her, snapping his fingers. They could hear Cormier cursing as he stormed towards the lounge, Joseph giggling.

"Angelo!"

"I'm in here," Angelo said, highly amused as Cormier, livid, dived at him furiously but slipped right through Angelo's body, crashing to the floor.

Bianca burst out laughing, Joseph clapping his tiny hands.

"Again!"

Scowling, Cormier got to his feet, dusting himself off.

"You see what I have to endure, chick pea?"

"I see," said Bianca amusedly, and Cormier smiled at her.

"Have you eaten?"

"Not yet."

"All right. Come and have dinner."

Smiling, Bianca obeyed, standing and following him out of the lounge, Joseph toddling at her side. He was so tiny!

Angelo scooped him up in a cuddle, stroking his curly hair. Joseph beamed, clinging to him as they all headed for the dining area.

* * Cormier * *

"Marissa should awaken in the next two, maybe three days," Cormier said, looking at Angelo. Angelo nodded.
"I know."
"I do it," said Joseph shyly, as Bianca fed him some macaroni, and Bianca smiled and handed him his little fork, showing him how to use it. Joseph stabbed at the macaroni happily, making them all laugh.
Finally he'd gotten some on his fork, popping it in his mouth.
"Mmm!"
Bianca smiled and sat down in her seat properly to eat her own meal, and Angelo and Cormier resumed their conversation.
"I think you should place her back in her home, brother."
"No, Cormier. She is weak. She will be bloodthirsty. She needs to be kept an eye on."
Cormier and Bianca both scowled at him, Cormier saying "She is not our problem, Angelo."
"She is my problem," Angelo answered. "She put herself in this state because of me. The least I can do is rectify the situation."
Cormier sighed. "You truly have a heart of gold."
Angelo smiled at that. "Thank you. Now, let's eat. You see Joseph has eaten the majority of his dinner and we have hardly touched ours?"
Joseph smiled shyly as they looked at him.
"Good boy, Joseph," smiled Angelo, and Joseph giggled. "He hasn't really eaten his carrots or broccoli, though."
"What wolf do you know eats carrots and broccoli?" demanded Cormier, and Bianca burst out laughing as Angelo scowled at him.
"A wolf doesn't eat macaroni either, but Joseph did. So be quiet. He is not a wolf, he is a human at present. So he will eat as humans will, and eat his vegetables to become a healthy, strong boy."
Cormier opened his mouth, then closed it. "Touché."

* * Bianca * *

Joseph was falling asleep in Bianca's arms as she sang a lullaby, Angelo watching dreamily with Cormier. They were in the lounge, Bianca cradling Joseph.

"Chick pea," Cormier whispered, and she smiled at him. "I leave now, for the club. I will see you tomorrow afternoon if you wake."

"Bye," whispered Bianca, and Cormier smiled and vanished after saying goodbye to his little brother.

Angelo stood, shaking himself a little. "I'll put him to bed."

Bianca let Angelo take little Joseph. He smiled as Joseph slept on, leaving the lounge with him. Bianca sighed, leaning back on the loveseat.

"I wish it could be like this forever."

* * Angelo * *

Joseph mumbled in his sleep before settling down properly, cuddling his teddy. Angelo smiled, stroking his curly hair before he left the room, taking care to leave Joseph's lamp on.

He turned into the lounge, where Bianca was waiting for him. She smiled at him: what a smile.

"Now we're completely alone."

"I know," Angelo said softly. "Come here, Bianca."

Bianca smiled and got up, walking over to him. When she was within reach Angelo pulled her into his arms, bringing his mouth down on hers in a passionate kiss.

Bianca threw her arms around his neck as she kissed him back, heart racing as her body temperature shot up.

When they couldn't kiss anymore and breathing was a must, they broke apart, panting.

"I need you, Angelo," she said weakly, and he looked at her. Taking a deep breath, she whispered "I need you inside me."

"What about Joseph?"

"Joseph's asleep," she said, kissing his neck and making him practically melt in her arms, but he fought to stay under control.

"What if he hears us and wakes?"

"Put a charm on your suite. A noise block or something so we don't disturb him."

Angelo stared at her, surprised. "Why are you so smart?"

"Because I am," Bianca said saucily. "Shall we go to your suite?"

Angelo paused to think it through, then she kissed him before he could start.

"Stop thinking, Angelo. Don't think. Just do."

"Fine," he said, highly amused, and she kissed him again.

* * Bianca * *

Bianca closed her eyes as Angelo moved, slowly.

Music was playing, the lights were dimmed.

"It's so romantic," she whispered, though she could barely get the words out she was feeling so much pleasure.

Angelo smiled down at her. "It always will be."

* * Ricky * *

Gran's gasp made Ricky snap awake instantly.

"What, Gran? What's the matter?"

"Nothing," lied Gran. "My, look at the time. Why didn't either of you wake me up?"

"You looked peaceful asleep in that chair. Did you have a nightmare?"

"I did," Gran lied. "Where's Samuel?"

"He went to bed," shrugged Ricky. "You'd better go too, it's nearly two a.m."

Gran did as she was told, heart racing. She prayed it was just a dream.

* * Angelo * *

"Oh, Angelo!"

Her shuddering moan did things to him as he watched her climax, knowing his own orgasm was not far behind. Angelo pumped as slowly as he did when he'd started making love to her, then his limbs almost gave way as he too came, groaning her name.

"Bianca…"

Panting, Bianca didn't reply. Angelo slowly lifted himself away, pulling out of her gently, then he laid beside her.

"Are you all right?"

"I'm fine," she said softly. Her eyes were closed. "I just… I wish it could be like this forever."

"As do I," Angelo admitted quietly, and she opened her eyes to look at him, speaking just as quietly.

"You do?"

"I do."

Bianca reached up and kissed him again, emotion clawing at Angelo's heart as he responded.

She cannot know I love her. She must never know.

Bianca pulled herself up his warm body and broke the kiss, laying her head on his chest and closing her eyes as sleep caught up with her. Angelo kissed her on the forehead.

"Sweet Dreams, Bianca."

"Sweet Dreams," she whispered, and Angelo snapped his fingers.

The lights in the suite went out.

* * Cormier * *

"So Cormier, tell us. Is it true?"

"Is what true?"

"That Count Angelo is definitely off the market."

Cormier rolled his eyes as he served behind the bar, ignoring the three vampire women.

"Cormier!"

"What!" he snapped, the vampires glaring at him. "What do you want me to say?"

"Give us a yes or no, that would be helpful. Morcheeba said-"

"Said what?"

"Said that Count Angelo took a vampire to the restaurant, and that vampire made him laugh. Is it true?"

"How can I know if it's true?" said Cormier, annoyed. "I didn't go to the restaurant with them, did I?"

"Well I'm taking Morcheeba's word for it. She was very upset."

"Angelo wouldn't touch Morcheeba if the world depended on it," Cormier said flatly. "Nor any of you three."

The female vampires hissed simultaneously, making him smirk.

"You sound like a bag of snakes."

Sebastian burst out laughing, saying "Away with you, ladies. Leave Cormier be. It's not his place to talk about the Grand Vampire. Notice I said the *Grand Vampire*. He won't appreciate his business being talked about."

"Can't you convince him to come to the club, Sebastian?" sighed a vampire, and Sebastian said "I'll suggest it. That's all."

"And don't hope he brings his lover," Cormier added. "Because he wouldn't. Angelo doesn't want her being ogled."

"How would you know?"

"Because I'm his brother. I know how he'd feel."

* * Bianca * *

Exhausted, Bianca crawled atop Angelo and rested her head on his chest, arms around him. Angelo kissed her on the forehead.
"You're an amazing young woman, Bianca."
"Thank you," she said quietly. "And you're the most wonderful man I've ever met."
Angelo smiled, touched. "Get some sleep, Bianca."
"Won't you?" she asked softly, and he nodded.
"Yes, but after I check on Joseph."
"I'll wait for you to come back."
"Would you like a hot drink while I'm up?" Angelo asked as he gently moved away from her and stood, reaching and putting on his robe.
"Yes please," she said shyly, and he bent and kissed her.
"Hot chocolate?"
"Sure. Thank you."

* * Angelo * *

Angelo smiled and left the suite, tightening his robe around him as he walked towards Joseph's room, popping his head around the door.
Joseph was fast asleep, thumb in his mouth, arm around his teddy. Angelo smiled, bending and kissing his little brow before he left the bedroom and proceeded to check on Marissa.
He sighed when he saw no change. She was still unconscious.
"Marissa, why do this?"
He lifted her duvet gently and tucked her in, shaking his head as he left the room and went into his kitchen, turning the kettle on with a snap of his fingers.

* * Bianca * *

Bianca smiled when Angelo entered his suite, two mugs hovering in front of him. He got back into bed and put his arm around her, the mugs sailing towards them.
Taking one, Bianca said "Thank you."
"You're most welcome."

* * Cormier * *

"Patricia!"

"Cormier," she responded icily. "Where is my sister?"

Cormier stared at his ex disbelievingly. "What are you doing here?"

"Am I still barred?" she asked dryly, and he said "No!"

"I'm glad to hear it. Now where is my sister? I haven't heard from her in over a week, which is strange."

"Haven't you heard?"

"Heard what?" she snapped, Cormier saying "What she did?"

"I haven't got time for idle gossip. What happened?"

"She… er… Would you like a beverage of some sort? Try the Cormi Colada."

"The what?"

"The Cormi Colada," Cormier repeated, unable to stop a smile. Patricia smiled back, saying "Another cocktail?"

"My latest. Try it."

"Are you trying to change the subject, Cormier Heathen?"

"No, but I know you'll need a drink when I tell you what went on."

* * Angelo * *

Angelo glanced at the clock.

It was four in the morning.

Knowing he wouldn't sleep until six, he sighed and looked at Bianca, and he couldn't help but sigh contentedly as she slept. She was perfect.

He couldn't help kissing her soft lips gently, making her smile in her sleep.

"What was that for?"

"For you. I love you."

"I love you too…"

Angelo stared as she fell back into a deep sleep, wanting to grab her and make her wake up. Did she just…?

After fretting for three minutes as he wondered if he'd been hearing things, he did just that, grabbing her and hauling her upright, startling her.

"Angelo, what's wrong??"

"You said you love me. Did you mean it? Were you sleep-talking?"

Bianca stared at him, then she kissed him. Angelo tried to break off but she didn't let him, hand at the back of his head as she deepened the kiss, making him groan and reach for her, pulling her closer.

* * Cormier * *

"It's a lie."

"It's no lie," Cormier said, a little haughtily. "If you don't believe me, come to the castle. That's where your sister is lying. Unconscious, in her bed, basically in a coma."

Patricia stared at him. "All of this for Count Angelo?"

"Yep."

"It's madness! I want to see her. I can wake her up if I share my energy-"

"And put yourself in a weak state? No," Cormier said flatly. "I won't allow it."

"Cormier-"

"You may come to the castle and see her. You can even spend the night, as dawn is near and you have a long way to go. Tomorrow night you may go home to… to your fiancé."

Patricia looked away, then she nodded. "Thank you."

Cormier looked at Sebastian, who nodded and rang the club's bell, signaling the club's closure.

One by one the vampires vanished, Cormier saying to Sebastian "You'll be all right locking up here?"

"I'll be fine," Sebastian said. "Go."

Cormier nodded, saying to Patricia "Take my hand."

"I'd rather not."

"Fine, fly to the castle rather than have me teleport. But no windows will be open."

Patricia scowled and took his hand. Cormier inhaled sharply at her touch, remembering everything about her.

They vanished.

* * Angelo * *

Bianca stepped out of the shower, Angelo as well.

"You cleverly used making love as a decoy, which I fell for. Now answer my question."

Bianca sighed, then she said "Let me get dressed and settled first."

Angelo scowled, then he said "Fine."

* * Cormier * *

"We will have to be quiet. Bianca may be asleep."

"And this *Bianca* is the one who caused Marissa to act like a madwoman over the man she cannot have?"

"Yes. Angelo's lover."

"Marissa must be extremely disappointed."

"A lot of women are," shrugged Cormier as they walked down the corridor, past little Joseph's room. "Wait here."

Patricia obeyed as Cormier popped his head around Joseph's door, checking on the little boy. He smiled when he saw Joseph was fast asleep. "All right. Come."

* * *

Patricia gasped and ran towards the bed. "Marissa!"

She knelt down, taking her sister's hand. Cormier rolled his eyes.

"Must you be so dramatic? She will be fine."

"She's ice cold!"

"She will be bloodthirsty," shrugged Cormier. "When she's had her fill her body will resume it's lukewarm temperature."

"You're sure?"

"I'm sure."

Patricia nodded, getting up. "Thank you for keeping her safe."

"Angelo is the one to thank, not me. You know me and Marissa do not get along. I told him to place her in her own home, but he refused."

Patricia glared at him. "Then I will thank Count Angelo."

"Do not disturb him at this time, Patricia. Come, I will show you to your

room."
Patricia looked at Marissa again, then she nodded.
"Good," Cormier said. "Follow me."

* * Bianca * *

"I didn't mean to let it slip out. I was half asleep."
"Well did you mean it or didn't you?"
"You know I did," Bianca said quietly. "I love you."
Angelo stared at her, and Bianca said "I know you don't feel the same."
"What?"
"You heard me. This may just be some sort of brief affair for you, like a wham-bam-thank-you-Ma'am-never-see-you-after-two-months thing, but it's much more to me."
Angelo raised an eyebrow. "A wham-bam-thank-you-Ma'am-never-see-you-after-two-months thing?"
"Yes."
"How can you think so low of me?!" he exploded, startling her as he began to glow scarlet. "You think I took your virginity for the fun of it?! That I don't love you?? That's it's just about sex?!"
"Well isn't it??"
"No!!"
Cormier appeared, startled. "Is everything ok??"
"Get out, Cormier!" spat Angelo, and Cormier looked at Bianca.
"Bianca, are you all right?"
"She's fine," snapped Angelo. "Now get out!"
Cormier ignored him, looking at Bianca. "Bianca?"
She looked at him, and he saw the fear in her eyes. That was enough.
"I'm staying. Have your argument while I'm here. I won't interrupt."
Angelo glared at him but he knew his brother wasn't going to budge. So he turned back to Bianca.
"How can you think that the feelings are one sided??"
"Because I know they are! I know you don't love me and I was hoping so much that you would, I know that it's just about sex!"
"WHAT!!"
"Angelo, calm down," Cormier said warningly, as Angelo began pacing the room.
"So you think I don't love you and it's just about sex."
"That's not what I think, it's what I know," Bianca replied flatly, and Angelo turned and slapped Cormier across the face. "Angelo!"
"What on earth was that for?!" shouted Cormier, and Angelo spat "I'd never hit a woman so you'll have to do instead."
Bianca nearly burst out laughing. "Can we drop the subject please?"

"No," snapped Angelo. "You honestly think I don't love you?"

Bianca shrugged. "That's what you told Clover. I heard you."

"Bianca, I was just- I couldn't tell Clover the truth-"

"And what is the truth?" she asked, not daring to get her hopes up.

Angelo looked at Cormier, who said "I'm not leaving. You have my word whatever you say will not be repeated from my mouth."

Angelo trusted his elder brother on that. Turning back to Bianca, he said "Bianca, I probably loved you from the first time we met. I'd never gone to such lengths to meet someone, especially a mortal. Women come to *me,* not the other way round. I had to know you. And ever since meeting you, I've grown to love you more and more with each thought of you, every time I see you. You are the first person on my mind when I wake up. I feel a sense of loss when I'm away from you. I don't know how I will bear it when the two months are over and you return to England. You have to know I love you. I love you so, so much."

Bianca's eyes filled, tears coursing down her face. "I love you too."

Cormier smiled and vanished on the spot, leaving them alone.

* * Bianca * *

"Bee? Bee!"
Bianca stirred, smiling as Joseph shook her shoulder with his tiny hands.
"Bee!"
"Hey," she said, and he threw his arms around her in a hug.
"Love you!"
"I love you too," she said, kissing him. "Are you hungry?"
Joseph shook his head. "Cormy."
Bianca knew he meant Cormier.
"Cormy fed you?" Joseph nodded happily. "Good."
She stood up, picking up Joseph as she did so, checking the time.
"Six," she sighed, then she snuggled Joseph. "Sit with Angelo while I get a shower, ok?"
Joseph nodded, holding his teddy. Bianca placed him next to Angelo, kissing him on the forehead.
"I'll be as quick as I can."
She was quick, too. Fifteen minutes later she was dressed, her hair done.
"Come, let's go and see what Cormier's up to."
She could hear him talking, and followed his voice, going into the kitchen. She gasped when she saw the beautiful pale woman standing there, talking to Cormier.
"Hello chick pea," smiled Cormier, and Bianca said hello whilst never taking her eyes off the female vampire, who stared back at her. "This is Patricia, Marissa's sister."
"Nice to meet you," Bianca said politely, Patricia staring at her. She looked Bianca from head to toe before she said "So you are the cause of my sister being unconscious for days?"
"Me??"
"Yes you."
"Patricia," started Cormier uneasily, but she held up a finger to silence him.
"What do you have to say for yourself, Bianca Davis?"
"How do you know my name?"
"Answer me!"
"Look, it's not my fault your sister's obsessed with Angelo, ok?" Bianca glared at her. "From what I've heard, she's been obsessed for years. She was mad about him *way* before I came into the picture, so don't try and blame me!"
Patricia's eyes lit scarlet. "Have you ever duelled with a vampire before?"
"Well before I came here I didn't think they existed," Bianca replied icily. "So no, I haven't."
"Well now you're about to!"

"Patricia, don't be stupid!" Cormier said angrily, as Bianca stated "You're as crazy as your sister, aren't you Patricia?"

"Bianca, don't wind her up," Cormier said warningly, Bianca saying "Who's winding her up? I'm stating facts."

Cormier couldn't help but smile at her, Patricia glaring at him.

"You find her amusing?"

"She's like a sister," Cormier replied, a little lovingly. "A cheeky, little sister."

"Well your cheeky little sister is about to duel with me!"

Bianca glanced at the clock, knowing Angelo would wake up at seven. It was six-twenty.

"You blame me for the way your sister is? Blame your sister! Nobody told her to drink two bottles of Courvoisier and a bottle of wine-"

Patricia vanished and reappeared in front of her- SMACK!!!

Bianca crashed to the kitchen floor, Cormier shouting "Patricia, have you gone mad??!"

"Bee!" cried Joseph, running to her. "BEE!!"

Dazed, Bianca spat blood out of her mouth and unsteadily got to her feet.

"All right, you want a duel? Bring it."

Patricia's eyes sparked before her hand lit: BANG!!!

"BIANCA!!"

* * Angelo * *

Angelo snapped awake.

He heard Joseph screaming, Cormier yelling, a woman shrieking.

Was he dreaming?

"Bianca, wake up!" said Cormier desperately- that was all he needed to hear. He pulled on his robe and ran out of his suite into the kitchen.

Bianca was lying unconscious on the kitchen floor, Joseph sobbing as he shook her shoulder. Cormier was holding a woman back as he begged Bianca to wake up, but Bianca didn't respond.

Silence fell when Angelo stared at Bianca's body, then he quietly asked "What happened?"

"She provoked me," spat Patricia, as Angelo's eyes lit scarlet. "We had a little argument and I hit her."

"A hit couldn't have rendered her unconscious," Angelo said icily, and Clover appeared with Sebastian.

"NO!!" screamed Clover when she saw Bianca, making Joseph jump and start crying again. Clover didn't care. "What is the meaning of this?! Who hurt her?!"

"I did," Patricia said flatly, and Clover whipped round.

"Are you *mad*, Patricia?! Why would you hurt Bianca??"

"She provoked me and I hit her-"

"That's not all you did," spat Angelo. "What else did you do?"

"I hit her and she fell," Patricia said flatly. "She got up, ready as ever, and I ended the argument by hitting her again. With a combination of cursed electricity and fire."

Angelo swore as he stared down at Bianca's lifeless figure.

Blood was on her face, on her mouth, trailing past her lips, scratches on her neck. Her clothes were singed.

Angelo ran a hand through his hair as he began to glow scarlet. He was furious and didn't everyone know it. But he was trying to stay calm for Joseph's sake. He took a deep breath, everyone waiting with bated breath. "Cormier, let go of her."

Cormier released Patricia, who seemed to have realised what a big mistake she made.

"Count Angelo-"

"Be quiet, Patricia," snapped Angelo. "Right now I want to rip you limb from limb for harming Bianca. But I won't. I don't hurt females. But cousin Clover will have no problem doing so. Will you Clover?"

Clover's eyes were burning with a scarlet glow. Glaring at Patricia, she said "None at all."

Angelo nodded. "Get her, Clover."

Clover dived at Patricia furiously, grabbing her by her long brown hair and hurling her across the kitchen.

Patricia slammed into the kitchen cupboards, Clover diving and pinning her to the ground, slashing at her face with her long nails as she screamed "So you think it's ok to hurt people dear to us?! Do you?!"

Angelo watched, face cold as ice. Sebastian and Cormier was gaping. Intrigued, Joseph watched without leaving Bianca's side. Pointing, he looked up at Angelo and said "Fight."

Angelo nodded.

"Answer me, you evil witch!"

"She provoked me!" Patricia screamed back as she tried to throw Clover off her, but Clover was too strong. She was a very powerful vampire, with the strength of ten men, though Angelo had the strength of eighty men put together. If he wanted, he could have torn Patricia's head clean off her shoulders, but he was content watching cousin Clover give the woman everything she deserved.

"Provoked?!"

"Yes!!"

"Don't lie! You just wanted to bully her!"

Patricia grabbed Clover by the neck and tried forcing her away- Clover saw that as a pro and grabbed her arm.

CRACK.

"Ouch," Cormier and Sebastian said together, as Patricia screamed in pain.

"My arm!!"

"Take your broken arm to your fiancé, tell him that it was me!" screamed Clover. "I welcome him and any other vampire to try and duel with me!"

Angelo knew Brian wouldn't dare duel with Clover. Everyone did. No vampire in their right mind would want to get on the wrong side of her.

Cormier couldn't help smirking.

"He's a coward."

Sebastian nodded. Angelo didn't react, waiting.

Clover opened her mouth, fangs unsheathed, and clamped down on Patricia's neck repeatedly, not drinking blood, but puncturing her nerves.

Patricia gasped then laid still, unconscious.

Disgusted, Clover stood, then kicked her in the side.

"Filth."

Angelo smiled. "Well done, Clover."

"Leave her in the forest," Clover replied, Sebastian saying "Isn't that going over the top, honey?"

Clover glared at him. Sebastian apologised. Turning to Angelo, she said "You can tell Brian he will find his filth of a fiancé with the wolves. I will take her there myself, with your permission?"

"Granted," Angelo replied, and he snapped his fingers. Patricia's body rose off the kitchen floor and floated towards Clover, who almost lost it and punched her again.

"I am so furious right now!"

"The walk to the forest should calm you," Angelo replied. "Sebastian, go with her. And take Joseph."

"Joseph?"

"Yes," Angelo replied. "He must see his old pack from time to time. He will know them."

"Won't he be afraid of going to the forest at night?"

"Not at all," Angelo replied. "He lived there."

Sebastian nodded, saying "Come, Joseph."

"Bee," Joseph said as he looked at Bianca uncertainly, and Angelo knelt next to the tiny child, speaking gently.

"She'll be fine. Go with cousin Clover. I promise she'll be ok."

Joseph nodded, letting Sebastian pick him up.

"We will be an hour or so," Clover said, still seething. "Come, Sebastian."

As soon as they left, Angelo looked at Cormier.

"You couldn't have stopped this from happening, brother?"

"Patricia took me by surprise," Cormier said, looking at Bianca. "She hit Bianca, Bianca got back up- then Patricia lost it and blasted her."

Angelo nodded. "All right. Take her to the lounge, lay her down. Make sure she's comfortable."

Cormier said ok, lifting Bianca into his arms with such care Angelo stared at him. Cormier stared down at Bianca's face, then he asked "What are you going to do while I take her to the lounge?"

"Get, as you say, fixed up."

Cormier smiled. "All right. Go."

* * Cormier * *

Bianca was out cold.

Cormier held her hand as he waited for Angelo, murmuring "You'll be all right, Bianca."

He pressed her hand to his mouth in a kiss. "You really are fire."

"That she is," said a voice, and Cormier looked around, but saw nothing. "Show yourself, Angelo."

Angelo appeared, fully clothed, looking handsome and devilish as he always did. His arms were folded and he had a scowl on his face.

"What's that look for?" asked Cormier. "And were you spying?"

"A little."

"Why?" Angelo's scowl deepened. "What on earth are you looking at me like that for??"

"For the tenderness you show Bianca. And the kiss you just gave her."

"This again?" sighed Cormier. "Angelo, if you didn't hear me tell Patricia, I'll tell you now. I love Bianca like a little sister. Trust me."

"All right."

Cormier smiled at him. "You're so protective of her. So *in love!*"

"Shut up," snapped Angelo, as Cormier started laughing.

Bianca coughed, and they both looked at her as she mumbled "Cormier..."

"I'm here, chick pea. Are you all right?"

Bianca opened her eyes, taking a deep breath. "What... what happened to me?"

"Patricia hurt you. You have to lay still. You're bruised pretty badly."

Bianca tried to sit up, but the pain was unbearable. She swore furiously as she slumped back on the cushions, cursing Patricia without caring who heard her.

"Where is she?"

"Clover took care of her."

"How?"

"I could give you a blow by blow account, or I could have Angelo show you. Angelo? Do the honours?"

Angelo smiled and snapped his fingers.

A screen appeared.

* * *

"Serves her right," said Bianca, wincing. "Can I have a hot drink, please?"

"You won't be able to hold the mug laying down," Angelo said. "And you are too weak to sit upright. You'll have to make do without for a while."

Bianca sighed. "You're so blunt."

"I can't help it. Cormier is the nice one."

"You can say that again."

Angelo smiled. "Cormier is the nice one."

"You can say that again."

"Cormier is the nice one."

They burst out laughing, Bianca wincing again. Sobering up, Angelo asked "Does it hurt?"

"Very much."

Angelo sighed. "I'm sorry, Bianca."

"You was zoned out, Angelo. It wasn't your fault."

"But I snapped awake as soon as you were knocked out. It should have been earlier."

Bianca shrugged with difficulty, saying "It doesn't matter."

Angelo sighed again. "Are you always so stubborn?"

"Are you?" Bianca replied with a smile, and he laughed.

"Yes."

"There, you got your answer."

Angelo laughed again.

* * Angelo * *

Cormier came back in the lounge, holding a hot water bottle.

"Here, chick pea. Rest this on your torso."

"Thanks so much," Bianca said appreciatively, smiling up at him. "Can you rest it for me? My arms feel like they're made of gold."

Cormier stared at her. Bianca was so *innocent*. She'd just asked him to rest the bottle on her torso without thought of him touching the upper half. Then he nodded, saying "Of course. Would you like it on your stomach or higher?"

Angelo snatched the bottle before Bianca could answer, saying "I'll do it."

"All right, keep your hair on," Cormier said, amused as Angelo gently laid the bottle on Bianca. "Does that feel better, Bianca?"

"Much better, Cormier. Thanks."

Cormier smiled at her, then he left the lounge.

Bianca smiled up at Angelo. "I guess making love is out of the question."

Angelo gaped at her. "You're thinking of that at a time like this?? You're in pain!"

"I can handle the pain, I promise."

"No," Angelo said flatly. "Until you're one hundred percent fit, we're not making love." Bianca pouted. "Don't look like that. What kind of man would I be if I thought we should make love regardless of you being in terrible pain?"

"A mean but sexy man. Who would make his woman very happy."

Angelo smiled. "You're a bad girl."

Bianca smiled back. "You brought out the bad in me."

"Is that right."

"Definitely."

Angelo smiled before he leant down and kissed her tenderly, murmuring "I will make love to you as much times as you want, when you're fit."

"You promise?"

"I promise."

"I still want that hot drink."

Angelo sighed. "Can you sit up?"

"Nope."

"Can you at least lift your arms?"

Bianca tried. "A little. Can't you just heal me, Angelo?"

"I wish I could. Patricia hit you with a very hard curse. It will leave your body in the next five hours. Until then, you'll have to sit tight and bear the pain, I'm afraid."

Bianca sighed. "I hope the wolves eat her alive."

Angelo smiled. "Sniff and prod her, more like."

"Won't the werewolves do anything?"

"Vampires and wolves are bonded, Bianca. We have lived harmoniously for centuries. They will not harm Patricia."

Bianca scowled. "She's as mad as Marissa."

"She was just angry, but her punishment was ideal and enough."

Bianca nodded. "Clover went *in.* And she's so calm and gentle normally! I didn't expect her to go ham like that. Will Patricia's arm mend?"

"Not for a while."

"Serves her right. She went ham on *me* for no reason."

Angelo shrugged a shoulder. "She blames you for Marissa's state."

"I didn't make Marissa put herself in that state. She did that on her own."

Angelo nodded. "I know."

"This hot water bottle feels so nice," sighed Bianca. "Cormier's a genius."

"Like I said, Cormier is the nice one."

"You can say that again."

"Cormier is the nice one."

"You can say that again."

"Cormier is the nice one."

They burst out laughing again, Cormier amused as he appeared.

"A joke at my expense?"

"Yep," Bianca said. "Angelo was just saying that you're the nice one."

Cormier smiled at her. "And you agree?"

"Of course!"

"Ego boosting again," said Angelo, shaking his head. "Cormier, why are you so vain?"

"If I were humble you couldn't possibly love me the same," was Cormier's amused reply, and Bianca said "Touché."

Cormier burst out laughing as Angelo pouted at her, and Bianca smiled at him, then she winced when she tried shifting.

"Aaargh, I can barely move it hurts so much!"

"Then stay still," scolded Angelo. "Why are you wriggling about?"

"I'm just trying to get comfortable," pouted Bianca. "I want to lay on my side but it's too painful to move."

"If you lay on your side the pain will double. Lay on your back and be content."

Bianca scowled at him. "Can we watch something? I can turn my head a little."

"Of course." Angelo snapped his fingers and his massive television turned on. "What would you like to watch?"

"Anything. As long as you and Cormier stay with me and wait on me hand and foot, taking care of me."

"Well I don't mind that at all," said Cormier pleasantly. "Would you like

to be fanned with a palm leaf and fed grapes, chick pea?"
Bianca frowned, unsure whether he was joking with her. His face was straight as heck as she asked "Are you being sarcastic?"
"I'm deadly serious."
"Well in that case-"
"No," said Angelo flatly. "Cormier, haven't you any new cocktails you want to make or experiment with?"
Cormier smirked at him. "Are you jealous, little brother?"
"He's nothing to be jealous of," smirked Bianca, and Cormier gasped.
"That's it! No palm leaves. And no grapes!"
Bianca burst out laughing, then she winced again and cursed Patricia.
"I can't do a thing but lie here!"
Angelo smiled, saying "In another hour or so you should be able to sit up. Then you can get your hot drink. Try flexing your fingers so you can move your arms a little more."
Bianca obeyed, bending her fingers. "If Dad or Ricky saw me like this they'd never let me out of their sight again."
"That I agree with," said Angelo solemnly. "Will you tell them you was attacked by Patricia?"
"No," Bianca said. "What they don't know won't hurt them."
"Wise," smiled Cormier. "Would you like a cocktail, chick pea?"
"Cormier, I can't move," Bianca said through gritted teeth, and he said "I meant for when you are fit and healthy again."
"She is having a hot drink," Angelo said curtly, as Clover appeared with Sebastian, Joseph in her arms.
"Bee!" cried Joseph, struggling in Clover's arms, and she put him down. Joseph ran towards the sofa where Bianca laid. "Bee!"
"Hey Joseph," she said weakly. "You ok?"
Joseph hugged her happily, and she clenched her teeth but bore the pain as he let go, beaming at her.
"Ok?"
"I'm fine," she lied, smiling at him. "Are you hungry, Joseph?"
Joseph nodded, and Bianca said "Feed him please."
"Krispies!" said Joseph happily, and everyone smiled at him, Cormier asking Angelo "Give him the cereal or make dinner?"
"Dinner," Angelo replied. "And we need to give him different cereals, not just Rice Krispies all the time."
"But he loves Rice Krispies."
Angelo glared at him.
"And we should give him different cereals like you said even so," Cormier said hastily, and Angelo said "Good."
"Bully," Bianca said amusedly, and Angelo smiled at her, Clover asking "Are you in pain, little sister?"

"So much pain," sighed Bianca. "But I just have to sit tight and wait for the curse to wear off, like Angelo said."

"Come Joseph," Cormier said, smiling at the little boy. "Come and choose what you'd like for dinner."

"Bee," said Joseph uncertainly as he looked at Bianca, and everyone smiled at Bianca, Cormier saying "Joseph loves you so much, Bianca."

Bianca smiled back weakly, hand on her hot water bottle.

"I'll be ok, Joseph. Go with Cormy."

Joseph smiled and lifted his arms, Cormier sweeping him up and leaving the lounge. Knowing Clover wanted to be alone with Bianca, Angelo and Sebastian left too.

* * Bianca * *

"Did you really leave Patricia in the woods, Clover?"

"Yes I did," Clover replied flatly. "She is a bully. Next time she will think twice before she attacks you again."

"Wow. Well... thank you. Thanks a lot."

Clover smiled at her. "You're welcome."

* * Angelo * *

Angelo showed Joseph some photos of food, asking "Which one, Joseph?"

"Chicken," Joseph said shyly, and Angelo had an urge to cuddle him.

"Chicken with what?"

"Rice?" asked Cormier, showing him a picture of white rice. "Potatoes? Or pasta?"

"It's nice you're involving him in meal choices," smiled Sebastian, when Joseph picked the potatoes, giggling. "How often?"

"Maybe two to three times a week," Angelo replied. "And he will still get vegetables, no matter what."

Sebastian nodded. "How much longer before Marissa wakes?"

"Two days, I believe. Between one and two." Angelo scowled. "I will be telling her exactly what Patricia did. No doubt she will run to her aid. But I want her to apologise to Bianca on her sister's behalf."

"And the bloodthirstiness?" asked Sebastian. "Marissa will be a danger to Bianca when she wakes."

"I will protect Bianca. Do not worry."

Sebastian nodded.

* * Bianca * *

4 hours later…

"Bianca," he said softly, and she stirred. "Bianca, honey. Wake up."
Bianca opened her eyes wearily. "Angelo?"
"Are you all right?" he asked gently, and she nodded, yawning.
"How long was I asleep for?"
"For a few hours. The pain should be gone now, but you will still be very weak. You need to eat something."
"Everyone ate already?" Angelo said yes. "What did you have?"
"Chicken and potatoes with vegetables. Joseph's choice."
Bianca smiled. "Where's Clover, Cormier and Sebastian?"
"At the club. Clover was reluctant to leave you, but Sebastian urged her with the point we should have some time alone. Every moment alone counts."
"I agree," said Bianca softly, and he smiled and held out a hand. Bianca took it, Angelo helping her up.
Her mind swam, head throbbing, and she sat back down.
"Angelo, I can't stand up. I feel so weak."
"I'll bring you some sweet tea, and something to eat."
Bianca nodded, holding her throbbing head. She laid back down on the sofa, sighing as she waited for Angelo to come back.
He came back ten minutes later, a smile on his face as a steaming plate of food and a big mug of hot chocolate sailed towards her.
"Chocolate is more efficient."
Bianca thanked him gratefully and took the mug, sipping delicately. She sighed, saying "Delicious."
Angelo smiled and sat next to her. "It should help get your energy back."
"Thanks so much, Angelo."
"You're welcome."
"Where's Joseph?"
"Fast asleep. He fell asleep at your side, and I took him to bed. No doubt he will find you when he wakes."
Bianca smiled as she took the hovering plate and began to eat. Angelo leant back on the sofa, saying "The pain is entirely gone I presume?"
"Yep. I'm just weak as a matchstick." Bianca cut her potatoes before forking a piece and popping it in her mouth. "Mmm."
"Tasty?" smiled Angelo, and she nodded. "I added spices."
"It tastes brilliant, Angelo. And the chicken-" She popped a piece of sliced chicken into her mouth and smiled, savouring the meat before swallowing. "Gorgeous."
Angelo smiled.

As soon as Bianca's dinner was finished and she was able to stand, he took her hand and kissed it, then he trailed kisses up her arm, making her weak again as he kissed her shoulder, then finally her neck.
Bianca closed her eyes as he hit her weak spot, whispering "Let's go to the bedroom."
Angelo smiled at her. "Now?"
"Now."

* * Cormier * *

"So one Bennett sister lies unconscious in the Heathen Castle and the other sister lies unconscious in the forest," Cormier said amusedly, and there were shouts of laughter.
Morcheeba did not laugh. "Don't you think that vampire is trouble, Cormier?"
"Which vampire?"
"Count Angelo's lover. She's trouble!"
"How do you mean?"
"Because of her, two vampires have been harmed-"
"Save it, Morcheeba," Cormier said, shaking his head. "Marissa harmed herself and Patricia brought harm *upon* herself. Bianca had nothing to do with it. You'd better leave well enough alone."
Morcheeba scowled. "When Patricia wakes up she won't be happy."
"Let her come back for revenge," Clover said coldly. "I welcome her."
Morcheeba scowled again but she didn't dare reply, picking up the drink she ordered and walking away.
Cormier scowled. "Bianca has no idea how popular she is. Everyone is craving to know her even though she has been here before."
"Everyone thought she was just a regular vampire, not Count Angelo's lover," Clover said, shrugging. "The males are interested and the females are jealous."
"Well I don't like it. If something happens to Bianca again-"
"Angelo will go crazy," Sebastian said, Clover saying "As will I. So they'd better stop at being intrigued and leave it there."

* * Angelo * *

Angelo laid next to Bianca, holding her to him.

Bianca's eyes were closed, her lips that he'd kissed thoroughly in a beautiful smile.

"I love you, Angelo."

"I love you more."

"Promise you won't forget me?"

Angelo looked at her properly. There were tears in her eyes.

"You're dreading the day you have to leave, aren't you?"

Bianca nodded.

Angelo kissed her again, on her forehead. "Don't worry about it."

"Sometimes I can't think of anything else," whispered Bianca, and he admitted "Nor I."

"But I swear- I'll find you again. No matter what it takes, or how long- I promise we'll be together again."

Angelo drew her closer in his arms. "You don't have to promise such a big thing, Bianca."

"So you really want it to be over?"

"No." Angelo spoke quietly. "I promise, Bianca Davis, that when you leave here for England, things will be far from over."

For Bianca, that promise was enough. And she believed every word.

Angelo kissed her again. "You should get some sleep. Maybe you can visit your family tomorrow in the day and I will collect you at nightfall, like before."

Bianca smiled. "Sounds like a plan. Although I'd rather stay with you."

"I know, sweetheart. But you need to balance it out before your father loses his cool and tries forcing you not to see me again."

"You know what? I don't think he will."

* * Ricky * *

"I don't want Bianca anywhere near those vampires."
Samuel and Ricky stared at her, surprised.
"Gran?"
"Something happened," Gran said, on edge. "I- I had a dream."
"It was just a dream, Mum," Samuel said kindly, and Gran snapped "It was no ordinary dream! A woman- there is a woman- no, *animals*- who will attempt murdering her, all because of Count Angelo!"
Ricky stared at her as Samuel stood.
"What shall we do?"
"We need to leave," Gran said. "As soon as possible."
"No," said Ricky, and they looked at him. "I'm not leaving Catherine earlier than I have to. You want to take Bianca out of harm's way then send her home to our mother. But I won't leave Catherine."
"You don't have a choice."

* * Angelo * *

Bianca and Angelo snapped awake at the same time.
"What did you dream?" they demanded at the same time, and Bianca said "You first. You're psychic."
"I dreamt of an attack, and then I dreamt of your grandmother," Angelo replied. "She dreamt of the attack too. Bianca, listen to me. This is going to seem very unfair. But she wants you and the family to go back to England right away, to keep you safe."
"I'm not scared of Marissa or Patricia," Bianca said flatly. "And I'm not leaving you."
"Bianca-"
"I've made up my mind."
Angelo sighed. "Why are you so stubborn?"
"We made a big promise to each other," Bianca said, glaring at him. "Why do you keep doing this?"
"Doing what?"
"Blowing hot and cold with me. One minute you want me with you the next minute you don't."
"I never said-"
"The next second you say I'll see you, now you're implying you won't!"
"Bianca-"
"No! Angelo, I love you and I'm staying with you. Don't make me leave- please." Bianca's eyes filled. "Please."
Angelo sighed. "You will have to talk to your family. And if they decide

to return to England as soon as possible then-"

"Then I'll run away," Bianca said flatly. "And I swear I'm not joking."

"If you run away I'll find you in less than a minute," Angelo said just as flatly. "So-"

Suddenly her mouth was on his, cutting him off and surprising him as she gripped his hair- he almost lost his sanity.

Groaning, he kissed her back desperately as an icy voice whispered "Blood."

Startled, they broke apart and whipped around.

Marissa was standing there, eyes burning scarlet. Not looking at Angelo, her gaze was locked on Bianca.

"Bianca, don't move," warned Angelo quietly, and Bianca obeyed.

"What's wrong with her?"

"She is bloodthirsty. Marissa?"

"Yes," Marissa said, still in that cold voice, and Angelo said "I want you to come with me."

"Blood," Marissa repeated icily, eyes still on Bianca. "She is mine."

Angelo sighed before he snapped his fingers, a metal dome appearing around the bed. Startled, Marissa looked at him.

"You deny me??"

"Yes, I deny you," Angelo said flatly. "You will not touch Bianca."

Marissa hissed angrily before she vanished on the spot, gone.

Unnerved, Bianca looked at Angelo.

"Where did she go? Is she still in the castle?"

Angelo said no. "She has gone to quench her thirst. She'll be back."

"Keep this dome around us please," Bianca said nervously, and Angelo said "Very well. Now... you were kissing me with that amazing mouth of yours."

Bianca smiled before she moved closer and kissed him, heat rising within Angelo and arousing him to high heaven.

* * Cormier * *

"Marissa!"

Shocked, Clover and Sebastian stared at her. Everyone was staring. Marissa was drawing deep breaths as she walked towards the bar, Cormier amused.

"Look who has risen from the coma," he said, smirking at her. "And oh, so *bloodthirsty!* Why did you come to the bar, Marissa?"

"Count Angelo, he... he denied me Bianca."

"What!"

Marissa drew a deep, shaky breath before she repeated herself, Cormier saying "And this surprises you because? Of course he'd deny you Bianca!"

"I... I want... Blood."

"Well blood isn't a drink we serve, unfortunately," Cormier said dryly. "Would you like some Tequila?"

"I am not- not in the mood... for your games, Cormier- Cormier Heathen!"

"Who's playing games?"

"Cormier, don't wind her up," Sebastian said quietly, as the vampires began to whisper, then he called "DJ, why did you stop the blasted music??"

The DJ jumped, startled, and immediately music blasted throughout the club again. Cheers erupted, everyone distracted as they started dancing again.

"Here, Marissa," Clover said quietly. "Drink from my wrist."

Marissa stared at her, eyes glowing. "You... you would give?"

"Of course," Clover said gently. "Am I not your friend?"

She pulled down her sleeve, Marissa staring at her arm.

"Clover, you'll weaken yourself," Sebastian said anxiously, and Clover said "I have the strength of ten men. It's nothing I can't handle."

"There is truth in that," Cormier said. "Don't worry, Sebastian."

Marissa licked her lips as Clover held her arm out, then she pounced, sinking her fangs into Clover's flesh.

Clover closed her eyes but bore the pain, knowing Marissa needed it. Sebastian watched with bated breath as Marissa groaned happily, holding Clover's wrist to her mouth, sucking hard, drawing as much blood as possible, swallowing in huge gulps.

Cormier said nothing, eyes on Marissa. He watched as the scarlet glow in her eyes died out, and Marissa gasped, releasing Clover.

Clover took a step back and smiled. "Better?"

"Much better," Marissa said weakly. "Thank you, Clover."

"You're welcome."

* * Angelo * *

"Nothing compares to you," sighed Angelo. "Nothing at all."
"I feel the same about you," Bianca said softly. They were in the lounge, holding hands as they watched Angelo's giant television. "Look, the tourist park is on the news."
"Odd," frowned Angelo, turning up the volume.

"And it seems the tour may be over sooner than we think as these overseas folk are slowly starting to wonder about their safety…"

Bianca and Angelo listened to the story, both of them frowning now.
"This has something to do with my family, I swear it," Bianca said. "You said my grandmother dreamt of an attack, right?"
"Right," said Angelo, and sure enough Bianca's father came on screen.

"Bianca, if you're watching this- come to the tourist park right now. Say your goodbyes, we're getting out of here."

On screen Bianca saw her brother Ricky, blood on his face and all over his clothes. Paramedics and his girlfriend Catherine were with him, the reporter asking what happened.

"Wolves," Ricky said weakly. *"They came right for my family. I got them away from Gran and- and they tore me up good and proper."*

"Did they bite you?"

Angelo and Bianca waited with bated breath, but Ricky said *"Nah. Slashed at me. They ran off when other people came to help."*

"This can't be happening!" cried Bianca, when Angelo stood.
"This attack was planned. Patricia must have awoken and sent them after your family, as an act of revenge."
"I'll kill her!"
"Bianca, don't be ridiculous. Get dressed- now. I'll send a message to Cormier, Sebastian and Clover."
Five minutes later the three vampires Angelo mentioned and a fourth- Marissa Bennett- stood in the lounge.
"What should we do, Angelo?" Clover asked softly, and as Bianca came into the lounge fully dressed Angelo replied "I want all of you to come with me, as guards for Bianca while I return her to her family."
"What?!" cried Bianca. "Angelo, don't do this!"

"Bianca, you must leave. I'm thinking of your safety. Your family was attacked by wolves, sent by Patricia."

Marissa said "Angelo, I apologise for Patricia's attack on Bianca and for her influencing the wolves. Please forgive her-"

"No," snapped Angelo. "I will not forgive her for this. Apology not accepted. Now prepare yourselves for what's out there and Clover, wake Joseph and bring him to me."

Clover nodded and vanished, returning five minutes later with tiny Joseph.

"Bee," said Joseph happily, and Bianca took him off Clover, hugging him. She knew what was going to happen.

"Those wolves are not wolves we know," Angelo said, pacing the lounge angrily. "They may have been the ones who savaged Claire. We won't know until we speak with Phoebus. So come now, everyone."

He snapped his fingers and a small travelling case appeared along with an envelope. He pocketed the envelope and picked up the case, Bianca asking "What's in the suitcase?"

"Everything I got you," Angelo said, a little sadly, and her eyes filled.

"If I stay in the castle-"

"The wolves will return," Angelo cut across. "Bianca, you must go. Your brother wasn't bitten by a werewolf, but he could be next time."

"So this is it?" she asked angrily. "We're just done? I have to go back to England before my time?"

Angelo saw the hurt look on her face, but it couldn't be helped.

"Yes. Put this travelling cloak on and take my hand."

Bianca didn't want to touch him. She was starting to get angry. *Beyond* angry, though she knew he was only trying to protect her.

"Do as he says, Bianca," Cormier said softly, and she obeyed reluctantly.

Angelo took a deep breath, then he said "Let us go."

* * *

"It was the Nefarious Pack," Phoebus said solemnly. "We chased them right back into the depths of the forest where they came from. They were indeed sent by Patricia Bennett."

Marissa shifted uncomfortably as another wolf said "She knew she couldn't attack your mortal friend, so she targeted her family."

Angelo swore angrily. "I'm certain the Nefarious pack is behind savaging Claire. The majority are female werewolves and six male werewolves. Where is Trevor?"

"I'm here, cousin." Everyone turned and saw Trevor leaning against a tree. "The Nefarious Pack are deadly. Unless Bianca gets out of here or Patricia calls off the attack, they will return to the tourist park."

"Trevor, persuade them to refuse to comply with Patricia's order." Angelo was starting to get agitated. "We should look at all options-"

"Yes we should," murmured Clover, Angelo saying "Before we ship Bianca off. But I do think the best thing possible right now is to send her home to England until this madness dies."

"The Nefarious Pack will not conform easily," Phoebus said solemnly. "Remember, they have always been fascinated by you, Angelo- you are the Grand Vampire."

"Fine," said Angelo stoutly. "Tell them it is *my* order."

"Do you think they will listen, brother?" asked Cormier. "They may want something in return."

"I am willing to negotiate," Angelo started, but Phoebus said "You should not have to. I will send the Virtuous Pack with Trevor. But Angelo, I think you should send the mortal-"

"Bianca."

"Apologies," Phoebus said. "I think you should send Bianca home. Back to England. Return her maybe, but right now, this minute, her name is hot on everyone's tongue. The vampire Morcheeba has been discussing her relentlessly along with other nosy vampires. No doubt she found Patricia in the forest and gave her energy after Cormier said she was lying there unconscious."

Angelo glared at his brother, who apologised feebly.

"All right. She goes back to England. But the entire vampire and wolf community will be punished." Angelo was cold as ice. "We had time to spend together, and that time was snatched from us. I am livid."

"I know. But it's for the best."

* * Ricky * *

"Does it hurt, son?"

"Nah," said Ricky. His face had eleven stitches, his side and legs much more. "I'll be fine. I'm just waiting to hear from Bianca-"

There was a knock on the caravan door, Samuel ripping it open. He gasped hotly, staring at the gorgeous man.

"Count Angelo!"

"Greetings to all of you," Angelo said, Bianca stepping into the van, eyes seeking Ricky. She gasped when she saw her brother, who said "Don't worry, Bianca- I'm fine."

"This is all my fault," said Bianca, eyes filling. "I'm so sorry, Richard."

"Here is a suitcase with Bianca's belongings," Angelo said, handing Samuel the suitcase he conjured. "And this- these are tickets for the earliest flight to England out of here. Your caravan will be taken care of."

Samuel took the envelope, not daring to look into Angelo's golden eyes. "Thank you so much."

"You're welcome," Angelo said. "You must leave- now."

"What happened to negotiating with the pack?" Bianca said angrily, eyes filling. "They may agree to call off the hunt!"

"They may take a while to agree and in that time they may attack again." Angelo almost couldn't look at her. "Bianca, please don't make this harder than it has to be."

"Listen to him, Bianca," Gran said firmly. "We're leaving, right now."

"Can I at least say goodbye?" Bianca whispered, and Samuel nodded. "We'll wait here."

Bianca stepped out of the caravan, tears trailing down her face.

* * Bianca * *

"Bee," said Joseph happily, and Bianca took him off Clover, kissing him as she wept "Bye, Joseph. Be a good boy for me, ok? Don't give Angelo any trouble, and make sure you eat all your vegetables like he said."
Joseph beamed at her, and she kissed him again before handing him to Sebastian, saying "Goodbye Sebastian. You're one of the kindest vampires I've ever met."
Clover's eyes filled as Bianca looked at her, and she pulled Bianca into a hug.
"Farewell little sister," she whispered, making Bianca sob a little.
"Chick pea," said Cormier, and she looked at him. "Do not forget me."
"I won't, I promise I won't."
Bianca turned to Angelo, who pulled her into his arms and brought his mouth down on hers, Bianca kissing him back with twice as much ardour.

* * Ricky * *

Ricky gaped, Samuel as well.
"Where the hell did she learn to kiss like that??"
"Come away from the window," snapped Gran. "Give Bianca some privacy."
They obeyed reluctantly as Angelo released his hold on Bianca.

* * Bianca * *

"It's not the end," Angelo said softly. "Remember what I promised you."
"Promise I'll see all of you again?" wept Bianca, and Angelo said "I promise."
Joseph seemed to understand what was happening at last, looking at Bianca uncertainly.
"Bee?"
"Don't," said Angelo, when Bianca looked at the child, tears streaming down her face. "Get in the van, Bianca."
"Let me hug him last one time. Please."
Angelo nodded, and Bianca swept Joseph into her arms and cuddled him, Joseph clinging to her tightly.
"Be good," whispered Bianca, and Angelo gently took him, saying "Say goodbye, Joseph."
"No!" cried Joseph, bursting into tears as Bianca turned to get inside the caravan. "Bee!"
"Go, chick pea," Cormier said, gently wiping Bianca's tears away, then he pulled her into a tight hug. "When you feel sad, remember Count

Angelo never breaks a promise."
Bianca nodded, and Cormier opened the caravan door as Joseph sobbed.
"In you get."
Bianca stepped inside the caravan, and one by one the vampires vanished.
Tears streaming, she sat down as Samuel started the van, and it started
moving. Bianca ran to the back window and stared out.

* * Angelo * *

Angelo stood alone, watching the van pull away.
He felt as if his world was crashing down around him. Thunder boomed
in the sky, lightning streaking through the clouds as rain began to fall.
Angelo locked eyes with Bianca, her expression mirroring his. He raised
a hand, and she raised one too.
Then Angelo vanished.

* * Bianca * *

At the airport...

Bianca's mother Barbara Smith was yelling down the line, Bianca wincing as she said "Mum, I'm fine, ok?"
"You're coming right back home, Bianca! And so is Richard!"
"You said that already and we said ok!" Bianca's temper snapped. She was so angry and upset. "You said we're coming straight to you and we don't have a problem with it-"
"I don't know what the hell your father was thinking, leaving you alone with some guy you just *met-*"
Bianca whipped round to glare at her father. "Why did you tell her?!"
"She called loads of times to check on you," Samuel said uneasily. "What did you want me to say??"
"Does she know he's a-"
"No," Samuel cut across. "Nobody does. Keep it that way."
"And your brother is just as bad," Barbara said, still talking. "Getting sliced up by a pack of wolves when he should have been inside the blasted van-"
"He was with his girlfriend, Mum!"
"I don't care!"
"Mum, they've just announced our flight is ready," Bianca said, when Samuel and Gran stood, Samuel helping Richard up. "I have to go."
She hung up before her mother could reply.

* * *

Bianca and Ricky were jetlagged.

They listened to their mother yelling her head off at their father, Gran's angry words as she said "Don't blame my son for this!"

"I *am* blaming your fool of a son! He lets my daughter run off with a stranger for God knows *how* long-"

"No point listening," yawned Ricky. "I'm going to bed."

"Me too," said Bianca, as they heard Samuel shout back at Barbara. "Looks like we're not going on any more trips for a while."

"Yep." Ricky limped into his bedroom. "See you later."

Bianca went into her own bedroom and laid down on her bed. She couldn't sleep, thinking about Angelo. And Cormier. And Joseph. And Clover and Sebastian. Even Marissa and Patricia.

"Count Angelo never breaks a promise," she whispered, repeating what Cormier said to her. "I really hope he doesn't."

* * *

Bianca's mobile rang.

She snapped awake, reaching for it and pressing answer. "Hello?"

"Bianca! Why the hell didn't you call as soon as you was back?!"

"Shanaid!" Excited, Bianca sat up in bed as she recognised her best friend's voice. "Who told you I was back??"

"I called your dad's house and your gran said you was back at your mother's with Ricky." Bianca could imagine Shanaid Durant smiling broadly. "How was the trip??"

"It was amazing," Bianca said truthfully. "When can I see you, Shan?"

"Tomorrow, you're coming right over!"

"Great!"

"Oh- Jacob wants to say hi-"

"Don't put him on the-!!"

"Bianca," said Jacob Durant, his voice so silky and sexy. "How are you?"

"Uh… I'm fine, Jake. You?" Bianca's heart hammered against her ribs as Jake said "I'm ok. I can't tell you how much I missed you."

"Really?"

"Really."

Bianca smiled, Jake asking "Vice versa?"

"No," she said honestly. "You didn't cross my mind at all, I had too much going on."

Jake chuckled. "All right. So are you coming to ours tomorrow?"

"Um, yeah. I'll see you then. Put Shanaid back on the phone."

"Bianca, Jacob wants you so bad." Shanaid was amused at her big brother. "He used to deny it but now he just agrees. You've both loved each other since you were tiny."

"I know."

"So are you coming to spend time with him or time with me?"

"You, nutcase!" Bianca burst out laughing. "What kind of dumb question is that?? I *always* come to spend time with you! Jake just hangs around!"

"Oh, and I heard about Ricky. Some of our neighbours saw his face when you got back and they were proper shocked. Will he be all right?"

"He'll be fine," Bianca said reassuringly. "He'll have scars, though."

"What happened to him?"

"Wolf attack," Bianca said bitterly. "A pack came to the tourist park."

"See, that's why I worry so much when you go away with your dad," Shanaid said worriedly. "That could have been you."

"It was meant to be."

"What??"

Bianca sighed. "Forget it. I just felt it should have been me, not Ricky."

"Bee, don't talk like that. Everything happens for a reason."

"Shanaid, if you knew-"

"Knew what? What happened?"

Bianca bit her lip, not answering.

"Bee?" Shanaid said timidly. "What happened?"

"I... I met this guy out there. And... and I think... I mean I just-" She stopped, Shanaid saying "Just what? You're scaring me!"

"I love him," Bianca said softly, and Shanaid inhaled sharply.

"Bianca, can you come to mine now?"

"No," Bianca said, checking the time. It was almost midnight. "I'll come first thing tomorrow, I promise."

"All right."

"And don't say anything to Jake," Bianca added. "I'll tell you everything tomorrow."

She ended the call, knowing her best friend was going to interrogate her as soon as she saw her.

Bianca's stomach grumbled. Scowling, she made her way downstairs into the kitchen and began raiding the fridge.

"Bianca!"

Bianca whipped round. "Mum!"

Barbara stood in her dressing gown, pouting. "If you want something to eat then make it. Don't a raid the fridge like savage. Are you a dog?"

Bianca scowled. "No Mum."

"Then make yourself a sandwich. And put down my hot wings."

Bianca placed the box of chicken wings back in the fridge and took out the bread, butter, ham and pickle.

"So tell me about this foreigner you met and stayed with."

Bianca cringed. "Are we really doing this? Why are you trying to get information out of me? You don't need to know about him."

Barbara sighed. "It's not like you to do something so improper."

"Yes, because your world is *so* proper, Mum." Scowling, Bianca buttered her bread and added the ham. "I'm going back to Dad's as soon as I can. I can't stand it here!"

"You can't stand it here or you can't stand me?"

"There's no difference," Bianca said coldly, and Barbara stared at her, hurt. "And don't bother getting upset. You knew from day one I wanted out. I had to get away from you and your *properness*. Being with Dad is like being at the beach. Pure peace, calmness, fresh air."

"Well you're going to be here a while yet," snapped Barbara. "So get used to the properness and decorum. Your father's gone."

Bianca stared at her. "Gone where?"

"He had to get away, clear his head. It looks like the trip wasn't his favourite and he took what happened to Richard very hard. He'll be back in three or four months."

"Three or four months!"

"That's right."

"What about Gran? Where is she?"

"At the house, I expect. He didn't say she was going with him."

"So can I go and visit her at least?"

Barbara shrugged a shoulder. "If you must. But you're not spending the night. Visit in the day and get straight back home."

"But Mum-!!"

"But nothing. Now eat your sandwich. Tidy back up before you go to bed, and for Heaven's sake put your phone on silent."

Bianca glared at her and bit her sandwich, not answering.

* * Angelo * *

Angelo laid on his back, listening to the rain falling.
He hadn't left his suite in hours, and no one came to disturb him.
He didn't even have a picture of her. Why didn't they take any??
Cormier popped up at the foot of his bed. "Brother."
"Leave me be, Cormier."
"I know you don't want to be disturbed. But can you please ease the storm outside? Joseph is still crying for Bianca, and the thunder is frightening him."
"I don't care. I just don't care anymore."
"Angelo, snap out of it," Cormier said firmly. "If you want a picture of Bianca I will give you a blasted picture. You're a father figure to Joseph and he needs you. Snap out of it."
Angelo sat up, staring at him. "Where did you get a picture of Bianca?"
"I took them," Cormier said sheepishly. "Don't worry, I didn't take them secretly. She was a willing participant."
"When did this undercover photo-shoot happen?" demanded Angelo, and Cormier said "Not long ago. You were in a deep sleep."
"And how many pictures of Bianca do you have?"
"I have about seven or eight."
"Bring them to me."
Cormier obeyed.
Angelo snatched the pictures from him, heart racing as he stared at them. She was so beautiful. He knew she'd grow more beautiful each day.
"You may keep them, if you tend to Joseph. Otherwise I burn them."
"You wouldn't dare."
"Wouldn't I?" Cormier said, eyebrow raised. "Don't test me."
Angelo glared at him. "All right. I'll see to Joseph. Where is Clover and Sebastian?"
"In the lounge with Marissa. Clover failed to comfort Joseph. All he wants is Bianca."
Angelo sighed. "I know exactly how he feels."
"We all do."
    Angelo ran a hand through his hair, saying "Bring him to me."

* * *

"Bee," wept Joseph, and Angelo put an arm around him.

"I know, Joseph. I know."

They were in his suite, Joseph snuggled under Angelo's covers. He hadn't stopped crying since Bianca left. Angelo had eased the storm he caused, but that didn't mean he wouldn't start it again.

Cormier appeared at the foot of his bed again. "How is he?"

"Very sad since Bianca left," Angelo replied. "As we all are."

"The club is closed. I didn't think you would want it open."

"No. I don't." Angelo sighed as he looked at Joseph. "Where is Marissa?"

"In the lounge with Clover and Sebastian. Do you want her?"

"No. I want her sister." Angelo was ice cold, Cormier saying "She would be with the Nefarious Pack, I'm guessing. And she must know Bianca is no longer with us."

"Call a meeting," Angelo replied. "Decisions must be made."

* * Bianca * *

It was eight in the morning.

Bianca stirred, opening her eyes to look at Angelo. She gasped when she realised she was in her own bed, recognising her laptop which sat on her desk, her wardrobe.

She was back in England.

Bianca wanted to scream frustratedly as she got up, then she remembered her brother. She quickly pulled on her dressing gown and went out onto the landing, heading for Ricky's room.

"Morning," a voice said, and she turned and saw her mother.

"Morning Mum," she said stiffly, knocking on Ricky's door gently. "Ricky? Are you up?"

"Yeah," Ricky said, Bianca saying "Can I come in?"

"Sure."

Bianca went in quickly, closing the door behind her. Ricky was sitting up in bed, in shorts and a vest top.

"Got to give the slashes air," he said, smiling when she frowned at him. "Feels better than having layers of clothes on blocking the circulation."

Before Bianca could answer their mother came in, saying "Breakfast is at nine. Make sure you're both washed and dressed please."

"Yes Mum," Ricky said; Bianca didn't reply. Barbara looked at her, as if expecting a "Yes Mum" from her too, then she shook her head and left the room.

As soon as her footsteps died Bianca said "Ricky, I am so, so sorry. The attack was my fault. A vampire attacked me, knocked me out. My sister Clover-"

"Sister?"

"Well, we're really close. She calls me her little sister." Bianca sighed. "Anyway, Clover dealt with the vampire who attacked me, and that vampire called the werewolves to attack my family, because she knew she couldn't attack me again. Angelo would have gone nuts."

"But why attack you in the first place?" asked Ricky, frowning at his sister. "What did you do?"

"Nothing, I swear. Patricia (that's her name) hit me across the face and attacked me because she thought it was my fault Angelo didn't want her little sister Marissa. Marissa put herself in a coma just to get Angelo's attention. Patricia blamed me for it, and she just went ham. Attacked me, then sent wolves after you, Dad and Gran. I didn't see any of this coming, Ricky- I swear." Bianca's eyes filled. "I am so, so sorry."

"It's all right," Ricky said gently. "None of it was your fault."

"It was totally my fault. I should have been slashed, not you."

Ricky sighed, knowing he couldn't change her mind. Then he said "I'm not even too bothered about it. I just want to see Catherine again. She lives in Manchester. I'm definitely going to see her when I'm fit. For now I'll be content talking to her on the phone and emailing her and talking to her on Facebook."

"Too bad I can't do the same with Angelo," sighed Bianca. "I'll see you when breakfast is ready."

* * Angelo * *

Angelo woke up. "Joseph?"

There was a sniffle in reply, and he sat up. Joseph was sitting by the window, holding his frog teddy. Sadness was on his tiny face as he looked back at Angelo.

Angelo held his arms open, and Joseph scrambled to his feet, running to him. Angelo swept him up and hugged him tightly as Joseph began to sob.

"I know, Joseph. I know. Here."

He reached for his bedside drawer, selecting a photo of Bianca which he framed. He'd framed all of them.

Joseph took the picture uncertainly, looking at it. "Bee!"

"Yes Joseph. Bee."

"Mine?" asked Joseph, and Angelo said "All yours."

Joseph beamed, wiping his tears away. "I put it down."

Angelo set the tiny child on his feet, and Joseph ran out of the room, Angelo following him with a small smile. That seemed to have done the trick. It closed the gaping hole of loss a fraction, anyway.

Cormier appeared, hair tousled. "What are you doing up before I, brother?"

"Tending to Joseph," Angelo replied, as Joseph's tiny feet pattered, then he turned into his bedroom, Angelo and Cormier following him.

Joseph placed Bianca's picture on his bedside drawer, next to his lamp. His eyes filled, then he quickly wiped them, mumbling "Be brave boy."

"He's trying to be tougher," Cormier said, when Angelo frowned at the child. "Me, Clover and Sebastian were saying yesterday he must be a brave boy for you. He seems to have understood."

Angelo nodded, emotion clawing at him. "Did Clover and Sebastian go home? And where is Marissa?"

"All three are asleep, although Clover will be up soon probably."

Angelo nodded again.

* * Bianca * *

Bianca rang the doorbell and waited.

Jacob Durant answered the door, smiling at her. "Hey stranger."

"Hey," she said, smiling back. "Where's Shanaid?"

"Still sleeping. Come in."

Bianca smiled and stepped inside the house, Jake closing the door behind her.

"Want a drink of anything?"

"No thanks. I had a mug of hot chocolate before I left."

Jake nodded. "So how was your trip?"

"It was great. Um. How's basketball going?" she asked, looking anywhere but at him. Jacob Durant oozed sex appeal every time she saw him, since they were in their early teens. Bianca would have given her right arm and leg and shaved her head just to be with him, be his girl- before she met the Grand Vampire. He was reminding her so much of Angelo she couldn't think straight.

"It's going all right. Training is vigorous." Jake smiled at her, lifting his t-shirt. Bianca stared at his hard abs, heart racing, before he lowered it. "I work out nearly every day. Thursdays are my day off."

Bianca nodded, throat tight.

"Bianca?"

"Yes Jake," she whispered, and he came closer.

"Do you know what day it is?"

"No," she admitted, and Jake lifted a hand and caressed her cheek. Bianca closed her eyes at his touch as he softly said "It's Thursday."

"Oh."

"I missed you so much, Bianca."

"Really?" she said quietly, and he said "Really."

"Jake, I-"

"Don't speak, Bee. Let me kiss you."

"I can't."

Jake smiled. "Why?"

"I just… things are-"

"Things are what?"

"Just confusing," Bianca mumbled, eyes closed still. "I'm not in a good place right now."

"Because of what happened to your brother?"

"Because of everything."

Jake chuckled, taking a step back. "All right."

Bianca opened her eyes to smile at him, and was just about to say something when Shanaid trailed down the stairs.

"Bianca!"

"Hey," smiled Bianca. "Good sleep?"

"Why didn't you wake me??"

"I was talking to Jacob," Bianca said, Shanaid eyeing her suspiciously.

"About what?"

"About mind your damn business," Jake said, highly amused. "Go and get fixed up before you show yourself to others. Rule number one."

"At Bianca's house, yeah," Shanaid said, amused. "Not here. I'm dying for a coffee!"

"We're fresh out of coffee," Jake said. "Go and buy some or have tea."

Shanaid pouted. "Are you for real? You're dressed plus you have a car. *You* go and buy some!"

"Shanaid, I'm about to watch a basketball match. That's why I'm in the living room. There's no plus channel for me to watch it later. Just get fixed up and run for the coffee, it's only going to take twenty minutes."

That's all we need, Bianca thought edgily. *Twenty minutes.*

Shanaid sighed. "Fine. Bee? You coming?"

"I'll wait here, Shan. I walked all the way here from my mother's. My feet kill."

She was lying about her feet hurting, but it did take a while to get there. Shanaid didn't seem to suspect anything, going back upstairs.

"All right. Jake, can you make pancakes?"

"Did you not hear what I said about the match?" Jake burst out laughing. "Make your own pancakes when you get back."

Shanaid uttered a curse word before she went into her bedroom, slamming the door behind her.

* * *

"So why can't I kiss you, Bee?" Jake asked quietly, after the front door closed behind Shanaid. "I've been dying to for over two months."

"I'm just not cool with this 'friends with benefits' thing," Bianca said honestly, avoiding his eyes. "Not anymore."

"Ok. Well, I feel the same."

Bianca's heart raced. "You do?"

"Yeah. I never was cool with it to begin with," admitted Jake. "I asked you out, you turned me down because... well, you said wouldn't be able to commit properly as you go away with your dad all the time. You was more focused on travelling than love."

"I know."

"But you admitted you love me, and I told you I love you too. Not often enough though," smiled Jake. "Do you still feel the same?"

Bianca swallowed. She was in love with Angelo. Yet her heart pounded furiously as she looked at Jacob Durant, pounded like it always did when she was around him. She remembered the walks through the park with him, the drives in his car. The trips to the movies together. The hot make out sessions that they never took too far because she was afraid. Everything.

It was like by coming to her best friend's house she had opened Pandora's box, unleashing her suppressed feelings for him instead of evil.

"Bee?"

Bianca looked at Jake, and she nodded. He smiled, pulling her into his arms and holding her close.

"I love you too."

* * Angelo * *

Angelo couldn't believe it.

Cormier and Clover was in shock. Marissa was smirking, Sebastian rubbing his neck awkwardly. He knew Angelo was going to go nuts in less than five minutes.

Bianca's image dissolved, the giant mirror showing their stunned reflections again.

"Bee," said Joseph indignantly, looking up at Angelo. "Daddy, Bee!"

"No more Bee, Joseph." Angelo forced calmness into his voice. "It's time for you to have dinner."

"I'll take him," Sebastian said. "Come, Joseph."

Joseph took Sebastian's hand, Sebastian taking him up the many flights of stairs into the dining area.

"There must be an explanation to what we saw," Clover began uneasily, Cormier nodding.

"Brother, don't get upset. Bianca loves you."

"She just told another man she loves him," spat Angelo, glowing scarlet. "And it hasn't even been a week. How can you tell me not to get upset?"

"Bianca couldn't mean it," Cormier said. "I know she doesn't."

"And she didn't exactly say it," Clover said gently. "She just nodded."

"Who is he to her?" demanded Angelo, and Cormier said "We will find out sooner or later. Come and eat, Angelo."

"No," said Angelo angrily. "I have to know who he is to her."

"Someone very close," Marissa said, speaking for the first time. "He may have been her boyfriend but is now an ex."

"No," said Cormier. "I'm not sensing that."

Everyone looked at him. "Sensing?"

"I'm concentrating. Look."

The mirror reflections dissolved again, everyone silent. Then everyone gasped harshly as images flashed across the glass, feeling a weird sensation, a hotness in their eyes as they kept them on the glass.

A six year old girl was crying, a ten year old boy saying "Don't cry!"

Angelo recognised the little girl as Bianca immediately.

"You won't let me play with you!"

"You've got your dolly!" said the boy huffily. "Play with that!"

"But I want to play with *you,*" wept Bianca, and Angelo's heart melted. It looked like the boy's did too.

"All right. You can play."

"Promise?"

"I promise."

Bianca hugged the boy and he patted her back, saying "You're such a baby."

"That's Jacob," Clover said softly, and everyone stared harder.

Fury erupted within Angelo as he recognised the boy- especially when he smiled at little Bianca.

"So they grew up together?"

"It looks that way."

The images changed again, Angelo never taking his eyes away. This time Bianca was fifteen, Shanaid at her side as she complained.

"Why does he treat me like I'm a little kid all the time?"

"He's nineteen," shrugged Shanaid. "He thinks you're too young for him. Plus you going out with him could pretty much be illegal. Jake would get in big trouble. But he does fancy you, I promise."

"Did he tell you that?"

"No, but I can tell. He's my brother."

Bianca started to smile, then she stopped, looking at Shanaid suspiciously.

"How can you tell?"

"He always watches you when you're at ours," shrugged Shanaid. "And he knocks on my bedroom door to check on us and what we're doing when he doesn't with other friends. And he always asks me if you have a BF."

"What is a BF?" demanded Angelo, Clover saying "A boyfriend, Angelo. Jesus."

Angelo scowled at her.

"Did you tell him I have one?"

"No."

"Good, because I don't want him to go off me."

"He might. Brittany from Sixth Form totally wants him."

"She'd better back off," Bianca said, heat rising. "He's mine."

Their images dissolved, then they saw Bianca's brother Richard.

"He's too old for you!"

"Age is just a number," sang Bianca, as a car horn beeped. "That's Jake. Dad, I'll see you tonight."

"Nine on the dot," her father called, as she checked herself in the mirror. Richard was scowling at her.

"You're only seventeen."

"Save it, Richard. You're only eighteen but you act like eighty. Even Dad doesn't mind me seeing Jacob."

"Mum will!"

"Tell Mum and I'll tell her you're not a virgin," Bianca said flatly, and Richard gaped at her.

"You wouldn't!"

"Try me," Bianca replied, putting on her jacket. "Bye!"

Richard slammed the front door behind her, cursing.

Cormier couldn't help but laugh. "She is such fire."

"I know," agreed Clover; Marissa and Angelo didn't reply. Marissa seemed interested in what she was watching and Angelo was beyond furious as the image changed again, to Bianca in Jacob's car.

"Bee?"

"Yes Jake?"

"Do you love me?"

"You know I do," Bianca said quietly. "I just don't know if *you* love *me.*" Jacob turned to look at her properly. "Why do you say that?"

"When I say I love you, you don't say it back. You just kiss me in reply. I don't know how I feel about that," admitted Bianca. "And I'm going away in three days with my father."

"Your mother's actually letting you go?" said Jacob amazedly. "How did that happen?"

"My grandmother. She kind of lost it with her. Said she couldn't keep me cooped up all my life like a chicken, smothering me with rules and perfection. She told Dad not to be a coward and speak up. So Mum's letting me go for three weeks."

"Damn. I don't know what I'm going to do without you in those weeks."

"I'll call you every night, I promise."

"Ricky will go nuts." Jacob smiled at her. "Don't let him catch you."

"Dad doesn't have a problem with me and you. He knows you and he trusts you."

"Maybe I shouldn't be trusted," Jacob said softly. "Bee, listen-"

"You really like me. I know."

Hurt flashed across his face. "I wasn't going to say that."

"Well what was you going to say, Jake?" Bianca sighed. "I'm tired of being your unofficial girl. I want us to go steady."

"I know. I've been unfair to you, baby. I know we should be in a proper relationship, but-"

"But what? What possible excuse is there aside from the fact you don't love me enough to be with me?"

"I do love you," Jacob said quietly. "So much."

"Then be with me, Jake," Bianca pleaded softly. "Make me your exclusive. Forget being a gyallis."

"What the hell is a gyallis?" spat Angelo, livid. "Someone answer me!"

"Someone who gets a lot of female attention," Marissa replied. "Basically yourself."

Angelo scowled. "I'm a gyallis?"

"Yes you are."

"It's not about being a gyallis," Jacob said. "I just... I don't want you to get your hopes up about being with me and then when we are together, you're disappointed."

"That would never happen, I swear. I don't care about material things. I want to be with you."

Jacob kissed her, touched. Angelo wished he could go back in time and drag him off her, but all he could do was rage as the kiss got deeper, Jacob Durant pulling Bianca into his arms, Bianca moaning. Angelo shivered at the sound, remembering all the times he made her moan like that in his bedroom, bathroom and even the lounge.

Then he got angry again. "So he is her childhood sweetheart and the one she adored all her life. Fantastic!"

Clover said nothing, thinking. Marissa shifted, rubbing her neck, and Cormier looked anywhere but at his brother.

Breaking away, Jacob said "When you get back from your holiday, I'll be waiting for you."

"You promise, Jake?" breathed Bianca, and Jacob said "I promise."

The image disappeared, the mirror showing everyone's reflections again. Nobody spoke.

After thirty seconds Clover said "I think we should study this. Angelo, we need to know the depth of Bianca's relationship with this man."

"We already know the depth," Angelo said angrily. "He is her childhood sweetheart and she adored him for years. When he finally got involved with her she fell even deeper in love with him and wanted to be his only. That's all there is to it."

"There is much more to it," Clover said. "Was he her first?"

Angelo knew what she meant. Clover waited as he pondered whether to answer his cousin. Finally he said "No. I was."

Marissa's jaw dropped. Clover was stunned too.

"You made love to Bianca?"

"Yes." Not wanting either of the women to berate him, he added "It was what she wanted and I wanted it as well."

"Did you use protection?" demanded Clover, and Angelo scowled.

"No I did not. And I do not regret not using any either."

"Angelo, think of what you're saying! Did you not stop to think of the consequences?" Clover said exasperatedly. "What if Bianca is carrying your child?"

"She can't be."

"You can't know that for sure, Angelo!"

"Clover, I am the Grand Vampire. I order you to drop the subject. Now."

"Order obeyed," said Clover angrily. "I pray you know what you're doing."

"I definitely know what I'm doing. I'm just so angry right now." Angelo turned back to the mirror, Cormier saying "Come and eat, brother. We'll come right back down afterwards."

Angelo sighed, then he obliged.

* * Bianca * *

Jake and Bianca quickly separated from each other's arms when Shanaid closed the front door, calling "I'm back! Bee, I bought you those strawberry and banana muffins you're mad over. You can have one with coffee- all right, tea," she said exasperatedly, when Bianca said hell no. "Jake, you want one?"

"Nah. Tea is fine. Thanks." Jake smiled at Bianca. "You still can't stand coffee."

"Nope."

Bianca's mobile went off, Bianca answering reluctantly. "Hello?"

"Bianca, you didn't make your bed before you left the house."

"Mum!" said Bianca, annoyed. "Are you serious?? And why are you in my room, anyway? Get out!"

"Well as soon as you get back you're going to make that room spick and span, do you hear me young woman?"

"I hear you," Bianca snapped. "Now can I go please?"

"Yes. Go."

Bianca hung up, fuming. "That woman! We'll never get along."

"You both have issues with each other," Shanaid said amusedly as she went into the kitchen. "You want to be wild and free while she's determined to make sure you're a proper lady."

"I like you being wild and free," Jake murmured, and Bianca smiled at him.

"Thanks, Jake."

* * Angelo * *

Clover was deep in thought. Marissa seemed to be fuming. Cormier was watching Angelo, who was fuming as well.

"Can we go back to the Mirror of Truth now please? It won't work without the presence of three people."

The Mirror of Truth worked in a peculiar way. It needed more than one person present so more than one could see the truth, so that the truth couldn't be lied about and if it was, two other people would know it was a lie.

Clover nodded and stood. "Let us go. Sebastian, put Joseph to bed."

Sebastian nodded. "Come, Joseph. Say goodnight."

Joseph ran and hugged Angelo's leg. "Night night Daddy!"

"Night," Angelo said, sweeping him up and cuddling him. "Sebastian, make sure you leave his lamp on."

* * Bianca * *

Shanaid gaped as Bianca finished speaking. They were sat in her bedroom. Bianca had basically told Shanaid everything about Count Angelo, excluding the fact he was a vampire. She also told her about little Joseph, but she didn't mention he was part wolf.

"So you're not…" Shanaid hesitated. "Not… a virgin anymore?"

"Well… no. I'm not."

They heard someone curse outside the bedroom door, and Shanaid snapped "Get out of it, Jake!"

Jacob opened the door, saying "I need to speak to Bianca. Alone."

"No," said Shanaid angrily. "She's been through a hell of a lot and she needs me, ok? So whatever you've got to say, say with me here."

"Shanaid, now isn't the damn time, ok?!"

Bianca flinched at his tone, Shanaid said "Exactly! Now isn't the time for you to let rip either!"

"This is the perfect time to let rip," snapped Jake. "Bianca."

She didn't reply.

"Bianca, please. I need to talk to you. We can go for a drive, we can get something to eat- anything." He was pleading with her now. "Please."

Bianca looked at Shanaid, who said "Up to you."

So Bianca got up, looking at Jake as she said "Ok."

Jake breathed out, relieved. "Thank you."

"Don't stay out for the whole evening," Shanaid said. "I'm making tuna and pasta for dinner. And Bianca has to get home."

"I'll drop her home," Jake replied. "And don't make too much food either, we might eat out. I'll text you."

"You are so sprung," was Shanaid's amused reply. "All right, go."
Bianca left the room, mumbling "See you in a bit."

* * Angelo * *

"Dad, I need ten pounds for my phone."
"Bianca, I gave you money for your phone two days ago."
"It's gone, Dad! Please lend me ten pounds again- I have to speak to Jake!"
"Jake this, Jake that." Samuel shook his head. "He's coming back in a week, Bianca. It's not a big deal if you don't see him."
"But we're leaving for Pennsylvania the same day he gets back!" said Bianca angrily. "I won't see him, will I? At least let me say goodbye, Dad! Please, I'm begging you now! *Please!"*
"All right," said Samuel exasperatedly. "But you're not going to the shop at this time. Ricky can for you."
"I'm not going anywhere," Richard said flatly. "Bianca can go without a night talking to precious Jacob Durant."
Bianca clenched her fists before she stormed out of the kitchen.
"So they spoke regularly on the phone when they were away from each other," Clover said thoughtfully. "I do believe they really did love each other."
"Well we know what happened after that scene," Angelo said haughtily. "She came here and I basically ruined her life."
Talk broke out at that, Cormier saying "Brother, don't be stupid!"
"You didn't ruin her life, Angelo!" Clover said angrily. "She had the most amazing, magical experience because of you-"
"And now it's over," snapped Angelo. "She had a life before I. This was meant to be a simple trip for her and her family. But I complicated things. All I am is a complication."
"Let us see what she's doing now," Marissa said, as the mirror showed Bianca fast asleep in the caravan, her father yelling to wake up. "We know what happens after this."
Angelo nodded, saying "Mirror of Truth, show us what we seek."
The image of the caravan driving beside the forest dissolved, then the mirror showed Bianca in Jacob Durant's car.

* * Bianca * *

"So you forgot me when you met this guy, yeah?" Jake kept his eyes on the road, though anger was evident in his voice. "You slept with him?"

"Jake, I... I'm really sorry-" Bianca's voice cracked as tears fell down her face. "I know you was meant to be my first. But I fell in love with him, I loved him so much!"

"Love or loved? Which is it, Bianca?"

"I don't know," wept Bianca. "When I saw you again all these feelings just came back- I love you and I always will! But- look, I already told you I'm in a bad place right now. I can't think straight, a lot has happened."

Jake sighed. "I really wanted to be the one."

"You are, Jake-"

"But I'm not, am I? He is."

Bianca looked at him, knowing he was hurt. "Stop the car."

"What?"

"Stop the car," she repeated, and he obeyed before he said "You don't have to explain yourself. You was always a hopeless romantic."

Bianca smiled through her tears. "You've been calling me that since I was fourteen."

"And all of this just proves I was right. Come here." Jake pulled her into his arms and kissed her on the forehead. "I love you."

"Still?" she asked softly, and Jake nodded.

"Still."

* * Angelo * *

Everyone looked at Angelo but he didn't react, arms folded.

"Brother?" Cormier said warily, but Angelo didn't reply. Clover hesitated, then she said "Maybe you could contact Bianca, Angelo. By post? I know you don't like using the phone."

"Contact her for what reason," snapped Angelo. "She loves Jacob. Maybe I was simply used."

"You know that's not true," Clover said quietly. "Used for what exactly? She loves you as much as you love her, her soul still screams your name."

"Well eventually her soul will scream Jacob, " snapped Angelo. "I am not fazed by her still wanting me. Eventually she will forget me."

"And you want that?" demanded Cormier, furious at his attitude. "You want to just let her go without a fight? You promised her things will be far from over!"

"I know!!" exploded Angelo, eyes lighting scarlet. "What do you want me to do?! What's your suggestion, Cormier?? I'm all ears!"

"Get her back!"

"How?!"

"Don't answer him," Marissa said smoothly, when Cormier opened his mouth. "Let him think for himself."

"I agree with Marissa," Clover said, thanking her. "Angelo needs time to think, Cormier, and he doesn't need you pressuring him. Be quiet," she snapped, when he glared and started to say Angelo needed to be pressurised. "He doesn't. It hasn't even been a week. Angelo is angry and upset, and a little confused. Just let him be."

"Fine," scowled Cormier, the mirror showing their reflections again. Angelo simply said "Enough watching Bianca for tonight. Let's go to the lounge."

"Are you sure?" asked Marissa. "We aren't tired of it."

"I'm sure," Angelo said. "We may watch again tomorrow. Right now I need a drink. A strong drink."

* * Bianca * *

Bianca was asleep in Jake's arms, Jake holding her close.

Shanaid pouted when she saw them, whispering "What happened to not taking long? And her mother is going to kill her! Look at the time! Didn't Barbara call?"

"I switched her mobile off," Jake whispered. "I didn't want to wake her."

* * Angelo * *

Cormier rubbed his chin, Marissa and Clover watching.

"You'd better wake her up."

"No. She can spend the night, it's no problem."

"Well if she's spending the night she's sleeping in my room," Shanaid said, scowling as Jacob said "The hell she is."

"Jake!"

"She's staying with me, ok?" Jacob glared at his little sister. "She's still jetlagged. She needs to rest. I won't trouble her."

"Well take her up to bed, then. I'll call her mother before she goes nuts."

Angelo watched, invisible.

They couldn't feel his presence. Another perk of being an all-powerful vampire, he thought with a wry smile, when Clover said "There's no denying Jacob cares for her. Bianca must be as confused as Angelo."

"I agree," Marissa said. "Would you like me to talk to him?"

"No," said Cormier sharply. "Your art of talking will become an art of seduction."

"What!"

"Cormier, don't be silly," said Clover, highly amused as Marissa glared at him. "Marissa and Angelo are very close. You know that already."

"I will talk with him," Marissa said. "He needs to let off some steam. I don't mind listening to him."

As soon as she stepped away from the mirror, it showed their reflections again. Angelo was already at the top of the stairs, so the mirror couldn't sense a third person anymore.

He really did need to let off some steam.

* * Bianca * *

Bianca woke up in Jake's arms.
His curtains were drawn, blocking the sunlight from brightening the room. She smiled a little, then she realised Jake was awake, watching her.
"Morning."
"Morning," she responded softly. "Did you have a good sleep?"
"Yeah. I had to keep you with me tonight. You don't mind, do you?"
Bianca said no, checking the time. It was almost eleven in the morning.
"Shanaid's probably still asleep," said Jake. "She hasn't come knocking on my door for you yet."
Bianca smiled at him. "I have to go."
"I'll drop you back," Jake said. "Do you want me to make you breakfast while you get ready? I'll make you pancakes."
"Yes please. Thank you."

* * Cormier * *

Cormier and Clover were eavesdropping on Marissa and Angelo's conversation, standing with their ears to the library door.
"She should have told me about him." Angelo was agitated. "Would that have been so hard? To tell me about him? Even a little?"
"Angelo, this was a whirlwind romance if not a holiday fling," sighed Marissa. "You barely knew her."
Clover and Cormier scowled as Marissa added "Two days may be like two months in the vampire world, but Bianca Davis is not a vampire. It seems you forgot that while you were with her. Of course she will be confused. She has no idea what she wants anymore."
"But I fell in love with her regardless, Marissa! I don't expect you to understand. I would have killed for her! And I still would," Angelo added, hating himself for admitting that. "I love her so much. And even if I barely knew her, we would have gotten to know each other much more in the two months she had left here, if your stupid, *stupid* elder sister didn't pull a crazy stunt to avenge you."
"So now you blame me?"
"Yes," said Angelo angrily. "If you hadn't put yourself in a coma, Patricia wouldn't have come looking for you, Bianca and her family wouldn't have been attacked, and she would still be here!"
"Touché," said Marissa dryly. "Look at me, Angelo Heathen."

* * Angelo * *

"No."

"I said look at me," Marissa said softly, and Angelo sighed and obeyed, looking into her blue eyes.

"You are the Grand Vampire. You need to be stronger than this. If you want her back, by all means go and get her. You are still connected in a fierce, strong bond. You can still be together. If you bite her, she will truly be yours-"

"No," said Angelo sharply. "I am not biting Bianca. At least not without her consent."

"Time will run out, Angelo. She is soon nineteen. What happens when she becomes too old and frail to be yours? You will regret not taking her while you had the chance, and you will never stop loving her. If she dies, you won't forgive yourself for not acting sooner."

"I vowed never to bite a human again. Even if I was bloodthirsty. I'd rather bite an animal than a human. I cannot bite Bianca."

* * Ricky * *

Two months later…

Ricky listened as Bianca threw up in the toilet, Barbara listening too.
"Bianca? You've been vomiting constantly for the past two weeks. Is everything all right?"
"Does everything sound all right?" snapped Bianca. "Leave me alone."
Ricky shook his head when Barbara opened her mouth. "Leave it."
"Bianca, dinner is soon ready," Barbara said curtly. "Fix up and come downstairs."
Bianca flushed the toilet, not answering her. Barbara sighed, then turned and went downstairs. Ricky followed her.

* * Angelo * *

"She's pregnant," Angelo said softly. Dazed. Shocked.
Clover smiled at him as his emotions took over, emotions he'd been suppressing for the past two months.
"I must see her, I… I have to see her!"
"How will you do that, brother?" Cormier asked quietly. "Will you travel there? You cannot function in the day."
"If the spirits of the Underworld grant me the power I beg of them I will surely be able to function in the day, for the time I need to sort things out," Angelo said just as quietly, and Cormier said "Brother, be careful. The spirits will want something in return."
"Whatever they want I will give them," Angelo replied, and Cormier said "And if it is your blood they demand from you? You will become weak and bloodthirsty-"
"I will easily regain my strength," Angelo replied, shrugging a shoulder. "And I will quench my thirst. Now are you going to support my consulting the spirits or simply be a thorn in a rosebush? I will need all the help I can get."
"We will support you," Clover said softly. "Cormier, do not try and change his mind. Bianca is carrying his child. The least you can do is support him."
"I want to come with you," Cormier said to Angelo, but Angelo said no.
"You need to stay and look after Joseph. It will only be the two of you here in the castle. He will need caring for to the highest point. And he still misses Bianca terribly. He will miss me terribly also."
"If something happens to you out there-"
"I will be fine. The spirits can grant you the power to come to my aid if something happens if you're so worried."

Cormier sighed. "All right. Where will you stay?"

"I'll rent an accommodation or stay in a hotel."

"Just like that?" said Clover, and Angelo said yes. "All right. When will you leave?"

"As soon as possible."

* * Bianca * *

One week later…

"You're carrying his child," whispered Shanaid amazedly, and Bianca nodded miserably. "Jake is so going to go mad."
"Don't tell him," begged Bianca. "Please, Shan."
"Bianca, you can't keep it a secret-"
"I'll keep it a secret for as long as I can," Bianca said, then her mind swam and she felt dizzy, swaying on the spot. Shanaid grabbed her quickly, making her sit down.
"Do you feel sick?"
"Real sick," mumbled Bianca, Shanaid saying "I'll take you to the bathroom- come, quickly."
When she pulled open the door they saw Jake standing there. The fury on his face told them he heard exactly what they said.
"Can you stop eavesdropping?!" Shanaid lost her temper. "Is there no privacy in this flipping house?? Screw you!"
Jake ignored her, saying "Bianca-"
"I'm going to be sick," gasped Bianca, and Jake swept her into his arms, carrying her into the bathroom and placing her next to the toilet with care. Shanaid followed as Bianca threw up, eyes filling over.
"Jake, please don't shout at her-"
"I'm not going to shout at her," snapped Jake. "I just want to make sure she's ok."
"She's pregnant," said Shanaid exasperatedly. "She's not ok. And don't tell anyone either, especially Richard and her mother. Here Bee, use the mouthwash."
Bianca obeyed, shivering. "I need Angelo."
"Has he got a phone number?"
"I don't know it," said Bianca, eyes filling. "I don't even know if he has a phone. But I need him, Shan- I need him so much."
Jake nodded. "We'll have to find a way to contact him and let him know what's happening."
Bianca smiled weakly, grateful he was being so understanding. Jake seemed to know what she was thinking.
"I could never hate you or be angry at you for this. Don't worry. We'll find a way to contact Angelo."

* * Angelo * *

Angelo woke up, startled as he looked around.

He was in a hotel in Central London. His bedroom, which he'd kept tidy for the past week and hardly left, was spotless. He guessed the staff had come in when he was asleep to do their job.

Angelo stood, checking the time. He snapped his fingers, the television across the room turning on. It showed the news.

Angelo switched the telly back off. He had no interest whatsoever in what was happening in England. All he wanted was to find Bianca.

"Come on Angelo, concentrate," he murmured to himself. "Where could she be? What is her number? Focus."

Angelo had been listening sharply, hearing Bianca's soul scream his name every time he slept. But from where?

He closed his eyes, concentrating. Unleashing his telekinetic power as he whispered her name: *"Bianca Davis."*

The answer hit him suddenly, his senses incredibly high, eyes burning scarlet. Angelo got dressed quickly and left his hotel room, then he quickly closed his eyes and waited until the glow died before he walked down the stairs into the lobby and out of the hotel.

* * Bianca * *

"I've looked him up but there's no result," Jake said, shaking his head as he looked at Bianca and his little sister. "No results for his brother Cormier either."

"What about the club?" demanded Shanaid. "Search for Nocturnal and see what comes up. You said that's the club's name, right Bee?"

"Right," said Bianca, and Jake typed the name, muttering "Club Nocturnal... Pennsylvania. Just one picture, which is weird for a club- no pictures of the owner either... wait, there's a number!"

"Dial it!" said Shanaid, and Jake obeyed, pressing loudspeaker.

"Club Nocturnal! How can I help you?"

"Cormier!" said Bianca, shivering as she stood up, and Cormier said "Chick pea! Bianca, what took you so long to contact me, hmm?"

"Cormier, I can't flatter your ego right now- where's Angelo?"

"He has gone to find you, he's in England right this minute! London!"

"What!"

Cormier repeated it, saying "He left a week ago, but he was very weak and couldn't function. I'm guessing now he has his strength back-"

"Cormier, where in London is he?" Bianca said desperately, when Jake and Shanaid frowned.

"Strength back?"

"Cormier, please tell me how to contact him," begged Bianca. "I have something to tell him-"

"He knows you carry his child, chick pea- and he knows about Jacob Durant." Bianca swallowed, Jacob shifting uncomfortably as Cormier said "He was very angry about you not telling him about Jacob but he has calmed down. He's desperate to see you. We all are."

Bianca's eyes filled over. "Do you have the exact address of the hotel he's in?"

"Of course, do you have a pen and paper?"

"Yes," said Bianca, Shanaid handing her a pen and notepad. Cormier gave the details, Bianca saying "How's Joseph?"

"Joseph is doing fine. Much better than when you first left. He talks a little more too. And he always kisses your picture goodnight."

Tears fell down Bianca's face at that.

"I miss him so much! I miss all of you!"

"Angelo promised you things will be far from over," Cormier said gently. "Remember, he never breaks a promise."

"But it's been two months-"

"Time does not matter, chick pea. Angelo will find you. I know it."

"Thanks, Cormier." Bianca smiled through her tears. "You're the best."

"I know, I know. Oh- Clover wants to speak."

"Little sister, where are you?" Clover asked urgently. "Angelo is on his way to you right now."

"He is?" said Bianca, startled. "I'm at my friend Shanaid's house-"

"Leave there, Bianca- Angelo wants you to meet him at your closest park."

"There's no park near here! Where's the closest park, Shanaid?" asked Bianca, turning to her best friend with urgency. "Shan!"

"Duckworth Common," Shanaid replied. "Bee, it's like ten at night- your mother's going to go mad if you don't get home by half ten latest-"

"I don't care, I have to see Angelo."

"I'll drop you," Jake said. "Shanaid, call Barbara and say Bianca's staying here."

"She won't be happy-"

"Just do it, Shan!"

Shanaid obeyed, holding the phone away from her ear as Bianca's mother yelled down the line.

"Yes Ma'am but Bianca's feeling really poorly- she was sick three times today. Jake isn't here, he can't drop her back." She glared at Jake as she spoke, warning him with her eyes not to speak. "She'll be back first thing tomorrow mor- evening," she said quickly, when Bianca shook her head quickly. "Tomorrow evening. She's so tired and she has no energy.

Please let her stay."
Barbara sighed and obliged, saying "Seven in the evening latest. As a matter of fact, I will pick her up. So if you're playing games with me, Shanaid Durant-"
"I'm not," Shanaid said quickly. "You can pick her up at seven sharp."
"Good."
Shanaid ended the call the same time Bianca said goodbye to Clover, then Cormier, saying to Jake "Let's go."

* * Angelo * *

She is on her way, brother.

Angelo, I spoke to Bianca. She's on her way.

Angelo breathed out, relieved at the mind messages from cousin Clover and Cormier. He waited, invisible, staring across the lake at the park entrance. He sighed, tightening his cloak as the wind blew.
Twenty minutes later a sleek silver car pulled up at the park entrance, Angelo watching with bated breath as two figures stepped out.

* * Bianca * *

"You want me to come with you?"
Bianca shook her head. "No."
"Sure?" asked Jake, and she said yes. "Bee, I'm not comfortable leaving you in a pitch black park far from home, alone with some guy you had a fling with overseas. You haven't know him that long, I mean… anything could happen."
"Nothing will happen, Jake. Angelo will protect me like he always has."
Jake scowled. "All right. I'll wait here."
"It's okay, Jake. You can go."
"No way," said Jake incredulously. "I'm waiting right here. Take however long you need to with him, I don't mind. But I'm not leaving."
Bianca sighed her ok. "I'll be back soon."
She turned and walked away, taking a deep breath.
He was here. She knew it. She could feel him. The closer she walked towards the lake the stronger his presence felt. She didn't know how she could feel him so intensely, but she could.
"Angelo," she whispered, heart racing as she stopped by some trees. There was no reply. "Angelo, show yourself."
Angelo materialised, staring at her. Bianca stared back at him, then he walked towards her and pulled her into his arms in an amorous hug.

Bianca couldn't stop the sob as she hugged him back, tears falling as she whispered "I missed you so much."

Angelo's eyes pricked as he softly said "I missed you more."

Bianca stood on tiptoe and kissed him, Angelo kissing her back urgently, arms around her as he deepened the kiss, making her moan and pull herself away with a gasp.

"We need to go somewhere."

Angelo raised an eyebrow. "Where?"

"Anywhere," she said quietly. "I want to make love with you, Angelo. I want you."

Angelo tried to stay in control, but she was doing a hell of a good job breaking his barriers as she kissed him tenderly.

"You're with child, Bianca. Is it safe to make love to you?"

"Of course it is, and you know it is. You're psychic."

"We need to talk about the baby."

"Mmm." Bianca kissed his neck. "What about it."

"It will be here sooner than you think."

"How soon?" asked Bianca as she curved her arms around his waist, and Angelo said "In another two months."

Bianca froze. "What?"

Angelo repeated himself calmly, and she panicked: "My dad will be back in two months! You're saying he'll come back to his children and a grandchild??"

"No. He won't. Not if you come back with me to Pennsylvania."

Bianca stared at him, and he quickly said "Just until the baby's born. Then you can return, if that's what you want."

"With or without the baby?" demanded Bianca, and Angelo replied "That's entirely your choice. But it won't be a good look, you being fully pregnant in the next two months. Your mother wouldn't know what to do, what with neighbours gossiping about you, and your brother will be furious. I'm trying to keep you safe, just like I did in Pennsylvania."

Bianca smiled up at him. "I love you."

"And I love you, sweetheart." Angelo kissed her. "I'm worried, though. A decision must be made."

"I'll come back to Pennsylvania," she said quietly. "As soon as possible."

"Are you sure?"

"I'm definitely sure. When can we go?"

"We'll give it a week before we leave," Angelo said. "In that time-"

He broke off, shuddering.

"Angelo?" said Bianca worriedly, as his eyes began to glow scarlet. "Angelo, are you all right?"

"It... it seems I am losing my strength... rapidly," he said, taking a deep breath. "I must return to the hotel. I have a mobile phone, though. I purchased one."

"How?" said Bianca curiously. "You can't function in the day."

"I can, but only for five hours. I made a sacrifice of my blood to the spirits of the Underworld, to find you in three weeks. I had to find you, Bianca. I couldn't wait any longer."

Touched, Bianca took his hand. He looked at her, eyes gleaming as she said "Never make such a sacrifice for me again. Promise me."

"I cannot promise," Angelo said weakly. "Take my mobile number, Bianca, and use it to contact me. I must leave."

Bianca obeyed, then she pulled him and kissed him one more time before she released him.

"Go," she said softly. "Get your energy back."

"Will you be all right getting home?"

"Sure I will. Now get out of here."

Angelo obeyed, vanishing.

Bianca slowly walked back through the park towards the entrance. Jake got out of the car, spotting her immediately.

"Everything ok?"

"Everything's great. But complicated. I need to talk to my Dad."

* * Angelo * *

Angelo fell into bed, panting.

He'd never felt so weak in all the time he'd been a vampire. He needed his elder brother, sending him a mind message.

Brother. Help me.

* * Cormier * *

Cormier teleported right away without a second thought, reappearing in Angelo's hotel bedroom.

Angelo laid unconscious, on top of his bed covers. Cormier swore, looking around for a knife or sharp object as Angelo stirred.

"B-brother..."

"I'm here, Angelo. I'm here."

Angelo was bloodthirsty. It looked like six years without blood was the maximum length of time he could go without it.

Finding a knife, fork and spoon, Cormier neatly slit his own wrist and held it to Angelo's mouth, murmuring "Drink, Angelo."

Angelo obeyed, weak as ever, eyes still closed. He seemed to grow stronger with each pull on Cormier's wrist, each swallow of his brother's blood. Cormier watched as the scarlet glow in his eyes grew dimmer and dimmer, finally disappearing.

Angelo pushed Cormier away with a sharp intake of breath, then he placed a hand on Cormier's wound and removed it, Cormier glancing at his wrist.

It was healed.

"Thank you."

"Thank *you,* " Angelo said, then he shook his head. "I saw Bianca."

"Yes, I know. I spoke to her."

"You did?" Angelo looked at him sharply. "When?"

"Moments before cousin Clover and I sent you a mind message."

"All right." Angelo stood, feeling revitalised. "You realise she carries a child that is part vampire?"

"I know."

"But if I bite her, then she and that child will be full vampires."

"I don't think that's a good idea, Angelo. The child will need to go to school."

"It can go to the school for vampire and wolf children. What's wrong with that?" asked Angelo. "Joseph will be going there in a year's time."

"You have to discuss this with Bianca, not I," Cormier said, shrugging a shoulder. "And don't call her. It's not something you put in a phone conversation. Oh, and your time is running out. You have just under two weeks before your gift from the spirits expires."

"I know," Angelo said. "Will you go back now?"

"Yes. If you need me, send me a mind message."

"I will. And thank you for helping me."

"You're my brother. I couldn't do anything else."

Cormier vanished.

* * Bianca * *

Bianca finished speaking, Jake and Shanaid shocked.

"So you're just going to go back to Pennsylvania with him? What if he bites you?" demanded Shanaid. Bianca had finally told the pair of them totally everything, from the night she met Angelo till the time she had to leave. "Or you're attacked again? This doesn't sound like a good idea-"

"I never said it was a good idea but it's what I want. In another two weeks, I won't be able to hide my stomach. The baby will be here in two months and it's part vampire. I don't even know if it can handle daylight," Bianca added thoughtfully. "What do you want me to do?"

"I want you to see sense," Shanaid said desperately. "Anything could happen to you out there-"

"Shan, I'm nineteen years old. Relax, ok?"

"Listen to her," Jake said, when Shanaid opened her mouth to retort. "I'm down for it, Bee."

"You are?" said Bianca, looking at him as he said yes. "Really?"

"Really," he said softly. "But you need to call your dad and tell him exactly what's going on. He needs to know you're pregnant and he needs to know you're leaving."

Bianca's mobile went off: she glanced at the screen. It read Private Number.

"Hello, who's calling please?"

"It's me, sweetheart."

"Angelo," she said breathlessly. "Are you ok now?"

"I'm fine. I was very weak but I'm all right now."

"Well, I told Jake and Shanaid everything," Bianca said. "Jake thinks it's a good idea to go."

She couldn't see him, but she knew Angelo cringed.

"Does he."

"Yep. Um… how are we getting there?"

"By flight," Angelo replied. "Are you sure this is what you want, Bianca?"

"I'm sure," she said firmly. "I just need to talk to my Dad."

* * *

The next evening, Barbara was at Shanaid's house at seven p.m. on the dot, beeping her car horn.

"Exactly on time," grinned Shanaid. "Good luck, Bee."

"Thanks," muttered Bianca, and Jake kissed her on the cheek.

"Call me if you need anything."

"Jake, I-"

"It's okay. Really." Jake looked heartbroken as he spoke, and Bianca's eyes filled. "I guess I took too long to make you mine."

Shanaid pulled Bianca into a hug, saying "Will you visit this week? You have to visit before you go-"

Barbara beeped again, then she rolled down her window and shouted "Bianca!"

"I'm coming!" said Bianca irritably, and Barbara said "I'm going to count to seven! If you're not in this car by the time I count to seven, you live here!"

"Wouldn't that be great!" snapped Bianca, and Barbara said "Four!"

"You're meant to start at one!"

"Five!"

"I'll see you guys later," Bianca said dully, and she walked towards her mother's car.

"Six!"

Bianca hurriedly got in the passenger seat and buckled herself in as Barbara said "Seven."

"I need to talk to Dad," Bianca said, and Barbara replied "You're not going on any adventures, Bianca- not after what happened to Richard."

"Look, I never said I want to go away with him! I said I want to talk to him! So can I please call him? I know you have his number!"

"Fine. You can use my phone," Barbara answered as she started the car and pulled away from Shanaid's house. "And I think tomorrow me and you need to go to the hospital."

Bianca looked at her mother sharply. "For what?"

"You've been vomiting almost every day for over three weeks," was her mother's reply. "I want to know why. You might have some sort of bug that could infect others."

"FYI? It's been two months," Bianca said angrily. "If it could infect others you and Ricky would be vomiting too. And it's not a bug. I know what's wrong with me."

"Well whatever it is, it needs fixing. So we're going to the hospital."

"I need to talk to Dad," Bianca repeated stonily, and Barbara replied "Well if you think you're talking to him in private you've got another thing coming."

Bianca lost her temper. "Why are you so difficult?!"

"Why are you so stubborn?" Barbara retorted. "What I say goes. It's my house. Abide by my rules or get out."

"I will get out," Bianca said frustratedly. "If I never see you again I'll be over the damn moon!"

"You don't mean that."

"The hell I don't!"

"What have you got against me?" demanded Barbara, Bianca saying "Everything! You just-" She stopped, feeling nauseous. "I'm going to be sick."

Barbara pulled the car over, Bianca getting out and vomiting over some bushes. She held her stomach as she threw up again, Barbara watching curiously.

"Bianca?"

"Just leave me alone," gasped Bianca, and a hooded stranger walked up to them as Barbara angrily said "What's wrong with you?!"

"Leave me alone!"

"Bianca-"

"Leave her," the hooded stranger said smoothly, making Barbara stop short. The stranger helped Bianca to her feet, Bianca shivering. "Sweetheart. Are you all right?"

"Angelo?" she said weakly, and Angelo said "Yes."

Bianca hugged him, and he held her tightly as she whispered "I love you."

"And I love you."

"Wait wait wait. What the *hell* is going on?!" cried Barbara, when Angelo kissed Bianca's forehead. "Who are you?! Where did you come from- and how the hell did you know Bianca was here in this exact spot?!"

"Mum, can you not freak out?" snapped Bianca. "I don't want to deal with that. This is Angelo Heathen, the man I stayed with in Pennsylvania. He knew I was here because I saw him and I spoke to him on the phone."

"Well how did he know *exactly* where you were?? We was driving, for God's sake!"

"I always know where Bianca is," Angelo said politely. "I'm just making sure she is ok. Travel sickness, was it not?" he said to Bianca, and she nodded, saying "Definitely travel sickness."

"I can walk you the rest of the way home if your mother obliges."

Bianca looked at her mother. "Mum?"

"We're fifteen minutes away by car," Barbara started, Angelo saying "Then it should be roughly half an hour by foot. Will you allow me to walk Bianca home? I'll bring her straight there but I do need to talk with her. Alone."

Something in his voice, maybe the smoothness, made Barbara shiver.

And in a very heated away.

"All right. Bring her straight home. Bianca, will you be all right with-with-"

"Angelo Heathen," Angelo said. "And yes, she will be fine."

"Show me your face," Barbara said, unable to handle Angelo's baritone. She thought she was going mad. When Angelo said no, she added "Please."

"If I show my face you will not forget it," Angelo said kindly. "Maybe you will see it in due time."

"Mum, just go," Bianca said weakly. "I'll see you in a bit."

Barbara hesitated, then she slowly got in her car, started it up, then pulled away.

Angelo turned and looked at Bianca, who threw her arms around him in a hug as she whispered "I can't wait to go to Pennsylvania with you."

"I can't wait either," admitted Angelo. "The flight is booked and I have the tickets. You just need to pack whatever you want to bring and break the news to your family."

He took her hand, and they began walking.

"You're nineteen now."

Bianca nodded. "Yep."

"Would you like a belated gift for your birthday?"

Bianca shook her head, smiling "No. You being with me is all I need, all I'll ever need."

Angelo smiled. "That was sweet of you to say."

"I don't know if I'll be all right on the plane," Bianca said thoughtfully. "I might keep vomiting."

"The plane staff will help you. You just need to let them know the condition you are in. I'm sure they can treat you."

Bianca nodded.

* * Ricky * *

Ricky walked into the kitchen where his mother sat drinking a glass of red wine. She finished her glass, then poured herself another.

Ricky frowned at her. "Mum? What's up?"

"I saw a man- a very, *very* appealing sounding man," Barbara said, shaking her head as Ricky frowned at her.

"An appealing *sounding* man?"

"Yes."

"What the hell does that mean? You like his voice?"

"His voice," sighed Barbara. "I couldn't see his face, but his voice-"

"Why couldn't you see his face?" demanded Ricky, then he stopped, a sense of dread creeping up on him. "Where's Bianca?"

"She's with him. He said if I saw his face, I wouldn't forget it, but he said his name was Angelo Heathen-"

"Count Angelo!" gasped Ricky. "He's here??"

Barbara stared at him. "You know this man?"

"Of course I know him! He's the flipping guy Bianca stayed with in Pennsylvania- what the hell is he doing here??"

Before his mother could answer Bianca let herself in the house, calling "I'm back."

Ricky limped towards her, demanding "Where's Count Angelo?"

"He's gone, you gay pig. I know you want him."

"Shut up," snapped Ricky, when Barbara gaped. "Where is he staying?"

"In a hotel in Central London," Bianca replied. "I need to call Dad."

"What for?"

"That's private. Mum, can I have the number please?"

Barbara obeyed, blasting Bianca with questions that Bianca didn't answer, dialling on the house phone.

"Come on Dad, pick up…"

"Hi!"

"Dad!"

"Sorry, I can't take your call right now. Please leave a message, and if it's important, I'll get back to you as soon as possible."

Bianca slammed the phone down, tears falling down her face as she swore.

"Why the hell isn't he answering?!"

"What's so urgent that you have to call your father?" demanded Barbara, Ricky staring at his little sister. "Bianca!"

* * Bianca * *

Bianca ignored her, trying Samuel's phone again.

"Don't ignore me, Bianca! I will cut the phone cord on you fast as lightning, so you'd better start talking fast! What is going on?!"

"Mum, can you just be quiet!" said Bianca angrily, then her face lit up. "Dad!"

"Sorry, I can't take your call right now. Please leave a message, and if it's important, I'll get back to you as soon as possible."

Bianca swore angrily as Barbara yelled she wanted an explanation.

Bianca closed her eyes and tried to block her mother's voice out, then Ricky started too: "What's going on, Bianca? Why is Count Angelo in England?"

"For me, you idiot!! Why else?!" Bianca nearly screamed the words. "He came for me because he couldn't stand being away from me!"

"Well when is he going back?!" Ricky was shouting back at her now. "He just comes down here like it's normal?? How the hell did he manage getting around in daylight, anyway?! When is he going back?!""

"At the end of the week!" screamed Bianca. "And he's taking me with him! He asked me to come and I said yes, and we're leaving at the end of the week! Want to know something else?! I'M PREGNANT WITH HIS CHILD!!!"

Ricky and Barbara gasped as Bianca, sobbing, slammed the house phone down again. She ran out of the kitchen up the stairs, Barbara shouting "Bianca!"

Her bedroom door slammed in answer.

* * Ricky * *

"Hello, Samuel speaking."

"Dad! Dad, you've got to come home," said Ricky angrily. "Count Angelo's here and he's taking Bianca at the end of the week, and Bianca's having his flipping baby!"

"WHAT!!"

"You heard," snapped Barbara, snatching the phone off her son. "Bianca nearly had a nervous breakdown, the way she was screaming at us. She's been vomiting for weeks. And now we find out she's pregnant for a foreigner! A very sexy foreigner, mind! But *she's pregnant!!"*

"Calm down," Samuel said, though he was taking deep breaths. "I want to speak to her. Go and get her, Ricky. Now!"

Ricky obeyed, limping into the hallway as his mother took the phone to berate his father.

* * Bianca * *

Bianca sobbed and sobbed, not answering Ricky when he knocked on her door.
"Bianca, come out. Please."
"So you can shout at me with Mum?"
"No," he said gently. "When was you going to tell me you slept with Count Angelo?"
"I wasn't," Bianca replied, sitting up as her stomach churned. She leapt up and dashed out of her bedroom into the bathroom, being neatly sick in the toilet as her mother called her name sharply.
"Bianca! Come and speak to your father."
Shivering, Bianca stood and flushed the toilet, then she quickly used the mouth wash and, still shaking, made her way downstairs.

* * Angelo * *

Angelo removed his cloak and sat on the edge of his bed, thinking. Would the baby be a boy or girl? What would it look like? And would it have his last name or Bianca's?
He smiled, thinking that whatever the child's name would be, he'd still love it as much as he loved it's mother.

* * Bianca * *

"So you're going to have the baby and come back?"
"I don't know," wept Bianca, and Samuel said "What do you mean you don't know?? Bianca-"
"Dad, don't do this- please," she sobbed. "I'm leaving with Angelo and I'm going to have the baby in Pennsylvania. I've made up my mind- please don't try and talk me out of it. Please, Dad."
"And if you decide to stay," Samuel said, dreading the idea but being realistic, "Will we be welcome in Count Angelo's castle to come and visit you and the baby?"
"I'll ask, but I know you'll definitely be welcome," Bianca said, smiling through her tears. "Does this mean you'll let me go?"
"You're not a child, Bianca. You can make your own decisions," Samuel said gently. "I just want you to be safe, protected. I know Count Angelo will make sure you are."
Bianca breathed out, relieved. "I love you, Dad."
"I love you too. Put your mother on the phone."
Barbara snatched the phone, furious.
"So you're just going to let her go, Samuel? Just like that?!"

"Barbara, give it a rest," Samuel said wearily. "You've been chewing my ear off about Bianca since we got back. She's not a kid, ok? I've met this guy, I've met his brother. I've seen the castle. She's not going to live in a tiny rundown flat, she's going to live in a *castle*. Angelo Heathen rules the land, he's well known and respected. I trust him. You should do the same, and for Heaven's sake stop smothering Bianca. That's why she's so wild. You keep trying to force properness down her throat. Just let her be, Barbara. Please."

Barbara opened her mouth, then closed it. "All right. Fine."

Bianca and Ricky gaped at her.

"Fine??"

"You heard," Barbara said curtly. "Bianca, we're going shopping for the baby tomorrow. And Ricky, you need your scars to be checked and a blood test at the hospital, dead on three, so Bianca, we'll have to go shopping in the morning. Set both of your alarms and go to bed while I talk to your father."

When both of them still stood staring at her disbelievingly as if she'd just sprouted eagle wings and a crocodile tail, she snapped "Bed. Now!"

"Night," muttered Ricky, Bianca mumbling the same.

* * Angelo * *

Angelo smiled as he listened to Bianca speak, then he said "That's wonderful, sweetheart. I'm so glad your family isn't going to try and stop you. That would have made things very awkward."

"I spoke to my grandmother. She's all right with it as well, but she's worried about Patricia and the Neffy Pack."

"The Nefarious Pack."

"Yep, that's what I meant."

Angelo laughed. "What did you tell your grandmother?"

"I told her not to worry. I said I'd call as often as I can and I'll definitely see her soon. She was crying, you know."

"I can imagine."

"So what did you say to Cormier and the rest? What did they say?"

"They are all overjoyed you are returning. And they're excited about the baby."

"And the vampires out there? Your community? What will they think?"

Angelo smiled. "They will want to celebrate, of course."

"At the club?"

"Probably all over town and in the castle. It has at least five halls everyone can come and party in. Bear in mind many may have to stay over."

"Well I don't mind as long as you trust them," Bianca said. "I don't want to get bitten. Unless it's by you."

Angelo smiled at that. "I couldn't bite you, Bianca."

"You could."

"All right, I *won't* bite you. Is that better?"

"I suppose. So what happens if a vampire wants to bite me at the celebrations?"

"Cormier and Sebastian will keep them all in check. As will I." Angelo shuddered, head swimming as Bianca said "All right. I trust you."

"Something is wrong with me," Angelo said, a little weakly. "I keep getting peculiar urges for blood. Cormier satisfied me with his own, but now it seems I want more."

"Six years was a long time to go without it," Bianca said softly. "I'm not surprised. Are you actually bloodthirsty, though?"

Angelo said no.

"If I were, I couldn't talk to you so easily. I'd be terribly weak."

"Well it sounds like you're growing weak," Bianca said, a little worriedly. "Call Room Service and ask them for raw meat and a large glass of milk. Do it, Angelo."

"Bianca-"

"Now," she said firmly, and Angelo sighed and obeyed, Bianca saying

"I'm staying on the line until they bring it."

"You worry for me."

"Of course I do-"

Angelo heard someone rap on Bianca's door.

"Bed, Bianca!"

"I am in bed!"

"Well get off the phone," Barbara Smith said. "It's late and we're getting up early tomorrow."

"Look, Angelo isn't feeling too good and I'm staying on the line until Room Service brings him something to eat, ok?!"

"Twenty more minutes, and if you're not off the phone I'm taking it from you," was Barbara's reply. "I'll be checking."

"Fine, whatever!"

Angelo chuckled. "I do like your mother, Bianca."

"She drives me up the wall," Bianca replied, as there was a knock on the hotel door, someone calling "Room Service!"

Angelo stood and opened the door, ushering the people in.

"Leave everything on the desk."

"Yes sir," the man and woman said humbly, then the woman said "Would you like me to stay with you, sir?"

Angelo stared at her, sensing the woman's lust. "Stay?"

"Yes sir."

"What for?"

The maid smiled naughtily. "For whatever you need."

"For Heaven's sake Susan," snapped the male servant. "Sir, I apologise. She's had a thing about you ever since you checked in. You didn't notice she's the one who does all the chores in this room?"

"I-"

"The bed making? The bathroom cleaning? Everything??"

"I truly didn't notice," Angelo said truthfully. "Now if you'll excuse me-"

"What'll you do with all that bloody meat, sir?" Susan asked interestedly. "You got a pet doggy in here or something?"

"Angelo," Bianca said, startling him; he forgot she was still on the phone. "Put me on loudspeaker."

Angelo obeyed as the staff continued to gaze at him, and Bianca said "To the maid who's desperate. Back the hell up or get *smacked* the hell up. I won't hesitate to come down to that hotel and dun you."

"And who are you?" demanded Susan, while Angelo made a mental note to ask Bianca what "dun you" meant.

"I'm his girlfriend. His wifey. His *baby-mamma.* Do you want me to come down there and make a complaint after I whoop your behind?"

Susan didn't reply.

"Didn't think so. Now find someone else to clean after my man. If I find you've so much as *breathed* in his direction-"

"Easy, Bianca," Angelo murmured, highly amused as Bianca said "I will come down there fast as lightning. Do we understand each other?"

"Yes," said Susan, and Bianca said "Good. Now leave. Both of you!"

The hotel staff quickly hurried out of the room, and Angelo couldn't help but chuckle admiringly.

"Fire will always be a word to describe you, Bianca Davis."

* * Bianca * *

Bianca smiled, head on her pillow. "Thanks. Now eat your meat and drink your milk. That should sustain you."

"How can you be so sure?"

"Cormier told me when we met," Bianca replied. "He said milk gives vampires energy when they aren't feeding on another. Raw meat does too, I know it does. So eat and drink up."

"Yes Ma'am."

"Good. Now-"

"Bianca, get off that phone this minute!"

"Mum! Five more minutes, ok?!"

"Five more *this* minute! Tell the person you'll speak tomorrow." Barbara opened Bianca's door and stood, hand on hip. "I'm waiting."

"Angelo, I'll call you tomorrow," Bianca muttered, and Angelo said "Goodnight, sweetheart."

Bianca pressed the red button, lifting her head to scowl at Barbara.

"Happy now?"

"Very. Have a good night."

Bianca rolled her eyes and dived under her covers, not answering.

* * Angelo * *

Fully energized, Angelo sat up and looked at his phone, knowing he had to thank Bianca. The girl was a genius.

But he knew her mother would go ham if he called, so he sent a text before settling down in bed, turning on the television.

* * Bianca * *

"Thank you so much, sweetheart. I feel much better. C.A."

Bianca smiled, then her phone rang. Quickly turning off her bedroom light, she pressed answer and whispered "Hello."
"Bee, it's Jake."
"Hey," she said softly. "You ok?"
"I'm just overwhelmed, Bee," sighed Jake. "You're leaving."
"You'll see me again, Jake. I promise."
"But you'll never be mine like you was before you went to Pennsylvania."
"Well that was your fault." Bianca was nonchalant as she said "You never made me yours so I was pretty much available to whoever took my fancy."
"Yeah. I know."
Bianca sighed. "Let's not do this. I'd rather we stay as friends instead of enemies."
"But we was never really friends, were we Bee?" Jake said quietly. "From day one we loved each other."
"Well like I implied, you're the one who screwed up by stalling us being together. I guess I got tired of waiting," she added thoughtfully. "I'm with Angelo now. You may as well accept that."
"I'm trying to. I just want you to know that-"
"That what?"
"That I've always loved you," Jake said softly. "And I always will."
Bianca's eyes filled. She took a deep breath, then she whispered "Goodnight, Jake."
"Night."
She hung up, stuffing the phone under her pillow.

* * *

Bianca and Barbara walked through Mothercare World, Barbara selecting yet another baby outfit.

"This is gorgeous!"

"Mum, it's blue. Can we stick to unisex colours please?" Bianca said, sighing. "Like yellow and pastel green and that. And red, I guess."

"Look, they have it in yellow." Pleased, Barbara switched outfits, then she looked at her daughter thoughtfully. "Your stomach isn't as flat as it was a few days ago."

"Must be all the muffins I ate," shrugged Bianca, and Barbara said "Don't be silly, it's obviously the baby."

"Can we hurry up and buy the clothes, please? I'm starving."

"What do you fancy?"

"Chinese food."

"Well I'm taking you straight home after we buy the baby clothes. You can have Chinese food for dinner."

"So what can I have for lunch?" said Bianca, highly amused as her mother said "Whatever you fancy, I suppose."

"All right. I want a foot long sandwich from Subway."

Barbara turned to pout at her daughter. "You'll get incredibly fat if you keep eating like a pig."

"Mum, all I had was tea this morning. Give me a break, ok? I'm hungry."

"All right, we'll get your sandwich. Minus the cheese."

"Cheese is what *makes* the sandwich, Mum."

Shaking her head, Bianca followed her mother to the checkout.

* * Angelo * *

Wincing, Angelo woke up.

Sunlight flooded his bedroom, harsh on his skin, which was burning at the feel of the sun. Angelo quickly got up and drew his curtains, then he picked up his mobile to call Bianca.

* * Bianca * *

Bianca sipped from her cup of Coke, gazing out of the car window.

"So will you come back after the baby's born, Bianca? Or not?"

"Mum, I don't know. The baby hasn't even been born yet. If I did come back, it would be when the baby's one probably."

"So you'd be gone for an entire year??"

"Yep. There a problem with that?"

"There's plenty of problems," Barbara said, and Bianca sighed, waiting for it. "Your father doesn't seem to mind. Well, he does a little, but he says it's your choice and he accepts that."

"So why can't you accept it?" Bianca asked shrewdly, and Barbara said "Because I'm your mother. I really think that you should have the baby here."

"I can't."

"Why not?"

"It's hard to explain."

"Try me."

Bianca's mobile rang as she pondered telling her mother the baby would be part vampire and may not be able to handle the light of day.

"Hello?"

"Bianca, it's Shanaid. Can you come to mine?"

"I wish I could Shan," Bianca said apologetically. "I'm real tired. I went clothes shopping with my mother, for the baby. I just want to sleep."

"Oh," Shanaid said disappointedly. "Well, what about when you wake up? I want to spend as much time with you as possible before you go jetting off to Pennsylvania."

"I'll call you when I wake up, Shan. I promise."

Bianca ended the call, sipping more of her Coke, then Barbara said "So tell me. Why can't you have the baby here?"

"Because-"

Bianca's mobile rang again, Barbara saying "For Heaven's sake! Is your mobile a hotline all of a sudden??"

"This is the second call, Mum! Jesus! Hello?"

"Hello," he said softly, and Bianca said "Angelo," just as softly.

Barbara said nothing, trying to listen while she drove.

"I can't thank you enough for helping me last night. The meat and milk really did the trick."

"I thought it would." Bianca smiled. "Now you know what to do if you feel weak again."

"I do. Thank you."

"You're welcome."

"What are you doing now, Bianca?"

"I'm on my way home in my mother's car, sipping on Coke and digesting a Subway sandwich. You?"

"I'm in my hotel room, rubbing oil all over my body."

Bianca swallowed at that. "Oil?"

"Yes." Bianca's heart began to race as he said "The curtains were open when I woke up, so the sun pretty much stung my skin."

"Must have been the hotel staff," Bianca said, trying to sound as casual as she could, but she couldn't help picturing Angelo topless, oiling his brown chest and eight pac. She could barely get the words out as she said "Mum, can I go see Angelo please?"

"I thought you said you wanted to sleep?" Barbara replied, and Bianca said "Mum! I'm going to a *hotel*. There is a *bed* in the hotel. I will *sleep* in that bed, in the damn hotel! Can you drop me please? It's only one o clock, you'll get back in time for Ricky's appointment."

"No."

"Please!!"

"All right," snapped Barbara, not wanting Bianca to start whining. "But you're not spending the night there. You know how I feel about you spending the night at places. I'm picking you up tonight."

"Ok, fine! Just call me when you're on your way so I can get dressed-"

"What?!"

"Get ready!" gushed Bianca, and Angelo burst out laughing. "I meant get ready. Stop laughing, Angelo!"

Still she couldn't help laughing a little as well, Barbara glaring as she drove.

"Bianca, I will see you when you get here," chuckled Angelo, and Bianca smiled as she said "All right. See you soon."

* * Ricky * *

"So it will just be me and you with Gran it looks like."

"Yes Dad."

"And Ricky, don't do anything to spoil this. I know you don't like the vampires. I have my reservations too," Samuel said, Ricky holding the phone to his ear. "But if we put our foot down Bianca will never forgive us. I just want her to be happy. So let her go."

"Just until the baby's born, right?" Ricky asked, and Samuel didn't answer. "She has the baby and then she can come back, right?"

Silence.

"Dad?" said Ricky uncertainly. "She's coming back when the baby's born, right?"

Samuel sighed. "It's totally up to her."

"What!"

"You heard me, Ricky."

"But-"

"Richard!" called Barbara sharply as she let herself into the house. "Are you ready to go to the hospital? Are you dressed!"

"I'll be down in a minute," Ricky called, then he said "Dad, you can't possibly be thinking of letting her stay with them- what if they bite her or something??"

"Count Angelo will protect her."

"Dad! Are you serious?!"

"Look, discuss it with Bianca. You've got a week before she leaves," Samuel said. "If you change her mind it will be a miracle. But I doubt you can."

* * Angelo * *

There was a timid knock on his door.

Angelo got up instantly, taking a breath before he walked towards the door, sensing her.

"Who is it?"

"Room Service!"

Angelo frowned as he opened the door. "I didn't order any-"

Bianca reached up and kissed him before he could finish his sentence, making the hotel staff stop and stare enviously. When she broke away with a smile, he breathed "Bianca."

"Who else?" she smiled, and he drew her inside the room, closing the door behind her.

Bianca smiled as she stepped out of her shoes, looking around.

"It's so neat in here."

"Well, I'm not an untidy Count. Besides, all I have to do is snap my fingers and everywhere is spotless."

"True."

"Would you like to speak to Joseph, Bianca?" Angelo asked. "I was going to call Cormier and check how he is."

"Umm, no. I want to surprise him," smiled Bianca, and Angelo smiled back, saying ok as he dialled on his mobile.

"Looks like you've got the hang of mobile phones," said Bianca, and Angelo said "I was against it at first, but now I realise I do need one. Especially to reach you."

He held the phone to his ear, smiling when Cormier answered.

"Brother! Somehow the news has leaked that Bianca is returning to Pennsylvania."

"With child?" asked Angelo, eyes lighting scarlet, and Cormier said "No, not with child. But everyone knows she's coming back."

Angelo calmed down a little. Taking a breath, he said "And the reaction was?"

"Mainly positive. Plus everyone is desperate for the storms you've been causing to cease."

Angelo smiled. "I suppose I can stop the storms. I am feeling jubilant, after all."

"Good. Because cousin Clover and Marissa were complaining about their shoes being ruined by the heavy rain." Cormier chuckled. "And I don't want to take Joseph out in the storm in case he falls ill. So ease them!"

"I'll ease them when I return," Angelo said, smiling broadly now. "For now, I really must get back to-"

He broke off with a gasp, staring at Bianca, who was laying on his bed-
wearing nothing.

Nothing at all.
Angelo gaped at her, heart racing. How did she undress without him noticing??

* * Cormier * *

"Brother? Are you there?" said Cormier. "Get back to what?"
"Nothing," said Angelo hoarsely. "I must go, brother."
"Get back to what?" Cormier repeated curiously. "What is so urgent?"
"I... I-"
"Angelo, you're not making sense," said Cormier, growing annoyed, then Clover took the phone, saying "Angelo? Are you all right?"
"I must go," gushed Angelo, and before Clover or Cormier could say something else the line went dead.
Cormier and Clover looked at each other, bemused. Then Clover said "He must be with Bianca."
"I don't doubt it," said Cormier, amused now. "I wonder what she did that distracted him so?"

* * Angelo * *

Panting, Angelo fell to Bianca's side.
"Don't you ever do that again," he said weakly, Bianca taking deep breaths as well as she managed "I will if it takes my fancy."
Angelo smiled at her. "You're a bad girl."
Bianca smiled back. "I was as good as gold before I met you."
"That's a lie," Angelo said, highly amused. "You was a rebel from day one."
Bianca snuggled up to him, and he put his arm around her.
"I love you, Bianca Davis."
"And I love you, Angelo Heathen."
Sleep was creeping up on both of them, like it always did when they were sexually satisfied.
"Does this hotel have good food?" mumbled Bianca, eyes closed, and Angelo drew her closer into his arms as he replied "Not as good as Cormier's but I suppose it will do when we wake up."
"Mmm. Ok."

* * Bianca * *

When Bianca snapped awake, it was dark outside.

Angelo was fast asleep, though he stirred when she sat up, hearing her stomach rumble.

Smiling, he muttered "I think it's time for you to eat."

"All right. Is there a menu?"

"Of course. On the desk," he said, sitting up and running a hand through his hair. "I'm surprised your mother hasn't called."

"She probably has," shrugged Bianca as she got up and picked up the hotel's menu. "Mmm, pizza. I fancy pizza."

Angelo smiled at her as she picked up her mobile and looked at the screen. She sighed, saying "Yep. Thirteen missed calls."

Angelo gaped at her. "But I didn't hear a thing."

"I put the phone on silent," shrugged Bianca, and he stared at her. "Don't look at me like that. I didn't want her to disturb us. And I needed to sleep, get my energy back."

"Call her," Angelo replied, and Bianca pouted.

"Can't I have my pizza first?"

"No."

Bianca scowled at him before she obeyed, calling her mother. She winced when Barbara answered, because she was yelling down the line.

"Bianca Davis, if you ever pull a stunt like this again-"

"What stunt? You knew where I was! It's not like I ran away for six days, is it??"

"I'm coming for you right now, so get ready!"

"I'm about to get something to eat!" said Bianca angrily, Barbara saying "And how long will that take you?!"

"Wait for an hour, then come and get me. I really, *really* have a craving for pizza and I'm about to order some."

Barbara sighed. "Fine. Richard was really worried about you."

"Richard is gay," Bianca said flatly. "He probably asked you to tell Angelo to bring me home."

Barbara paused. "Yes he did."

"See? Totally gay. He wants Angelo so bad, you'd be shocked. He'd sweat like a pig if Angelo kept his eyes on him for ten seconds."

Angelo burst out laughing. "Don't be so mean, Bianca."

"It's the truth," smirked Bianca. "Mum, I'll see you in a bit."

* * Angelo * *

"Would you like me to walk you to her car?" Angelo asked, but Bianca said no.

"I don't want the female staff ogling you."

Angelo laughed. "All right. Well, I will see you soon I hope?"

"Tomorrow night," Bianca promised. "I have to see Shanaid before she murders me for not seeing her."

"The two of you are very close."

"Yep. BFF's for life."

Angelo frowned at her. "BFF?"

"Best Friends Forever," smiled Bianca, and he smiled back.

"That's very sweet."

Bianca's mobile went and she answered, annoyed: "I'll be right down!"

"Hurry up!" said Barbara, just as annoyed. "I can't stay outside of the hotel entrance or even this street without buying a parking ticket, so say your goodbyes and get down here!"

"All right," snapped Bianca, and Angelo smiled as she hung up, pulling her into his arms and lowering his mouth to hers in a tender, almost shy kiss.

"Tomorrow?"

"Definitely tomorrow," breathed Bianca, and he kissed her again.

* * Bianca * *

Bianca fell into bed, smiling as she sent a text to Shanaid.

Saw Angelo. Had the greatest time. Wuu2?

Shanaid called instead of texting back.
"Had the greatest time, huh?"
"Yep."
"Did you pick out some clothes for the baby?"
"Of course. Well, Mum picked most of them," Bianca said thoughtfully. "But they were all super cute."
"Great!"
"Where's Jake?" asked Bianca, and Shanaid said "Jake's gone for a drive with some chick he met at McDonalds."
Bianca sat up. "What?"
"Don't make me repeat it. He's so stupid sometimes."
"Well, I'm not bothered anyway," lied Bianca. "I'm leaving at the end of the week so it's cool. I-"
She stopped as she heard Shanaid's front door open and close, Jake calling "I'm back, Shan."
"I'm on the phone to Bianca. How was your time with that chav?"
"She's not a chav. And it was ok. I think I'll see her again. Can I speak to Bianca?"
Shanaid obliged and put Jake on the phone.
"Hey Bee," Jake said casually. "You ok?"
"So you've moved on just like that?" was Bianca's icy reply, and Jake replied "Isn't that exactly what you've done? Don't be a hypocrite, Bianca."
"Jake-"
"You think when you go to Pennsylvania I'll just be sad, distant, and depressed? Sorry Bee, it's not going to happen."
"Yeah, you won't be depressed. But you'll be angry," Bianca said. "And you'll take it out on Shanaid and anyone close to you when you really should be taking it out on me."
"Well that's my problem. Why are you even bothered?"
"Because I care about you, and I always will. So just get whatever you have to say off your chest."
"Can you please come back after the baby's born?" Jake melted just like that. "I can't bear the thought of not seeing you, of you being in a totally different part of the world."
"I won't be that far away," Bianca replied. "And it's not like I'll never see any of you again."

"But you'll be in danger over there."

"Everyone's in danger at some point in their life. They could leave home and get hit by a bus. Or have a stroke at home. No one knows what their day will be like. Life is a risk, Jake."

"You're going to a town full of vampires," Jake said, heat rising. "It's not like you'll be safe and your Count will make sure of it-"

"That's exactly what it's like."

"And what happens if-"

"Jake, stop the ear bashing and give me the phone." Shanaid took her mobile off her brother. "Bee? You there?"

"I'm here," Bianca said, sighing. "Jake said he was down for me leaving before."

"Yeah, I think he's just realised you'll be gone for a long time. It's not like you're going on a trip with your dad and he can count down the days until you come back."

"Jake used to count down the days?" Bianca asked, heart racing. "I thought only I did that."

"Nope. He did too. He'd get dead excited when you was like two or three days away from coming back to London. He was like a kid waiting for Christmas," Shanaid said amusedly, and Bianca's eyes filled. "He's going to take it so hard when you actually leave. Everyone is."

Bianca sighed as her mother rapped on her bedroom door.

"Bianca, get off the phone and go to sleep. It's nearly midnight."

"All right," said Bianca huffily. "Shan, I'll see you tomorrow."

"Brace yourself for a moody Jacob."

"Will do. See you."

Bianca hung up and turned off her bedroom light before settling down to sleep.

* * Angelo * *

"Daddy, I good!" Joseph said happily, and Angelo smiled, head on his pillow.
"Have you been eating all your vegetables, Joseph?"
"Yes," said Joseph happily, "I eat lots, Daddy!"
"Good."
"Daddy, I miss you now," Joseph said sadly, and Angelo gently said "You'll see me at the end of the week, Joseph. I promise. Put Uncle Cormier on the phone."
"Uncle Cormy, phone!" said Joseph happily, Cormier taking the phone.

* * Cormier * *

"Brother, are you well?"
"I'm fine," Angelo said truthfully. "I just can't wait to get back to all of you."
"Marissa has been missing you something fierce," Cormier said, scowling a little. "She hasn't said anything to me, but Clover told me."
"Tell Marissa she will see me soon. Five more days and then I am back."
"I'll tell her," lied Cormier. He had no intention of doing so.
"Good," said Angelo. "Now I'd better get some sleep. Put Joseph to bed at a decent time, brother."
"I will."
"Good," Angelo repeated. "How is the weather?"
"You know exactly how the weather is," said Cormier amusedly. "Your storms are still wreaking havoc."
"All right. I'll end the storms as soon as I get on the plane with Bianca."
Cormier said ok. Then he asked "Do you know the child's gender?"
"No. I don't want to know, either. I'll be happy either way."
Cormier nodded, then he remembered Angelo couldn't see him.
"Well, we're all looking forward to both of your return."
"I don't want any kind of celebration," Angelo replied. "I just want to get Bianca settled and keep her pregnancy as calm as possible."
Cormier said ok again.

* * Bianca * *

Bianca woke up to the feel of her baby bump.

She sat up slowly, running her hands over her stomach amazedly.

"Mum!"

"Yes?" called Barbara, and Bianca called "Do you have any big t-shirts I can borrow just for today?"

"What for?" demanded Barbara, already on the stairs, and Bianca said "To hide my baby from nosy neighbours!"

"Bianca, don't be ridiculous. You've naught to be ashamed of," Barbara said, entering Bianca room. "You- oh!"

"Exactly," Bianca said, looking at herself in her mirror. "I think I can still pull off my clothes. But they'll be tight and everyone will see the bump. And they'll ask questions probably."

"Let them ask," said Barbara stoutly. "There's no reason you can't wear your own clothes, Bianca."

"Well like I said, there'll be nosy neighbours out there," Bianca said, shrugging a shoulder. "If you want to risk being the talk of the town-"

"If the bump gets bigger then I will buy you maternity clothes to wear when you leave. Actually, I will. You'll need some," said Barbara, hardly listening to her daughter. "Especially if it does get bigger, which it will. Still, I'm glad you only have two months of pregnancy left to endure."

"What?" Bianca stared at her mother. "Who told you that?"

"I spoke to your father last night," Barbara replied, shrugging a shoulder. "He told me everything. He didn't leave anything out. I suppose he felt I should know."

Bianca nodded, then she said "So you understand why I should have the baby in Pennsylvania and not here in England?"

"I understand. But that doesn't mean I'm for it. The baby should know it's family."

"Oh, for God's sake-"

There was a knock on Bianca's door. "Bianca? You up?"

"I'm not decent, Ricky- I'll see you at breakfast."

Ricky said ok.

Barbara sighed as Bianca pulled her nightdress down after staring at her bump some more in the mirror.

"This is so much to take in. So the man you're going away with, by all means shouldn't exist."

"Correct." Bianca stepped into her slippers. Barbara sighed again.

"And the baby... *his* baby- will be like him? A vampire?"

"Partially," Bianca said, shrugging a shoulder. "It's nothing to worry about, Mum. I promise."

"Will the child drink milk when hungry?" demanded Barbara. "Or blood?"

Bianca burst out laughing. "Definitely milk. I promise. Now can you excuse me so I can get my shower and get dressed please?"

Barbara had a lot more to say, but she nodded and left the room.

Bianca sighed, looking at herself in the mirror.

Suddenly she felt warm inside, knowing she and Angelo had created this life. And she knew the baby would be loved dearly by both its parents.

* * Angelo * *

When Angelo woke up, it was seven in the evening. He sighed, getting up. He knew it was too late to see Bianca.

His mobile went off, and he grabbed it.

"Hello."

"Angelo?"

"Bianca," he said relieved. "Apologies for not contacting you sooner, but I've only just woken up."

"That's ok. I'm at Shanaid's, guzzling ice cream."

"How much ice cream have you had exactly?" asked Angelo, and she replied "Almost a whole tub. We're watching Titanic."

Angelo smiled. "It's a nice love story. But with tragic events."

"Yep. That's why me and Shan love it."

"All right. I'll leave you to it. What time will you be home? I'll call you then."

"Umm, Mum's picking me up at eight, so I guess you can call me at nine."

Angelo said ok, ending the call.

* * Cormier * *

"Any news on your wretched sister, Marissa?" asked Clover, Cormier serving both ladies a drink. "No one has heard from her. Is she still with the Nefarious Pack?"

"Clover, if I knew I would tell you," Marissa replied. "Patricia hasn't contacted me or even Brian. Nobody knows where she is. She's basically missing."

Clover scowled. "Well I believe she's in the depths of the forest with the werewolves."

"She may be," shrugged Marissa, "But that doesn't mean I will go looking for her. I have always been loyal to Count Angelo. What Patricia did was unacceptable."

Cormier rolled his eyes. "For the love of peace, Marissa. Now you're choosing my brother over your sister? That is pathetic."

"Shut up," snapped Marissa, as he smirked at her. "Serve the vampires waiting instead of listening to our conversation."

Cormier glared at her and turned to the vampires waiting.

"As much as I enjoy being your mixologist I must head home to a child that needs me. Sebastian will be here soon to serve my cocktails. Until then, be content with the normal drinks."

"Yes sir," the vampires said, and Cormier said goodbye to Clover, glared at Marissa again, then vanished.

* * Bianca * *

"Bianca!"

Bianca snapped awake. "What??"

"We're home," Barbara said flatly, and Bianca glared at her.

"You couldn't have nudged me awake instead of yelling the car down??"

Barbara gave her a pointed stared before she got out of the car, Bianca following suit.

"So I take it you didn't see Angelo Heathen today?" Barbara asked, once she'd made herself and Bianca a drink and they were seated at the dinner table.

"No, I didn't see him," Bianca replied, adding "You can call him Count Angelo, Mum."

"I'm not calling him that. It just reminds me of what he is."

Bianca glared at her. "Meaning?"

"Meaning I'm afraid of you going to a town full of vampires-"

"How many times must we go through this?" Bianca said exasperatedly. "I'll be fine. I promise."

"I'd feel much better if Count Angelo promises."

"Ha, you said Count Angelo."

Barbara scowled at her.

* * Angelo * *

Angelo's mobile rang.
"Hello?"
"It's me, Angelo."
"Bianca." Angelo smiled, head on his pillow. "Are you home now?"
"Yep. Um… my mother wants you to promise her you'll keep me safe from harm. You're on loudspeaker, so just promise before she does her nut."

* * Bianca * *

"I solely promise to you, the mother of Bianca, that-"
"Please, call me Barbara," Barbara said quickly, sitting down at the sound of Angelo's voice. Bianca smirked at her, saying "You have a fourth admirer from my family, Angelo."
Angelo chuckled, and Barbara shivered as he said "I solely promise that I will do whatever it takes to keep Bianca safe from harm."
"And if- if…" Barbara took a deep breath. Bianca burst out laughing.
"For God's sake, Mum! You're as bad as Richard."
"Is that Count Angelo?" Ricky asked from the hallway, and Bianca said "Yes. You want me to give you the phone?"
"What for?"
"So you can speak to him one on one."
Ricky swallowed. "About what?"
"About how much you love his chocolate skin, his golden eyes, his straight black hair-"
"Shut up, Bianca!"
Angelo burst out laughing as Barbara said "Stop teasing your brother, Bianca. Count Angelo, you have a very beautiful laugh."
"Ugh. Angelo, just make the promise and get off the line," Bianca said, shaking her head at her mother and brother. "Do you promise to keep me safe from harm?"
"I promise."
"And if I am somehow harmed, what then?"
"Then I will punish the being responsible severely."
"And is that a promise?"
"That is a promise also."
"Good." Bianca looked at her mother. "Satisfied?"
Barbara smiled. "Very."
"Good. Angelo, can you call me back in an hour?"
"Of course."
Bianca ended the call, saying to her brother "You seriously need to get a

grip. Are you always going to be a mess when you hear or see Angelo?"

Ricky opened his mouth to shoot back, but no words came. He swallowed, then he quietly said "I don't know."

"And you, Mum! You need to get a grip too," Bianca said amusedly, and Barbara pouted at her.

"What did I do?"

Bianca smirked before she batted her eyelashes and pretended to swoon.

"Please, call me Barbara. Count Angelo, you have a beautiful laugh."

"I was being friendly! And he does have a beautiful laugh," Barbara said huffily. "And a beautiful chuckle. And... just a beautiful voice. He sounds so breath-taking."

"He's gorgeous," Bianca said grudgingly. "Keep your paws off."

Ricky burst out laughing, Bianca adding "You keep your paws off too, Richard."

"Me! I didn't do anything!"

"That doesn't mean you're not sexually attacking Angelo in your imagination. I know you are."

Ricky glared at her. Barbara burst out laughing.

"Right, I'm going to make us all a mug of hot chocolate. That should calm our nerves."

"You and Richard's nerves," Bianca retorted. "Angelo isn't Jesus, you know. Can we have muffins with our hot chocolate?"

"Fine," Barbara said. "Get ready for bed, both of you, and come back down for your hot chocolate and muffins. Go."

Bianca left the kitchen, smirking at her brother.

"You may as well admit you're attracted to Angelo."

"Shut up."

* * Angelo * *

"How is everything, brother?"

"Everything is fabulous," Cormier said amusedly. "Joseph is asleep, therefore I do not have to listen for the sound of tiny pattering feet until some hours later. I'm going to have a cocktail and relax."

"And how is Marissa?"

"Marissa is pining after you as usual. Oh, and she has basically chosen you over her sister. I overheard her talking to Clover at the club."

Angelo smiled, touched. "Marissa is definitely-"

"Pathetic? I agree. I called her pathetic."

"Loyal," Angelo said, annoyed. "I was going to say loyal."

"There's a difference between being loyal and being mad in love, brother."

"Marissa is very loyal to me, Cormier."

"So she implies. She doesn't fool me nor does she fool Bianca."

Angelo sighed. "All right. Stick to that notion if it makes you feel better."

"I shall."

There was a scream in the background, Angelo sitting bolt upright.

"What was that?"

* * Cormier * *

"DADDY!!"

"Joseph has awoken," said Cormier, getting up. "He must have had a nightmare."

"Don't hang up," Angelo said. "Let me talk to him."

"All right."

* * Angelo * *

"Daddy," wept Joseph, and Angelo gently asked "Are you all right?"

"Yes Daddy."

"Are you sure?"

"Yes Daddy."

"Ok. Me and Bianca will be back soon, ok Joseph? You'll see Daddy soon."

"Bee?" said Joseph uncertainly, and Angelo said yes. "Bee come back?"

"Yes, Joseph. Bee's coming back."

"Yes!" shrieked Joseph, suddenly happy. Angelo smiled as he gushed "Uncle Cormy, Bee come back! Bee come home!"

* * Cormier * *

Cormier took the phone, smiling. "He's over the moon."

"Good," Angelo replied. "We'll see you in five days, brother."

"All right. Have a good night."

Cormier hung up, smiling as Joseph beamed up at him.

"Shall we have some hot milk and biscuits as you're awake, Joseph Heathen?"

"Yes please," Joseph said shyly. "Then see Bee?"

"We'll see Bee in four days come tomorrow. And Daddy too."

Joseph clapped his hands excitedly. "Ok!"

Marissa Bennett appeared, startling Cormier.

"Marissa!"

"Cormier," she responded coldly, and he glared at her before he spat "What are you doing here?!"

"I was hoping to catch Angelo on the phone," Marissa said stoutly. "I could feel his presence whilst walking by the castle."

"Oh, I cannot *wait* for Bianca to get back." Cormier smirked at her. "You will rile her so badly you'd be scared to come and go as you please."

"Bianca does not scare me," Marissa retorted, and Cormier laughed.

"She should."

"Well she does not."

"Uncle Cormy, milk," said Joseph huffily as he pouted up at Cormier, and Cormier swept him up.

"All right. Let's give you your milk and biscuits. Marissa, see yourself out. And don't come back without Angelo being here. I will not let you speak to him on the phone, so there's no point in asking."

"Then I will ask Clover," Marissa replied with a shrug, and Cormier almost lost his cool, but remembered little Joseph.

"I will order Clover not to let you speak."

Marissa smirked. "She will not listen to her little cousin."

"Get out, Marissa."

"I will stay," she replied flatly. "You may need help looking after little Joseph."

"I am fine with him," snapped Cormier. "I see putting yourself in a coma did nothing to change your mind about having my brother in any way. Suddenly you just *have* to be near him even though he is not present? You are losing it, Marissa Bennett."

"Just let me stay for tonight. I'm not up to travelling all the way home. My feet ache."

"Then fly," Cormier answered flatly, and she scowled at him.

"Have you no heart??"

"Not when it comes to you and your sister."

"I'm sure Angelo wouldn't mind me staying. I'd like some milk and biscuits too," she said as she smiled at little Joseph, but Joseph didn't smile back, looking at her haughtily.

"Marissa, you're not staying," Cormier said, glaring at her. "Now, I'm going to make some hot milk and biscuits for me and Joseph, and then put him back to bed. If you're still here by that time I will get rid of you. And don't think for one moment I won't."

"But I am in pain-"

"I don't want to hear it," snapped Cormier. "I suggest you leave now."

"I'm going to my room," Marissa replied flatly. "Like I said, my feet ache. And I am not up to flying. I just need to rest."

"Can you not go to Clover's if you feel this way?" demanded Cormier. "She doesn't live far from the castle. It's a half hour walk."

"A half hour walking and my feet will drop off." Marissa sighed, looking at him through innocuous blue eyes. "Let me stay, Cormier. I promise I won't be any trouble."

"No."

"Please?"

"Finally some manners," smirked Cormier. "But the answer is still no."

Marissa sighed. "Cormier, what are you afraid of?"

"I'm afraid of Joseph getting cranky. He doesn't like strangers."

"But I'm not a stranger."

"To him you are. "

Marissa sighed. "Fine, give him his milk. Have your uncle-nephew bonding session. I will be in my room resting my legs. And if I feel better before dawn, I promise I will leave. Do we have a deal?"

Cormier thought about it, then he nodded. "Deal."

* * Bianca * *

Bianca woke up, whispering Angelo's name.

She'd had a very vivid, very heated dream about her Count, and needed to wash away the feeling with a cold shower. Bianca stood, then gasped at the feel of her baby bump, which was much bigger. There was no way she'd be able to fit into her tops now. She'd have to borrow Ricky's.

Bianca threw on her dressing gown and walked out of her bedroom, crossing the landing to knock on her brother's door.

"Ricky, are you up?"

"Yeah, why?"

"I need to borrow a t-shirt. Give me a red or black one."

"For what?" Ricky asked curiously, and Bianca said "To hide my baby. My stomach is bigger and I can't wear my tops."

"Let me see?"

"No!"

"Then I'm not giving you a t-shirt." Ricky smirked and opened his door, his little sister glaring at him. "I'll give you a t-shirt if you let me see."

"How about I let you see if you give me a t-shirt?" Bianca smirked back at him, Ricky scowling at her.

"You can't reverse the deal!"

"The hell I can't. Give me a t-shirt! Actually, give me three."

Ricky obeyed, still scowling as he handed her a black, red and yellow t-shirt.

"Now let me see the baby."

"You will. When it's born." Bianca smirked at him and walked back across the landing holding the shirts. "See you later."

* * *

Shanaid pulled Bianca inside the house excitedly, saying "Walk to the sofa and back?"
"Why?"
"I just want to see something."
Bianca rolled her eyes before she obeyed, and Shanaid nodded.
"Yep. You're definitely waddling."
Jake was standing at the living room door, arms folded as he leant against the doorframe. He said nothing, Bianca saying "I'm not waddling."
"You are," Shanaid retorted. "And did you even eat before you left your mother's to come here, Bee?"
"I had tea."
"Just tea?"
"Yep."
Shanaid sighed. "You need to eat something, Bianca."
"I'm not hungry-"
"Eat something," Jake said softly, and she looked at him. "You're eating for two now. You want me to make you chocolate chip pancakes? Glazed with maple syrup for my number one girl?"
"Take the offer," Shanaid said, while glaring at her brother. "He never ever makes me chocolate chip pancakes. He always makes them when I'm out and then tells me he made them when they're gone."
Bianca burst out laughing, Jake grinning at his sister.
"All right. You can have two. That ok?"
Shanaid beamed at him. "Great."

* * Cormier * *

"Uncle Cormy, I hungry," Joseph said, shaking Cormier's shoulder. He was in Cormier's bed, Cormier asleep. "Uncle Cormy?"
Cormier stirred, mumbling "All right. I'm up, Joseph."
Joseph giggled as Cormier sat up, hair tousled. He yawned, lifting Joseph into his arms and standing.
"Come on, let's get your breakfast. And then I'm giving you a bath-"
Thunder roared outside, making Joseph jump in his arms, as the rain pounded on the windows. Cursing Angelo under his breath, Cormier said "Don't be afraid, Joseph."
He walked into the kitchen, placing Joseph in his high chair.
"Rice Krispies?"
Joseph nodded shyly, Cormier taking down a bowl.
"I could murder a Cormi Colada."

* * Bianca * *

"Best pancakes ever," sighed Bianca, and Jake smiled at her.
"Thanks, Bee. You want a hot chocolate to wash them down?"
"Yes please."

* * Angelo * *

Angelo woke up with a smile on his face. For what, he had no idea. He just felt really good. He stood up and stretched, checking the time on his mobile.

It was almost five in the evening.

Angelo scowled at that. What was the point of being granted power to function in the day if he still slept throughout the majority of that day? Angelo shook his head and headed into the bathroom to shower.

* * Bianca * *

"The Lion King?" said Jake, highly amused. "Seriously?"

"Watch it with us," said Bianca, and he said hell no. "Please?"

Jake shook his head even as he mumbled "Ok."

Shanaid burst out laughing. "You're such a sucker for Bianca!"

"Shut up, Shanaid."

* * Cormier * *

Cormier knocked on Marissa's bedroom door. "Marissa?"

Silence.

Cormier entered the room and gaped.

It was empty.

It looked like Marissa kept her word and left after she felt better. Cormier smiled and closed the door, walking back into the lounge, where Joseph sat happily playing with his toys.

"It's soon time for dinner, Joseph Heathen."

"Ok."

* * Angelo * *

Angelo sat drinking tomato soup, dipping a little buttered bread in and eating it. He wondered what Bianca was doing.

* * Bianca * *

"I wonder what Angelo's doing?"
"You'll know when you see him another time," Shanaid said, prodding her in the chest, because she didn't want to prod her in the stomach. "Jeez, you lovebirds can't stand being away from each other."
"You'll have ages to spend with Angelo when you leave with him," Jake added, a little jealously. "So stay with us and chill. Tomorrow you'll only have three days left here."
"Exactly," Shanaid said. "Text your Angelo if you can't bear not to have contact. No calls until you get home. And no accepting calls either."
Bianca smiled and said ok.

* * Cormier * *

"Uncle Cormy, I want Daddy." Joseph pouted at Cormier as he held his teddy, and Cormier smiled at him.
"Daddy will be home soon, I promise." Rain pounded the windows outside, Cormier adding "Then you'll see Bee again."
Joseph beamed at him.

* * Angelo * *

Bianca wasn't answering her mobile, for some reason.
Angelo frowned as he decided to send her a text. He'd called five times now and still no answer or form of communication from her. He hoped everything was ok.

* * Bianca * *

"He's going to do his nut if he doesn't hear from me." Bianca looked at Shanaid and Jake reproachfully. "I feel bad for not answering."
"He'll get over it," Jake replied flatly. "Now are we going to finish watching this or not?"
A text came through on Bianca's mobile before she could answer.

Sweetheart. Is everything ok? C.A.

"Don't tell me I can't answer," Bianca said as she pressed the reply button. "I'm going to."

"All right, fine," Shanaid said amusedly; Jake scowled and said nothing. Bianca glared at him before she began typing on her phone.

* * Angelo * *

*I'm fine, Angelo. Shanaid and Jake didn't want
me to answer any calls. Don't worry, I'm ok.*

Angelo breathed out, relieved.

* * Bianca * *

*Do not scare me like that, Bianca. I thought
something may have happened to you.*

"See?" Bianca said, showing Shanaid the text. "The next time he calls I'm answering."

"Ask him if I'll be allowed to visit you in Pennsylvania," Shanaid said eagerly. "You said he's head of the land, right? Right??"

"Right," Bianca said, amused. "I'll ask him when-"

She stopped, placing a hand on her stomach. Jake sat up straight, looking at her.

"Bee? You ok?"

"I'm fine, Jake," Bianca muttered. "I just... I felt the baby."

"It kicked?" Shanaid said excitedly, and Bianca said yes. "Did it feel like a boy or a girl?"

"What kind of dozy question is that??"

Jake burst out laughing as Shanaid said "I don't know, I thought you could tell and stuff!"

"Shan, I swear you have the brain of a goldfish." Bianca shook her head as Shanaid pouted, then she smiled and hugged her best friend. "I will miss you so much."

"Right, so you have to beg Count Angelo to let me come every two weeks or something, to spend time with you and the baby-"

"Every two weeks?? Shan, you can't afford that-"

"And they need time alone, nutcase," Jake said, prodding his sister. "Stop getting carried away."

Shanaid glared at him, then she brightened up again.

"Let's watch another film."

* * Angelo * *

Angelo spoke happily to Joseph, who was equally happy to be talking to his Daddy.

"Daddy, you back soon?"

"Very soon, Joseph. Two days come tomorrow."

"Bee come too?"

"Of course. I promise you. Now it's time for you to sleep, Joseph Heathen."

"Yes Daddy. Night night."

"Goodnight."

* * Cormier * *

Cormier took the phone, smiling as Joseph tottered out of the lounge.

"I'd better go and tuck him in. He's too tiny to get into bed on his own."

"I can't wait to see all of you again," sighed Angelo. "I miss my bed. I miss Clover, Sebastian and Marissa. You, Trevor, and Joseph. The wolves. I'm not content anymore. I have half a mind to just come tomorrow instead of two days' time. I'm very, very homesick."

"Well, you did what you had to," Cormier replied. "You'll be content when you step back on Pennsylvanian soil. Just relax and don't think about returning too much. Time always flies when you're having fun."

* * Bianca * *

"Bee?" Bianca stirred. "Bee. Wake up."
Bianca opened her eyes wearily, Shanaid looking at her concernedly.
"You ok?"
"I'm fine…" Bianca yawned, asking "What time is it?"
"Three in the morning."
"What?!"
"You fell asleep and we didn't want to wake you," Shanaid said uneasily.
"Don't worry, we called your mum and Ricky. Jake told her you felt the
baby and was tired. He kind of milked that fact so she'd let you stay."
"Bianca nodded. "Where is he?"
"He's coming down the stairs. I can hear him."
He was, too. Jake called "Is Bianca awake yet?"
"I just woke her," Shanaid said, Jake coming into the living room with a
smile on his face as he looked at Bianca.
"Hey you."
Bianca smiled at him. "Hey."
"Hot chocolate with blueberry muffins for my number one girl?"
"Yes please."
"What about hot chocolate and muffins for your number two girl?"
demanded Shanaid, glaring at him, and Bianca and Jake burst out
laughing, Jake saying "All right. Hot chocolate and muffins for all of us."
"Great."

* * Ricky * *

"Mum, what…? What are you doing up?" said Ricky amazedly.

Barbara was back at the dining table with a glass of wine again.

"Mum?" said Ricky cautiously. "You ok?"

"I'm fine, Richard. I'm just trying to come to grips with everything. Bianca's leaving in less than three days."

"Yeah, I know. But getting drunk isn't going to solve the problem, Mum." Ricky took the bottle of wine and put it away. "You seemed ok with her going before."

"It's not that I'm not ok with her going. I just don't want her to go with us on bad terms, that's all. You know she can't stand me."

Ricky felt bad for her. "She just doesn't want to be smothered, that's all."

Barbara looked at him. "You think I smother her too?"

"Well-"

"Your father and grandmother do. I'm only trying to look out for her."

"I know, Mum."

Barbara sighed and stood. "You'd better go to bed, Richard. It's five in the morning."

"You go to bed too," Ricky answered, and Barbara said "I will."

* * Bianca * *

Bianca woke up in Jake's arms. Smiling as she eased out of them carefully, she whispered "Morning Jake."
"Morning," he whispered back. "Your last free day, right?"
"Right," she said softly. "Let's make the most of it."

* * Angelo * *

Angelo woke up, sensing someone's presence.
A maid was staring at him- her eyes raking over his face, then his body. Angelo wore only black pyjama bottoms, his torso bare. She inhaled at the sight, Angelo sitting up.
"Can I help you with something?"
"Are you taken, sir?"
"What do you mean by taken?" frowned Angelo, and she smiled.
"I mean do you have a girlfriend."
"Oh," said Angelo. "Yes I do."
"Where is she?"
"That's not your concern. Why are you in here?"
She blushed big time, but she didn't back down. "I was just coming to see if you needed anything."
"Doesn't Room Service cover that?"
"Well-"
"I don't need anything," Angelo said, standing up. "But thank you for your concern. Please leave."
The maid bowed as she mumbled "Yes sir," and left the room.
Angelo sighed. "I should make a complaint about these maids."

* * Bianca * *

Shanaid helped Bianca stand up off the sofa, saying "What will you do when you get home?"

"Start packing," shrugged Bianca. "I'm leaving tomorrow night, so I guess the logical thing would be to pack as soon as possible."

"And don't forget to ask Count Angelo if I can come, ok?"

"Ok."

A car horn beeped outside.

"That's my mother," sighed Bianca. "Will you guys come and say goodbye?"

"Of course we will," Shanaid said, Jake as well. "Go on, get going."

Bianca smiled as she said bye, eyes lingering on Jake for a moment, before she left the room. Jake and Shanaid followed her to the door as Barbara beeped again, Bianca saying "I'm coming! Jeez!"

Jake smiled as Shanaid laughed, Bianca saying "See you guys later."

* * *

Bianca stepped out of her shoes, Barbara saying "Straight into the kitchen for some food and a hot drink. I know you haven't eaten much. You're not going to bed on a half empty stomach."

"All right, fine," sighed Bianca. "Where's Richard?"

"He's gone out with some friends of his," said Barbara. "Now, about tomorrow. Have you packed your things yet?"

"No I haven't," shrugged Bianca, and Barbara pouted at her.

"Bianca, you can't leave it until the last minute."

"Can't I just get Angelo to do it?"

Barbara frowned at her. "How on earth will Count Angelo do it?"

"He'd just snap his fingers and boom! Everything's packed."

"No, young woman. You're packing your things yourself in the suitcases I bought you. Stop being lazy."

Bianca scowled at her.

* * Angelo * *

Angelo called Bianca, smiling as she answered.

"Hello?"

"It's me, Bianca."

"Angelo," she said, pleased. "You ok?"

"I'm pretty annoyed with the staff here."

Bianca laughed. "The maids?"

"Yes."

"Well, you've only got one more night left there. Just bear it for another night, ok?"

Angelo sighed. "Ok. What are you doing now?"

"I'm having something to eat with a hot drink. You?"

"I'm about to go on a walk."

Bianca said ok. "Angelo, I need a favour."

"Anything."

"Can you please pack everything of mine magically before you go on your walk?"

"Of course." Angelo pictured Bianca's bedroom in his mind's eye and snapped his fingers. Everything was packed. "Done, Bianca."

"Great!"

"Bianca!"

"What??"

"Tell Count Angelo to unpack everything," Barbara said, and Bianca said "No way. It's done now, there's no point. Now I can relax until tomorrow night."

Angelo smiled and ended the call.

He couldn't wait to see the fiery young woman that was his.

* * Cormier * *

The next evening...

The town was buzzing about Angelo's return with Bianca.

Cormier was serving and serving Angelo's Hurricane cocktail, nobody wanting Cormier's cocktails for the moment, not until their beloved Grand Vampire returned.

Marissa and Clover ordered a Hurricane as well, Marissa saying "I can't wait to see Angelo again."

"Nor I," smiled Clover, and Cormier rolled his eyes.

"Marissa, get over my brother."

"Shut up," snapped Marissa, and he smirked at her. "It's been almost a month. Everyone feels the same as I do. Are you going to tell the rest of the community to get over Count Angelo as well?"

Cormier opened his mouth to retort, then closed it. "Whatever."

Marissa smirked, knowing she put him in his place. "Aren't you going back to the castle to wait on him now?"

"He won't be back until the early hours of the morning," Cormier said grudgingly, hating that he was speaking to her normally. "I will leave in another hour or so."

"I must leave," Clover said, glancing at the clock. "Sebastian will soon make his way here, so I will go to the castle to tend to Joseph."

"Ok," Cormier said, Marissa as well. "I will be there shortly."

* * Bianca * *

Bianca stared out of the plane window, Angelo seated beside her.
"Are you all right, Bianca?"
"I'm fine," she said softly. "I just wish I could have said goodbye to my Dad. And my Gran was in bits on the phone. Even Ricky had tears in his eyes. Now he knows how I felt when he left to go travelling with my Dad."
Angelo took her hand. "And your mother?"
"She was crying," sighed Bianca. "Whatever she wanted to say, she didn't say. She just said to look after myself out there and that's it."
"She was no doubt holding what she wanted to say in."
"I know."
Angelo smiled and kissed her on the forehead. "Do you regret leaving?"
"No," Bianca replied flatly. "It's not like I'll never see any of them again."

* * Angelo * *

She was such fire.
"I like your train of thought, Bianca Davis."
Bianca smiled at him. "Thanks, Angelo. How much longer until we get there?"
"I'd say another three hours. Why don't you go to sleep?"
"I'm too excited to sleep. I can't wait to see Clover, Sebastian, Cormier and Joseph-"
"And Marissa?"
"Marissa too, I guess."
Angelo smiled at her. "Well, unless you want to be fully jetlagged I suggest you try and sleep, even for a little while. Then you can snuggle down in our giant bed when we get home."

* * Bianca * *

Home.
He'd said it like he already thought of the castle as his and Bianca's, not like Bianca was a guest or something. Bianca smiled and closed her eyes, mumbling "Wake me up in an hour."
"I'll wake you up in three."
Bianca sighed. "All right."

* * Ricky * *

"She's gone already?!"

"Yes Dad." Ricky was really upset. "She didn't change her mind."

"I didn't even get to say goodbye," said Samuel sadly. "Will she keep her mobile number?"

"She said she would."

"Excellent. I'll give her a call as soon as possible."

* * Bianca * *

Excited as they walked toward the airport exit, Bianca gasped.

"A limo?! We're going in a limo??"

"Of course," smiled Angelo, as the people he passed bowed to him.

"Welcome back, sir!"

"Thank you," Angelo replied, taking Bianca's hand. "Are you ready to go home, Bianca?"

"Definitely," smiled Bianca, and he smiled back at her.

"I'll let Cormier know we'll be there soon."

* * Cormier * *

Jubilant, Cormier ended the call.
"He's on his way with Bianca. And not even after dawn."
Clover beamed, Sebastian grinned. Marissa gave a fleeting smile.
"Should I wake up Joseph?" asked Cormier, but Clover said no.
"He'll see Angelo and Bianca in the morning. Don't disturb him."

* * Angelo * *

As the limousine cruised through the town, Angelo and Bianca heard
cheers upon cheers from the residents, joyous shouts of welcome back to
the Grand Vampire and Miss Davis.
Bianca smiled, amused. "Is my name still hot on everyone's tongue?"
"Yes," admitted Angelo. "But in a good way, I promise you."
"Where's Patricia?"
"Nobody knows," Angelo replied. "I assume she's in hiding."
"For over two months??"
"Yes. And time does not matter. I haven't forgotten that she attacked you
and your family."
"Angelo, I don't care about it anymore. Her friends and family must be
real worried-"
"They're not," shrugged Angelo. "Marissa cares not for her."
"I can't see why," Bianca said sarcastically. "Angelo, Marissa is really-"
"Loyal," Angelo said, cutting her off. "She has always been loyal to me."
"Because she wants you," Bianca said, annoyed, and Angelo replied "She
has always been a very close friend, Bianca. I've already told you that."
Bianca nodded. "All right. But if she gives me a reason to let rip, then just
know I'm letting rip."
Angelo smiled and dropped a kiss on her forehead.
"I won't let her give any kind of reason. I promise you she is just a
friend."
The castle loomed ahead, Bianca sighing happily when she saw it.
"I can't believe this is my new home."
Angelo smiled. "I just hope you'll be happy."
"I will be. I promise."

* * Cormier * *

"Chick pea!" Cormier smiled broadly as Bianca walked towards them, beaming. "Come here and give me a cuddle."
Bianca smiled as he pulled her into his arms, giving her a big hug.
"I've missed you so."
"I've missed you too," said Bianca, eyes filling as she looked at Clover. "Clover, Sebastian-"
Clover gently pulled her out of Cormier's arms into her own.
"We've missed you, little sister. I'm so glad you're back without a fuss."
"And I," added Sebastian, smiling at her. "And- where is Angelo?"

* * Angelo * *

"I am so glad to see you again, Angelo."
"And I you, Marissa." Angelo took her hand and kissed it. "How have you been?"
"Miserable without you." Marissa shivered as he released her hand, saying "Cormier was less than hospitable."
"I can imagine."
Marissa smiled at him. "So how did it feel, being in daylight?"
"Very odd," admitted Angelo. "I'm glad to be back."
Marissa smiled at him. "You'd better get back to them before they realise you're missing."
"They probably have," shrugged Angelo, and right on cue Cormier appeared.
"You must be joking."
"Good to see you too, brother." Angelo smiled at him as he glared at Marissa. "I was just speaking to Marissa one on one."
"I can tell that much. Now can you get back to Bianca please, Angelo?"
"All right." Angelo took Marissa's hand again. "Another time?"
"Of course," Marissa said softly, and he said "I will see you soon."
Marissa dissolved into nothingness, Angelo smiling at his brother, who was scowling.
"Turn that frown upside down, Cormier. It's a lovely night."
Cormier gaped as he realised Angelo had ceased the storms he caused. Angelo smirked at him, asking "Where is Bianca?"
"Talking to Clover in the hall. Your belongings are unpacked."
"Good," said Angelo, glancing at the clock. "I should make Bianca call her family to let them know she has arrived safely."

* * Bianca * *

"I'm fine, Gran. We got here safe and sound," smiled Bianca, holding her phone to her ear. "Can you call Dad and tell him for me?"

"Of course, darling. Was there any trouble on the plane?"

"Nope. I didn't throw up once."

"Good, good. Will you go to sleep now, darling? You must be tired."

"I will in a bit. I still need to call Shanaid."

"Did you call Richard and your mother?"

"Yes Gran."

"And have you eaten properly?"

"Yes Gran," Bianca repeated, smiling. "I'm going to go now."

"Now you just be careful out there," Gran said worriedly. "Call me as often as possible."

"I will, Gran. Have a good night."

Bianca ended the call, Angelo smiling at her.

"Will you call Shanaid?"

"I'll text her," Bianca replied, hand on her stomach. "I just want to relax right now. The baby feels tense. Must be because I've been active all day."

"Mmm. Go and relax in the lounge," smiled Angelo. "I'll bring you in a hot drink and a muffin. I know you like a hot drink and a muffin with it."

"I do," said Bianca shyly, and Cormier and Clover smiled at her. "Ok, I'll be in the lounge."

* * Angelo * *

Clover smiled at Angelo. "You look so happy, Angelo."

"I am very happy." Angelo smiled back at her. "Will you stay the night?"

"Not tonight, cousin. Me and Sebastian will head home."

"All right."

"I hope you don't mind me closing the club earlier than usual, Angelo," Sebastian said. "I also wanted to be there when you arrived."

"I don't mind at all, Sebastian." Angelo smiled at him. "Clover, if you're leaving, it would be best to leave now. Dawn is approaching."

"All right. Have a good night, cousin."

"You too."

"See you, Angelo." Sebastian clasped Angelo's hand in a firm handshake. "It's good to have you back."

Angelo smiled, Clover and Sebastian vanishing.

Cormier appeared, scowling at his little brother. Angelo sighed, saying "Whatever the lecture is, it can wait. I'm going to Bianca."

* * Bianca * *

Bianca smiled as Angelo entered the lounge, a steaming mug of hot chocolate and a blueberry muffin sailing through the air towards her and settling on the coffee table not far from the loveseat she sat on.

"Thanks, Angelo."

"You're most welcome." Angelo joined her, smiling. "Are you tired?"

"Not really. Are you?"

"I won't be for now. Not until dawn. But you should rest after you have your hot drink and muffin."

"All right, I will. Can you come with me?"

"Of course."

* * Angelo * *

Bianca fell asleep in Angelo's arms, back to his chest, his arms around her waist, a hand on her stomach. Angelo himself was asleep.

Cormier appeared at the foot of his bed, smiling as he looked at them. They looked like the perfect couple.

"Angelo." Angelo stirred. "Brother. Wake up."

Angelo inhaled, muttering "What is the problem..."

"There's no problem," Cormier said, quietly so as not to disturb Bianca. "I was just going to tell you to settle down in bed properly before you fall off the edge."

Angelo smiled, doing as he was told, gently laying Bianca down before he laid down himself.

"Satisfied?"

"Yes," Cormier said amusedly, as Bianca shifted slowly, snuggling up to Angelo. "Goodnight, Angelo."

* * Cormier * *

Cormier sank into bed, closing his eyes.

Patricia Bennett stood before him, eyes burning scarlet. Sensing her presence, Cormier leapt to his feet, staring at her.

"Patricia?"

"Cormier," she responded coldly. "I see everything is cosy once more."

"Do not do anything to disrupt that," Cormier said warningly. "Bianca does not feel anything about what happened anymore. You'd better rid yourself of this uncanny hatred you bear for her and return to your fiancé. He's worried about you. A lot of people are."

"I cannot return to him. I am a part of the Nefarious pack now."

"What??"

Patricia repeated herself icily, Cormier staring at her disbelievingly.

"But you're a vampire, not a wolf. How can you be a part of that pack?"

"I was bitten by the leader of the pack," shrugged Patricia. "I am now part vampire, part wolf. I am very, very strong."

Cormier's jaw dropped.

Patricia smirked as she watched him try and come to grips with what she just told him.

"Are you afraid, Cormier Heathen?"

"Cross-breeding is against the law of magical beings," spat Cormier. "You'll be killed by the vampires and wolves out there if they ever find out what you've become, what you did to yourself-"

"They won't find out."

"They will!"

"They won't," Patricia repeated. "Now tell my little sister that I love her and I always will. I didn't mean for things to get out of hand. I was only doing it for her."

Before Cormier could retort she was gone.

Cormier cursed angrily, knowing he had to tell Angelo as soon as he woke up.

"This is madness."

* * Angelo * *

"DADDY!!"
Angelo snapped awake, startled as Joseph shrieked happily, trying to climb into his giant bed to get to him.
"Daddy, you back now!"
Bianca woke up too, in Angelo's arms. Joseph stared at her.
"Bee?" Bianca nodded, smiling. "BEE!!"
Angelo swept him up into his arms and hugged him, Joseph hugging him back before he reached for Bianca. Smiling, Bianca took him off Angelo and kissed his forehead.
"Bee," said Joseph happily, clinging to Bianca like a little monkey. "Ok?"
"I'm fine, Joseph. Have you been ok?"
"Yes," said Joseph happily, Angelo gently taking him out of her arms. "Come and eat, Joseph."
"Bee come too," said Joseph happily, and Bianca smiled at him, getting up carefully.
"All right. Let's all go and get something to eat."

* * *

"Brother, we need to talk. Urgently," Cormier said, and Angelo and Bianca looked at him curiously, Joseph eating his cereal happily.
"What is the problem?"
"Patricia Bennett," Cormier said. "She appeared before me in my room. She told me she was bitten by one of the werewolves and is now a part of the Nefarious Pack. And she is now very strong; part vampire, part wolf. She left a message for Marissa-"
Marissa Bennett appeared, eyebrow raised. "What message?"
Normally Cormier would have berated her for eavesdropping and turning up without notice, but he was too unnerved to care at the moment.
"She said to tell you that she loves you and she always will. That she didn't mean for things to get out of hand, and that she was doing it for you."
Marissa didn't respond to that, looking at Angelo.
"What should be done, Angelo?"
"I have no idea," admitted Angelo. "I need to think about this. And speak with the wolves. Patricia is no doubt very strong now. It will take a lot to bring her down, especially when she is guarded and worshipped by the Nefarious Pack. It's obvious she leads them now."
Cormier thought, then he said "Cousin Clover could take her down."
"There is no way I'm letting cousin Clover even attempt it," Angelo replied flatly. "Even if she did manage to reach Patricia, she will be

facing at least ten werewolves which she'd have to deal with before her."
Bianca sighed. "I really thought this was over with."
Angelo took her by the hand and gently pulled her to him, already protective of her.
"I will make sure you're guarded, Bianca. And please, try to stay as calm as you can for the baby's sake. Don't get stressed out."
Bianca nodded. "All right. What are you going to do?"
"For now, look after you and Joseph. Marissa, I want you to stay here. If Patricia comes back, maybe you can get through to her."
Marissa glowered. "I thought Cormier had done that."
Angelo sighed. "Marissa, please. Do this for me."
Marissa sighed too. "Fine. For you, Angelo."
Angelo smiled at her. "Thank you."
Cormier and Bianca scowled, Joseph saying "Finished!"
"Good boy, Joseph," smiled Bianca, and he lifted his little arms happily. Bianca lifted him out of the high chair and snuggled him, Angelo running a hand through his silky black hair as he thought.
"Cormier, get Clover over here. I want her and Sebastian on the premises."
"As guards for Bianca? Angelo, you should get the usual vampire guards, those that are skilled against any form of enemy, even a Necromancer from the Underworld." Cormier rubbed his neck uneasily. "If angered, Patricia could summon one."
Bianca was nervous. "What's her problem exactly?"
"I wish I could tell you, chick pea." Cormier shook his head. "Nobody has a clue why Patricia has rebelled in such a ghastly way."
"I have something to do with it though. Right?"
Everyone exchanged looks, not answering her.
Bianca sighed. "Right."
"I want Clover here anyway. She could be a target of Patricia just like Bianca," Angelo said. "No doubt Patricia will want revenge."
"I'll go to Clover's and get her," Cormier said uneasily. "In the meantime make regular checks about the castle and summon the guards, brother. I'll be back soon."

* * Bianca * *

Bianca sat in the lounge, hand on her stomach as she watched little Joseph play with his toys on the carpet.

The castle was alive with vampires. Guards were stationed almost everywhere, and Bianca knew they weren't going to be dismissed anytime soon, nor would they leave on their own account. They were honoured to serve Count Angelo, the Grand Vampire. And also Bianca.

"Why me?" she asked Clover, who entered the lounge with a smile on her face. "They respect me as much as Angelo for some reason."

"Bianca, you carry Angelo's child. An heir. And you are also the future Grand Countess of Pennsylvania," said Clover gently. "You are basically royalty."

"I am?"

"You are."

"Oh," said Bianca nervously, as they heard a fierce howl from outside.

Clover stood quickly, Angelo appearing at her side. Bianca would have liked to have stood too, but she was too relaxed, and she didn't want to upset the baby.

Marissa and Cormier appeared too, Marissa saying "It's nothing to worry about. They're only howling at the full moon."

"They're in werewolf form," snapped Cormier. "There's plenty to worry about. If the Nefarious Pack are sent here-"

"I doubt they will be," shrugged Marissa. "Patricia was never one to act rashly. I know her. Angelo? Do you agree?"

"I agree, Marissa." Cormier rolled his eyes, Angelo saying "The only thing I'm worried about is Patricia in werewolf form. I want to see what we're up against. So I'm going out there."

"What!"

"Angelo, are you mad?!" said Cormier angrily. "You can't do that!"

"I know they are an unruly pack, but they respect and are in awe by me," Angelo replied, shrugging a shoulder. "I will use that as a leverage."

Cormier thought about that, then he nodded.

"I'm coming with you."

"And I," said Marissa, and Angelo shook his head as Clover opened her mouth.

"Clover, you must stay here. You are not one of Patricia's favourite people right now. Stay with Bianca and tend to Joseph."

Clover nodded.

* * Cormier * *

"Stay on your guard," Angelo said quietly, and Marissa and Cormier nodded as they walked deeper and deeper into the forest. Four more vampire guards were with them; they pleaded to come to defend the Grand Vampire lest he need defending.

"Count Angelo!"

Everyone whipped round, staring at the group of wolves.

"Phoebus," said Angelo, relieved. "What are you doing so far into the forest with the Virtuous Pack?"

"Keeping a watchful eye on the Grand Vampire," growled Phoebus. "Angelo, turn back. You have nothing to gain by going to the Nefarious Pack."

"Patricia Bennett leads them," Angelo replied, and there were more growls of anger at that. "I must speak with her."

"There are rumours," Phoebus answered. "Whispers from the trees and animals. She has become something evil, terrifying. A cross between a vampire and a wolf. Is it true?"

"Yes," Cormier said, speaking for the first time. "She appeared before me, and she told me that she is now part vampire, part wolf."

"Then only the Grand Vampire can take her down," Phoebus replied. "Angelo, is that what you intend to do?"

"She is not a threat," Angelo replied, shrugging a shoulder. "I want to-"

"Talk?" Phoebus cut across. "Negotiate?"

Angelo said yes, and Phoebus growled angrily.

"Angelo, she is a monster. She will not negotiate!"

"I can at least try talking with her."

"She needs to be killed before she does something to the future Countess. Two months and more may have passed, but I know that does not matter to Patricia Bennett. She will want revenge on both Miss Davis and your cousin Clover."

"Both are heavily guarded at the castle," Angelo said. "Now we must head on to the Nefarious Pack. I have to talk with Patricia."

"And if Patricia does not listen to you?" demanded Phoebus, the other wolves nodding. "What then?"

"Then I will think of something, and fast," Angelo replied, ready to go. "Cormier, Marissa. Come."

"Be careful, Angelo," called Phoebus as Angelo walked into the trees. "We will be close by in case we need to come to your rescue."

Angelo called thank you, Cormier and Marissa keeping as close to him but as far as away from each other as possible.

A fierce howl shot through the trees, Cormier and Marissa stopping, but Angelo carried on walking, ignoring the noise.

"Cousin!"

Everyone whipped round, staring at the werewolf, which breathed "Cousin, it is not safe here. Turn back!"

"Trevor," said Angelo, surprised. "What are you doing so far out in the forest? You are with the Virtuous Pack, are you not? It is not safe for you here either."

"That I know, cousin." Trevor stood on his hind legs, walking towards them as if he were still in human form. "I had to get away. You know I like to be alone when the full moon is out. I'm a danger to any human who crosses my path, including Miss Davis."

"Bianca is safe at the castle, Trevor. But thank you for thinking of her."

"What are you doing so far out in the forest?"

"I'm going to Patricia Bennett."

"Angelo, I have seen her. It's not safe for you to be here. Return to the castle with your company. If you want to speak to Patricia, at least wait until she is in human form."

"I've come this far so I'm continuing my journey, cousin." Angelo began walking again, Cormier, Marissa and the guards following him. "If I can't speak to her, I at least want to see her in wolf form. What she is."

Trevor sighed. "I will come with you."

"If you'd like that then you may."

* * Bianca * *

"Awhoooooo!"
Bianca stared at Joseph as he howled, on all fours like he was still a wolf
cub. Clover smiled at him, saying "He's just reacting to the howls outside
and the full moon. He did that at mine as well."
"Should I be concerned?" Bianca asked uncertainly, and Clover said no.
"Don't worry about it."

* * Angelo * *

"There she is," said Trevor quietly. "Angelo, Cormier, Marissa. Vanish.
Guards as well."
They obeyed, unnerved by what they were seeing. The werewolves and
wolves of the Nefarious Pack surrounded a gigantic wolf, a beast with
twelve inch claws and burning red eyes. She was tearing away at the body
of a bear, clamping down on it with her gigantic jaws.
"Patricia," whispered Marissa, stunned like Angelo and Cormier.
A wolf looked and saw Trevor, growling angrily as he approached them
cautiously.
"What do you want, Trevor Gordon? Son of the Virtuous Pack!"
There was harsh insults towards Trevor from the other wolves and
werewolves as they stood, glaring at him.
"I've come because of the Grand Vampire," Trevor replied, eyes on
Patricia, who hadn't stopped eating or even looked at him. "His lover,
Bianca Davis, is back in Pennsylvania. I'm sure you're aware of that."
"We're very aware. Is that all you've come to tell us?"
"I want you to leave the girl alone," Trevor replied, and there were shouts
of laughter.
"Leave the girl alone?! Why, we hadn't thought of troubling her."
"You lie," Trevor answered coldly. "Count Angelo isn't stupid. What do
you plan to do to her?"
"Tear her limb from limb," sneered a wolf, another saying "Slice her
face, carve Patricia's name on her forehead."
"But why?" demanded Trevor, making them stop. "Why? What has Miss
Davis done to any of you?"
"It matters not if she has done anything, Trevor Gordon. We have
orders."
"And orders must be obeyed!" shouted a male werewolf, and there were
cheers.
"You are fools," spat Trevor, and there was silence. "Have you not your
own minds? Are you not individuals? Some of you must think that there
is something wrong about these orders!"

"Well we don't."

"Another lie," snapped Trevor. "Since when did the Nefarious Pack harm the innocent? You may be unruly, but you never touched a hair on an innocent person's head!"

Patricia stood on her hind legs like Trevor, but she was much larger than he, broader, more muscular, taller- more than four times his height. She towered over him, eyes glowing.

Trevor didn't back down, never taking his eyes off her for a second.

"You love the mortal, do you Trevor Gordon?" rasped Patricia, Trevor staring up at her, totally stunned like Angelo, Cormier and Marissa. "Well? Do you?"

"I love no one," Trevor replied, voice steady.

"Kneel before me, Trevor Gordon. I am the new Queen of this forest. Kneel, and I will let you live."

"I kneel before no false ruler," Trevor answered icily, and Cormier hissed "Now would be a good time to appear, Angelo!"

"Wait," Angelo hissed back.

"I am not a false ruler. I am a *new* ruler."

"You are false," Trevor replied flatly. "And foolish with it."

"You dare?!"

"Yes, I dare," Trevor said coldly, glaring up at her. "You may kill me, but what good it will do you, I have no idea. You may give yourself any name you want; queen, ruler, monarch of the forest. You will *never* have my respect. And the Nefarious Pack shouldn't give you any either."

Silence, the wolves and werewolves looking at each other uncertainly. Patricia laughed, her voice booming through the trees.

"Trevor Gordon, your death will be an example to the Nefarious Pack, the Virtuous Pack, the vampire community and anyone else who tries to oppose me. I am stronger than any but the Grand Vampire. And I know Count Angelo will not challenge me."

"I wouldn't be too sure about that," snarled Trevor, on all fours now. "You want me dead? Come and get me."

He shot away through the trees before Patricia could drop on all fours, already gone. Screaming with rage at his agility, Patricia shrieked *"After him!!"*

The Nefarious Pack stood, howling, and ran through the trees, Patricia bounding heavily behind them, tearing trees out of her way angrily.

"I want him alive!"

Angelo appeared, shocked. Marissa, Cormier and the four vampire guards appeared as well, looking at him.

"What on earth are we going to do, brother?"

"For now, get back to the castle," Angelo replied. "I really need to think."

"What about Trevor?" asked Marissa worriedly, and Cormier and Angelo smiled at her, Angelo saying "Trevor can handle himself, Marissa. Don't worry."

* * Bianca * *

His tender kiss woke her up.

Bianca smiled, mumbling "What took you so long?"

"I got here an hour ago," Angelo said softly. "I just didn't want to wake you or Joseph. Are you all right?"

"I'm fine," Bianca said just as softly. "Did you see Patricia?"

"She is a startling sight," Angelo said, shaking his head. He was still amazed. "I've never seen any kind of wolf that size before. Werewolf or normal. I was shocked. She has paws five times bigger than Cormier's head."

Bianca burst out laughing at that. "Did you actually speak to her?"

"No. We stayed invisible. Cousin Trevor did the talking. He riled her pretty badly."

"Which means he's in danger too, right?"

"Right, but he can take care of himself. Trevor is as unruly and dangerous as the Nefarious Pack."

Bianca nodded, Angelo helping her up.

"Are you ready to go to bed, sweetheart?"

"Will you come too?" Bianca asked shyly, and Angelo smiled at her.

"Yes. I'll bring you in a hot drink. Would you like tea or chocolate?"

"Tea please. Wait- where's Joseph?"

"I put him to bed," Angelo said, taking her hand and walking with her. "It seems he wants to stay with you as much as he can, just like before."

Bianca smiled. "He was howling earlier."

"He'll do that from time to time. Especially when he hears other wolves howling and the full moon is out."

"That's what Clover said."

"And she's right. It's nothing to worry about."

Guards bowed to them as they walked past, Angelo asking "How is the baby feeling?"

"The baby's ok. I just can't wait until it's born. I feel like a whale."

Angelo burst out laughing, Bianca smiling grudgingly.

"Well I do."

"You're not a whale, sweetheart. You're beautiful."

"Thanks, Angelo."

* * Angelo * *

Bianca slept soundly in his arms.

Angelo held her to him, deep in thought about Patricia and the Nefarious Pack. Something had to be done before they caused harm to someone, be it a human, vampire, werewolf or wolf, even a fairy- something had to be done.

But what?

There was a timid knock on the door of his suite, Angelo looking at it sharply as a tiny voice said "Daddy?"

Angelo relaxed, gently laying Bianca down and getting up, walking across the suite and opening his door to the tiny boy.

"Joseph? What's the matter?"

"Scared," said Joseph, eyes filling as they heard another fierce howl from outside, and Angelo understood immediately, Cormier appearing.

"He understands the wolves. There must be threats in their howls towards us, and he's picking up on that."

"It's the Nefarious Pack howling," Angelo replied. "That is why he's scared. I don't doubt their howls are ferocious. Patricia must have sent them to unnerve us."

He picked up Joseph and cuddled him, saying "He can stay with me and Bianca tonight. Tomorrow I will do something about the howls."

* * Cormier * *

Cormier nodded and left them, heading into the kitchen for a drink.

Cousin Clover and Marissa Bennett were in there, talking.

"It was unlike anything you've ever seen, Clover. I couldn't believe my eyes when I saw Patricia."

"I bet I could have taken her down."

"You couldn't have," Cormier said flatly, and they turned and saw him. "And don't even think for one second of trying to, Clover. Patricia is a monstrous beast. Even Angelo was shocked when he saw her."

"We all were," said Marissa, and Cormier glared at her.

"Did I ask you to join this two-way conversation?"

"This was a two-way conversation before you arrived," snapped Marissa, and Clover burst out laughing.

"Will the pair of you ever get along?"

They said no, looking daggers at each other.

"I only came in for a drink," Cormier said, scowling as Clover continued to laugh. "A cocktail will do me nicely for the night."

"I'd like one, cousin."

"All right. Coming up." Forcing politeness into his voice, Cormier said

"Marissa? Would you like a drink also?"

"Red wine please. And try not to spike it with poison."

Clover burst out laughing again, Cormier amused as he served both ladies their drinks.

"Where is Angelo, Cormier?" asked Clover, and Cormier replied "In his suite with Bianca and Joseph."

Clover frowned at him. "What is Joseph doing in there? He was asleep when I checked on him not long ago."

"The howls woke him up." Cormier sighed. "There are threats in the howls from the Nefarious Pack and he understands them. He was scared, so naturally he ran to his Daddy."

Clover and Marissa nodded.

Cormier smiled, sipping his cocktail. "I doubt they caught up with Trevor."

"If they did they wouldn't be howling at the castle," Clover said, amused. "I'm just annoyed they woke and frightened Joseph."

"He'll be fine, Clover." Marissa smiled at her. "When he's with Angelo he's always happy."

Cormier raised an eyebrow as he looked at her. "And you know this because?"

Marissa glared at him, ignoring the question. Clover burst out laughing again as Cormier smirked at Marissa.

"I cannot see the pair of you getting along even though you are under the same roof."

"Yes, well, I will be having words with Angelo about Marissa being here. She is not under threat," Cormier said, a little harshly. "There is no reason for her to be here, though she is loving every moment of it. Angelo has too good a heart."

"Go to bed, Cormier Heathen," Marissa said dryly, sipping her wine. "It was not I who asked Angelo to stay. He insisted I do. So I'm staying."

Cormier scowled at her and sipped his cocktail.

* * Bianca * *

"You are mine, Bianca Davis..."
Bianca stirred in her sleep, frowning a little.
"All mine..."
"Angelo, shut up," muttered Bianca, snuggling up to him, but Angelo didn't answer, in a deep sleep.
"You have turned what I know against me, and you will pay..."
Bianca's frowned deepened and she opened her eyes, looking into burning scarlet ones.
Patricia Bennett stood over her in human form, holding a knife directly over her heart. Bianca screamed *"What the hell are you doing?!"*
Angelo snapped awake with Joseph as Cormier and Clover appeared.
"Patricia!"
Patricia spun on the spot and vanished with a cruel laugh, Angelo standing quickly. Joseph burst into tears, startled at the commotion as Angelo said "How did she get inside the castle??"
"You lifted the barrier charm for the guards' arrival," Cormier reminded him. "Now that they're here, you'd better put it back on."
Bianca was furious. "What the hell is her problem?!"
"Don't worry about it, chick pea." Cormier smiled at her. "She just wants to frighten you."
"Well I'm not frightened. Just friggin' annoyed." Bianca scowled as she stood, hand on her stomach. "I don't need all of this aggravation. I'm pregnant!"
Clover smiled at her. "We'll protect you, little sister."
"If I wasn't carrying a baby she would have got it," Bianca said angrily. "She's a nutcase just like her little sister-"
Marissa Bennett appeared, looking at them curiously. "What's going on?"
"Your sister appeared holding a knife over my heart," Bianca said, trying not to glare at her. "Did she come to you at all?"
Marissa said no. "She wouldn't have struck. She just wants to scare you."
"That's what Cormier said," Clover said, and Cormier scowled at Marissa, who said "It's true. But it doesn't seem as if you are scared, Bianca. Are you?"
"No I'm not," said Bianca through clenched teeth. "Like I said, I'm annoyed. You're out of your friggin' self-inflicted coma. It's been over two months. I've been out of the country and I've only just got back. Your sister needs to let this go, and I'm being so serious when I say that. I'm so vexed right now."
Marissa nodded, Angelo taking Bianca's hand.
"Come, sweetheart. Let's go to the lounge."
"We'll come too," Cormier said, Bianca lifting Joseph into her arms and

cuddling him. "Unless you want to be alone?"

Bianca said no while Angelo said yes.

Amused, Cormier said "Which is it?"

"Come with us," smiled Bianca, and he smiled back at her.

Angelo scowled but said nothing, Marissa glancing at him and smiling. Angelo smiled back.

* * Cormier * *

Cormier noticed the look on Marissa's face as Angelo held Bianca in his arms, his hand on her stomach. Clover smiled at them, saying "I really can't wait until the baby's born."

"Nor I," smiled Angelo, Cormier as well. Marissa said nothing. Joseph sat sucking his thumb, holding his frog teddy. Clover smiled, asking "Will it be a boy or girl?"

"We don't want to know," Angelo said, smiling at her. "We made a decision on the plane to keep it as a surprise for all of us."

"How sweet," said Marissa, a little stiffly. "I'm going back to bed, everyone."

"Bye," said Cormier coldly, and Clover hit him on the arm. "Ouch!"

"Stop being so mean towards Marissa," Clover said, hitting him again, and Angelo said "Clover, you may as well leave it. I gave up on that a very long time ago."

Marissa smiled briefly before she vanished, and Angelo said "Bianca?"

"Mmm?"

"Would you like a hot beverage of some sort?"

"Umm, yes please."

"What would you like?"

"Hot chocolate please," she said shyly, and Angelo kissed her on the forehead. "Joseph needs some milk or hot chocolate to settle back down."

"I'll make it," Clover said, standing. "Stay with Bianca, Angelo."

Angelo nodded, Cormier saying "I'm going to get a cocktail."

Angelo and Bianca said ok, Bianca closing her eyes as Angelo took to stroking her hair.

"Are you tired, Bianca?"

"Not so much. But Joseph needs to go to bed, and this baby needs rest as well."

"I agree," smiled Angelo, and Bianca asked "Where will I give birth?"

"At the hospital of course," said Angelo, surprised. "Where did you think you would give birth?"

"I don't know," said Bianca, embarrassed. "I was just thinking, because the baby will be partially a vampire-"

"Bianca, do not worry. You'll have the baby like any other woman in the

community. You'll get the treatment you need, and you'll be taken care of. There are vampire nurses who will be there to look after you, and I will also be there. I won't leave your side."
Bianca looked up at him. "You promise?"
Angelo kissed her. "I promise."

* * Cormier * *

"I make a mean hot chocolate," smiled Clover, and Cormier smiled back. "I add mint and all sorts."
"As does Angelo," smiled Cormier. "His hot chocolate is the meanest. It's almost addictive."
"As is everything about him," smiled Clover. "Come, help me with these mugs. I made some for all of us."

* * Angelo * *

Joseph was asleep, snuggled in Bianca's arms. Bianca herself was snoozing. Angelo checked the time: it was almost six in the morning. The sky was a very light blue.
Cormier and Clover were asleep in their chairs, Clover's head in her arms. Angelo smiled, gently getting to his feet and lifting Joseph up into his arms.
"Angelo," a voice said softly, and he turned, then he smiled.
"Marissa."
"You should be in bed," she said quietly, and he replied "I'm going now after I put Joseph to bed."
Marissa nodded, and he asked "Why are you up?"
"I couldn't sleep. I was pretty much waiting for dawn to arrive," she admitted. "Would you like me to leave you be?"
"I don't mind the company."
Angelo smiled at her and left the lounge carrying Joseph, Marissa walking behind him as he walked down some corridors before turning into Joseph's bedroom and placing him in the bed, tucking him in.
Marissa smiled as Angelo straightened up, saying "Would you like a glass of wine before we depart for bed, Marissa?"
"I'd love one."
Angelo offered his arm, and she took it, pleased as they walked.
"I cherish every moment alone with you, Angelo."
"And I you, Marissa." Angelo smiled down at her. "I have truly missed our talks and walks together in the forest."
"Would you like to walk there now?"
Angelo looked at her. "Now?"

Marissa nodded.

"Marissa, we will surely pass out from the power of daylight."

"We won't be long. I promise."

Angelo hesitated, and Marissa smiled at him.

"Angelo, you are the Grand Vampire. What's the worst that could happen?"

* * Bianca * *

"Bee?" Bianca stirred, Joseph looking at her. "Bee!"
Bianca opened her eyes to find the little boy looking at her earnestly.
"Hey," she said gently, and he beamed at her. "You ok?"
Joseph nodded, then he said "Hungry."
Bianca started, realising she was still in the lounge. Cormier and Clover were just waking up.
"Hello chick pea," smiled Cormier, then he frowned at her. "Did you not go to sleep in you and Angelo's suite?"
"No," she said, frowning as well. "I woke up just now."
"Angelo didn't put you to bed?" asked Clover, and Bianca said "No."
"Odd," said Cormier curiously. "I'll go and see where he is."

* * *

Bianca fed Joseph, who smiled at her happily as he ate. Clover stood by her side, Cormier appearing.
"Angelo isn't anywhere in the castle. Neither is Marissa."
"What?" said Bianca amazedly, and Cormier repeated himself.
"Do you think something happened to them?" asked Clover worriedly, and Cormier said "I doubt it. They probably just went for a walk."
"In the light of day?? Cormier, you know that's not safe!" said Clover anxiously, and Cormier replied "They must be in the forest. It's basically night time all the time there. They'll be fine. If they wasn't I would know."
"How?" demanded Clover, and Cormier changed what he said: "If *Angelo* wasn't ok, I would know. We are connected. I'd immediately know if my little brother was in danger."
"But what about Marissa?? Don't forget Patricia is lurking in that forest!"
"Patricia would never harm Marissa. She loves her dearly."
Bianca didn't take part in the conversation, Cormier saying "Marissa probably convinced him to take a walk in the bleeding light of day. Angelo isn't reckless. He's the most practical and logical man I've ever met. We'll wait for them to come back."

* * Angelo * *

Angelo could hear voices, and loads of sniffing.

Something prodded his shoulder, a firm voice saying "Angelo."

Angelo stirred, mumbling something before he tried going back to sleep-

"Angelo! Cousin, for Heaven's sake wake up."

"Trevor?" said Angelo uncertainly, opening his eyes to look into his cousin's glowing ones. "How did you find me?"

"I could sense your presence. And so could the rest of the Virtuous Pack," Trevor said, scowling at him. "What are you doing passed out in the forest?"

"I took a walk with Marissa Bennett," Angelo said, sitting up. "Where is she?"

"I'm here, Angelo."

Angelo looked at saw Marissa, getting to his feet.

"How long was I asleep for?"

"For as long as I was," Marissa replied. "I woke up ten minutes ago, then the Virtuous Pack arrived."

"Count Angelo, go back to the castle," growled Phoebus. "Night has fallen. Get back to Miss Davis and the rest of your family."

Angelo stood, dusting himself off. "I will. Come, Marissa. And Trevor, be careful. You're still being hunted."

Trevor grinned at him. "Cousin, I can handle the Nefarious Pack. Get back to Bianca and Joseph. Farewell."

"Farewell," Angelo responded, offering his arm to Marissa, who took it and they began walking. "Bianca must be very worried."

Marissa cringed, but nodded. Then she said "Let us fly instead of walking. We'll get there quicker."

"All right."

* * Cormier * *

Angelo appeared in the lounge, Marissa on his arm.

Cormier stood, Bianca and Clover glaring at them as Cormier said "A note perhaps, brother? Rather than have us worried sick about where you could have gone and what might have happened to you?"

"Apologies," Angelo replied, eyes on Bianca, who didn't look at him.

"Bianca was very troubled," Clover said angrily. "You have a mobile, Angelo- why didn't you even send some kind of message to any of us?"

"I was unconscious," said Angelo, heat rising. "I woke up less than an hour ago. Marissa came to me this morning and suggested a walk-"

"I'll bet she did," Cormier said furiously; Bianca still hadn't spoken. "Marissa, did you forget about the light of day having the power to kill a vampire? Yes you did," he said, when Marissa opened her mouth. "You forget everything when you're with my brother!"

"That's not true," snapped Marissa. "Angelo said he missed our walks so I suggested we take one. That's it. So get off my back, Cormier Heathen!"

She was still on Angelo's arm.

"Get away from him," snapped Cormier, and Marissa let him go. "Go and get cleaned up, Angelo. You look like you wrestled with an ox."

Angelo vanished, Marissa awkwardly standing there. Clover warmly said "You too, Marissa."

Marissa nodded and vanished as well, Clover looking at Bianca.

"Are you ok, Bianca?"

"I'm fine," sighed Bianca. "I'm just glad he's ok. Don't forget that nutcase Patricia is out there with a wild wolf pack. Anything could have happened to him."

* * Angelo * *

Angelo stepped out of the shower, sighing. He could hear Cormier fuming a mile away.

"Angelo?" Bianca said softly, making him whip round. She was standing outside the bathroom doors, but he could see through them, see her.

"Yes Bianca?"

"We're soon going to have something to eat. Will you come to the dining area to eat with us?"

"Of course I will. I…" Angelo hesitated. "Are you angry with me, Bianca?"

"No," she said, and he breathed out, relieved. "I was just worried."

Angelo wrapped a towel around his waist and opened the doors, pulling her into his arms and holding her to him.

"I'm sorry."

"It's all right. I…" she stopped, Angelo looking at her.

"What's wrong?"

"The baby kicked," she said softly. "Feel."

Angelo nervously placed his hand on her stomach, then he gasped when he felt what she did.

Bianca smiled at him. "It definitely knows it's Daddy."

Angelo smiled back. "I can't wait until it's born."

"Me either. So how much longer?"

"A month and a couple of weeks." He smiled and kissed her tenderly. "I really cannot wait. Have you thought of any names?"

"Well… if it's a girl I may call her Chanice Heathen or Davis. But I'm not too sure about that name."

Angelo smiled at that. "And if it's a boy?"

"Micah Heathen. Or Davis."

"Micah." Angelo breathed out. "I love it."

* * *

Bianca lifted Joseph into her arms and cuddled him, Joseph smiling up at her. Clover, Marissa and Cormier sat contentedly, listening to the vampire guards patrol the area.

Angelo was looking at his phone. "Sebastian asked for you, Clover."

"Tell him I am fine," Clover responded, and Angelo obeyed. "If he misses me he can always come over."

"As I told him," Angelo replied, Bianca snuggling Joseph. "Is anyone hungry at all?"

Everyone said no.

* * Bianca * *

One month, one week later...

"I don't want to spend my last week of pregnancy in the hospital."
"Bianca, you must." Angelo kissed her forehead as she pouted. "It's safer that way. You don't want to have the baby here with no professional midwife at hand, do you?"
"No," she said grudgingly. "But what about Patricia and the Nefarious Pack?"

* * Angelo * *

The Nefarious Pack had gone on a rampage through the town and had made several attempts to enter the castle. Patricia's orders, Cormier had said disgustedly.
Cousin Trevor was no longer being hunted; Patricia had lost interest in him. Now it seemed she was hell bent on capturing the attention of everyone inside the castle.
She couldn't get to Bianca again in person, but she had managed to make a connection with her while she slept. Bianca kept having vivid dreams of Patricia snarling what she was going to do when she finally got her hands on her, but Bianca laughed it off, angering her greatly.
Angelo smiled, Bianca looking up at him.
"Why are you smiling?"
"Because of you, sweetheart. It seems you aren't even a tiny bit afraid of Patricia."
"Nah. I'm not. She just has issues," shrugged Bianca. "Maybe you should send Marissa to talk with her. Patricia loves her so much."
"Marissa wouldn't do it. And besides, I wouldn't let her venture deep into the forest alone. I would accompany her of course."
"Or you could send the vampire guards like last time."
"The Nefarious Pack injured them greatly recently, Bianca. I couldn't let that happen again."
Bianca rolled her eyes. "They're *guards,* Angelo. If they didn't get hurt while guarding you something would be wrong."
Angelo smiled at that. "Do you have everything?"
Bianca nodded. "Yep."
"Are you ready to go?"
"Nope."
Angelo laughed. "Bianca, the midwife and nurses are waiting to look after you."
"You said you'd come too," pouted Bianca, and Angelo said

"Unfortunately I'm not allowed to stay over at the hospital. But I promise I will come every night."

Bianca sighed. "You're the Grand Vampire. Can't they make an exception?"

"If they did the other fathers wouldn't think it fair at all."

Bianca sighed again, reaching for her suitcase-

"No, Bianca. You're heavily pregnant." Angelo smiled and picked up the case. "I'll carry it. Come, the limo is waiting."

Bianca followed him out of his suite, Clover and Cormier appearing, Joseph in Cormier's arms.

"Bee," said Joseph happily. "Where you go?"

"To the hospital," smiled Bianca. "I'll miss you, Joseph."

Cormier came closer with him, allowing Bianca to kiss his forehead.

"Be a good boy, ok?"

"Ok," said Joseph, smiling still. Bianca knew he wasn't going to be smiling when she left.

Two guards stepped forwards, saying "We shall accompany you, sir."

"All right," Angelo replied, then he turned to Cormier and Clover. "I will be back soon."

"Daddy?" said Joseph uncertainly, and Angelo smiled at him.

"I will be back soon, Joseph. Don't worry."

"Bee too?" asked Joseph, and Angelo shook his head.

"No."

Joseph's eyes filled over, and Bianca said "I'll be back soon, Joseph. With the baby, ok? You'll have a baby brother or sister to play with. I'll be back soon." She kissed his forehead. "I love you."

"Love you," wept Joseph, and Cormier said "I'll take him to the lounge. I don't want him to watch you leave again, chick pea. He was in a terrible state the last time."

"Ok," Bianca said evenly, and Clover hugged her as Cormier carried Joseph away, distracting him with his teddy.

"I'll visit every day, little sister."

"I'll be fine," mumbled Bianca. "Look after Joseph for me."

"I will do both," smiled Clover. "Are you afraid?"

"I am a little."

Angelo took Bianca's hand. "Come, Bianca."

"Bye Clover," sighed Bianca, and Clover said goodbye. "Tell Marissa I said bye."

"I will."

Angelo smiled as they left the castle, his guards looking around sharply as they neared the limousine.

"Sir?"

"Yes?"

"I can sense someone's presence."

"As can I," Angelo replied, "But ignore them and head for the limousine."

"Sir, please grant us permission to stand guard at the hospital for Miss Davis. Just in case anything happens."

"Granted," Angelo said, as they heard leaves crackle. Angelo stopped, turning to look at the figure. "What is your message from Patricia, son of the Nefarious Pack?"

"She wants the baby," growled the figure. "I have come to warn you. The Nefarious Pack do not harm the innocent. Trevor Gordon was right about Patricia. She is evil, cruel. We cannot allow her to harm that child."

"So what are you going to do?" asked Angelo, eyebrow raised. "If Patricia tells you all to jump, half of you will automatically leap in the air and the rest of you will shyly ask how high."

"Not anymore."

"And I should believe you?"

"Yes sir, you should. We have left Patricia alone and have abandoned our headquarters. We stand with the Virtuous Pack now."

Angelo said nothing for a moment. "What does she intend to do with our child?"

"Bite it, sir, turn it into a werewolf... and raise it as hers. If not, murder it."

"I'll murder *her* if she comes near my baby," spat Bianca, and the figure bowed to her.

"Miss Davis, rest assured the Virtuous and Nefarious Pack will not allow anything to happen to you or your child."

Bianca wasn't assured at all. "I want to be heavily guarded by vampires and wolves alike while I'm away from the castle. I'm being so serious when I say that."

"As you wish."

"Come on, Angelo. Let's go."

"Wait," said Angelo, looking at the figure. "Do I have your word you are no longer under the instructions of Patricia Bennett?"

"Yes sir. I would not lie to you, sir."

"And you really want to keep Bianca and our child safe?"

"Yes sir," they repeated. "I will give word to send ten werewolves to stand guard at the hospital. Five from the Virtuous Pack and five from the Nefarious Pack."

Angelo couldn't find a fault in that.

"You realise, if you are trying to find a way to get to Bianca and our child for Patricia and I find out, I will murder you?"

Bianca's jaw dropped but nobody else seemed surprised.

The werewolf nodded. "I realise that, sir. Yes."

"Good. Go back and get your guards. I will wait in the limousine with Bianca."

The figure morphed into a wolf before their eyes and bounded away.

Angelo led Bianca to the limo, his driver opening the door for them. Bianca stepped in and got comfortable, sighing. Angelo sat next to her, putting his arm around her.

"Are you all right, sweetheart?"

"I'm fine." Bianca sighed. "All of this because of Marissa's coma."

Angelo smiled grudgingly. "Patricia has slowly become obsessed with you. As time passes and you don't respond, she becomes angrier."

"Crazier," Bianca corrected. "I really think Marissa should talk to her."

"And you should talk to Marissa."

"I do," Bianca said indignantly. "I do talk to her."

"Both of you force conversation," Angelo replied. "I noticed it."

Bianca scowled. "What should I talk to her about? About how she's in love with you and she wishes it was her having your child? Or should I talk to her about her sexual fantasies about you?"

Angelo burst out laughing. "Her sexual fantasies about me?"

"I know she has them. When she looks at you, I see the love in her eyes," Bianca said amusedly, making Angelo laugh again.

"Bianca, I think you are obsessed with Marissa the same way Patricia is obsessed with you," chortled Angelo, and Bianca smiled at him.

"Nah. I don't mind her. But I do mind when she puts you in danger like she did when she took you for a walk in broad daylight."

"I apologise again for that." Angelo took her hand in his. "If the wolves take longer than forty minutes to get here we are leaving without them."

"Ok. Can they all fit in here?"

"Of course."

* * Cormier * *

"This week is doing to drag," Cormier said, Joseph sniffling on his shoulder. "Stop crying, Joseph."

"I want Bee," wept Joseph, and Clover smiled at him.

"She'll be back soon, sweetie. Do you want to read a story with me?"

Joseph nodded, Clover gently taking him off her cousin.

"I'll put him to bed afterwards. Angelo should be there when he wakes up."

Cormier nodded.

* * Angelo * *

Bianca was fast asleep in her bed, Angelo gazing at her.

"Um… Count Angelo? Sir?" a nurse whispered, and he glanced at her.

"Yes?"

"It's sleep time on the ward," she said humbly, and Angelo smiled.

"In other words, I must leave."

"Yes sir. Apologies, sir."

Angelo indicated the crowd outside Bianca's door. "They stay."

"Yes sir. As you wish, sir."

Angelo bent and kissed Bianca's forehead. "I shall return tomorrow at nightfall. Take care of her."

"It will be an honour to do so sir. Good night."

Angelo said good night, stepping outside Bianca's room and closing the door behind him. Looking at the vampires and werewolves, he said "Vampires guard at night along with the werewolves. When a vampire cannot function, werewolves take over. When the full moon is out in two or three days and the werewolves cannot be near Bianca, vampires take over. Understood?"

"Yes sir. Understood."

"Good."

Angelo glanced at Bianca's door, and reluctantly vanished.

* * Cormier * *

Angelo appeared in the lounge, falling into an armchair with a sigh.
"What's wrong, Angelo?" Marissa asked softly, making Cormier cringe.
Angelo sighed again. "I didn't want leave her."
Clover looked sorry for him. Cormier felt so too.
"Brother, it's only a week. You'll have a child at the end of this week or even earlier. Stop being so dependent on a female. It's not like you can't live without Bianca."
"I can't," Angelo replied flatly, and Cormier rolled his eyes.
"You will have to."
"Maybe you'd like to talk with me, Angelo?" Marissa offered, but Angelo declined, surprising her.
"I don't want to talk. I just want the hours to pass quickly so I can go back to the hospital."
Marissa nodded, looking slightly put out. Cormier smirked at her, and she glared at him but said nothing, Clover saying "How shall we kill the time?"
"We could watch the television," Cormier suggested; Angelo didn't speak. "We may find something interesting to watch. A movie of some sort, or a documentary."

* * Bianca * *

It was morning.

Bianca winced at the sunlight streaming through her window directly onto her face, sitting up and looking around.

She was in the hospital, and could hear doctors and nurses bustling around outside the room. Bianca glanced up, then her jaw dropped.

Four men hung over her, arms folded, eyes closed, their feet on the ceiling. Steam was issuing from their skin, she could hear the hissing. But the vampires felt nothing, in a deep sleep.

Bianca quickly drew her curtains, blocking the sun and plunging the room in semi-darkness. She listened, ears pricked, for the hissing sound to stop. It did, and she breathed out, relieved. She didn't want four dead vampires on her conscience.

There was a knock on her door, and a nurse entered, smiling.

"Good morning Miss Davis."

"Good morning," Bianca replied, and the nurse's smile grew.

"You must be hungry. Are you ready for breakfast?"

"Um. Yes please."

"We have pancakes with maple syrup or lemon, would you like that? Or would you like a healthier alternative such as a large bowl of cereal? Or fruit with a glass of fruit juice?"

"I'll have the pancakes, thank you."

The nurse bowed and left, five men entering the room and staring at her.

"Good morning to you, Miss Davis."

"Good morning," she said nervously, and they smiled, one saying "Don't be afraid. We're from the Nefarious Pack, here to protect you."

"Where's the wolves from the Virtuous Pack?" asked Bianca, and they pouted at her.

"They're looking around the hospital for anything suspicious. You prefer them to us?"

"No, I was just asking."

Immediately their expressions cleared, all of them smiling again. Bianca couldn't help but think they were very good looking men, or werewolves. They were gorgeous!

"Dwayne will stay with you at all times, Miss Davis. He will be your company for the week."

Dwayne the werewolf stepped forwards, a smile on his roguish face. Bianca smiled back at him, the other men or wolves promising to be just outside the door.

Bianca said ok, the nurse she saw entering with a tray of food and a drink.

"Here you are, Miss Davis."

"Thank you," smiled Bianca, shifting and sitting up properly, Dwayne taking a seat next to her.

Bianca tucked into her food fast, suddenly really hungry. Dwayne laughed, saying "You didn't eat for a week I presume?"

Bianca laughed as well. "I'm starving."

Dwayne smiled at her. "I can tell."

Bianca averted her gaze, not wanting him to notice her attraction to him.

"So, um, do you have a partner? A werewolf girlfriend?"

Dwayne laughed. "No."

"Don't you want one?"

Dwayne shrugged. "I wouldn't want a werewolf girlfriend or even a vampire one. I'd prefer a mortal."

"Oh," said Bianca. "Why?"

"Because then she could choose to be with me, out of her own choice. Then, I would turn her. Some werewolves think they must be with another werewolf. That's not the case at all."

"Right," said Bianca slowly. "So… if I was your girlfriend, you'd turn me without my consent? Or would you give me a choice?"

"A choice of course. I wouldn't risk you hating me forever."

Bianca smiled at that. "Good."

Dwayne smiled back.

* * Angelo * *

Angelo gasped in his sleep, vivid images flashing before his eyes.

Bianca was laughing at something a man said, the same man feeding her food off a fork.

Bianca accepted the food with a saucy smile, Angelo staring as pink light swirled around her, light invisible to them, but light he could see.

Her attraction to him.

"No…"

Bianca smiled as the man leant forwards, Bianca too, and their lips met in a soft, tender kiss.

Then he saw Patricia Bennett, laughing her head off.

"Be careful, Count Angelo! She may be your downfall."

"Away with you, Patricia!" spat Angelo, furious. "You can't turn us against each other. Stop this madness!"

"No."

Bianca was before his eyes again, in Dwayne the werewolf's bed, her eyes closed as he kissed her- Angelo saw red as he watched Dwayne slowly unbutton her blouse.

"Patricia! Stop!!"

Her evil cackle rang in his ears as he snapped awake and leapt to his feet,

Cormier, Clover and Marissa appearing.

Angelo was breathing hard, Cormier saying "Brother? What is it?"

"Patricia planted false images of Bianca being intimate with another in my head."

"And you are angry?" said Cormier, surprised. "Angelo, it wasn't true!"

"I know. But having to see it angered me. I need a drink."

* * Bianca * *

"Mmm. That feels nice."

"Count Angelo will have my head," Dwayne replied amusedly, hands on Bianca's shoulders, massaging her. "Are you sure we should be doing this?"

"I'm sure. My back kills and I can't lay on my stomach. My shoulders ache too and you're making them feel so good."

Dwayne smiled at that, choosing not to answer.

There was a knock on the door but Bianca didn't reply, eyes closed.

* * Angelo * *

Angelo's eyes glowed as he was about to stare through the door, but Clover slapped him on the cheek, startling him as he looked at her.

"What-"

"Just go in. She may be asleep," she whispered, so he did.

And stopped dead.

"Bianca!"

"Hey," she said, Dwayne releasing her shoulders immediately. "What took you so long to get here? I was starting to think you wasn't coming."

"Patricia Bennett was winding me up," Angelo replied, eyes on Dwayne, who took a step away from Bianca.

"Sir, if whatever Patricia said to you has you angry with me-"

"I'm not angry with you," Angelo said, slightly untruthfully. "Please, join the other wolves. I'm here now."

"Yes sir."

"Thanks for the massage," smiled Bianca, and Dwayne smiled back at her.

"Anytime."

Angelo sat in the seat next to Bianca's bed, Clover standing.

"Little sister, how are you?"

"I'm great. The food is excellent and Dwayne hasn't left my side all day. He's great company."

Clover smiled at her. "I'm going to talk to the vampire guards and the werewolves. I'll be back in a little while."

Bianca said ok, Angelo nodding.

Clover vanished.

"Angelo?" said Bianca, and he looked at her. "Are you ok?"

Angelo said no.

"What's wrong?"

"That evil woman Patricia. She showed me images of you... cheating." Angelo looked at her. "I was so upset."

"I'm not going to cheat, Angelo. I love you," Bianca said softly. "I left everything and everyone I know for you. I might make you angry over some things, but I promise you, it will never be because I've cheated."

Relieved, Angelo leant forwards and kissed her.

"I love you so much."

"I love you too. I-" Bianca gasped, Angelo looking at her.

"Bianca? Are you all right?"

"Call a nurse or doctor- anyone," panted Bianca, holding her stomach. "Quickly, Angelo!"

Angelo vanished and reappeared in the corridor.

"Can we get some help in here!"

Nurses came running, and the next thing Angelo knew Bianca was being wheeled away to theatre, joyous shouts from patients and staff alike.

"The baby's here!!"

"Angelo, don't leave me!" gasped Bianca, and Clover said "I'll come with you, little sister- Angelo, you wait here with the guards."

Angelo wanted to go with Bianca, but Clover pushed him back.

"Wait here!"

"Angelo, listen to her," panted Bianca. "Clover, please come!"

Clover vanished and reappeared at Bianca's side, in an elevator. Angelo locked eyes with Bianca, who breathed "See you in a bit."

Angelo opened his mouth but nothing came out. He nodded, the doors of the elevator closing.

Angelo ran a hand through his hair, a nurse saying "Sir?"

"What?" he snapped, and the nurse hesitated before saying "Maybe you should go home? We can call you when Miss Davis is out of theatre-"

"I can't leave her-"

"She's with ten werewolves and five vampires including Clover. Please Count Angelo, you'll only tear your hair out with nothing to do. I promise you, we will call you."

Angelo sighed, then he vanished.

* * *

Almost seventeen hours later…

Angelo's mobile rang.

He snapped awake, grabbing it. "Hello?"

"Angelo, it's Clover. Come with Cormier and Joseph to the hospital. And Marissa as well, if she'd like to come. It's time you saw your child, cousin."

"Why did no one contact me sooner??"

"Apologies," Clover said humbly. "The hospital tried calling in the day but obviously you wasn't available-"

"I understand, Clover. We're on our way."

Angelo ended the call, heart racing as he ran into the bathroom to get a shower.

As soon as he was dressed, he called his brother.

"Cormier, dress Joseph and ready yourself. We're going to the hospital."

Marissa appeared at his side, Cormier saying "No Marissa, you aren't coming."

"Fine," she said stoutly. "I will be here when you get back."

"Are you sure, Marissa?" said Angelo, and she nodded.

"I'm sure. Now go and see your child."

Angelo smiled at her, Joseph reaching for him from Cormier's arms. Smiling, Angelo took him.

"Are you ready to see your little brother or sister, Joseph?"

Joseph nodded. "Yes Daddy. Bee too?"

"Yes Joseph. Bee too."

Marissa smiled a little. "I'll be waiting for you, Angelo."

Angelo nodded, leaving the castle with Joseph in his arms.

* * *

Angelo took a deep breath, standing outside Bianca's door.

Sensing her cousin, Clover appeared at his side, saying "Cormier, wait here with Joseph. Let Angelo go in on his own."

Cormier nodded, Angelo taking another breath before he entered the room, closing the door behind him.

* * Bianca * *

"Hey," Angelo said softly, and Bianca smiled at him weakly.

"Hey."

Angelo cautiously came closer, eyes on the bundle in her arms. Then he stopped, suddenly scared.

"Bianca?"

"It's ok," she said gently. "Come and look at your son."

"Son?" he whispered, and she smiled and nodded.

"Son."

Angelo took a deep breath before he walked closer and stared down at the tiny brown face of his baby- their baby.

Angelo couldn't speak.

The baby gurgled a little before opening his eyes- Angelo gasped.

"He has my eyes! My... my golden eyes."

"He's beautiful," Bianca said softly, as Angelo's eyes filled, a nurse standing by Bianca's bed. Angelo looked at the nurse.

"Can I hold him?"

"Yes sir. Of course."

Angelo inhaled sharply as the nurse gently took the baby from Bianca and walked over to him, placing the tiny boy into his arms.

Angelo stared down at the baby as he gurgled, looking around, then up at Angelo.

And Angelo felt a love for his child so intense he was glowing pure white, and he kissed the child's tiny forehead before looking at Bianca, who smiled at him as he asked "Micah Heathen?"

Bianca nodded. "Micah Samuel Heathen."

Angelo nodded, loving the name as he looked at Baby Micah.

"Hello, Micah Samuel Heathen. Welcome to the world."

Baby Micah closed his eyes, the nurse taking him and gently giving him back to Bianca.

"The rest of the family may come in now."

Cormier and Clover tiptoed in, Joseph in Cormier's arms.

"Bee!" said Joseph happily, and Bianca smiled at him.

"Hey Joseph. You ok?" Joseph nodded. "Come and look at your baby brother."

Joseph stared as Cormier carried him to the bed, looking down at Baby Micah, who opened his eyes again.

"Baby," said Joseph softly, and everyone smiled at him, Cormier putting him down. Still, Joseph stood on tiptoe so he could peer at the baby some more. "What it's name?"

Bianca smiled at him. "Micah."

"Micah?" asked Joseph, and she nodded, and Joseph beamed at the baby. "Hello Micah!"

Everyone could have kissed tiny Joseph as he smiled, saying "My brother!" He looked up at Angelo. "My brother, Daddy!"

"Yes Joseph." Angelo smiled at him. "Your baby brother."

"He's a beautiful baby, chick pea." Cormier smiled at Bianca. "He must take after you."

Everyone burst out laughing, Cormier dodging Angelo's playful hit and turning to the nurse.

"When can they come home?"

"The doctor says in two days," the nurse said, and Cormier pouted.

"Where is the doctor? They are both in good shape, healthy-"

"Miss Davis is still very weak," the nurse said firmly. "She needs to recuperate here at the hospital with the baby. If she has recovered in two days from giving birth, then rest assured she will come home. If not, she stays a little longer."

Cormier and Angelo nodded.

* * Bianca * *

Bianca spoke happily to Angelo, Clover and Cormier, letting Clover hold Baby Micah as she cuddled Joseph happily.

Joseph was excited at the thought of having a brother, and happy being with Bianca again. Bianca kissed him on the forehead, Angelo saying "Bianca, you'll have to call your family and let them know the good news."

"I will," smiled Bianca, "When me and the baby come home. I need to rest, calling my family is off limits until I'm one hundred percent fit."

"Well said chick pea." Cormier smiled at her. "We'll have to go soon."

Bianca pouted, the nurse saying "Sleep time is coming up, Miss Davis. But maybe I can bend the doctor's ear a little about letting Daddy stay."

"Would you?" said Angelo, smiling as she nodded. "Thank you."

An hour later Cormier, Joseph and Clover was gone.

Bianca was snoozing, Angelo holding Micah in his arms. He was staring down at his son's tiny face as he slept. Angelo took a deep breath as he looked at Bianca, who seemed to be in a deeper sleep now.

He stood, holding the baby, who stirred a little at the movement before settling back in his father's arms.

The werewolf and vampire guards stood outside the door, talking in low voices.

Angelo slipped right through the closed door with his child in his arms, saying to them "Guard Bianca until I get back."

"Yes sir."

Dwayne the werewolf went inside immediately, followed by two vampires as Angelo began walking. A nurse followed, saying "Count Angelo? Sir? Where are you going with the baby?"

"I'm just taking him for a walk. Come with me if you'd like."

The nurse blushed, then nodded.

Angelo smiled at her, and she smiled back shyly.

* * Bianca * *

Patricia Bennett stared down at Bianca as she slept, stroking her hair.

"You must be the only one who does not detest me."

Bianca didn't respond, Patricia sliding a finger down her cheek.

"I like that about you, Bianca Davis."

Dwayne was bound and gagged, unable to move, though he was trying to wake Bianca up, struggling with the thick rope wrapped around him, his voice muffled. The vampire guards were unconscious on the floor.

Patricia smiled, eyes burning red as she placed a hand on Bianca's chest.

"So kind a heart... so pure. I can feel it beating under my fingers."

Dwayne struggled harder, Patricia's fangs unsheathed as she lowered her mouth to Bianca's neck.

"I am so glad I get the first bite."

Dwayne burst free of his bindings, eyes glowing as he tore the tape off his mouth, then he threw his head back and howled.

Startled, Patricia looked at him. "You dare ruin this?!"

"I dare," snarled Dwayne, the door bursting open as Bianca snapped awake, Angelo appearing with the baby in his arms.

"Patricia!" Furious, Angelo bellowed *"Get away from her!!"*

Patricia spun on the spot and vanished, Baby Micah crying as the other guards helped Dwayne up, Dwayne staggering a little as he panted "She was going to bite Bianca. I couldn't let that happen."

"No you couldn't have," Angelo said, feeling a rush of gratitude. "Thank you so much."

Dwayne nodded, looking at the unconscious vampires. "Anytime, sir. Your vampire guards need to get their strength back. They were no match for Patricia."

Angelo nodded, gently handing Baby Micah to Bianca, who was slightly in a daze as she asked "What… what exactly-?"

"Patricia had you in some sort of stupor as you slept," growled Dwayne, and everyone looked at him. "She paralysed me and tied me up, and taped my mouth. But the werewolf in me, the brute strength inside me, overcame the paralysis in no time. She almost plunged her fangs into your neck before I howled for backup."

Bianca held Micah close and kissed his tiny brow before she placed him in the bassinet beside her bed.

"Thank you."

"Anytime," Dwayne said, rubbing his arm, which was bleeding. Angelo placed a hand on Dwayne's arm and removed it, Dwayne and everyone else looking at his arm.

It was healed.

"Thank you, sir."

Angelo nodded, then he knelt and prodded both the unconscious vampires, both of who snapped awake at his touch.

"Where is she?!"

"She fled," Angelo replied. "Did you not use your sceptres on her?"

"Sir, she caught us off guard- our weapons were in the corner-"

"I don't want to hear it," said Angelo coldly. "You stay on your guard at all times aside from daylight and keep your weapons at hand, do you understand the words issuing from my mouth?"

"Yes sir."

"Good. Now I'm going to watch over Bianca and our son for tonight. Go and get your strength back, take a walk. Be back before sunrise."

"Yes sir," they mumbled again, Bianca feeling sorry for them as they sauntered out of the room.

"Don't be so hard on them, Angelo. Nobody knew Patricia would come here-"

"Bianca, they didn't have to know. All they had to do was expect it." Angelo scowled. "Anything could have happened to you if I didn't hear Dwayne's howl."

Bianca sighed and nodded.

* * Cormier * *

"Micah is such a beautiful baby boy, Marissa." Clover smiled at Marissa. "He has his father's amazing gold eyes and such perfect, dark brown skin. He's like a little chocolate bar, I could gobble him up. He is perfect, just like little Joseph."
Joseph had only just fallen asleep, too happy and excited about everything to settle easily.
Marissa smiled as Cormier served them both a drink, saying "I can't wait to meet the little bundle of joy. Were there no disturbances?"
"Not that I know of."
"I'm   glad   to   hear   it."

* * Angelo * *

Angelo woke to a soft caress on his cheek.

Smiling, he opened his eyes to find Bianca on his lap. "Hello."

"Hey," she said softly, kissing him. "Wake up. I miss you."

Angelo was amused. "You miss me and I'm right next to you."

"Yep. I just fed Micah."

"Did he feed well?"

"Of course."

"Good." Angelo inhaled deeply before he held her in his arms and stood, saying "I must go home to freshen up, and check on things. I'll be back."

Bianca nodded, and Angelo kissed her before he placed her back on her feet.

"I'll send in the guards-"

"Angelo, wait-" Bianca stopped him, looking out of the window, at the sky. Angelo looked up too, then he swore.

The full moon was out.

"Werewolves," Bianca said softly as the vampire guards entered the room, and Angelo said "Stay in here at all times, Bianca. Do not leave this room."

"The wolves have fled from the hospital, sir, back into the forest. I think they were trying to stay away from Miss Davis, resist temptation," a vampire guard said, looking at Angelo. "Dwayne was blocking the door from the other nine. They wasn't prepared to fight him, so they ran."

"Oh," said Angelo, wondering why Dwayne the werewolf was resisting biting Bianca and also stopping the others from getting to her. To stay in his good books? That had better be the reason. "Where is Dwayne now?"

"Gone as well, sir. I expect he shall keep away with the rest until dawn."

"All right. I'm going back to the castle. I will be back in less than two hours. Guard Bianca in that time. All four of you be on your highest guard, understood?"

"Yes sir."

"Good."

Angelo looked at Bianca, who was back in bed. She beckoned him closer, and he came curiously; Bianca smiled and pulled him down so his lips met hers, the guards shifting as they tried not to stare.

"Hurry up," Bianca said softly once they broke the kiss, and Angelo said "I'll be as fast as I can."

He vanished.

* * Cormier * *

"Daddy!" cried Joseph as Angelo appeared, and Angelo smiled at him. "Hello, Joseph."

Joseph got up from his toys and ran to Angelo, who swept him up in a big hug.

Marissa smiled, asking "How is the baby?"

"The baby is doing fine. Bianca fed him before I left."

Marissa nodded. "And…" She took a deep breath. "How is Bianca doing?"

Cormier knew it had killed her to ask that. Angelo smiled, saying "Bianca is amazing as usual. She wasn't even fazed by Patricia-"

"What?" said Cormier sharply, Clover as well. "Patricia came to the hospital, brother?"

Angelo's expression darkened as he told them what happened, Clover saying "Thank the Heavens for Dwayne! And he wouldn't let the werewolves near Bianca once they'd transformed?"

Angelo said no, once again relieved at that. "I'm so grateful for that."

"As am I," Cormier said, Clover saying "And I."

Marissa sipped her wine and said nothing, Cormier glaring at her as Angelo said "Anyway, I'm only stopping by quickly to freshen up. I need to get back to them. Hopefully they let me stay another night."

Amused, Cormier said "And if they don't, brother?"

"Then I shall just charm the lot of them into letting me. I don't want Bianca unguarded."

Cormier frowned. "The vampire guards are more than capable of-"

"They are no match for Patricia. And the wolves aren't there either. This will be the most vulnerable night for Bianca to be protected," Angelo said grimly. "I just hope Patricia doesn't realise that. And if she does, I will be ready."

Marissa and Clover nodded, Angelo putting Joseph down.

"Was Joseph all right?"

"He was fine," Cormier said reassuringly. "He just can't wait for you all to come home."

Angelo smiled, then he left the lounge.

* * Bianca * *

Bianca held Baby Micah in her arms, gazing down at him.
The vampire guards watched her in silence, saying nothing as they listened to the doctors and nurses bustle in the open ward, on guard.
Bianca gently kissed Micah's forehead before she laid him back in his bassinet beside her bed, then she began to settle down herself, closing her eyes as she mumbled "I wish Angelo will hurry up."
"He'll be here, Miss Davis. Don't worry," a guard said kindly, and she smiled at him.

* * Angelo * *

Marissa knocked on Angelo's door as he was buttoning up his shirt.
"Angelo?"
"Yes Marissa."
"Can I come in?"
"Just a minute."
Angelo fastened his cape, his collar upturned as he reached for his gloves. After he pulled them on and wore his shoes, he said "Come in."
Marissa entered, then her jaw dropped.
"You look magnificent."
"Thank you," smiled Angelo. "Did you need something? I really must get back to Bianca."
"I need to be held by you," Marissa said quietly, and he said "Is that all? Come."
She smiled and walked forwards, almost falling into his warm embrace. Marissa closed her eyes as Angelo rested his chin atop her head, whispering "I needed this, Angelo."
Angelo could sense the lust, the intimate feelings she was experiencing from being in his arms. But he didn't let her go.
Cormier appeared, startling them.
"Brother, I think Joseph- what-?" he stared at them, then looked at the dreamy expression on Marissa's face. "What the hell is going on?!"
"Marissa needed a hug, that's all," Angelo said. "I didn't mind giving her one."
"It may have been just a hug to you but it meant more to her," spat Cormier as he glared at Marissa, who slowly let Angelo go.
Angelo sighed. "Cormier, control your emotions for once. What was you saying about Joseph?"
"I was saying that I think Joseph's speech is improving. He's using proper sentences now. Bianca had the right idea when she said it's good to read with him."

* * Cormier * *

Angelo smiled. "Bianca is perfect."

The scowl on Marissa's face was delicious. Cormier couldn't help maliciously adding "That she is."

Marissa's eyes were starting to glow red, Angelo looking at her.

"Marissa? Are you all right?"

"I'm fine, Angelo." Marissa glared at Cormier. With a hint of ice to her tone, she said "I'll go and see what Clover is doing. Farewell, Angelo."

"Farewell," Angelo replied, and Marissa vanished. "Brother, please ready a room for Micah before Bianca brings him home."

"Consider it done, brother."

Angelo vanished, and Cormier's smile faded as he teleported to the lounge, where Marissa sat fuming.

"You just can't let him go, can you Marissa? Even after the birth of his child?"

"Go to Hell, Cormier."

"Well that would be easier for you, am I correct?" Cormier smirked at her as she snapped "Just keep out of my way!"

"Not when you're trying- *still* trying, should I say- to seduce my brother."

"This again?" sighed Clover as she walked into the lounge. "Cormier, change the record."

"Yes Cormier," smirked Marissa. "Change the record."

"Clover, she was in Angelo's arms a moment ago," Cormier said angrily, and Clover shrugged, answering "So? Everybody needs a hug from time to time. Come and give me one, cousin."

"Clover, be serious!"

"Come and give me a hug!"

Cormier cursed before he walked and gave Clover a hug, Marissa laughing now. Cormier released Clover, scowling as she said "Didn't that feel good, cousin?"

"No," Cormier said, though he didn't mean it. "I'm going to check on Joseph."

"Don't disturb him," Clover said. "I left him asleep."

"I won't."

Cormier threw a dirty look at Marissa before he left the lounge.

* * Angelo * *

Angelo woke as he heard Baby Micah gurgle, a nurse saying "He needs to be fed now, Miss Davis."
"All right."

* * Bianca * *

Bianca held Micah in her arms, holding up his bottle. She didn't notice Angelo watching her until she glanced at him as the baby fed, then she smiled.
"Hey. Good sleep?"
"Pretty good," smiled Angelo. "Yours?"
"It was ok. Micah woke me up a few times though. But he always goes back to sleep when I hold him."
"He loves and misses the touch of his mother, that's why." Angelo smiled and stood. "I'm pretty hungry. I'm going to go to the castle and freshen up, get something to eat, then come back."
"Ok."
Almost as soon as she said it Angelo's vampire guards came in, sceptres at hand. Four werewolves including Dwayne also came in.
Dwayne smiled at Bianca. "How are you feeling, Bianca?"
"Much stronger than I did when I first had Micah." Bianca smiled back at him. "I can walk without getting dizzy now."
"That's good to know." Dwayne jammed his thumbs in his pockets. "Well, you're stuck with me again as your personal guard. There won't be another full moon for a while so there's no reason for me not to guard you."
"Great. Wow," she said as she looked down at Baby Micah. "He pretty much finished the whole bottle of milk."
Angelo smiled and kissed her on the forehead, then he kissed Baby Micah.
"I will be back soon."
"Ok."
Angelo looked at Dwayne. "Take care of them."
"Yes sir. I will," Dwayne replied, and Angelo said "All of you be on guard, not just Dwayne."
"Yes sir," the vampire guards said, the werewolves as well.
Angelo looked at Bianca, who softly said "We'll be fine. Go."
Angelo vanished.

* * *

A cackle made Angelo stop dead as he neared the castle. He glanced around sharply, then he saw her.

"Count Angelo," she said softly, eyes burning red.

"Patricia," he responded icily, and she bowed. "What do you want?"

"I want Bianca Davis. If I can't get her, you will pay."

Angelo rolled his eyes. "Is that a threat?"

"I challenge you to duel with me," snapped Patricia. "If I win the duel, I get Bianca Davis and the baby."

Angelo smiled coldly. "And if you lose?"

"Then I will leave all of you alone. That is a promise. I won't even contact Marissa."

"No deal." Angelo began walking again, Patricia following him.

"Are you afraid to lose, Count Angelo?"

"I'm amused, actually."

"Amused?!" Enraged, Patricia morphed in front of him. "You think I jest?!"

"You may as well be jesting." Angelo looked at her icily. "Because you can't honestly think I'd gamble my lover and my newborn son in a duel with you."

"Then face the consequences-"

"No. *You* face the consequences," Angelo said, eyes lighting scarlet along with his body. "Come near Bianca or my son again and I promise, I really promise, I will not rest until you are dead. Do you understand?"

Patricia didn't answer.

"You have been playing games with me and my loved ones for a while now and it's starting to get under my skin. So do the right thing, Patricia Bennett, and slink back into the depths of the forest where you belong. Otherwise I really will take matters into my own hands and deal with you." Angelo grabbed her by the neck, making her gasp out loud. She didn't struggle, scarlet eyes on scarlet eyes. "I will kill you, Patricia. Is that what you want?"

"You don't have the guts," spat Patricia, though she was shaking and he knew she was just putting on a front.

"You think so?" She didn't answer. "Give me a reason. Give me the slightest reason and I swear to you, you will be dead within that hour."

Angelo's golden eyes had bypassed scarlet and were now pitch black.

"Angelo!"

Surprised, Cormier appeared with Marissa and Clover, but Angelo ignored them.

"Do we understand each other, Patricia?"

"Yes," she said, afraid as he let her go.

"Good. Now get out of my sight. And don't ever think of challenging me again."

Patricia vanished, Cormier dashing over to Angelo.

"Brother! Are you all right? What happened??"

"I'm fine," Angelo replied, taking a deep breath. "I will tell you inside the castle."

* * Cormier * *

"So that's the end of it?" said Clover, and Angelo nodded.

"I expect so."

"She will not dare disobey you, Angelo." Marissa spoke with much admiration in her voice, annoying Cormier to the max. "I've never seen you so angry that your eyes were pitch black."

"Not many have," Angelo replied, shrugging a shoulder. "She had the nerve to challenge me and claim Micah and Bianca lest she win. It had me sick to the stomach. That woman is deranged, twisted. No offence, Marissa."

"None taken," smiled Marissa. "So when can Bianca and little one come home?"

"If all goes to plan, tomorrow night. If not, the following night, I believe. I'll check with the doctor."

* * Bianca * *

Bianca woke up to Angelo's soft, tender kiss.

"Hey," she said softly, and he replied "Hey. Were you ok while I was gone?"

"I was fine. You?"

"I wish I could say the same."

Bianca sat up in bed as Angelo sat down in the chair next to her bed. "What happened?"

"I ran into Patricia Bennett. I was so angry." Angelo sighed. "I think she will leave you alone now, Bianca."

"Oh." Bianca didn't feel the need to ask what went down. "Are you sure?"

"I'm sure."

* * Angelo * *

Two days later...

It was soon time for Bianca to come home with the baby.

Angelo was smiling broadly as he checked Baby Micah's room. It was pastel yellow with splashes of green, blue, and silver, with a tall, brown wooden grand cot in the middle, a small table with a baby monitor on it next to it, and a rocking chair.

"At night you can dim the lights to suit him," Cormier was saying, "Just turn the knob here on the wall and it will either get brighter or darker. However you prefer it. Oh, and did you check the drawer, Angelo? He has plenty of clothes from Bianca's mother and then some."

"Brother, it's perfect. Thank you so much."

Cormier smiled, pleased. "You're welcome."

* * Bianca * *

"I suppose it's time to say goodbye to you, Bianca Davis." Dwayne the werewolf smiled at her, and her eyes filled. "It has been a pleasure guarding you."

"Please don't go," she said sadly, and he came closer. "You've been such a good friend to me. Don't go."

"I must, Bianca. I'm sure our paths will cross again in the future."

"I want us to stay in contact. Please, I'm begging you." Dwayne looked at her as she said "It doesn't have to be the end."

"Hmm." He pondered that before he said "Hand me your mobile phone."

Bianca obeyed, Dwayne tapping something in before giving it back to her.

"My mobile number is in there now. If you ever want to talk, text me."

Bianca pouted. "This still feels like a goodbye forever."

Dwayne laughed at that. "I can see why the Grand Vampire chose you to be his. You have all the qualities a man desires in a woman."

Bianca opened her mouth, then closed it. "Thank you."

Dwayne took her hand and kissed it, murmuring "You have my number now. Feel free to contact me at any time. I will still protect you as I have done here, in the forest if you decide to see me."

"I will," said Bianca, and Dwayne left the room.

"Count Angelo!" she heard people call excitedly in the ward, and she smiled as she looked at Baby Micah.

"Daddy's here for us, Micah. I hope you'll be comfortable in your new home."

Micah gurgled, dressed in a blue and white striped babygro, a matching hat on his head. He sat in a baby chair, buckled in.

Angelo entered the room, smiling. "Miss Davis, the limo awaits."

Bianca smiled back as Angelo's four vampire guards appeared, picking up Bianca's suitcase and other belongings.

Angelo smiled and picked up the baby chair by the handle, a guard saying "Would you like one of us to carry him, sir?"

"No," Angelo replied. "I want to carry my son to his new home."

Bianca smiled at him as they left the room, the hospital nurses, doctors and even patients calling goodbye to Bianca, wishing her all the best.

"Thank you so much," Bianca called back, then she went and pulled a female vampire nurse into a hug. "Thank you especially, Veronica."

Pleased, Bianca's personal nurse beamed at her, eyes glowing.

"You're welcome, Miss Davis. You see vampires don't only bite?"

"I see," smiled Bianca. "Thank you so much."

"I will be at the castle weekly for the next two months to check on you and Micah," Veronica replied, then she looked at Angelo. "Is that ok, sir?"

"Of course it is, Veronica." Angelo smiled at her. "Thank you so much for everything you have done."

Bianca was excited as they left the hospital. "I can't wait to climb into that big bed of yours and just roll around in it."

"It's our bed, Bianca. Not just mine."

Bianca beamed at him.

* * Cormier * *

Joseph ran about excitedly, saying "Bee come home with my brother!"
"That's right," smiled Cormier, Clover saying "Joseph is so adorable. I love him."
They heard the doors open on the floors below, and Cormier swept Joseph up as he made to run to Angelo, saying "Wait, Joseph."
"Ok!"
Almost ten minutes later Angelo entered the lounge with Bianca, carrying Baby Micah in his chair.
Joseph squealed and ran to Bianca, who swept him up and cuddled him, kissing his forehead.
"Bee!" said Joseph happily, and Bianca smiled at him.
"Hey, Joseph. You ok?"
"Yes Bee! I miss you lots!"
"I missed you too," smiled Bianca as she set him down, and Cormier pulled her into a warm hug.
"I missed you also, chick pea."
"Same here," smiled Bianca as she hugged him back, and Baby Micah gurgled contentedly, Joseph jumping up and down to try and see him.
"Daddy, I want to see my brother!"
Angelo smiled and moved to the centre of the lounge, placing the baby chair down.
Joseph knelt next to the chair and looked at Micah, beaming. Micah looked back, then he gurgled again, kicking his tiny legs. Pleased, Joseph said "I love my brother, Daddy!"
"And he loves you too, Joseph." Angelo smiled at the tiny boy, loving him more than ever. "We all do."
"He's a beautiful baby," Marissa said, slightly amazed as she looked at Micah. "You didn't tell me he had your eyes, Angelo."
"Did I not?" she said no. "Apologies, Marissa."
Micah gurgled again, Joseph sitting close to the baby chair, already protective of his baby brother.
"Are you hungry, chick pea?" asked Cormier. "I will make whatever you fancy."
"Really?" said Bianca, and Cormier said yes, smiling. "All right. I fancy chocolate chip pancakes."
"At this time?" said Angelo amusedly, and Bianca nodded.
"Yep."
Everyone laughed, Cormier saying "Coming right up. Does that go for everyone else? Pancakes for dinner?"
Everyone said yes, highly amused.

* * Bianca * *

"Bianca, sweetheart. You must call your family and let them know about Micah," Angelo said quietly, and she said "Snap, I forgot. Shall I do it now?"

Angelo said yes.

An hour later Bianca's family; her father, mother, grandmother and brother all demanded they come and stay with them in Pennsylvania for at least a week- and that they come the following week. Bianca said no way, but Angelo said they were more than welcome.

"Angelo, I want to get settled and used to life with you and our baby and Joseph, our family," pouted Bianca after she ended the calls. "Can we at least have a month with just us first?"

Angelo thought about it, then he said "I suppose. But your family do want to share the excitement with us, Bianca. They'll be fit to burst if we make them wait for a month."

"Then let them burst! Angelo, please," begged Bianca, following him around, then she paused as she looked around. "Where's Micah?"

"In his crib, sound asleep," Angelo said, and Bianca relaxed, then remembered what she was saying.

"Angelo, I'm begging you. Let them come in a month."

Angelo sighed. "Call your family back and request it. If they say no, they come next week. If they oblige, they come in a month. Deal?"

"No deal," pouted Bianca, then she smiled. "It's kind of a bet."

Barbara, Samuel, Gran and Ricky all said there was no way they'd wait for a month to see Bianca and Micah.

"Please, Count Angelo! Let us come sooner," begged Bianca's mother. "Don't listen to Bianca. We have to see Baby Micah!"

"No!" said Bianca, when Angelo opened his mouth. "Mum, I'll send you pictures or something, ok? I just left the hospital, I can't handle you and the rest yet!"

"How about you arrive in two weeks?" suggested Angelo. "More than a week from now but less than a month."

"That sounds fair," Ricky said quickly. "Can we do that then? Come in two weeks?"

"Of course," said Angelo: Bianca scowled and said nothing. Angelo burst out laughing, ending the phone call to Bianca's mother and brother before he looked at her. "Come on, sweetheart. Be nice."

Bianca pouted. "The two weeks before they come is going to go by so quickly. Then I won't have you to myself."

"Of course you will," Angelo reassured her. "I will make myself scarce so you can spend the time you need to with your family. I will make sure Cormier and the others do too."

"Wait- what? You're going to just ghost while they're here??"

"If they aren't comfortable being around vampires, then yes," Angelo said, then he smiled at her down expression. "Bianca, I'm trying to make sure they're comfortable in our home."

"They will be," said Bianca. "And if they're not, they can go to a hotel."

Angelo laughed. "That wouldn't be very hospitable."

"They can go to a hotel," Bianca repeated. "I'd prefer that, actually. They can visit every day instead of staying here."

"I think they had their minds set on staying in the castle, Bianca."

"Well too bad," pouted Bianca, and he laughed again.

"What about Shanaid? She will want to come too."

"Shanaid can come another time. Let's get the family visit over with."

"Chick pea, your pancakes are now lukewarm," Cormier said, appearing suddenly. "We was waiting for you to get off the phone."

"Sorry, Cormier. My mother wouldn't get off the phone," said Bianca apologetically, and Angelo snapped his fingers.

"There. I cleared the table. I will make fresh pancakes."

"No, I will," pouted Cormier. "You just relax, brother."

Clover appeared before Angelo could reply, saying "If we must wait for supper again we may as well go into the lounge."

Bianca and Angelo said ok, Joseph in Clover's arms.

"Where's Marissa?" asked Bianca casually, and Clover said "She's in her bedroom, I believe. The last thing she said was she was so stunned by Baby Micah."

Bianca froze, and she turned on her heel and walked down the corridors and made a right, into the corridor where the bedrooms were, almost running now. Angelo was right behind her with Clover and Cormier, Joseph squirming in Clover's arms.

Bianca gently opened the door to Micah's room and stopped dead.

"He woke up," Marissa said quietly, before Bianca could demand what the hell she was doing. Micah gurgled in Marissa's arms, Marissa gazing down at him as he looked around curiously. "I held him before he could start crying."

Bianca opened her mouth, then closed it. Forcing calmness into her voice, she said "Thank you. But please don't touch him again."

"Bianca!"

"All right, you can touch him," she said irritably as Angelo scowled at her, and he said "Marissa, you may hold Micah, but please alert us if he wakes. He may be hungry."

Marissa nodded, Bianca glaring at her as Joseph wailed "I want to see my brother!"

"You can, Joseph." Bianca smiled at him, taking him from Clover and carrying him towards Marissa. "See? He's looking at you."

Joseph beamed down at Baby Micah, and Angelo said "I'll take him, Marissa."

Marissa hesitated, Bianca coldly saying "Give my son to his father."

Marissa handed the baby almost reluctantly, Cormier glaring at her. Clover broke the icy atmosphere as she clapped her hands and said "Shall we go to the lounge then? Cormier's going to remake everything, so we may as well do something while we wait to eat."

Bianca nodded, Joseph clinging to her like a little monkey as she walked. She was seething and everyone knew it.

* * Angelo * *

After dinner, everyone went to the lounge to relax.

Bianca was holding Micah, deep in thought as everyone smiled at her and the baby. Marissa said nothing, eyes on Angelo. He met her gaze questioningly, and she sent him a mind message:

If comforting the baby was out of line, I apologise. I just wanted to keep him calm before he started to cry.

It is fine, Marissa. I promise.

Angelo smiled at her reassuringly, Cormier and Bianca looking at him curiously as Marissa smiled back.

Bianca detests me.

No. She's just protective of her child, that's all.

She does not like me, Angelo.

She does.

All right, if you say so.

Angelo's smile grew, Marissa smiling back at him with an even bigger smile, and Cormier said "Would you care to share why you are both grinning like Cheshire cats?"

"No," Angelo replied flatly, and Marissa said "Mind your own business, Cormier Heathen."

Joseph suddenly got up, staring at the door. "Daddy?"

Angelo looked at him. "Yes Joseph?"

"Lady out there," said Joseph, pointing, and everyone got up immediately.

"Patricia," spat Cormier, and Clover's eyes lit scarlet as Patricia morphed in the middle of the lounge, everyone standing. Every vampire's eyes burned bright red.

"I take it you didn't heed my warning about toying with me and my family, Patricia?" Angelo asked coldly, and Patricia smiled at him.

"I was never one to heed for long."

"What do you want?"

"The death of you," she replied casually; Clover hissed and took a menacing step forward. "Relax, Clover. I wouldn't want Sebastian to take his life after I murder you also for challenging me."

Micah gurgled in Bianca's arms, and Patricia glanced at him and Bianca.

"Bianca Davis. Congratulations on your newborn child."

"Thank you," Bianca said icily, and Patricia smiled.

"You have fascinated me for so long. But I am done chasing you. The child will need it's mother, I realise that now. So instead of taking the mother's life, I shall make do with the father's."

"You are insane," Angelo said, and Patricia smiled.

"Call me what you like. When I am done with you, you will be so weak and bloodthirsty that you won't even be able to heal yourself. No vampire's blood will sustain you." Angelo didn't reply. "You will die, Angelo Heathen. And there will be nothing you can do about it."

"Why do you want him dead?" spat Bianca as she held Micah, Joseph holding onto her leg. "You'd better have a good reason."

Patricia shrugged a shoulder. "He threatened my life."

"And you didn't threaten mine?!"

"It's not about you anymore, Bianca Davis." Patricia smiled at her. "When I murder the Grand Vampire, the castle will be mine. I will be the new Grand Countess of Pennsylvania. Everyone and everything will fall under my rule."

"If you believe everyone will worship you just like that you really are insane," Angelo said, amused now.

"They will have no choice," Patricia replied. "Now, Count Angelo. You will follow me into the grounds of the castle. Everyone has been summoned there, vampires and werewolves alike. I want them to watch their beloved Grand Vampire die at my hands."

Suddenly everyone could hear the roar of the crowd outside the castle.

"It's either that or I make you," Patricia added, and she snapped her fingers.

Baby Micah vanished from Bianca's arms and reappeared in Patricia's.

"What the hell?! *Give me my baby!!*" Bianca screamed, and Patricia said "For every second Count Angelo hesitates I will cut him. So talk to your lover, Bianca Davis, if you want your son to remain unscathed."

Bianca turned to Angelo immediately. "Go with her, Angelo."
"Bianca, I need to think about this-"
"Brother, there is no time!" said Cormier fearfully, as Patricia conjured a knife with a smile. "Do you want a dissected child?! Just go with her!"
"We're right behind you," Clover added, and Angelo nodded, his body lighting scarlet.
"All right."

* * Bianca * *

The wind blew, icy cold.
Vampires and werewolves alike stood together fearfully as Angelo stood with Patricia, speaking quietly.
Bianca held Micah, Clover at her side with Cormier and Marissa. They were cut off from the rest of the crowd, Joseph fearful as he looked around.
The massive crowd of vampires and werewolves were shouting furiously at Patricia, yelling abuse and pleading she not do this. Patricia ignored them, stepping away from Angelo with a smirk.
Angelo turned and walked to his household, taking a deep breath.
"I will duel with her."
"Good," said Clover cogently, and Angelo shook his head.
"Only one survives, cousin Clover. We fight to the death."
"Good," Clover repeated, Cormier saying "Rip her limb from limb."
"You can do it, Count Angelo!" yelled someone, and cheers went up.
Angelo turned to Bianca as well, who said "Look how slim she is, Angelo. Break her back first, then-"
Angelo crushed his mouth to hers in a hot, passionate kiss, taking care not to press on Micah. Bianca felt a tremble pass through her body and she couldn't help wishing she and Angelo was making love up in the castle with her underneath him, eyes on his face as he moved in and out of her body, not huddled on the grounds shivering in the cold and about to watch the love of her life duel with a deranged woman.
Angelo knew what she was thinking.
"I'll do my best to survive, Bianca."
"You will survive," Bianca said firmly, and Patricia laughed, a baby chair appearing and a tiny chair appearing next to it.
"He will not survive, Bianca Davis. Let Baby Micah have a front row seat and watch his Dada die. Little Joseph can sit by him."
"Go to Hell," spat Bianca, as there were more shouts of outrage at that.
Eyes burning scarlet, Clover begged "Let me duel with her, Angelo. You don't have to. I will kill her!"
"No," Angelo said firmly, though his entire body was alight he was so

angry. He waved his hand, a golden gate appearing around Bianca and the rest of his family, and Marissa. "Stay inside this gate until it's over. Do not leave."

"I won't obey," Cormier said flatly, Clover as well. "You may need us."

Sebastian ran across the grounds and joined them before Angelo could reply, taking Clover's hand.

"Angelo, be careful. Is there no other way?" he asked, and Angelo said "There is not. If she is not killed, this will only continue. We fight to the death. To be honest I'd have it no other way."

Sebastian nodded, face grave.

A bell gonged from somewhere, Patricia saying "Prepare yourselves, everyone, for the death of your beloved Grand Vampire. Count Angelo, come!"

Angelo took a deep breath, saying "Stay inside this gate."

"We won't obey," Clover said firmly, and Angelo said "It is an order from the Grand Vampire. Cursed you will be if you do not obey me."

"I don't care," said Clover angrily. "We are family, Angelo. You can't fight alone."

"I will fight alone just as she is fighting alone," Angelo replied, glancing at Patricia. "Nobody will come to her aid. It is only fair nobody come to mine."

Cormier swore. "You are too kind, brother. If it were me-"

"But it isn't," Angelo said quietly. "If anything happens to me, you must look after and protect Bianca and my sons. Promise me that, brother."

"I promise," said Cormier, heartache in his voice. Angelo nodded, then he turned and walked to Patricia, who said "Thirty seconds before this will start. Are you ready, Count Angelo?"

"I am ready," Angelo replied, and she smirked.

"Good."

She glanced up at the sky, then she smiled. Without warning her hand sparked- BANG!!!

Angelo was blasted high into the air before Patricia clapped her hands hard, and he slammed to the ground.

Everyone was screaming his name as he unsteadily got to his feet, wiping blood from his mouth. Joseph was screaming, Clover doing her best to calm him, but Patricia morphed into the terrifying gigantic wolf beast she could become at will and pounced on Angelo, making the poor child scream again.

Bianca bit her fist to stop herself screaming as Patricia's claws sparked before she slashed Angelo's face, three gashes appearing on there, her other massive paw holding him down, her eyes burning scarlet.

"Fight back!" a female vampire in the crowd screamed. "Count Angelo, *fight back!!*"

"FIGHT BACK!!!" everyone yelled, Cormier and Clover as well. Marissa was taking deep breaths as she struggled not to do so, trying to stay calm, though she wanted to jump in there and save the man she loved. Tears were trailing down Bianca's face as she held Micah.

* * Angelo * *

Panting, Angelo's hand sparked- BANG!!!
Patricia was blown off him, everyone cheering, but she landed on her feet and ran back towards Angelo, eyes gleaming as Angelo conjured a sceptre and swung hard- Patricia screamed, her face cut deeply.
"An eye for an eye, it's only fair," panted Angelo, then he ducked as she leapt at him, running under her massive body and thrusting the sceptre hard into her stomach.
Patricia tumbled onto the grass with another scream, wounded as Angelo walked towards her, taking deep breaths as blood ran down his face.
"Daddy!" cried Joseph, as he staggered a little. "DADDY!!"
Patricia tore the sceptre from her stomach, blood gushing onto the grass.
"You will not win, Count Angelo!"
"Finish her!" yelled someone in the crowd, and everyone started yelling the same thing.
"FINISH HER!!!"
Patricia was weak: her body was not capable of remaining in wolf form. Angelo watched as she changed back into a human, hesitating as if unsure if he should kill her.
"Kill her!" yelled Cormier angrily. "You are too kind, brother! Send her to Hell!"
Patricia backed on her hands and knees as Angelo walked closer, unable to get up. Still, she goaded "You don't have the guts to kill me."
Outraged, Clover made to leave the segment Angelo placed them in and finish Patricia herself, but Angelo said "No, Clover! Stay where you are!"

* * Bianca * *

Bianca saw something glimmer in Patricia's hand as Angelo walked towards her, eyes burning scarlet.

What was it?

It looked like a star made of silver, jagged points all over it- Patricia was still goading Angelo.

Heart racing, she remembered what Patricia said.

"When I am done with you, you will be so weak and bloodthirsty that you won't even be able to heal yourself. No vampire's blood will sustain you. You will die, Angelo Heathen. And there will be nothing you can do about it."

She wants him to come closer, Bianca realised. She's going to use that star!

"Angelo, stay back!" she cried, but Patricia had already hurled the silver star at him, and it latched itself onto Angelo's chest, the pointed ends piercing his skin until the star was deep within him.

"The Star of Darkness!" said Clover, shocked as Angelo stumbled back with a gasp, and Bianca said "Please tell me that's not a bad thing!"

Angelo's body burst into bright yellow light and he was pulled high into the air by some invisible force, the Star of Darkness glowing as Joseph screamed "DADDY!!!"

Angelo was gasping for air, his skin tearing as his own blood poured from it, and Patricia laughed from the ground.

"You... you thought I believed that... that I could really duel with you and win?!" she sneered, panting. "The Star of Darkness was my plan all along! Goodbye, Count Angelo!"

Angelo struggled with the force holding him, but he was growing weaker and weaker as more and more blood poured from his body.

Patricia was still laughing.

* * Angelo * *

Angelo had two choices.

He could kill Patricia with the ounce of strength he had left, or he could try and tear the Star of Darkness from his body. He knew he would most likely fail to do so: blood was pouring from him, weakening him more every second.

Angelo gasped for air again, and then he made his decision.

* * Bianca * *

BAAAAAAAAAAAAAAAAANG!!!!!
Everyone screamed as it looked like Count Angelo exploded, then a huge
burst of golden light erupted from nowhere, heading straight for Patricia,
who tried to scramble away with a scream- another huge BAAAANG!!!
And Patricia exploded into dust, gone forever.
Cheers went up, everyone shouting with delight, but Bianca was staring
upwards. Everyone looked up too: Count Angelo was slowly falling to
the ground, his clothes singed and torn, soaked with his blood, his eyes
closed as he hit the grass with a soft thud.
"COUNT ANGELO!!!" everyone cried, as Angelo remained motionless.
"Clover, take Micah," said Bianca, but Clover said "I'm coming with
you."
"As am I," Cormier said firmly, and Marissa said "And I."
Bianca scowled at her, and Sebastian said "I'll take him, Bianca. I'll
watch him and Joseph."
Bianca nodded as she left the golden enclosure and walked towards
Angelo's body, Clover, Marissa as Cormier behind her.
Silence fell as Bianca knelt beside Angelo.
"Angelo?" she said softly, and his eyes flicked. "Angelo, wake up."
"Bianca…"
"Shh," she said gently. "We have to get you to the castle-"
"I- no!" suddenly wide awake, Angelo said "Bianca, listen to me. We
don't have much time. I am about to die-"
"What?!"
"I have lost a lot of blood- the chariot of Death will take me-"
Bianca heard horses neighing from in the forest, and she turned to look at
the gigantic chariot as it burst from the trees, glowing white, transparent-
her blood ran cold as she saw the hooded rider, his skeleton hands- Death.
"You can't take him!" she cried angrily, and Death laughed.
"There is nothing you can do now, Bianca Davis."
"But- but- Angelo?"
Angelo was unconscious again.
Bianca stood. "Please, you can't do this!"
"It is not my decision. I merely take the lives," Death replied, as tears
trailed down her face. "He has lost a lot of blood. He needs blood right
now to regain his energy, sustain his life- and you are all vampires. There
is nothing you can do. Your blood is tainted."
Bianca stared down at Angelo, whose lips were a faint blue. She was
doing some quick thinking.
"If he has untainted blood, he'll live?"

"Yes," Death replied. "Not the blood of vampires or werewolves."

"Do you have the power to awaken unconscious people?"

Death seemed to hesitate.

"Please," begged Bianca. "Please, I just need to talk to him for a split second. I'll owe you."

Everyone was silent, then Death nodded and snapped his fleshless fingers.

"You have five minutes, Bianca Davis."

"That's all I need," Bianca replied as she knelt next to Angelo again, and Cormier said "Chick pea… what are you doing?"

Bianca shook Angelo gently and he stirred. She didn't answer Cormier.

"Angelo? Please wake up."

Angelo opened his eyes, inhaling sharply. "Bianca…"

"Angelo, we don't have time on our hands. Death gave me five minutes."

"Four and thirty seconds," Death added, and Angelo frowned.

"Why? Am I not to die? We may as well not waste time."

Death shrugged. "As you wish-"

"No!" said Bianca angrily. "You gave me five minutes!"

"Bianca, when Death takes me, it won't be pretty," said Angelo weakly. "Take Micah into the castle with Joseph. I don't want you to witness this, Bianca-"

"Shut up and stop talking. Just listen to me." Angelo obeyed, waiting. "Angelo, I want you to bite me."

Gasps went up, Cormier, Clover and Marissa's mouths hanging open.

"What?" said Angelo incredulously. "I could never-"

"Angelo, you have to," pleaded Bianca. "I'm not losing you."

"You… you love me that much?"

"Three minutes," Death said flatly, and Bianca said "We don't have time to discuss this. But if there's a chance you'll live, I'm taking it."

"Do it," Marissa said softly, Clover as well. "Bite her, Angelo."

Fangs unsheathed, Angelo tried to protest even as his eyes gleamed scarlet.

Bianca shifted closer to him, and he took her in his arms.

"See you on the other side maybe," she whispered, and Angelo groaned before his fangs plunged into her skin.

Everything went black.

* * Cormier * *

Cormier waited with bated breath, Marissa and Clover also.

With each pull on Bianca's neck Death was a step further and further away from Angelo, Marissa whispering "It's working."

Angelo seemed to grow stronger and stronger, glowing pure brilliant white- with a large rear, Death's horses turned and charged back into the forest with the chariot, Death calling "Until another time, Count Angelo! You are blessed to have someone love you so much they sacrificed themselves for you!"

Angelo gasped and released Bianca, who was unconscious in his arms.

"Bianca?"

Silence.

* * Angelo * *

Angelo shook her, scared. "Bianca!"

"She's dead," whispered Clover, eyes filling, and Angelo felt Bianca for a pulse as whispers filled the air.

He felt nothing, and he felt her chest as well for a heartbeat.

Nothing.

"No! She can't be dead!"

He shook Bianca desperately, but he didn't get a reaction from her. He knew she wasn't playing games with him, otherwise he'd have felt her heart beating. He knew she was gone.

Dwayne the werewolf howled in pain and misery, the other werewolves following suit as Angelo lifted Bianca's body and stood, tears trailing down his face as he began to walk, away from them.

"My condolences, sir," a female vampire whispered as he passed her, and the rest of the crowd murmured the same thing.

Angelo didn't answer any of them, unable to think straight. He just knew he had to get Bianca's body to the castle, away from the public eye.

Cormier followed, tears trailing down Clover's face as she reached for Joseph, saying "Come, sweetheart."

"Where Daddy take Bee?" asked Joseph as he lifted his arms, and Clover picked him up without answering, kissing him.

Marissa reached for Baby Micah, but Sebastian said "I'll carry him, Marissa."

Marissa nodded.

* * *

Five hours later…

Angelo sat staring into nothingness, not speaking.

Everyone looked at him but said nothing as well, Micah gurgling in Angelo's arms.

"We should let Bianca's family know," Clover said uneasily, and everyone looked at her. "They will find out sooner or later- and they were meant to come here in two weeks' time, Angelo."

Angelo didn't reply, Clover looking at Cormier for help. Cormier shook his head, saying "We can't think of that now, cousin. We are grieving."

"Bianca's family must grieve also," Clover replied, and Marissa asked "Where is her body?"

"On the marble slab below, near the Mirror of Truth," Cormier replied. "Candles surround her."

"Very nice."

"I want Bee," said Joseph, eyes filling over. "I want Bee, Daddy!"

Angelo's eyes filled over. "Joseph, Bianca is… asleep."

"Oh," said Joseph. "Tired?"

"Yes." Angelo couldn't stop the tears trailing down his face. "She's very tired."

* * Bianca * *

Bianca woke up in a field of clouds, hovering in the air.

"Where am I?"

"You amazing girl," a voice said, and she whipped round and saw Death. "You sacrificed yourself to save the Grand Vampire."

Bianca nodded. "Is he ok?"

"He is far from ok, but not health wise. Health wise he is in perfect condition, as good as new."

Bianca breathed out, relieved. "Good."

"But he is mourning your death, like many others. You will be remembered years from now, Bianca, for what you did."

Bianca nodded again. "What now?"

"Well, it was agreed among the Dark and Higher Power, that you have a choice, and also a gift."

"A gift?"

"A gift for what you did," Death said. "From the Higher Power."

"So what's the Dark Power's part?" demanded Bianca, and Death replied "The Dark Power offers you the choice."

"Of what?" asked Bianca, though she had a good idea.

"Of returning to your loved ones... alive."

"As a vampire, right?" Death shrugged, and Bianca asked "What's the gift then?"

"That is entirely up to you."

"Ok, let me think about this for a minute."

"You've been dead for five hours," said Death flatly. "Almost six. When it reaches the sixth hour you have no choice anymore. You will be truly dead, Bianca Davis, and the gates of Heaven will open for you. Your body will be buried, and it will start to decay-"

"All right all right. How much time do I have to think about this?"

"Nine minutes," Death replied, and Bianca started pacing the clouds, thinking hard to herself.

She had to go back.

She had a son, a beautiful baby boy with stunning golden eyes, just like his father's. And there was little Joseph, who she loved dearly. And there was her family. Her parents, brother. Her grandmother. And her friends! Shanaid, Jake, Clover, Sebastian. Dwayne the werewolf. Even Marissa, who she didn't like and she knew it was vice versa, but Bianca was willing to be civil to her if she returned.

If.

She had a choice.

"Why chuck all that away?" she muttered to herself, Death saying "You haven't long, Bianca. It's better to make your mind up before the time runs out."

Bianca thought of Micah and Joseph, how she'd never be able to take them for walks or to school. She'd probably- oh!

"I'll go back," she said quickly, and Death nodded. "And I know what I want my gift to be."

"Excellent. Name anything you like."

"I'd like to be able to still function in the day and be able to go outside in daylight," Bianca said, trying to speak steadily. "I have a son, so much to do with him and Joseph. I can't miss out on that, and I will if I'll be trapped in the night. I have to be able to function in both day and night, and sleep when I want to, not by force. That is the gift," she said firmly, when she thought Death was going to interrupt. "Give it to me. Please."

Death nodded, and he snapped his fingers.

Everything went black again.

* * Angelo * *

Angelo and the others were still in the lounge, everyone but him asleep.
Joseph was in Clover's lap, sucking his thumb as he dreamt.
Baby Micah was fast asleep in his baby chair.
Angelo couldn't believe that Bianca had made such a grand gesture and
gave her life to save his. He just couldn't believe it.
"Why would you save me?" he whispered as his eyes filled again. "I
would have preferred it the other way. Now Micah will grow up without a
mother- and I will never fall in love with someone again. Because I will
never stop loving you, Bianca." Tears trailed down his face. "And I will
never love another the way I loved you."
Angelo heard a noise from below, and he frowned and got up. Everyone
woke as he did so, startled.
"Angelo?"
"Shh."
Angelo left the lounge, Clover handing Joseph to Sebastian before she
followed with Cormier and Marissa, Angelo picking up speed as he heard
the noise again.
He looked over the castle banisters below, then he gasped.
Bianca's body was gone.
"No!"
He charged down the stairs furiously, everyone right behind him as he
stopped at the marble slab, staring at it angrily, then he whirled round.
"What sick being would steal a dead body?!"
"I have no idea," said Cormier, disgusted as he walked around the slab,
inspecting it. "Nothing looks out of the ordinary. They must have lifted
her somehow without touching the candles."
"Or they flew," said Marissa, and Clover said "If they flew we still would
have heard their escape. Even if they were a bat. Bianca's body would
still be the same weight and length."
Angelo was furious. "Why steal Bianca's body?!"
Nobody replied, staring behind him in shock.
"Do they have no respect at all?? Now we have to throw a search party
for a missing body before I call her family and let them know-"
"Angelo," she said softly, and he said "Not now, Bianca!"
Then he stopped dead, whipping around.
"Bianca?!"
She stood before him, a smile on her beautiful face.
"Hey. You ok?"
"I- I…" Angelo's mouth hung open. Then he shook his head in disbelief.
"How is this possible?!"
"You're my vampire Daddy, Angelo." Bianca smiled at him, and they

saw the fangs. "Did I mention I have these amazing new teeth?"

Everyone laughed, relieved as Angelo pulled her towards him in a massive, relieved hug.

"I love you so much, Bianca Davis."

"I love you too."

"So my chick pea is a vampire now!" said Cormier, amused as well as relieved, and Bianca smiled at him, her teeth normal again.

"Yep. You'll have to tell me what the perks are aside from being able to read minds and unsheathing my fangs."

"You can fly," smiled Clover, "Either normally or as a bat. You'll pick everything up just fine, Bianca. Don't worry. We will help you."

Bianca smiled at her. "Thanks, Clover."

"And you can teleport," Cormier added; Marissa hadn't spoken. "But you won't be able to function in the day."

"Um, about that," said Bianca, trying not to smirk. "I can function just fine in the day. And aside from that I'll be able to go out in daylight."

"Why is that?" said Angelo curiously, and Bianca said "It was a gift from the Higher Power, for saving your life. Death told me."

"Death??"

"He's pretty cool, Angelo. Well, pretty calm given what he does anyway. He explained a lot to me."

Angelo nodded, then he pulled her into his arms again and just held her.

"Where's Joseph and Micah?" asked Bianca, arms around Angelo, and Clover said "Asleep in the lounge. We all wanted to just huddle together after- I mean, we thought you died, Bianca. I'm so glad you chose to return, even if you are a vampire."

"It's not a bad thing," smiled Bianca. "I'm still the same person."

"Indeed you are," smiled Angelo. "Come, let's go back to the lounge. I'm so glad I didn't call your family to tell them about your death."

"They don't have to know," shrugged Bianca, and Angelo asked "Are you sure?"

"I'm sure."

"All right." Smiling broadly now, Angelo said "Come, let's go to the lounge."

* * Cormier * *

Marissa was glaring at the floor, Cormier smirking at her.

He knew she felt thwarted by Bianca's return. If Bianca had remained dead, maybe she could have been Angelo's new lover. Cormier knew what she was thinking, and loved every minute of it.

Micah was awake, content in Bianca's arms. Joseph sat next to her, sucking his thumb.

Angelo was on cloud nine, Cormier thought amusedly as he looked at his younger brother, who was smiling dreamily.

"Brother. Are you all right?"

"I'm fine," sighed Angelo. "Bianca, Joseph and Micah need to go to bed. It's nearly dawn."

"In other words, he wants time alone with you," smiled Clover as she stood. "Go with him, Bianca. I'll put Joseph and Micah to bed for you."

"Thanks, Clover." Bianca stood carefully and gently handed Micah to Clover, who took him with a smile. "Night."

"Good night," everyone said, and Bianca smiled and left the lounge with Angelo, Clover leaving the lounge as well.

Sebastian picked up Joseph and followed her, saying "Good night, Cormier and Marissa."

"Good night," they replied; moments later it was just Cormier and Marissa in the lounge.

"What?" snapped Marissa, when she noticed Cormier smirking at her.

"You know exactly what, Marissa Bennett." Cormier's smirk grew. "You're not glad Bianca returned to Angelo. If she had remained dead, you may (note I said *may*) have had him."

"I'm glad she's back," lied Marissa, and Cormier arched an eyebrow.

"Really?"

"Really."

"All right Marissa, look. I know you're in love with Angelo. But really. He doesn't want you. You need to get that in your head before you do something crazy, like your sister Patricia. And her end wasn't nice," Cormier added, as if she didn't remember what happened. "I wouldn't want the same for you."

Marissa stared at him. "You talk as if you care."

"I..." Cormier swallowed. "I don't."

"Liar."

"It matters not if I care," snapped Cormier, and Marissa said "Don't lie to yourself, Cormier Heathen. I know you crave me."

Cormier stared at her, and she smiled.

"I see you don't deny it."

"I'm going to bed," snapped Cormier, and she shrugged a shoulder.

"Go if you may. I'm going to stay here and sit for a while. I have a lot to come to terms with."

"Like what?" demanded Cormier, and she glared at him.

"My sister is dead. Did you forget? She and Bianca Davis died less than twenty four hours ago."

"Well I would say I'm sorry for Patricia's death but I really couldn't give a damn," Cormier replied flatly. "She was evil. I'm glad she's dead."

Marissa opened her mouth, then she closed it and nodded, leaning back in the armchair she was in. Cormier wondered whether to leave her, then decided not to.

"Would you like a drink? A glass of red wine?"

"That would be nice. Thank you."

Cormier soon returned with Marissa's beverage and a glass of his own cocktail. Marissa accepted her drink with a soft thank you, and chills ran down Cormier's spine as he sat down opposite her on Angelo's loveseat.

They sipped in silence, then Marissa asked "Why do we hate each other, Cormier?"

"I don't hate you Marissa," Cormier said quietly, and Marissa said "You certainly act as if you do."

"And you don't act the same towards me?" Cormier said, arching an eyebrow, but before Marissa could reply Angelo appeared.

"Dawn is almost upon us, the pair of you. You'd better head to your rooms unless you want to fall asleep here."

Cormier nodded, eyes on Marissa. Angelo looked from his brother's face to his friend's, and realised he interrupted something.

"Apologies if I have disturbed you-"

"You didn't," Marissa said softly, making Cormier cringe. "We was just discussing the way we act towards each other. We pretty much established we don't hate each other, though we do act like it."

"You have repressed feelings for each other that you channel through hostility," Angelo replied with a shrug, and Marissa and Cormier's jaws dropped. "You act as if you hate each other because you both get angry with yourselves for wanting someone like each other. You think you don't stand a chance with each other and that makes you even angrier. The feelings are there," Angelo added, when they both stared at him. "You just need to let go of any other attachments toward anything and anyone and focus on each other."

"That's nonsense," said Cormier immediately, though he was uncertain and both Angelo and Marissa knew it.

"Is it, brother?" said Angelo, smirking. "Go to bed and sleep on it. It has been quite a crazy night. You may think differently later tonight."

"Good night Angelo," Marissa said quietly, and Angelo said good night. Hesitating, Marissa said "Good night, Cormier."

Cormier swallowed, then he said "Good night."

Marissa vanished, and Angelo smiled at his brother.

"Are you all right?"

"I have no idea what just happened or how I feel," Cormier admitted. "I will do as you say, brother, and sleep on everything. It has been a crazy night indeed. Good night, brother."

* * Angelo * *

Angelo slipped into bed beside Bianca, who was waiting for him.

"Everything ok?" she asked, and he smiled at her.

"Everything is amazing as long as we're together."

Touched, Bianca kissed him.

Smiling as they broke apart, Angelo decided to tell her.

"I believe Cormier has feelings for Marissa."

"That's obvious," shrugged Bianca, making him gape. "What else is new?"

"You believed so too?"

"Angelo, normally when a guy picks on a girl for no apparent reason it's either because he wants her to be his or he wants her dead. Cormier always picks on Marissa," Bianca pointed out. "He winds her up for no reason and says snide things to her."

"She does the same to him," Angelo said, and Bianca said "It's the same vice versa. Marissa and Cormier like each other. But Marissa loves you as well."

Angelo sighed and nodded. "I know."

"Let's go to sleep," smiled Bianca, and she snapped her fingers.

The main lights in Angelo's bedroom went out, the bedside table lamps turning on.

Angelo's jaw dropped. "You are a powerful vampire."

"I have the strength of sixty men and strong mental power. Call me Matilda," smiled Bianca, and she snuggled down under the duvet, shifting closer to Angelo, who put his arm around her as she closed her eyes, mumbling "I have a lot of skills to develop."

"I will teach you everything," Angelo reassured her. "For now, go to sleep, Bianca. You have been through quite a lot."

"You've been through worse," smiled Bianca without opening her eyes. "You have to sleep too."

Angelo smiled and dropped a kiss on her forehead. "Deal."

* * Bianca * *

Two weeks later...

"Mum, put him down," said Bianca exasperatedly, as Barbara cuddled Baby Micah happily. "I swear you haven't let him go since you got here."
"I will not put him down," said Barbara happily, Micah gurgling contentedly. "He's my baby grandson and I love him so much. Oh Bianca, you have to come on regular holidays so I can see him more."
"Do I have a choice in the matter?" Bianca asked amusedly, and her mother said "No you do not."
Joseph squealed as he ran into the lounge, Ricky behind him.
"I'm coming to get you Joseph!"
Joseph squealed again as Ricky swept him up and hugged him, saying "Got ya!"
Joseph laughed as Angelo appeared, and he said "Daddy, Daddy! Ricky come get me!"
Angelo smiled at Bianca's brother, who swallowed as he said "Joseph has taken to you brilliantly."
"Um... yeah. Thanks," mumbled Ricky, and Bianca sighed as Angelo asked "Is everyone ready for dinner? If you are, follow me to the dining area."
"Thinking Angelo is such a dish, Richard?" Bianca asked under her breath with a smirk, and Ricky snapped "Go to Hell, Bianca."
"Nah. That would be too easy for you. I'd rather stick around and watch you sweat because of Angelo."
"Shut up!"
"What's the matter?" asked Angelo as he looked back, and Ricky gushed "Nothing! Bianca was just winding me up."

* * Angelo * *

Angelo smiled and turned into the dining area, where Samuel was already seated with Gran. Both of them were staring at the mouth-watering food amazedly as if they'd never seen food before.
"I see you're stunned." Angelo smiled at them. "I hope you like my cooking."
"We will," said Ricky quickly as he took his seat, and Bianca placed Joseph next to her before she sat as well.
"Mum, give Micah to Angelo."
"Must I?" said Barbara adoringly as she snuggled the baby, and she smiled and handed him to Angelo, who gently took him with a smile.
"Bianca, does he need feeding?"

"I fed him not long ago. And I changed him," smiled Bianca. "Cormier can watch him while we have dinner if he won't come."

"All right."

Cormier, Clover and Marissa had made themselves scarce when Bianca's family arrived: Marissa was staying at Clover's (Clover moved back home as the immoral ordeal with Patricia was over), while Cormier kept to his bedroom and didn't leave unless necessary.

Angelo smiled and carried Micah from the dining room, heading for his brother's bedroom.

"Cormier?"

"Yes, brother."

"Will you watch Micah while we have dinner?"

"Of course," Cormier said, and Angelo smiled at him.

"You know you are welcome to join us for dinner, don't you? Bianca's family think you are being quite hostile."

"They have been here for less than three days," Cormier replied, stung. "Why would they think I'm being hostile?"

"Because you introduced yourself to them properly and pretty much vanished after that," Angelo replied flatly. "And you have made no attempt to reappear or mingle. At all."

Cormier scowled as Micah gurgled, saying "Shall I take the baby or not?"

"Come to dinner," Angelo replied. "I will put Micah in his baby chair."

Cormier sighed. "Fine."

* * Bianca * *

"Hey," smiled Bianca, as Cormier entered the dining room slowly. "You going to eat with us, then?"

"Good," said Barbara, when Cormier said yes. "For a while I thought you didn't want to be around Bianca's family."

"It's not that at all, Ma'am," Cormier said humbly. "I thought it was vice versa. I thought, because of me being what I am, that you didn't want me around."

"Nonsense," scoffed Gran, and Bianca and Samuel smiled at her. "That's all in the past. If we had a problem with vampires like we first did, we wouldn't want Count Angelo near us either."

"And we do want Count Angelo near us," blurted Ricky, and Angelo smiled at him.

"Thank you, Richard."

Richard swallowed, then he nodded.

Bianca smirked at him, and he scowled at her. He knew she was going to tease him around the clock as soon as she could.

"This looks delicious," Barbara said as Cormier took his seat, Angelo doing the same after placing Baby Micah in his chair. "Count Angelo, did you cook all of this?"

"Yes Ma'am, I did." Angelo smiled at her. "Tuck in."

"I'm dying to taste those ribs," said Samuel, and Ricky handed the platter to him after taking three ribs for himself.

"There, Dad."

"Thanks."

* * Angelo * *

Everyone held a glass of champagne except from Joseph, Samuel saying "To a new beginning."

"To a new beginning," everyone chorused, clinking glasses.

Angelo waved his hand and everything on the long dining table vanished, Richard's jaw dropping as Angelo said "Shall we go to the lounge?"

"Yes please," Gran said, Barbara saying "After that excellent meal that's all I want to do. Just lounge."

Angelo smiled at the double use of the word, Bianca picking up Micah.

"Come on then, let's go. We could watch a movie or something."

"Let me take him, Bianca," smiled Samuel, and Bianca smiled back as she handed her baby to his grandfather. Joseph ran towards her happily, and she scooped him up in a kiss and cuddle, holding him to her happily.

Bianca's family smiled at her. They knew she adored little Joseph Heathen.

Angelo smiled as they entered the lounge and got comfortable, Bianca sitting down still holding Joseph.

"So what do you think of the castle, Samuel?" Angelo asked, and Samuel grinned at him.

"It definitely beats a hotel. It's amazing. I love it."

Micah gurgled contentedly in his arms, Samuel adding "And I love my grandson Micah."

"Micah not grandson," pouted Joseph. "Micah my brother!"

"He's Samuel's grandson too, Joseph." Angelo smiled at him with everyone else. "And he's your brother as well. Both."

"Ohhhh." Joseph thought, then he smiled. "Ok!"

"Let me hold him," begged Barbara, as Joseph giggled. "Come now Bianca, you've been very protective of little Joseph. He should know his family."

"Go to Aunty Barbara, Joseph." Bianca smiled as Joseph climbed down from her lap and ran to Barbara, who scooped him up and cuddled him.

Ricky smiled, then he asked "Where's Cormier?"

"Back in his room," sighed Angelo, and everyone else sighed too, Bianca saying "I'll go and see if I can get him to come out."

* * Bianca * *

Bianca left her family and lover, walking down the corridor as she called "Cormier Heathen, get out here right now!"
Cormier morphed in front of her, arms folded. "You called, chick pea?"
"Come in the lounge with me."
"I cannot."
"Why??"
"You all seem perfectly fine without me being there," Cormier pointed out, and Bianca said "We are fine."
"Exactly."
"But it's not the same without you," Bianca said, prodding him in the chest. "Please come. For me?"
Cormier sighed. "All right. But if I feel uncomfortable I am leaving."
"Are you going to be like this with every mortal?" asked Bianca, annoyed. "Or is it because it's my family? Because you was fine when it was just me in the castle with you and Angelo."
"Bianca, you don't understand-"
"Try me."
"I can smell their blood," Cormier admitted. "Perfect, aged blood. It arouses me, and I crave it. I want it so much. I cannot be around your family, Bianca. I don't want to bite them."
Bianca understood. Taking Cormier's hand, she said "I smell it too. But I ignore it. And they don't know I'm a vampire. I'm doing a pretty good job of resisting temptation while they're here with us."
"I can't say I am doing the same, Bianca. I will soon become bloodthirsty."
Bianca sighed. "All right. Stay away. Why don't you go to town and bite someone?"
"You would recommend that?"
"Of course. I can smell fresh blood nearby." Bianca inhaled, then she said "It's a woman with her husband walking by the castle."
Cormier stared at her. "You are indeed a powerful vampire."
"Go," Bianca replied, and Cormier grinned at her.
"Come with me."
"What?"
"Your first bite, Bianca. Come and experience the hunting, the luring the innocent into your clutches. The blood. You'll love the taste."
Bianca hesitated, then she caught that strong whiff of blood again. The couple were right by the castle, gazing up at it in awe.
Bianca's heart was racing, her eyes were glowing. Her fangs were unsheathed.

She had to taste their blood. She just had to.

"All right," she said, when Cormier raised an eyebrow. "Let's go."

* * Angelo * *

Joseph was content in Barbara's arms as everyone watched the television, Angelo frowning as he wondered where Bianca was.

Baby Micah was looking up at his grandfather, Samuel smiling at him.

Ricky was staring at Angelo, and when Angelo met his gaze curiously, he quickly looked away.

"Are you all right, Richard?" asked Angelo, and Ricky mumbled "Yeah. Um. I'm just wondering where Bianca is."

"As am I," Angelo replied. "Would you like to come with me to find her?"

"Just me and you?" Angelo said yes. "You promise?"

Barbara frowned at her son with everyone else, saying "That's an odd thing to promise, Richard. Just go with the Count to find your sister."

"I'll come too," Samuel said, frowning as well.

"All right," Angelo said, standing. "Let's go."

* * Bianca * *

Invisible, Cormier and Bianca crept towards the couple who stood holding hands, gazing up at the castle.

"Do you think it's true about the castle, darling?" breathed the woman. "Count Dracula is in there?"

"No. Dracula didn't live in this castle," the man replied. "But another Count did. And generation after generation of his kind lived there. He wasn't evil like Dracula. This Count was loving, kind. And so were his successors. I believe the very last Count lives there."

"The rumours say he is called Count Angel."

"Count Angel??"

"Yes."

"Don't believe rumours, sweetheart. Stick to the facts. Angel is a pretty feminine name-"

"Indeed it is," said Cormier as he appeared, Bianca as well as the couple whipped around, startled. "The Grand Vampire is called Count *Angelo.*"

"Oh- I'm sorry," the woman said nervously, eyes on Bianca, who was gazing at her neck hungrily. "Do you know him?"

"Of course we know him," Cormier replied as he took a step closer, Bianca as well. The couple back away fearfully, the man saying "What do you want with us?? We're tourists- we mean no harm!"

"You stumbled upon our castle," Bianca replied coldly, and Cormier said

"Exactly. You are trespassing."

"We can give you money as an apology-"

"Your money is no good to us. We want something much more."

"Like what?" the man asked fearfully, then he stopped as Bianca's eyes glowed scarlet, her fangs unsheathed as she smiled. "Oh my God!!"

"Run!" cried the woman, and she and her husband turned and ran as fast as they could- Bianca shot towards them like a bullet, at the speed of light it looked like, marvelled Cormier, then he whistled admiringly as Bianca gave the woman a vicious backhand across the face, sending her crashing to the ground.

"Meredith!" cried the man, and Cormier vanished and reappeared behind him, grabbing him as his own fangs unsheathed- without pausing, he sank his teeth into the man's neck and began to drink like the world depended on it.

Bianca stared at the unconscious woman on the grass, then she grabbed her and pulled her up, roughly turning her head to the side and, following Cormier, plunged her teeth into the woman's neck.

* * Angelo * *

"Bianca!!"

Shocked, Richard and their father stared at the scene in front of them as if they couldn't believe what they were seeing.

Angelo cursed under his breath as his brother whipped round, blood trailing from the corners of his lips down his chin.

"Bianca!!"

Bianca swore as well before she released the woman, who thudded to the grass in a heap as she stood.

Samuel and Ricky recoiled as she walked towards them, blood on her mouth, her eyes glowing bright red.

"Bianca, what... what the hell is going on?" spat her father, as Ricky stared at his little sister in shock. "What happened to you?!"

Bianca touched her mouth with two fingers and looked at them. Blood was on her fingertips.

Cormier hesitated, then he said "It's not what it looks like-"

Wiping her mouth with her sleeve, Bianca said "It's exactly what it looks like."

Annoyed, Cormier turned to her. "You were meant to stick with what I say, chick pea."

"No point in lying," shrugged Bianca. "Dad, Ricky- I'm dead."

"What!!"

"I died," shrugged Bianca. "And I came back as a vampire."

"Who bit you?" spat Samuel, and Bianca hesitated. "Well?!"

"I did," said Cormier quickly- outraged, Ricky pounced on him, slamming Cormier to the ground and punching everywhere his fists could find.

"You killed my sister, you son of a crackpot!!"

"I'm still here!" cried Bianca, as Samuel said "Give it to him, Ricky!"

"Get off him- please! It wasn't him!" cried Bianca. "He's lying!"

"Then who bit you?!"

"I did," Angelo said quietly, and silence fell as everyone looked at him. "Think twice before you try and attack me, Richard."

"I'm not going to," breathed Ricky as he pushed Cormier away and stood up. His reaction to Angelo was the total opposite to his reaction to Cormier, and everyone noticed that as he said "Why did you bite her, Count Angelo? I thought you wasn't going to!"

"Believe me when I say I didn't want to." Angelo sighed. "Bianca made me. She saved my life."

Samuel and Ricky turned to Bianca curiously.

"Bianca?"

Bianca took a deep breath, then she spoke.

* * Cormier * *

Cormier inspected his bruises in the kitchen, everyone back inside the castle.

Bianca stood with him, wrapping some ice cubes in a flannel and gently pressing it to his arm.

"Here."

Cormier cringed at the feel, then he said "Thank you."

"I'm sorry my brother attacked you, Cormier."

"It's all right. I expected nothing less," Cormier said, slightly disgruntled.

Everyone was in bed aside from Bianca and Cormier. Angelo was putting Joseph to bed along with Micah.

Bianca sighed, then she smiled. "The taste of blood was awesome."

"I know." Cormier smiled at her. "I believe the couple will turn."

"Into vampires?" Cormier said yes. "Won't they have a choice like me?"

"Not everyone will. But come, let me show you something."

Bianca followed him out of the kitchen down the corridors, into the lounge towards the gigantic windows.

"Use your powers and look through the frosted glass," Cormier said gently. "Look out at the castle grounds."

Bianca obeyed, staring through the windows down at the grass. "What am I meant to be seeing?"

"The bodies are gone," Cormier said softly, and she stared at him. "Either they are now vampires or the werewolves have taken them for a snack."

There was a bang on the castle doors before Bianca could reply.

"Count Angelo!!" screamed a voice from outside, and Cormier and Bianca whipped round as Angelo appeared. "COUNT ANGELO!!!"

Angelo cursed as he heard his startled baby start crying.

"What's going on?" said Barbara, in her dressing gown as she entered the lounge with Gran and Samuel, and Ricky as well. "It's the early hours of the morning! Who's out there at this time?"

"The woman I turned," muttered Bianca, and Cormier chuckled. Angelo slapped him hard on the back of the head.

"You think this is funny?!"

"No!"

"Then?!"

"I was a little amused- okay, not amused!" said Cormier quickly, as Angelo raised his hand again furiously. "I just-"

"Shut up," snapped Angelo. "Everyone aside from Cormier and Bianca stay here. Barbara, please see to Micah and try to settle him."

"Of course."

Glaring at Cormier, Angelo held out a hand to Bianca, and she took it.

Angelo led her out of the lounge towards the banging on the giant doors downstairs as the enraged tourist banged on the castle doors.

Angelo pulled the doors open to find the woman there, tears falling down her face as she glared angrily.

"My husband is dead," she spat. *"He-"* She pointed at Cormier. "He killed my husband!"

"Apologies," Cormier said amusedly, and Angelo quickly blocked the woman's way she made to attack Cormier, saying "Please, calm down. What is your name?"

"Meredith Butcher," she replied, eyes glowing scarlet. Then her expression changed as she looked at Bianca, who stared back at her nervously. Softly, Meredith said "Hello, Bianca Davis."

"Hello," Bianca replied timidly, and Meredith stepped closer, gazing at her hungrily.

"I will do your bidding. I am your slave."

"You are?"

"I am," Meredith said quietly, and Angelo said "She is. You are her Vampire Mother, Bianca. She falls directly under your rule."

"Oh," said Bianca. "Um. Well, I'll look after you, Meredith. I'm really sorry about your husband."

Meredith's eyes filled, tears coursing down her pale cheeks. Bianca didn't know what to do as she watched the woman sob uncontrollably.

"We- we hadn't been married that long and- and- oh, his family- they have to know-"

"We'll sort that," Bianca said gently. "How old are you, Meredith?"

"I'm twenty four," wept Meredith. "John was all I had and *he-*"
Cormier flinched, obviously feeling guilty now.
"He took him away from me!"
"Don't worry about that," Bianca said, still gentle as ever. "Angelo, can we give her a room? Just for tonight?"
"I won't stay in the castle, not with the vampire that killed my husband!"
"All right," said Bianca exasperatedly. "What about the inn that's in town? Can you spend the night there and then wait for me to visit you tomorrow night?"
"I... I-"
"I'm your Vampire Mother," Bianca cut across before Meredith could give her a yes or no. "So I order it."
Bianca's eyes were glowing bright red, Meredith staring into them as Bianca softly said "Go to the inn. I'll be with you tomorrow night. Go, Meredith."
"I will go, Mother," Meredith said quietly. "Goodbye."
Angelo and Cormier's jaws dropped as Meredith turned and walked away just like that, Angelo amazed as he asked "Is she in a trance, Bianca?"
"No," shrugged Bianca. "She just did as I asked, that's all."
"Oh."
"Let's go inside," Cormier said, and Angelo gently took Bianca's hand and led her back inside. "Meredith made me a little uncomfortable."
"Because you killed her husband," Angelo said dryly. "Now I am going to tell you once, Cormier Heathen. When you go on your little blood hunts do not take Bianca with you. Anything could have happened to her."
"I liked it, Angelo," protested Bianca as they went up the stairs. "I want to hunt again. I have real high senses-"
"I'd rather you hunt with female vampires, Bianca. Clover and Marissa will teach you everything you need to know."
Bianca pouted. "All right. Fine."
They heard Micah wail, Barbara cooing him gently, and Bianca sped up, Angelo as well as they went into the lounge.
"He must be hungry, Mum. Let me take him," said Bianca, and Barbara smiled and handed Micah to his mother.
Micah calmed down almost immediately once he was in his mother's arms, Angelo saying "I will bring him a bottle of milk."
Marissa Bennett appeared, startling Barbara as Angelo smiled at her.
"Greetings Marissa."
"Greetings," she responded with a smile, Bianca glaring at her.
"Why are you here, Marissa?"
"Bianca," Angelo said warningly, and Marissa said "I came to see Angelo, Bianca. Is there a problem?"

Micah gurgled in Bianca's arms before Bianca could retort, distracting her from saying something harsh.

Marissa smirked at her before turning to Angelo, saying "I will wait for you in the library if that is fine?"

"Of course it is, Marissa. Go on ahead," said Angelo, and Marissa smirked at Bianca before she vanished, Cormier scowling.

"Brother, it is soon dawn. Marissa-"

"Can stay here," Angelo replied. "She has her own room, did you forget brother?"

"And you have a son and lover to put first," Cormier retorted. "You was about to make Micah a bottle of milk."

"And I shall," Angelo replied, then he noticed the expression on Bianca's face. "Sweetheart? What's the matter?"

"You said Marissa would make herself scarce while my family is here," Bianca said angrily. "Clover and Sebastian have, so why the hell can't she? Does she want you that much?"

"Bianca-"

"No," she spat. "Go to the library and have your precious chat with her. I'll make Micah his milk and I'll put him to bed with me in our bedroom. Have a good night, Angelo."

* * Bianca * *

Angelo hesitated, then he vanished.

Bianca swore angrily, Cormier saying "It matters not, chick pea."

"The hell it doesn't," snapped Bianca. "She is really starting to get under my skin. And it's like Angelo's putting her first! I have half a mind to go to the library and let rip."

"Don't do that," Barbara said gently. "Talk to Angelo when he comes back from the library."

"He knows how I feel about that flipping woman. I don't give a damn if he's known her for years," Bianca said angrily. "I swear to God I'll punch her face in and I am not joking."

* * Cormier * *

"Good," Cormier said ruthlessly. "She annoys me. I have half a mind to go to the library and demand she leaves at once. But Angelo will not have it."

Micah started to wail again, Bianca shushing him gently and kissing his tiny cheek as she walked out of the lounge down the corridor, towards the kitchen. Cormier and Barbara followed her, Barbara saying "Bianca, please calm down-"

"I am calm," snapped Bianca as she waved her hand; the kettle started to boil. The baby milk powder sailed out of a cupboard along with a baby bottle, and settled on the counter.

Barbara smiled at her daughter's use of magic, and Cormier knew Bianca's mother would always love her dearly, even if she was now a vampire.

"Bee?" said a tiny voice, and they turned and saw tiny Joseph. "Bee? Ok?"

"I'm fine, Joseph. Come here."

Joseph toddled over to her anxiously, Cormier saying "He must have sensed you was upset, chick pea."

"Take Micah," Bianca replied softly, and Cormier obeyed, taking his baby nephew from her. Bianca knelt and picked Joseph up, kissing his forehead. "I'm fine, Joseph. Do you want to sleep with me and Micah tonight?" Joseph nodded, and Bianca said "All right. I'll make you some hot chocolate and biscuits. I'm sorry I woke you."

Joseph stuck his thumb in his mouth as she set him down, and Cormier smiled down at him.

"You get to sleep with Bee and Micah, Joseph. Aren't you a lucky little boy?"

Joseph said yes, giggling. "You come too, Uncle Cormy!"

"Me??"

"Sure," Bianca said, and Barbara and Cormier looked at her. "You can rest in the recliner and keep me company until whenever your little brother decides to rest. I doubt he'll come to bed anyway as he's so into Marissa."

Cormier laughed. "All right. I'll come."

* * Angelo * *

Two hours later…

Angelo kissed Marissa's hand, and she shuddered.

"Dawn is almost upon us, Marissa. Please, use your bedroom."

"I couldn't, Angelo. My being here has already put you in the dog house."

"Well, I gave her over an hour to calm down. Hopefully she has."

"I don't think she has, Angelo. Shall we have another drink?"

Angelo thought about it, then he shook his head.

"If we do Bianca will murder me."

"Are you the Grand Vampire or not, Angelo?" purred Marissa, and Angelo smiled at her.

"You are already intoxicated on your feelings for me. A glass of wine and who knows what you will do."

"I'll do this," she said softly as she moved closer…

* * Cormier * *

Cormier snapped awake, eyes glowing scarlet as he sat up in the recliner.

"The hell she did!"

Bianca mumbled in her sleep, her arm around Joseph. Joseph slept on as well, his thumb in his mouth as he snuggled up to Bianca. Baby Micah was sound asleep in his crib also.

Cormier left the suite quietly, gently closing the doors behind him, then he stormed towards the library, livid.

"Angelo!"

"Yes, brother."

"Where the hell is Marissa?!"

"She is sound asleep in her bedroom," Angelo replied, looking at him curiously. "Why?"

"Did she try and kiss you?"

"I'm sorry?"

"Did she try to kiss you!!"

"Of course not! Were you asleep?" demanded Angelo, and Cormier said yes. "You must have been dreaming, brother. Marissa went to bed almost an hour ago."

"Oh," said Cormier, frowning. "Apologies, brother."

Angelo nodded. "Would you like a sample of my new cocktail?"

"You made a cocktail?" said Cormier, impressed as his little brother nodded. "What do you call it?"

"The Love Drug. I'm hoping to serve Bianca some tomorrow."

"So she will fall into deeper love with you?"

Angelo burst out laughing. "It's a cocktail, not a potion, brother."

"All right, give me a sample."

Cormier sipped curiously, then he gasped at the taste. He tasted strawberry, cherry, and a hint of apple merged with just the right amount of alcohol.

"Do you like it?" smiled Angelo, and Cormier downed the rest of the cocktail before he said "It's heavenly! Your cocktails always are. I love it! Let me have a full glass."

"Help yourself," Angelo replied. "I'm going to bed now. Don't drink all of it, brother. Good night."

* * Angelo * *

Angelo quietly slipped into bed, as gently as he could so as not to disturb Joseph or Bianca, but Bianca opened her eyes to look at him. Angelo stared back at her, then he said "Bianca, I apologise if-"

"If you chose talking to Marissa over tending to our son? No problem," Bianca said sarcastically. "Really, I didn't mind at all. Please do it more often."

Angelo sighed. "Would you like me to sleep in the recliner?"

"Sleep where the hell you like." Bianca scowled and closed her eyes again. "I couldn't care less."

Bianca shrieked as Angelo grabbed her and teleported, both of them reappearing in the lounge.

"Angelo, what-"

Angelo kissed her hard on the mouth, reaching for her hairband and pulling it out so Bianca's hair tumbled around her shoulders, Bianca moaning as she reached for his trousers.

Angelo broke the kiss, making her whimper as he asked "Are you mad at me, Bianca Davis?"

"Angelo, not now- please, just make love to me," she panted. "Now, Angelo- please!"

Angelo smiled at her before he leant down and kissed her again, snapping his fingers.

The lounge doors swung shut.

* * Bianca * *

One week later…

"I can't believe we only have a week with you left," pouted Barbara as she sipped her Love Drug cocktail. "Please let us come back soon when we raise the money, Count Angelo."

"You will always be welcome here," smiled Angelo. "Maybe you could come for two months next time instead of just a couple of weeks."

Bianca's family cheered while Bianca choked on her cocktail.

"Two months?!"

"Of course," smiled Angelo, and she pouted at him.

"You've been sipping too much Love Drug juice, Angelo."

"No, you've been sipping too little." Angelo smiled at her. "Come on darling, don't be mean. Your family will always be welcome to stay however long they want to."

Bianca's family cheered again, Samuel saying "Raise your glasses in a toast!"

Everyone obeyed, Micah gurgling in his baby chair.

"To the Heathen and Davis family," smiled Samuel. "My beautiful daughter, my future son in-law, my grandsons Baby Micah and little Joseph. To any future grandchildren-"

"Not too soon though," Barbara interrupted, and everyone laughed.

"To happiness!" said Samuel, and everyone said "To happiness."

And for the rest of their immortal lives, surrounded by friends and loved ones, Bianca and Angelo lived in just that.

* *

Thank you for reading Count Angelo!

Follow me on Twitter @misskelz90 and look out for posts about other available books and more!

You can also follow my Amazon Author Page if you search for me; "Makala Thomas".

I really hope you enjoyed reading this book but like any book, some will not like it and some will love it.

Be sure to leave a review!

Happy reading!

xxx Makala Thomas xxx

COUNT ANGELO

MAKALA THOMAS

Other Titles by Makala Thomas

The Link: Matthew's Beginning

The Link: Colette's Beginning

The Link: Colette's Fame

The Link: Colette's Return

The Link: The Betrayal

The Link: Psycho Eruption

Integrity

The Angel (Who Knew Not Love)

Jeiklee

Count Angelo

A Witch Like No Other

Skylar Grey

Kenco: The Goddaughter

Kenco: The Return Of Her King

Krissie Taylor

Beast

Lost

Love Conquers All

The Stranger In The Woods

Unrequited Love

The Tail Of A Queen

Amaris

Gadget Girl

Contact Makala Thomas here:

Facebook Page:

The Diverse Works Of Makala Thomas

Twitter:

@MissKelz90

Email:

misskelz90@gmail.com